License to Ill

by

Russell T. Wright

OLD WORLD LIBRARY

New York, New York

Library of Congress Cataloging-in-Publication Data

Wright, Russell T., 1964

ISBN13: 9781503033894

ISBN10: 1503033899

To Tor Eckman

Acknowledgements

I'm deeply indebted to Catherine Adams, an editor in New York. Due in part, no doubt, to our shared heritage, working with Catherine to produce this novel was one of the most fulfilling experiences of my professional life.

As for influences, I'm grateful for the books of Eckhart Tolle and Robert Persig. And not least, I'm beholden to Jerry Seinfeld and Larry David. Their combined brand of humor pervades this novel well beyond the many references to the TV show they created.

Chapter 1

"Hey, Jerr."

Jerry Riggs cringed a little and then looked around, feeling like he'd been caught browsing a porn shop. Finding the man's eye, he raised his chin in recognition, picked up the large flat box of Krispy Kreme's, and turned to leave.

He couldn't remember the guy's name. Jewish liberal Democrat from Justice was all he could come up with that early in the morning...Harvard guy. For a lawyer, that was one route to DC, the easy one. If you came from one of the flyover states the path wasn't so direct. This was not so much a thought for Jerry as an attitude—a constant attitude—as he reached the man, a few paces behind him in line.

Eisen—yes! Still got it, Jerry thought. That politician's knack for remembering names. Justice Department. Anti-trust. Good guy. Everybody in DC's a politician.

"Morning, Saul."

"You're a good boss." Saul pointed his chin toward the box of donuts as he grasped Jerry's free hand.

Jerry looked at the box, too, then back at Saul. Comprehending, he said, "Yes," and smiled at Saul Eisen just a tick too long. "Yes. These donuts aren't for me, they're for my staff. That's right." The line moved forward. "Good to see you, Saul."

Did he suspect anything? No, don't think so. Jerry moved on through the press of people like a waiter with a tray, then out into the dark. He clicked the keychain to open the Cherokee passenger door, placed the box longways on the seat, then in one fluid motion closed the door and ambled around to the driver's side. Squeezing himself behind the wheel, he pulled the door closed and angled into the greater-DC traffic like clockwork. This pit stop had come in under eight minutes, as usual. Those NASCAR boys would be proud.

Jerry tugged at his collar where shirt met tie and tried to adjust himself in the seat. Taking a sip of coffee from the insulated cup that waited in the holder by his knee, he glanced at the box of steaming donuts. With his teeth, he pulled a glove off as he drove and lifted the corner of the box like a corrupt Congressman opening his war chest.

* * *

Inside the Capital Annex parking garage, Jerry slid the neatly folded green, red and white box into the trash can beside the elevator door. A moment later, the door slid open and he stepped inside, dabbing at the corners of his mouth with the back of his hand. When the elevator dinged his arrival, Jerry stepped out and wended his way to his office inside the Speaker's suite. The Chief of Staff was already there.

"You ready?" the COS said from his own office.

"I'm like a Marine," Jerry said. "Always ready. *Semper Fi.*" His overcoat was on the hanger but the hanger was not yet back on the coat tree. "Ready for what?"

"The Republican leadership breakfast?" the COS said as if it were a question. James Wiedemann was called "COS" by his staff, as in "Just Cause." He had retired from the Army as a Brigadier. Supply Corps. He'd begun his career with the Riverines, riding the boats as a First Lieutenant through the Mekong Delta to keep the Green Berets stocked with MREs. He'd expected back then to be in some comfy supply depot in Saigon. He hated his lot in life so much that he rode standing up in the front of the boat, hoping to get home any way he could. Miraculously, he came though a year of that duty unscathed, but the experience changed his personality and he developed a reputation that would precede him the rest of his days, allowing him to get things done without raising his voice or his blood pressure wherever he went.

Jerry looked at his watch. "Shit. That's today?" He hung up the coat and strolled into the COS's office.

"You're nothing like a marine, by the way. *Semper Fi* is short for *Semper Fidelis,* which is Latin for 'Always Faithful.' Don't they teach Latin in law school anymore?" The COS put on his suit coat while inspecting his singular troop.

Jerry had merely forgotten about this rather routine and generally dull kick off to the winter legislative session this morning, but he knew what the COS would make of that, so he didn't respond at all, leaving his boss with the impression that he was unprepared, an impression he actually preferred. And he didn't mind suckering the COS in, truth be told.

"Don't tell me you already ate."

And that was *exactly* what Jerry knew he would make of it. "No, no," Jerry said. "Nothing much." The COS was now in Jerry's personal space, and as always Jerry felt the need to stand at attention, though he never actually did.

"You left some crumbs in the corner of your mouth there," the COS said, upon close observation. "Krispy Kreme again, if I'm not mistaken."

"Thanks for noticing," Jerry said, clearing the crumbs with his tongue.

"That's not helping your weight problem any. You could stand to lose thirty pounds." Though the COS maintained a paunch of his own, Jerry never mentioned it at times like this. Wiedemann was doing pretty well for a man his age. "And why don't you shave that beard? You're a Republican lawyer, for God's sake."

In the common area between the two offices, Jerry eyed his briefcase, left there in a chair the night before. He picked his iPad from it and followed the COS into the hallway.

"It balances out the receding hairline," he said. "You know that."

* * *

Jerry eyed the plate of bacon, eggs and toast the server silently placed in front of him, wondering how on earth he could be hungry again. The Speaker sat at the head of the main table, along with the Senate Minority Leader and his underlings, holding forth his views on the looming "fiscal cliff." As the COS sipped his coffee, he looked down his nose at Jerry, who now held a strip of bacon at the ready.

Jerry shrugged and whispered, "It'll balance out the

donut. Salty and sweet."

The Speaker handed control of the floor back to the COS, who's job it was each session to run this meeting. The COS stood and said, "The Speaker's Staff Counsel, Jerry Riggs, will now give us a run down of the Supreme Court's current session. Jerry." The COS sat down, unable to completely camouflage his self-satisfaction.

Jerry put down the bacon strip, wiped his hand on his napkin and rose slowly. Buttoned his coat, cleared his throat. He looked at the COS, who regarded him expectantly. Maybe this time, finally, he was going to catch the United States House of Representatives Speaker of the House's Chief Counsel, who always seemed to be flying by the seat of his pants, unprepared. Jerry knew this was what the COS was thinking, and he bore him no malice for the thought. This was a game they played from time to time to keep their working relationship lively, or to keep Jerry on his toes, depending upon whose perspective one was considering. And Jerry always won this game. If he didn't, of course, the COS would probably can him.

Jerry rotated his wedding band as he began speaking. "OK...well...Let's see...The Court heard oral arguments in Fisher versus the University of Texas back in October," he began, "an affirmative action case that should have little impact on the use of racial preference in the selection of students, though the ruling is expected to go in favor of Fisher, the student who challenged the practice at UT..."

Jerry went on like this for some fifteen minutes, detailing even those cases of no political interest, just to spite the COS. His lengthy presentation had the ancillary benefit of allowing everyone the chance to finish his and her breakfast without fear of interruption.

When he sat down finally, the COS whispered, "You really didn't know about this meeting?"

Jerry held up the limp and lifeless cold strip of bacon and took a bite. "Nope." This would maintain for a good while longer that aura of high intelligence, photographic recall and encyclopedic knowledge he had carefully nurtured over the years—all he needed to accomplish for the rest of the day.

"I didn't hear anything in there about Obamacare," the Speaker said. "The Chief Justice really let us down last term."

There was a lot of wound licking going on in Republican circles. Six months earlier, the conservative-leaning Supreme Court had stunned all sides of the debate surrounding the new healthcare overhaul, officially called the Affordable Care Act and more affectionately known as Obamacare, by ruling that its individual mandate provision requiring every taxpayer to acquire health insurance or be subject to the payment of a cash penalty was, in fact, constitutional. And the Bush-appointed Chief Justice John Roberts, no less, had provided the swing vote in the decision! Adding insult to injury, Republican leadership had hoped the decision would energize its base to sweep Obama out of office—that didn't happen. Republicans even lost a little ground in both the House and the Senate. Just weeks after that round defeat, this bloodied band huddled to rethink strategy.

Jerry looked across at the Senate Minority Leader, a Senator from his home state of Kentucky. He could see the man only in his chinless profile, but his smugness was nonetheless palpable. Senator Mack McCormick had had more to do with the success of Obamacare than Chief Justice Roberts, that was for sure. No one knew more about procedural wrangling that McCormick did. As Minority Leader, he held just enough votes to keep Obamacare from ever coming to the floor for a vote if he wanted to, but he didn't use that option. Oh sure, he talked a good game in opposition to the law, but with the largest insurer in the country, Populous Healthcare, situated in the largest city in his state, the Senator's hometown of Louisville, and filling his campaign coffers with cash, well...that's all it would ever be—talk—as long as McCormick was at the Republican senatorial helm.

His breakfast finished and his duties complete, Jerry tried to put Senator McCormick out of his mind. He placed his iPad on his knee and began flipping through the day's news. His beloved Kentucky Wildcats were third in the preseason college basketball rankings, with Indiana at number one, Louisville number two and Ohio State number four. All of the top programs were within a few hours drive of each other, with Cincinnati, the Speaker's home turf, right in the middle of them. It was a vortex that drew everyone in the region to it. Home to seven presidents, mostly from the Gilded Age, it was a dying vortex. Nicole, Jerry's wife, had been his own personal vortex. Cincinnati was her town. There was no way she was relocating to Bumfuck, Kentucky, that was for sure. That's how he became a Buckeye transplant and any political ambitions he might have harbored, himself, were summarily scarified to the greater good of marital bliss.

Jerry looked up to see the Speaker still railing against Obamacare, and the Speaker's frenemy, the Senate Minority Leader, who hailed from just up the road in Louisville, gazing disinterested out into nothingness, and thought: Cincinnati really is the middle of America, the navel, so to speak, lint and all, just far enough inland to balance out the west with the eastern seaboard, and perched right at the top of the south so as to keep a better eye on it. And Ohio as a whole had just made its deciding voice clear in the last election, summarily granting Obama four more years. Jerry thought about that for a moment, turned down the corners of his mouth in conclusion and then went back to the sports page.

"Overturning Obamacare remains my number one priority," the Speaker was saying. "But we've run out of options at this point. If anybody has any ideas, let's hear them. I don't care how off the wall they might sound. We're officially desperate at this point." The room rustled with polite chuckles. The Speaker chuckled too. "I'm serious."

"We have a different view in the Senate caucus," McCormick said in response. He sat across from the more amiable Speaker of the House, and looked him in the eye. "The Affordable Care Act isn't going anywhere. It's here to stay. The best thing we can do is to allow its implementation—which will be painful for the American people—to have its beneficial impact on the political horizon."

"But it's bad law," Jerry heard himself pipe up. All eyes in the room turned his way. There were times when the moment overtook him and he couldn't help but speak. This was one of them. He couldn't take Senator McCormick's hypocrisy. And yet, he was savvy enough not to take it on directly, he let his lawyerly authoritative tone do it for him, expressing in an unspoken way that of which everyone in the room was already well aware: that McCormick's political interests were at odds with the party and with the American people. "The President's assurances aside, our analysis indicates that a large minority of present policyholders will lose their coverage when the law is fully implemented. Is Populous Healthcare up for that? Or is there a provision in there we haven't found yet that immunizes them?"

"Mr. Riggs is making my point for me," McCormick said, addressing himself to his only peer in the room. "Mr. Speaker, if and when this large minority lose their healthcare coverage, will they see that as the fault of Republicans or Democrats?"

With his characteristic combination of candor and humor, the Speaker said, "The way the mainstream media spins things these days, I'm not so sure."

It was then that Jerry began to feel the searing pain in his chest again. He did his best to relax, took a drink of water, tried to hold himself still. How much longer would this meeting go on? Another hour at least. He'd done his part, spoken up in support of the Speaker. The conversation was moving on. Jerry wouldn't be missed. The COS beside him picked up on his discomfort.

"I'm just going to get some air," Jerry whispered. The COS nodded and Jerry stood up, tucked his seat in and then forced himself to walk as normally as he could to the door at the end of the room. Once outside, he steadied himself against the door jamb.

* * *

The COS flipped on the light to his office to find Jerry lying on his couch. "What happened to you?" Jerry shielded his eyes from the light. "Heart pains again? Go get yourself checked out, for God's sake." The COS dropped Jerry's iPad on his midsection as he passed en route to his chair.

"No doctors."

"That's an order, mister."

"You're not in the Army anymore, Jim," Jerry grunted. "Just give me a minute."

"Then get out of my office," the COS said. "I don't want you dying in here. I don't have time to write any extra reports." The COS stood with his hands on his hips, surveying the neat piles of paper on his massive desk. "Obamacare, Obamacare, Obamacare," he said. "Barely a word about the fiscal cliff."

"He knows the fiscal cliff is a no-win situation," Jerry said. "Nothing he does there will be good enough for Cantor and his gang. A Hail Mary on Obamacare is the only thing that's going to save him with that crowd."

"Just go get yourself straightened out, will ya?"

Jerry struggled to his feet, lifting his girth off the leather couch with a squeak, and made his way out into the reception area. The COS's Secretary, Naomi, was there.

"Morning, Jerry," she said. Blinker was there with her. Doug "Blinker" Garnett, young blond-headed guy just out of Xavier, ran constituent correspondence in the Cincinnati office. He'd picked up his nickname the first time he visited the DC office. His eyes appeared even wider than normal then, with more frequent blinking, mesmerized by the scale of government all around him.

What Blinker was doing here in DC, Jerry had no idea, and he didn't stop to ask. "Morning," he grunted.

Jerry opened the door to his side of the office and closed it as quietly as he could. His own secretary, Rita, was inside.

"Oh, there you are," she said. "I have a couple of messages for—"

Jerry closed the door to his office and found his way in the dark to his own identical leather couch and eased himself down on to it.

A moment later, the door opened and the light switched on. Jerry's intern, Pattie, stood in the doorway, her hat and coat still in place, her purse over her shoulder.

"Oh, gees," Pattie said. "What's with you?"

"What the..." Jerry shielded his eyes again. "Would you turn that off?"

Pattie complied. "Your heart again?" she said. "I want you to go see somebody."

"No way," Jerry said. "No doctors. They killed my old man. Cut him open and that's where he died, right there on the operating table." Though it had happened seven-teen years earlier, that formative event was always in the back of Jerry's mind. In a self-fulfilling-prophecy kind of way, it colored everything he did. "I'm feeling better now, anyway."

Pattie took her hat off and loosened her coat. She set her purse in the leather chair and walked around Jerry's desk. Once on the other side, she opened up the top drawer and lifted something from it. There was just enough morning light streaming in through the window behind her for Jerry to see that she held a small plastic bag with a few blue pills in it.

"No doctor," she said, "then no more of these."

"How did you know about those?" Jerry said, his head cocked suspiciously.

"Let's see," Pattie said. "Nothing going on down there, then you have to go to the bathroom, you come back and stall for twenty minutes, then all but one part of you is veritably passed out? Pretty easy to tell."

"Well, I uh . . ."

"It's a real thrill for me, let me tell you," Pattie went on, brow arched. "One step above doing it myself."

"All right, all right." Jerry said, staring at her. "Can't you see that I'm having a heart thing here?" He held the stare for a moment longer, then lay back into the couch cushions.

"The disclaimer on all the commercials states quite clearly that you should ask your doctor if your heart is strong enough for sex. And you're going to make an appointment to do just that."

Pattie dropped the pills into her purse, then picked up the purse and set it on the table and sat down in the chair.

"Did something happen?" she asked.

"Nah, nothing much." Jerry lay staring up at the ceiling. The two sat in silence for a moment. "McCormick is so smug."

"Mack the Knife? What about him?"

"He's the one who got Obamacare through the Senate. Without his support, there's no way it passes. He works for Populous Healthcare. Populous's headquarters are in Louisville. Obamacare isn't going to help the little guy, it's going to help Populous. It's going to drive a massive amount of business to Populous and all the other health insurance companies out there, and he knows it, that smug bastard." Jerry had argued otherwise in the meeting, but now he wasn't so sure his analysis was correct. Mack McCormick usually played the game with insider information.

"Am I interrupting?" Tim Hanrahan swung into the room in his characteristic fashion, blue pinstripe suit, teeth blazing. Pattie stood up, looked down, and smoothed her skirt, tucking a strand of hair behind one ear.

Heart problems or no, it was too early in the morning to be smiling like that, Jerry thought. "We were just having a broad-based, no-holes-barred discussion about the pharmaceuticals lobby," he said without moving from the inclined position. The son of a Cleveland industrial family, Tim Hanrahan had graduated first in his law school class at Case Western Reserve.

Hanrahan said, "I was just looking for the . . ." He searched the office. "There it is. Don't get up." He sprang to the desk and picked up a thick file. It was the Boudreau file. That was next on Jerry's list of things to do. The Speaker needed talking points on the legal aspect of Louisiana offshore drilling in advance of a sit-down with Obama's likely choice to replace Lisa Jackson as head of the EPA, scheduled for the end of the week.

"Working on the talking points for the meeting with McCarthy," Hanrahan said.

Even better, Jerry thought. Nothing beats delegation.

"You all right, Jerry?"

"I'm fine."

"Look after him, will ya, kid?" Hanrahan said to Pattie

with a wink.

When he was gone, Pattie said, "Pocket hanky? Get real. Watch that guy. He has ambitions."

"He's just punching a ticket," Jerry said. "He'll move back to Cleveland in a year or two and run for Congress, himself." Jerry thought for a minute. He was beginning to question his political analysis of everything and everybody. "Why do you say that? Did he say something?"

"Don't get yourself worked up," Pattie said. "Now, go get yourself checked out, ok?"

"No doctors," Jerry snorted.

"Little blue PI-ills," Pattie said with a singsong in her voice.

* * *

Jerry sat on the examination table stripped to the waist. Only the fear of the loss of sex was stronger than his fear of this place. After a few taps on his chest and back and a few deep breaths with the cold head of the stethoscope held against the pasty white skin of Jerry's torso in various places, the doctor had just left.

Dry mouth, cold sweat. Did the stethoscope register any of these symptoms? He could feel a trickle of perspiration in the curve of his lower back even as he sat there all alone, the worst of it presumably over.

Before he'd ever seen the doctor, he'd been run through the full battery of tests: EKG whilst walking on a treadmill, X-rays, MRI, CAT scan, PET scan, the works. Blood samples, urine samples, stool samples, everything but semen samples (which might have been fun), you name it, Jerry had done it. The only thing left was to turn his head and cough, and maybe that was all that was left of the doctor's job—he did say he'd be back in a minute.

When Jerry checked in, the receptionist had taken one look at his congressional-strength Cadillac of a medical card he had handed her and all but shouted to the back of the office, "We've got a live one here!" Someone had even come out to help him with the paperwork. Jerry had asked if this royal treatment included a foot massage and the poor woman almost looked as if it just might be within her job description to comply with the request.

Nothing but the best for Congress and its staffers, Jerry thought. Meanwhile, the rest of the country will soon be in a single-payer system. European-style socialized medicine, Medicare for everybody. Unless Mack McCormick knows something the rest of us don't, which is a distinct possibility.

Before he could rouse himself to get dressed, as he had been advised that he could do, the doctor was back with a fist full of prescriptions.

"It'll be a few days before all the tests are in," he said. "You do need to lose about thirty pounds, though."

"So I've been told."

"The main problem appears to be stress. I want you to consider taking a few days off."

"I can't do that right now," Jerry said. "The legislative session's just getting started."

The doctor didn't seem to be listening. He began going through the drugs. "I want to get you started on Lipitor to bring your cholesterol down and..."

This one is a blood thinner, that one is for blood pressure, and the litany seemed to go on and on. But the entirety of the consultation lasted less than a minute, the "any questions" was asked rhetorically and the little papers left on the desk rustled in the breeze of the opening and closing of the door.

"Really?" Jerry said. "This is the world's greatest healthcare system in action?" They let the machines do the work for them. "Hey, where's my foot massage!"

He sat there for a moment more before getting down off the table. Shirtless, he leafed through the prescriptions.

* * *

"He says it's stress," Jerry explained. "Whatever that means. He gave me a stack of prescriptions and told me to take a few days off."

The COS stood over his desk, looking like Churchill reviewing war maps. He'd just received an OMB report on the consequences of another government shutdown. It was massive. "Now?" he said. "We need all hands on deck right now."

"Isn't that Navy?" Jerry said. "Look, you're the one who told me to go see the guy."

"He gave you those pills. Just take them and see how you feel."

"I'm not big on taking pills," Jerry said. "Most pills, anyway," he revised, thinking of the blue ones Pattie had shaken in his face that morning. "Look, I'll leave Pattie here. I can talk her through whatever goes down. I'll fly back to Cinci for a few days."

The COS stopped what he was doing and read Jerry's face. "You're worried."

It took a moment for the admission. "I should have never gone to see that guy." Jerry finally said.

The visit to the doctor's office had triggered something in him that he could neither control nor fully explain. It was like one minute he was champing at the bit to get back to work, the next minute he wanted to bolt from everything and everybody, including himself, if that were possible.

"It's what killed my old man."

The COS knew the story about the botched heart surgery, so Jerry didn't elaborate. He didn't have to. The COS could read it on Jerry's face, hear it in his tone.

"All right," he finally conceded. "Go home, kiss your wife and kids for me."

"That's no cure for stress," Jerry said. "Believe me. Maybe I'll head down to London, see my mom."

"You got one week. Call in three times a day. And make sure your phone is always on this time."

"My mom lives on a farm," Jerry said. "Very bad reception out there, you know that."

"I have your mother's home phone number now."

"Right. Right. I forgot about that."

* * *

Jerry was back in Cincinnati by eight-thirty that night. Nicole picked him up. The twins, Sophia and Sarah Grace, were in their pajamas in the back seat. They had seen him just a few days before, but their reaction was always the same.

"Daddy! Daddy!" They both said. They seemed to know that he loved that. Jerry gave them each a big hug and then watched them strap themselves in before climbing into the Lexus SUV himself.

"What happened?" Nicole asked. "You weren't due back for another two weeks."

"No kiss hello?" Jerry said. "Nothing happened. Things were a little slow—"

"A little slow? The session just started."

"I had a few things to take care of back here, is all," Jerry said. "I thought I would motor down to London and see Mom for a few days."

"So it's your mother again," Nicole said.

"She hasn't been feeling well and she needs a few things done around the farm."

"I need a few things done around our 'farm,' too," Nicole said.

"She's getting up there, Nicole. What am I supposed to do?"

Jerry wondered how he had gotten himself into the same old fight—and could still get so worked up—when the premise wasn't even true. Nicole had taken the dutiful Republican wife route in life. She had seen something in Jerry during law school that led her to believe the traditional approach was her best bet, laying aside her own personal ambitions. She was as good a lawyer as Jerry was but she demonstrated little in the way of political acumen. She would have risen high in some sort of technical legal field, like mergers and acquisitions or corporate counsel for a large company like P&G there in Cincinnati. But it would have sucked the life out of her. Wouldn't it be more fun to hitch her wagon to another horse? One that could bring her either the money of a successful legal career or the fame and power of a political life? But Jerry had managed to give Nicole, by her standards, only moderate amounts of both.

His metaphor was different. Jerry was the fish out of water. Removing him from his natural habitat in rural Kentucky had put him in touch with the man who would eventually become Speaker of the U.S. House of

Representatives. But for Jerry's political potential, that connection came at a cost. He would likely forever be working for someone else.

"Stop fighting!" Sarah Grace and Sophia said, not quite in unison.

"We're not fighting," Jerry said. "We're discussing."

"Stop discussing, then," Sarah Grace said.

"There's also some free CLE going on tomorrow in Lexington. I can pick up a few credits on the way. That'll be sweet, huh?"

"Fantastic," Nicole muttered.

"What's the best kind of CLE, girls?" Jerry called out without turning around.

"What's CLE?" Sophia said for both of them.

"It's school that daddy has to go to so he can keep being a lawyer. You want daddy to keep practicing law, don't you girls? So he can keep buying you all the stuff you've come to love and expect, like a brand new Lexus so you can compete with all your country club friends, right?"

"We don't have country club friends," Sarah Grace said, both girls giggling. "Mommy does."

"See how often you say those things?"

"It'll just be a few days," Jerry said.

"It's always just a few days. A few days here, a few days there." Nicole abated momentarily. "Did you gain more weight?"

Jerry thought guiltily about the two Cinnabons he'd consumed while waiting to board his flight at Dulles.

"Thanks for noticing," Jerry said. "Maybe I'll come join your spinning class with whatsisname, Sergio."

"Sergio's gay." Nicole mouthed the second word so the girls wouldn't hear it.

"Whatever." Jerry stared out the window. Galvanized by ten years of marriage, this negative foreplay hardly bothered him anymore. It was Nicole's way of making sure he didn't want to have sex with her that night.

Chapter 2

Jerry was up and out before Nicole or the twins even began to stir. The night before, he'd helped himself to leftovers, then fortified himself in his office for the remainder of the evening until the far end of the house became noiseless. In the morning, he brewed a vat of coffee.

The "Hot Now Doughnuts" sign was flashing in the window of his local Krispy Kreme. "Sweet," he whispered. He was on I75 South a few minutes later.

* * *

Jerry glad-handed a couple of classmates he found waiting outside one of the conference rooms inside Heritage Hall in downtown Lexington. Then as he tried to duck into the first morning session already in progress, he heard that unmistakable Motor City brogue behind him: "No, it couldn't be Jerry Riggs."

"Hello, Orlando," Jerry said.

It was just like old times. Both hustled into the hall and sat down in the back, just as they'd done twenty years before in Professor Sturgis's early morning property class. African-American and older than the rest—a non-traditional student, as they were called—Orlando Broxton had been a class favorite. The only difference Jerry could see in him now was that his cropped hair was more salt than pepper. The old adage, "A-students make good law professors, B-students make good judges and C-students make good money," applied. Orlando Broxton was making good money. And yet he always showed up at the yearly law update, provided free of charge by the Bar Association. As Jerry had told his twin girls, the best kind of CLE (like beer) was free.

For Jerry, UK had been a step down after graduating college at the University of Virginia, academically speaking. But if statewide office were ever his aspiration, there was no better choice. Not only was it the most prestigious in the state, its location in Lexington was also critical. The divide between the urban-industrial powerhouse of Louisville, relatively speaking, and the rest of the mostly rural state was one that transcended even the Republican-Democrat divide. With a hundred and twenty counties, the fight was nearly always a hundred and nineteen to one against the states largest city. The Commonwealth had elected only two Governors from Louisville (Jefferson County, to be more precise) in more than two decades and a score, and one of those two, Lawrence Winchester Wetherby, required the benefit of incumbency to win at the ballot box, having gained office initially by succession from Lieutenant Governor.

For Orlando, UK had been a step up. With the twin benefits of affirmative action and family in Lexington, the move down from the urban decay of "DE-troit" to the idyllic, best kept secret of his present location had been the proverbial no-brainer.

"Shouldn't you be in DC right now?" Orlando whispered. "You slummin' comin' back down here, now."

"Just taking a little break before the session heats up," he said. "It's nice to be in button-down and khakis for a change."

"Tell me about it."

"I'm heading down to see my mom in London. Take care of a few things around the farm."

"All right. All right." Orlando may not have seen Jerry in a while but he knew him well enough not to buy into his story. "Let's do lunch and we'll talk about it."

Jerry nodded, but something told him that wasn't going to happen. Something inside made him want to bolt, just as it had back in DC, even from his old friend Orlando. He couldn't even keep his mind on chitchat, let alone an hour-long session of perfectly routine questions—How's Nicole? How's your health? How's the job?—every single one of which would send him back into that tailspin from which he was currently on the lam.

He'd left in his wake the only thing that lent his life any cohesion—his job, and that at a moment of utter crisis for the party—and to do what? Run home to mama. And all because of a routine medical check up. No sir, if his job wasn't going to get his attention at the moment, neither was his old buddy Orlando. But how did one say so politely? One didn't.

"Sounds great," Jerry responded on cue.

On the other hand, it was a cardinal rule of politics to know who you could lie to and get away with it. An old law school trench-mate that you dearly loved, and who knew you dearly loved him, though being men neither had ever said such a thing and never would, was not in that category. There would be recompense at some point from Orlando for his moral weakness, but Jerry couldn't think about that right now.

Orlando whispered: "You heard about Brad Vogel, didn't you?"

"I haven't heard about anybody," Jerry whispered back.

"He had some sort of a breakdown."

"Is that right?" The news didn't register at all with Jerry. He couldn't really pay attention. Wouldn't mind one of those myself, was all that came to mind.

"Patrice Patterson and Evan Daltry got married, went to work in the same firm in Louisville. They made partner at the same time too." Jerry didn't even feign interest at that one. "Dan Hernandez is still in the Commonwealth's Attorney's office. He does mostly murder cases now. I had one against him a year or so ago. It plead out at the last minute."

When an older gentleman in the row in front of them glanced back in their direction, forcing Orlando finally to break off his cataloguing of their classmates' movements since law school, Jerry was grateful.

CLE always made him feel like he was in jail. Something about its mandatory-ness. You couldn't leave, not even a minute early. And it was exceedingly rare those times when he ever remembered caring even slightly about the subject matter of one of the sessions. Hour after hour, all you could do was sit there with your thoughts—and that was under normal circumstances, if there were such a thing. This was altogether different. He had no use for his thoughts these days.

His mind latched on to Mack McCormick once again, and whether his analysis of the Senator's angle on Obamacare had been correct, and what he might be missing. It popped and pinged around inside his head until he got back to Tim Hanrahan. What did Pattie know that he wasn't seeing? That got him through the rest of the session without having had to listen to either the presenter or to Orlando.

* * *

The next session pulled Orlando and Jerry in different directions. Orlando wanted to sit in on a personal injury refresher, while Jerry opted for a lecture on elder care.

"End of life planning is so critical these days," the speaker commented, "because modern medicine has managed to increase life span by an average of 15 years, but it's done nothing to improve quality of life during that extra time they've given us."

"That's the very definition of hell, isn't it?" Jerry remarked to the lawyer sitting next to him. "Or at least purgatory."

"What's that?" the man said.

"Nothing," Jerry said. "Never mind."

How could he explain in a whisper to a man he didn't know that he had a father who'd managed to avoid this dilemma by submitting himself to a botched surgery, and a mother whom he loved and to whom perhaps he remained a little too attached who was about to go through those fifteen years, and that he himself had a problematic ticker and a predilection for Viagra, which could not coexist?

Then he thought of a way, a succinct question that would sum it all up: what are they keeping us alive *for*? But he kept that one to himself.

Jerry gritted his teeth and held out for as long as he could, but there came a point late in the session when all he could do was bug out of there. Though there were free credits to be harvested that afternoon, and the following day if he wanted to stick around, Jerry found himself once again on I75 headed south without a word to Orlando or anyone else.

On the way out of town, he stopped at Spaldings Bakery

for a box of the world's best donuts—far better than Krispy Kreme, in Jerry's studied estimation. He was just in time. Each day when their morning run sold out, that was it, they closed up shop. He got their last seven glazed—heavy, greasy and delicious. They were gone by the time he reached Berea.

* * *

Jerry sat at his mother's kitchen table, his legs crossed, the day's copy of the *Sentinel Echo* on his knee. She was greasing a cast iron cornbread mold. A pot of brown beans was warming on the stove. Jerry took in a deep breath. They smelled homey. A warmth washed over him. This was just what he needed, to relax for a few days in the comfort of home.

"You don't have to do that, Mom," Jerry said without looking up, though he was glad she did for the sake of ambiance. "I just ate a late lunch at Shiloh's."

"I had these beans already made yesterdee," she said. "You can have it whenever you're ready."

"We can go into town later," Jerry said. "How 'bout the Cracker Barrel?"

"I'm too tarred," she said. When she had filled the mold and popped it in the oven, she opened the cabinet beside the sink and took out a prescription pill bottle. "The doctor changed my medication a week or so ago and I cain't hardly keep a-goin'."

Jerry watched as his mother took the pill and chased it with a swallow of water. She left the cabinet door open. Inside was a multitude of similar bottles.

"My God, Mom," he said. "How many prescriptions do you have?"

"Watch your language," she said, closing the cabinet. "He's got me a-takin' pills all day long."

When Jerry arrived, he noticed that her face looked a little puffy, like she was retaining water. He hadn't said anything then and he didn't know what to say now—he had his own stack of prescriptions about which he knew not what to say, either, even as his chest had tightened up yet again on the drive down from Lexington, to the extent that he had to pull off at an exit and sit in his car at a Marathon station for a good long while until the pain subsided.

The TV was going in the living room. Jerry's mother took off her apron and sat down in the chair, her chair, across from it. The channel was set to the Fox News channel.

"You never did say what it is that brings you down this way," she said.

"You said you needed a few things done around here," Jerry said. "I thought I might come down here and do 'em."

"Eric come over and took care of the gate," she said.

"Eric," Jerry repeated as flatly as he could. His only sibling, ever dutiful. And ever martyred.

"He did a real nice job on it. You must have seen it when you come in."

"Yeah, yeah," he said. "I saw it. You had a whole list of stuff, didn't you?"

"No, not really. He did a couple of other things for me, too. Now that you mention it, you could bring a little hay down from the loft. They're going through it quicker than he can come around here and feed 'em."

"There you go," Jerry said. "I've come to feed the beef."

He laid out the paper on the kitchen table to read below the fold: the sheriff's office was running drills to prepare for the possibility of a school intruder. One hoped that the drills were going down after school hours, Jerry thought, when the children weren't there. But whenever the Laurel County Sheriff's Office was involved, one never knew. Your typical police blotter stories: man beats wife after a University of Kentucky men's basketball loss. That number three ranking would be short lived. Meth lab destroys mobile home, kills child—same stuff, different day.

Jerry opened up the paper and folded it back. He didn't immediately register the importance of the subject matter in the next headline his eye fell upon. He wasn't there on business, after all. He was there to get away from all that. Neither had the writer, who managed to wax eloquent about it for only a couple of paragraphs; nor the editor, who chose to place the story below the fold on page two.

A local attorney filed suit in Federal District Court in

London, the Honorable Stephen Van Doren presiding, challenging the so-called individual mandate, a cornerstone of Obamacare, under the free exercise of religion clause of the First Amendment.

As much as he tried, it was tough for Jerry to stay out of political mode, and by the time he came to the name of the attorney who had filed the constitutional challenge, he sat upright, as did the hair on the back of his neck. Jerry's attention was fully had.

Brad Vogel?

Could there be two Brad Vogels who were attorneys? No, there couldn't. What was Brad Vogel doing in London, Kentucky?

"This is too weird," Jerry said, his attention delving deeply into memory.

"What is?" Mrs. Vogel asked.

Orlando had mentioned something about Brad Vogel, what was it? Something about a crack up, yes, that was it. If Brad Vogel—*the* Brad Vogel—had somehow ended up in London, Kentucky, he must have had a breakdown, indeed, and one of major proportions at that, whereupon he must have been cast into outer darkness by the powers that be. *The* Brad Vogel that Jerry remembered would have considered relocation to the countryside the old "fate worse than death."

Brad Vogel? Jerry couldn't get his mind around the idea.

"What's the matter?" Mrs. Riggs asked when she saw the frown on Jerry's face.

"Nothin', Ma," Jerry said. "Just some legal…thing."

Yes! he thought. Some legal thing! And some political thing, too. Jerry snapped the paper open and read the short article once more, hoping for some additional information this time, but there was no more to be had. He laid the paper down again and put his political thinking cap on.

Not many could connect so few dots to form a complete legal picture. Jerry just happened to be one such personage. What this case must be arguing is that there are certain religious folk for whom the purchase of health insurance offends religious sensibilities. They have faith in

God, in other words, to heal them and keep them healthy, so if they bought health insurance, that would indicate a lack of faith. There was already an exemption for the Amish in Obamacare, who don't believe in insurance, so Vogel's challenge had to be even more fundamental then that somehow.

Jerry thought for a moment. What a boon this could be for a religion: all people would have to do to avoid paying the individual mandate (which the Supreme Court had just labeled a tax) would be to join that church. And if Republicans really wanted to bring down Obamacare, all they would have to do...was convert.

A slight involuntary smile creased Jerry's face. This was just the sort of thing the Speaker was looking for regarding Obamacare, a fresh angle of attack that no one had yet considered. The challenge under the Commerce Clause had just failed. Why not try the Free Exercise of Religion Clause? Sure, why not? He ran that through the political Cuisinart of his brain. He ran it through again. Sure, there were religious people out there who might consider health insurance a violation of their faith, Jerry got that. But Brad Vogel? That was the piece that wasn't computing. Vogel was no religious fanatic, that was for sure. Let's just hope he hasn't joined up with the Amish.

The political possibilities resonated with Jerry at a deeply unconscious level, intertwining themselves with the horrific memories of his father's death at the hands of a doctor all those years ago. And Jerry's own heart problems and his fear of doctors now. This struck a nerve.

"Weird," he said out loud. Hearing his own voice brought him back to the present moment. His mother had left the room at some point in his cogitation.

Jerry felt his cell phone vibrating. He pulled it from his shirt pocket and checked the number. It was Pattie. He walked into his mother's bedroom, closing the door behind him, and into the far corner of the room where he knew the cell phone reception would hold up, reading the article one more time as he went.

"I just need to know where the Boudreau file is," she said.

"The COS needs some talking points by the end of the day and I can't find it anywhere."

That's right, the talking points, Jerry thought. He knew he'd forgotten something. "Hanrahan has it," Jerry said.

"Hanrahan?"

"Yeah, Tim Hanrahan. He was supposed to do those." Damn that Harahan. Jerry didn't want to think about that right now. "Check this out," he said. "A guy I know from law school is challenging the Individual Mandate provision of Obamacare under the free exercise of religion clause. That should make the COS happy."

"Is he a religious nut or something?" Pattie asked.

"That's the thing," Jerry said. "He wasn't. I didn't know him all that well, but he seemed like an all right guy. It's a mystery how he ended up down here in London." Jerry was reading again. "The presiding judge was appointed by Dubya. A party hack. Should play ball with us if we need him to."

Jerry had met Judge Van Doren a few times, in fact, when he had been Chief of Staff to a Kentucky congressman back when Jerry was just starting out, well before his own Ohio congressman had become Speaker. They had been peers more or less. And who knew? If the political stars aligned for Jerry the way they had for Van Doren, with the right administration coming to power at the right time, they might one day be peers again. Jerry could imagine himself wearing the black robe of judgeship at some point in his life. Black, as they say, is very slimming.

"Hey, do me a favor. You at your computer?"

"Yes."

"Find his contact info for me. Name's Brad Vogel."

"You have a smart phone," Pattie protested.

"Reception's terrible down here."

After a moment: "I got an office address and phone number."

"Give it to me." He found a pen and wrote the information down on his hand. He checked his watch. It would have to wait until the morning. "One more: Orlando Broxton."

* * *

"What happened to you?"

"Sorry, Orlando," Jerry said. "Something came up. You know how it is."

"No, not really," Orlando said. "I'm just a lowly practitioner, unfamiliar with the duties of state."

Orlando's exercise of choice had always been jogging. Neither fleet nor small boned, as he pushed his way into his fifties, his knees no longer tolerated the abuse. Jerry had noticed that he had begun to take on just a little more of a pear shape when he had seen him earlier the same day up in Lexington. This late in the afternoon, Jerry imagined that he had ambled back from the afternoon CLE session to his home office where he was presently sitting behind his desk, filling out his leather chair just a little more than he used to, and could almost hear through the phone line the ice jingling in Orlando's glass of gin.

"It didn't have anything to do with that," Jerry said. "I just have some, you know, stuff going on."

"What's her name?"

"Orlando, come on, man," Jerry said. "It's my mom. I had to get down here to London."

"Um hmm."

"I need some information. You were telling me about Brad Vogel."

"And as I recall, you were less than enthusiastic about the information I had to offer," Orlando said. "If I were representing an alleged criminal and you were the prosecutor, I wouldn't be expecting much in the way of a plea deal, if you get my drift."

"I'm sorry, Orlando. Come on, buddy."

"He graduated in the top ten percent with y'all," Orlando said. "Landed a gig with Brackman-Hollis in their Lexington office. And he *was* on the fast track to partner."

Brackman-Hollis, the most prestigious firm in Louisville, Vogel's hometown. Its Lexington office was smaller and perhaps even more prestigious than the main. This was a choice very much in keeping with the Brad Vogel Jerry remembered.

"'Was?' What do you mean 'was'? Didn't you say something about a breakdown?"

"It was kind of a big deal at the time in certain circles," Orlando said coyly. "Old news now."

"What happened?"

"You know, you really should come a-slummin' a little more often," Orlando said. "You never know how long people will be in power. You may need us again someday."

"Come on, buddy," Jerry said. "I've just been busy. I'm working all the time. I'm working now. Help a brother out."

"He had some sort of meltdown, is what I heard. Left Brackman and just sort of disappeared. I have no idea where he ended up."

"Funny thing is, he's down here in London."

"Kentucky? Really? He has no connection to London, as I recall. About the only kind of person less suited to setting up shop in London would be a black man, such as myself."

"Tell me about it," Jerry said. "I'm from here and I wouldn't attempt it."

"She-it," Orlando said. "You would have been mayor of that town by now if you'd gone back home."

"Doubt it. More likely I'd be dead by now. Or a meth head like everybody else."

"I know, right?" Orlando said. "You want to tell me what this is all about?"

"You don't want to know, believe me." When Orlando waited for the answer to his question, Jerry said, "You know, I can't even picture the Brad Vogel I knew stepping foot outside of a city."

"Um hmm," Orlando said, still waiting.

"He just filed a lawsuit down here challenging the constitutionality of Obamacare."

"You damn Republicans," Orlando said.

"Orlando, Obamacare isn't about the little guy, okay? It's all about the fat cat insurance companies. Come on! Why can't you people see that?"

"'You people'?"

"Democrats. You know I meant Democrats."

"If it's about the fat cats, then you should be all about that."

"Here we go," Jerry said. "What are we, back in law school again? Look, I didn't want to bring it up." And then Jerry remembered: "And besides, Vogel's a Democrat. Or at least he used to be."

"You still know how to piss me off, don't you, Riggs?"

"Yeah, well, it isn't all one sided."

"And you better stop in when you roll back through, that's all I got to say," Orlando said. "Or we're going to finish this argument the easy way, if you know what I mean."

Orlando clicked off and Jerry stood there pondering the conversation for a moment, the odor of liniments hanging in the air, the bed neatly made beneath the vintage off-white chenille bedspread, with the familiar black and white picture of Pop as a young farmer smiling, twinkle in his eye, outside in bright sunlight, still prominently displayed on the beside table. He picked it up, looked at it more closely. He hadn't even noticed this picture in years. You could only see the strap of his overalls on his right shoulder, not the left. Late sixties, early seventies. Black and white photos seem to stand the test of time much better than color, Jerry thought. They have a timeless quality to them. He put it down and opened the door.

"Everything all right?" Jerry's mother asked when he came out.

"Oh, you know," Jerry said. "Just politics, as usual." He sat down again at the kitchen table.

"You got that from your daddy," she said. "That's how he was with the cattlemen. He could get hisself worked up into a lather over anything or nothing at all."

Jerry's heart was tightening up again, but not yet so much that he noticed. He was thinking about Orlando Broxton and Democrats and what he might find tomorrow when he dropped in on Brad Vogel.

A breakdown, huh? Jerry thought. I could use one of those, myself. Now he remembered, that's exactly what he had thought when Orlando told him about it the first time.

Chapter 3

Jerry ducked into Weaver's Hot Dogs for a cup of coffee to wait until the law office across the street opened up. His mother had link sausage and eggs waiting when he got out of the shower, but now in the dark of morning, something was missing. He felt as edgy as a junkie as he paid for his coffee. And then he saw the honey buns in cellophane wrappers hanging by the register.

"I'll take a cup of coffee and one of these," he said. After a beat: "Make it three." He had never practiced in London, the chances of him knowing any of these people from back in the day were slim. What difference did it make?

As the sun rose a little, Jerry sat and ate and waited until he saw a plump little thing unlock the front door to the office. He watched her turn on the lights and start up the copier as he bit into the next honey bun he had no idea he'd opened.

A little later, a man came into view and handed the woman a stack of papers, which she immediately began to copy. There must be a back entrance, Jerry realized.

He waited until the woman finished her copies, and he had finished his third honey bun, before heading over.

* * *

Jerry's intention was to retreat to his country home and relax for a few days, it really was. But this Obamacare thing just seemed too perfect. He couldn't resist its siren song. He would run it to ground as best he could while he had the opportunity. The COS would never forgive him if he didn't—if the COS found out about it, which, as Jerry thought about it, seemed a remote possibility at best. If the case turned out to have any merit, it might—repeat might—get national news coverage, at which point the COS would naturally assume that Jerry got wind of it the same way he did, via the O'Reilly Report or some other news-like broadcast. But there were plenty of constitutional challenges initiated in the lower courts that no one would ever hear about, nor would they ever need to. Jerry proposed to himself that he look into it just in case. If it was worth pursuing: great, feather in his cap. If not, no harm done, he'd keep it under that cap.

Something deep inside told him this must be part of his problem, never being able to leave work at work, always thinking, thinking, thinking. He couldn't help himself, and that was a big part of the problem too, not being able to help himself, in a few different departments of his life.

Jerry's instincts told him the ambush was the most appropriate approach. Why call when he could pop in? When he asked after Brad Vogel, the woman's face tightened protectively.

"I'm sorry," she said. "Brad's not in the office at this time. Could I perhaps take your name and number and have him give you a call?"

"Yes," Jerry said. "That would be fine." He took his wallet out of his jeans pocket and removed a business card from it. "I'm an old friend of his," he said, advancing the card across the high counter. "We went to law school together many moons ago."

The woman was wowed by the official seal. "Oh," she said. "Let me try to get him on the phone."

"I wouldn't want to impose," Jerry said.

"It's no trouble." After a moment: "No answer. Brad doesn't believe in voicemail," she said as she hung up. "But he'll see the number and give me a call."

"Should I wait?" Jerry said, ingratiatingly.

"We probably won't see him until this afternoon," she said. "He works mostly from home."

"I see."

He could probably get Pattie to find his home address, but why go that route if he didn't have to? Genuineness was the only thing that worked with these people. Jerry mustered what little he had left.

"I'm on a pretty tight schedule. Maybe I'll catch up with him another time." He turned to go.

"He just lives down the street," the woman said. "He walks

here when the weather's nice."

"Really?" Jerry said. "Must be nice. Working only in the afternoon, walking to work."

Jerry just couldn't believe that Brad Vogel had signed up for this kind of lifestyle. The Brad Vogel he remembered was more inclined to drop a Mercedes off with a valet at eight o'clock each morning than to walk a few blocks to work on a sunny afternoon.

And in turn, Jerry began to seriously reconsider his own decision to leave London all those years ago for the sprawling traffic of the Greater Cincinnati area, and then the snarl of Washington, DC—he was thinking of the government now—and all the traffic that went with it. Yes, the small town practice of law had its benefits, all right. Not to mention the fact that this receptionist became more pleasing the longer Jerry talked to her. "You know my name but I don't know yours."

"Amanda," she said. "I don't think he would mind if I gave an old friend his address." Amanda slid a slip of paper across the counter. "It is in the phone book, after all."

"London still has a phone book?" Jerry said, reading the slip. The woman pointed to the yellow book beneath the phone. "Good to know."

Amanda smiled up at him. Still got it, Jerry said to himself. He smiled back. Thirty pounds overweight and a receding hairline and I still got it.

* * *

Jerry drove around killing time until around 9:30, a respectable hour for an ambush. He swung by the address a couple of times searching for some sign of life inside, whilst hoping not to be noticed himself. He passed a rusted out Monte Carlo the first time, an old one, going in the opposite direction. He felt a little awkward when he passed the same car a second time fifteen minutes or so later.

What was this guy, a neighborhood watch, or something? Jerry knew this neighborhood—and all of London for that matter—was the kind of place that would notice a stranger in their midst pretty quickly. After all these years away, Jerry had to admit, that's what he was here, a stranger.

He pretended not to notice the man as they were about to glide past each other, but managed to get a sense of him nonetheless: deep blue eyes and otherwise scraggly and forgettable. He was driving slowly and paying more attention to the houses than the road, like maybe he was checking for a particular address. Just as Jerry was about to pass, the man began to drift toward and slightly across the centerline. No time for horns, Jerry swerved into the gravel shoulder and glared at the man, who looked up just in time to right his vehicle.

"What the hell?" Jerry scowled into the rearview mirror. What the hell was that guy doing!

Probably on a cigarette run, Jerry surmised as he watched the Monte Carlo pull around the bend, up and out of sight. He'd been into town and back, no doubt high on Oxycodone or some such substance. Yes, it was that kind of neighborhood, too. The man probably "had his disability" and sat at home all day watching Springer and the like, stoned out of his gourd. He probably got distracted by something shiny on a front porch.

No harm done, Jerry guessed, as he pulled a U-y and rolled to a stop in front of Brad Vogel's address. But he couldn't get that driver's blue eyes out of his memory. They were like something out of the *Andy Griffith Show* when the hillbillies come down from the mountains to play bluegrass music.

Jerry rang the doorbell to the little cottage-style house. Hearing nothing, he knocked on the wooden frame of the screen door, which caused enough rattle to startle anyone inside. As he waited, Jerry noticed that the field stone house had some charm to it, or at least it might come spring. The flowerboxes around the porch looked untended. After a moment the door opened.

"Yes?"

Hair a bit longer and unshaven, it took a moment for certainty to set in that this was in fact Brad Vogel, an acquaintance of his from the Clinton years.

"Hi, Brad," Jerry said. "Remember me?"

Brad frowned, struggling to remember.

"Jerry Riggs. We went to law school together."

Jerry waited the requisite interval for the unspoken exclamations, "Wow, you've gained a lot of weight!" and "Wow! You've lost a lot of hair!" to be considered and dismissed.

"Jerry, yes," Brad said. "Yes."

Jerry had to take his own moment to reconcile this Brad Vogel with the one he remembered. Brad stood in a sweatshirt and jeans, his white feet bare. Jerry had half-expected him to be sitting at home dressed in an Armani suit. Okay, he hadn't pictured him with the suit coat on, *per se*, but it would be close at hand. In law school, while others had come to class in sweats, Vogel had dressed as well as one could get away with and not be labeled antisocial. Collared shirts, usually button-down, as Jerry recalled, and gabardine slacks, maybe—maybe—cotton khakis, his version of a dress-down Friday. And jeans, never.

"Can I come in?"

Vogel, unprepared for visitors, seemed uncomfortable, a circumstance Jerry had counted on. Vogel looked around the living room behind him and must have decided that it didn't look overly unpresentable.

"Sure," he said. "Sure." Jerry followed him into the house. "Just let me straighten up a little."

As he took a couple of dishes left scattered on the coffee and end tables to the kitchen, Jerry said, "Please don't make a fuss." *This brings back fond memories of law school*, he considered saying but didn't. It was actually refreshing that Vogel had loosened up a little. Jerry wasn't quite sure this was the stuff of mental breakdown. Perhaps the opposite. And thankfully, Vogel didn't appear to be Amish. "I was just in town visiting my mom and I learned you had set up shop down here, so I thought I should pay you a visit."

Brad went through the open door of the bedroom and emerged a moment later wearing house slippers. He stood, sizing up his unexpected guest, and now it was Jerry's turn to feel uncomfortable.

"Please, sit down."

Jerry sat down on the leather couch, while Brad took up position in the matching chair, the ensemble a vestige of a prior, more opulent lifestyle.

"Are you still in politics?"

"Still in the game," Jerry said, smiling painfully for effect.

"In Cincinnati?"

"Still in Cinci," Jerry confirmed. "Cinci and DC. Back and forth all the time. I don't know if you remember this, but I went to work for a firm up in Covington right out of law school. Worked there for a while. I got to know some people on the Speaker's staff during some rallies and fundraisers and so forth. One thing lead to another and I ended up going to work for him."

"Interesting. Yeah, I remember hearing something about that."

"That was before he became Speaker, of course," Jerry felt the need to add. "Been there ever since." An awkward pause. "Ever since."

"He's lucky to have you on his staff," Vogel said, smiling slightly as if he were not sure how far to go with his comment. "You were one of the smartest guys in law school, and one of the most reasonable...for a Republican, I mean."

Jerry smiled, too. This was not the sort of compliment the old Vogel would have given. It was nice. Jerry recalled again that Vogel was a Democrat, but not staunch. More of a big money Democrat.

"Are you still active in the party?" Jerry asked.

"Me? No," Vogel said. "I switched my registration to independent some time ago."

This made sense somehow, Jerry decided.

"To be honest," Vogel said. "I was a little surprised when I heard you went that route."

"Really?" Jerry said, crossing his arms, rounding his shoulders. He wasn't quite sure what Vogel meant.

"You just seemed to be a guy with political ambitions of your own."

"Ah," Jerry said, uncrossing his arms. "Well...you never know." But sometimes you do. He was too long cut off from his London roots to ever hope to grow fresh political foliage from them again.

Then again, maybe it was Jerry's impolitic penchant for speaking up when he shouldn't—like with Senator McCormick in the leadership breakfast earlier in the week—that told the better tale of his political demise. He never listened to that voice that told him he shouldn't be doing this, whatever "this" was that he shouldn't be doing. He'd gotten away with it so far, but...

He had hoped to make Vogel ill at ease to better control the situation, but it wasn't working out that way. After the initial awkwardness of this impromptu morning visit wore off, Vogel didn't seem uncomfortable at all. It was as if he'd been expecting this reunion. Jerry was a little spooked by that.

This Vogel was incisive and insightful. He hadn't said more than two words and he had already made Jerry feel like lying back on this Italian leather sofa and telling him everything, opening up his vault, getting everything off his chest, telling his old friend all about how he felt he had betrayed his people and sacrificed his own ambition for the love of a woman who didn't seem to care for him very much anymore. How that union had seemed like a step up the socioeconomic ladder he couldn't pass up at the time, but he wasn't so sure about that anymore. A breakdown? Something wasn't adding up, that's what spooked him.

"I don't have that many visitors," Vogel said.

Another awkward pause ensued and Jerry weighed where he might take the conversation next. Maybe he should just come clean.

"I'm here about the lawsuit you filed."

Vogel nodded. "I see," he said. "Are you here in an official capacity?"

"Sort of," Jerry said. "I'm here in an unofficial official capacity."

"Okay."

Smiling, Jerry needed to come even cleaner. "Kind of a coincidence, really. I came down here to visit my mom, as I said, and I saw in the paper that you had filed a challenge to Obamacare and I was kind of blown away. I was like, small world, you know?"

"And the Speaker would like nothing better than to overturn Obamacare, is that it?"

Jerry looked him in the eye. "That's exactly right."

"Well, you know as well as I do that even if I prevail, the ruling will carve out only a very small exception. It's not going to bring the whole thing crashing down or anything like that."

"Could be a start," Jerry said, imagining again Republicans converting in droves to this new religion.

"Anyway, I don't think that's why I'm doing it."

"What do you mean, you don't *think* that's why you're doing it? You have backers that put you up to it?"

"I mean, who knows why we do anything? You wake up one morning and you know you have something that you need to do. I don't really take the time to judge why I do what I do anymore, you know what I mean?"

No, Jerry didn't know at all what he meant, so he sidestepped the question. "So why *do* you think you're doing it?"

"People are brainwashed," Vogel said. "Maybe I'll have the chance to tell the other side of the story."

Jerry took this in. After a moment, he chuckled and leaned back, resting both arms along the back of the sofa. His old acquaintance, Brad Vogel, had become a whole lot of crazy. And crazy he knew how to handle.

"Wow, Brad," he said. "You've changed a lot since law school. You were serious, hair slicked back, buttoned down. You're still serious but, I don't know, there's something different about you."

"Would you like something to drink?" Brad said.

"What d'ya got?"

"I could make some coffee."

"Too much trouble," Jerry said.

"No, I was making it when I heard the knock on the door. Just be a minute."

It was warm in the house. When Vogel disappeared into the kitchen, Jerry stood up and took off his jacket. A laptop,

Apple, sat on the table beside the chair where Vogel was sitting. It was plugged into the wall, charging. A chic glass-top dining room table was cluttered with books in the back. Jerry went to the doorway into the kitchen and watched Vogel start the machine. A table and two chairs to the right, some dirty dishes were piled up in the sink. Jerry shook his head: Brad Vogel with dishes in the sink. He backed away before he was noticed.

"Cream and sugar?"

"Black is fine," Jerry said as he stood in the middle of the living room with his hands in his pockets.

A few minutes later, Vogel brought him a mug and Jerry took a sip. It was good stuff, high end. Some indulgences burrow in deep and you can't get rid of them.

"I *have* changed since law school," Vogel said. "That's a fair statement."

Jerry was looking out the front window. The sky was overcast with a low cloud ceiling, the weather out there unseasonably warm.

"They said you had a breakdown."

Brad sat on the arm of the chair. "In a way, I guess I did."

Jerry turned and looked at him, his free hand still in the pocket of his jeans. "Care to talk about it?"

"I was working for Brackman-Hollis doing medical malpractice defense mostly. I'd been there about five years when my girlfriend and I began to have problems." This was indeed old news, as Orlando Broxton had said, even to Vogel, himself. "You may remember Candice."

"Yes," Jerry said. "Blonde, glasses."

"That's right," Vogel said. "I'd always had what you might call a preoccupation with neatness and order. My German heritage probably had something to do with that." Vogel smiled. "Everything had to be in its place and clean and neat."

"I remember that, too," Jerry said.

"And everything had to be the best. Candice was one of those things. When she ended it, I started having full-on OCD symptoms. One episode, I locked myself in the bathroom and didn't come out for 12 hours. Luckily, I had my cell phone with me and managed to call in sick, a no-no at Brackman-Hollis. I didn't know what was happening. I talked to a doctor about it, he told me what was going on, set me up with some pills and sent me to a psychologist. She ran a few tests and promptly told me there was nothing wrong with me. I guess by then I had calmed down and was back into a normal range of behavior. But the fact was, there was plenty wrong with me. I left her office and determined then and there that I was going to get to the bottom of it all, no matter what it took."

"So you quit and moved to London?" Jerry said.

"Not quite," Vogel said. "Not long after I made that decision, something happened to me. It was like I'd been encased in ice all my life and suddenly without warning, and for no particular reason that I can point to, except that decision I had made, the ice just cracked and fractured and fell away. That's the only way I know to describe it."

Jerry sat down on the couch and Brad slid down into the chair he'd been sitting on.

"I kept working at Brackman but everything started to look different. The firm, how we did business, how the hospitals did business—everything. We handled every aspect of the medical industry, from malpractice to lobbying in Washington, DC, and state capitals all around the country. Our biggest client by far was Populous Healthcare. The business became so lucrative over the years, with the largest health insurance company in the country right there in Louisville and all the support companies that sprang up around it and the explosion of government involvement in healthcare, that it consumed what had once been a prestigious, broad-spectrum legal services provider into what in many ways became, essentially, the *consigliere* for a healthcare mafia. I was starting to have qualms and I think they could sense that. That's all it really took to pull you off the partner track at Brackman. I wasn't their kind of guy anymore. I was out within two months of that profound experience."

"Really?" Jerry said. "They fired you just like that."

"At the time, it seemed like a crisis in and of itself, of

course. I wasn't ready to let go of all that just yet. The salary, the prestige. I groped around for a while but there were no jobs to be had, not for me anyway. That's the way it is in Lexington. Something like that happens, you're radioactive for a while. I had a friend who knew the County Attorney here in Laurel County. I came to work as an assistant for him. I was making subsistence wages, pretty much, but that was plenty for where I was at the time.

"Very monastic," Jerry said. "Country living has a way of restoring the soul."

"Right," Vogel agreed. "Exactly right. I never would have considered the move before, but that's how it's worked out. I worked there for about a year until some of the local attorneys took me under their wing and showed me how I could make a little more on my own. So I hung out a shingle. That was a couple of years ago."

"I had no idea," Jerry said, just to have something to say.

"Like a lot of people say, it was the best thing that could have ever happened to me."

"And the suit you filed," Jerry said, feeling his way, "that's somehow an extension of this...experience you had."

"Yes."

"This religious conversion, if you will."

"It has nothing to do with religion," Vogel said. "It's just life. It's the way things are. Religion is an attempt to institutionalize that which is spiritual. It can't be done. It can't be accomplished. The process of institutionalization kills spirituality, which can only be individual and personal. Spirituality is about how each of us lives his life in the here and now. It's not something that can be codified."

Jerry had long since left his Christian roots behind. It was nice, it was all very nice, but its moral tenants were such that he simply could not live up to them, and in many cases he didn't even feel that he should. In both his personal and his professional lives, he often felt the need to be more Machiavellian than the rules, if faithfully applied, would ever allow. And yet, organized religion was the largest part of his party's political base. It was a constant source of tension. He hated to go to church, but if rallying the base around a particular Republican agenda item required it, he could sing from the hymnal and speak from the pulpit alongside the most ardent believer.

If Jerry understood what he was saying, Brad Vogel experienced no such tension. He seemed to reject organized religion outright. Jerry even then foresaw that this could be a problem, if not for Vogel, then for the Religious Right, so called. If they got so much as a whiff that Vogel rejected their branding, he would be out, and any support the Speaker and his underlings—Jerry—had offered to him would become a political liability.

"Okay," Jerry said, drawing out the letters. "So the free exercise of religion under the First Amendment doesn't have to actually come from religion. It can pertain to any deeply held conviction."

"That's right."

"So what's the conviction?"

"That all medicine is a substitute for consciousness," Vogel said. "To the extent you're conscious, you don't need so-called healthcare and so you shouldn't have to pay for it. This is a completely different paradigm."

Jerry heard the words, but in a rational sense he had no idea what Brad Vogel was talking about. *Consciousness*? What the hell did he mean by *consciousness*?

At the same time, the spirit of it struck a chord deep inside him, but that's all it was, a vague feeling of kinship. He couldn't make the leap from what Vogel was saying to his own rejection of modern medicine after what the doctors had done to his father—not consciously anyway. He didn't recognize that he too was hoping there might be a better way to solve his own health issues, and that that was part of what was driving him to investigate Vogel's case.

"Boy, that's out there, my friend," he said, standing up and looking out the window once again at the brooding clouds. "You're right, we're not going to be carving out much of an exception with that one."

"As I said, that really isn't my motivation. People are being brainwashed and they have been for hundreds of years. And with the advent of mass media, modern marketing and ubiquitous advertising, the process of indoctrination into a fallacious philosophy has reached a critical stage."

"What the hell are you talking about?" Jerry said turning back to Vogel again, feeling a little threatened.

"Do you have time to take a ride?"

Jerry held out his hands. "I'm on vacation."

Chapter 4

Vogel exchanged his house slippers for shoes, grabbed a jacket and lead Jerry out the front door and around the side of the house to the detached garage. He lifted the door, revealing the contents of the flimsy structure to be none other than a BMW Z4 convertible.

"Nice ride." Now *this* was vintage Brad Vogel, a lifeline to their shared past that made Jerry more comfortable somehow.

"It was already paid for when everything went south," Vogel said. "Maintenance is a little pricey, but I couldn't bear to let it go. The local girls like it. That's about all it takes, really."

"I can understand that," Jerry said. "I'm a little attracted to you right now myself. And I say that with 'an unblemished record of staunch heterosexuality.'" The old repartee from law school was coming back to the relationship, replete with *Seinfeld* references. "So you still . . ."

"Like girls?" Vogel finished. "I had a spiritual awakening. I didn't become a priest."

"Certainly not," Jerry said.

* * *

Vogel drove out to I75 and pulled over to the shoulder just before the onramp. He got out and Jerry did likewise.

"See that?" He pointed at a billboard.

"'All Saints Hospital – Your Doctors for Life," Jerry read aloud. "Kentucky's Largest Health System. London Cancer Center: Because Cancer Can Strike Anyone at Anytime." The words were written over the face of a pretty woman in owl-like glasses, her shoulders clad in a white lab coat, draped with a stethoscope. "Yeah. So?"

"That's propaganda. It's the main tenant of their faith. It's a religion based on the belief that the world is simply a series of randomly occurring events. And doctors are the ministers of the religion."

"But cancer *can* strike anyone at anytime," Jerry said.

"How do you know that? How do you know that there isn't a reason why people get cancer?"

Jerry reached down deep into his argumentative lawyer nature but came up with nothing. He was stuck.

"Healthcare is a for-profit business. Businesses thrive by creating markets for themselves. That's all this is," Brad said ticking his head in the direction of the billboard. "You only accept this statement because of forty-plus years of indoctrination, of which this is simply more systematic reinforcement. But it ain't necessarily so. In fact, it definitely isn't so."

"How do you know that?"

"Because I've proven it to myself. And so can you."

A few cars whizzed by and Jerry's eyes traveled back up to the billboard and beyond. The goldenrod Cracker Barrel sign stood nearby, slightly swaying in the wind.

"Hey, have you had breakfast yet? I always get a hankerin' for Cracker Barrel when I come down this way."

Vogel looked at his watch, a nice one. "Sure, I've got time," he said.

* * *

Jerry had already had one breakfast, or perhaps two depending on how one counted. And all this talk about doctors and hospitals and cancer made him feel guilty for what he was about to do again. But then, he had registered not the slightest chest pain all morning. He realized this as out of habit he perused the menu, and when the waitress arrived he promptly ordered what he always did.

"Four stars," he said, noting the waitress's apron. "Nothing but the best for us. The manager must have pegged us as a handful." He smiled up at the woman, who smiled down at him, tired but appreciative. "I'll have the Uncle Herschel's, over easy, sausage, hash brown casserole, with three blueberry pancakes on the side."

Brad ordered three pancakes too and a side of bacon.

"Not a health nut, eh?" Jerry said. "Me, neither."

"I eat what my body tells me to eat," Brad said. "The body

has it's own intelligence. The best thing you can do is stay out of its way. I don't override my body's natural inclinations with rationality about what may or may not be good for me. There's no need for that when you're not cut off from your body."

"Is this part of the system, too?" Jerry said.

"It isn't the body that causes the problems, it's the self-destructive thoughts most people pump into their bodies, combined with a complete lack of consciousness. Most people are completely cut off from their bodies. And then when the body tries to get their attention through disease or...weight gain, they have no idea how to respond."

There was just enough of a pause to indicate that Brad realized, belatedly, the implication of what he was saying. It was unusual for Jerry, but he felt a little defensive. If he didn't want to bring his own health issues into this discussion earlier, he really didn't want to now.

"I'm sorry," Brad said. "I didn't mean—."

"It's all right," Jerry said. "You wouldn't be the first to tell me that this week." Changing the subject a little, he said, "So how exactly is medicine a substitute for consciousness?"

"I'll show you." Vogel stretched his leg out in the aisle and hiked up his pant leg. "See that?" He pointed to a small, inflamed spot just above his ankle.

"Looks like an infection," Jerry said. "An infected hair follicle."

"That's right," Vogel said, protracting his pant leg and retracting his leg. "Now I could easily put some antibiotic ointment on it and clear it up in a couple of days, right?"

"Probably."

"But instead, I can also use consciousness to heal it on its own."

"How do you do that?"

"By taking my awareness into that area as often as possible. This is the great secret of all positive change, whether it be a change of character or a change in a physical condition. There is really no difference between the two. It's awareness—not judgment—that brings about the improvement. Take your awareness into it, feel it from the inside. That's all it takes for improvement to come about. Medicine is a substitute for that because it keeps you from having to become aware of your body at all."

"Hm," Jerry grunted in response.

"And the beauty of it is, this process has a far greater impact than just healing that little spot on my leg. 'A little leaven leavens the whole lump of dough,' is the way Jesus put it. Even that small amount of body awareness takes you infinitely deeper into reality, and that depth is healing to your entire being."

Jerry grasped none of the foregoing. The voice in his head had latched on to a point it wished to make and everything after that had been tuned out. "Isn't that spot going to heal on its own eventually, anyway?"

"Maybe. Maybe not. You don't need to take my word for any of this. You can prove it to yourself the next time you have any kind of physical malady. Use something small like this." Vogel pointed to his leg. "That's what your body is for, to teach you the nature of the universe."

Too late for small physical maladies, Jerry thought, thinking of his heart. "What about big things?" he asked as nonchalantly as he could manage.

"I'm not recommending that people go off their medications," Vogel said. "Unconsciousness got them to the point where they required a substitute. But certainly they can use minor ailments to prove it to themselves and then supplement medicine with consciousness until they see the results. It's building faith, in a way, but I would actually call it building knowledge about the way things are. You have faith in what you don't see. This you can see. The results, I mean."

"Have you ever read any studies about this?" Jerry persisted.

"Do your own study next time you catch a cold," Vogel said. "A cow doesn't need a study to tell it to eat grass," Vogel said, gesticulating toward the window beside them. Jerry looked outside on cue. Across the interstate cows stood grazing in the field.

"No," Jerry said, "but they might benefit from a study that tells them to eat bluegrass instead of fescue, which has no nutritional value."

"You don't think cows know when they're getting nutrition?" Vogel countered.

Jerry shrugged. "Cows are pretty dumb," was all he said, but he had to admit, they knew.

"Drink coffee, don't drink coffee," Vogel gestured at the table beside them, where the occupants were already in mid-meal. "Eat eggs, don't eat eggs. They change their minds every other week. Why? Because the cause of disease is not in these factors. The cause is in the fact that to varying degrees people bombard their bodies with painful thoughts and they don't realize it because they remain otherwise cut off from their bodies. Dealing with sickness with medicine and surgery is only dealing with symptoms, not root causes."

Jerry thought: *I'm not cut off from my body and yet I have this heart problem to deal with, just like my father.*

Vogel seemed to respond to Jerry's thoughts. He said, "Want to find out if you're cut off from your body?"

Sensing a trap, Jerry went back to his thoughts. "What about genetics?" he asked.

"What about them?"

"Aren't genetics the biggest player in all this?"

"All right," Brad said. "Let's explore that." He reached into his shirt pocket and took out his iPhone and began searching for something. "Here's a recent article I came across." He handed the phone over the table.

"'DNA pioneer James Watson takes aim at "cancer establishments'," Jerry read, handing back the phone. "Okay."

Vogel scrolled down. "The article talks about mapping of the human genome. It says,

> "The great hope of the modern targeted approach was that with DNA sequencing we would be able to find what specific genes, when mutated, caused each cancer," said molecular biologist Mark Ptashne of

> Memorial Sloan-Kettering Cancer Center in New York. The next step was to design a drug to block the runaway proliferation the mutation caused."
>
> But almost none of the resulting treatments cures cancer. "These new therapies work for just a few months," Watson told Reuters in a rare interview. "And we have nothing for major cancers such as the lung, colon and breast that have become metastatic."

"Yeah," Jerry said. "So?"

"Let me give you the translation: 'We've mapped out the DNA and found that it doesn't explain everything.'" Vogel allowed a moment for his translation to sink in. When Jerry bobbed his head a little in uncertain agreement, Vogel said, "Could that be because there's a spiritual aspect to disease?" Jerry could find no response, so he shrugged and took a sip of coffee. "The article goes on to say:

> The main reason drugs that target genetic glitches are not cures is that cancer cells have a workaround. If one biochemical pathway to growth and proliferation is blocked by a drug...the cancer cells activate a different, equally effective pathway.

Jerry sat blinking as the waitress returned with the food.

"Don't you see?" Vogel said. "This result is predictable when you take consciousness and the impact of a person's unconscious thoughts into account. You can't have a positive result from negativity."

"Thank you, dear," Jerry said to the waitress.

"He's describing exactly what happens. You can treat one pathway, but if the painful, negative thoughts keep coming, and the patient doesn't feel them and stop them—by making them conscious—then the disease—which is merely a reflection of that negativity—will find a workaround and the body will eventually give up and die."

"That's how it all works, huh?" Jerry said. "You've figured it all out, whereas Sloan-Kettering is groping in the dark." Jerry began doctoring his pancakes and then his grits.

"Why are there no studies to back up what you're saying?"

"Because this runs counter to the faith," Vogel said, preparing his pancakes too with syrup and butter. "They're trying to solve the problem without recourse to consciousness, which they don't believe is anything of significance. The world is all neutral molecules floating aimlessly in space, responding to causes and effects that go back to the big bang. But the universe isn't that way at all. It's actually quite benevolent."

"If you say so," Jerry said, his mouth full of eggs.

Vogel took a moment to swallow before responding. "You don't have to take my word for it. You can try the experiment for yourself."

"The experiment?" Jerry said. "What experiment?"

"Finish your breakfast," Vogel said. "It just takes a few minutes. We have plenty of time. You're on vacation, remember?"

"So what are you trying to do?" Jerry said. "Live forever?"

"Not forever," Vogel said. "The point is, disease need not be part of the equation, that's all. Guys like me, we have a couple of options. We either live to a ripe old age, or we die a violent death in service to the Universal. Jesus, Gandhi, and thousands of others we've never heard of."

"You're comparing yourself to those guys?" Jerry said. "That's pretty bold."

"Something's happened to me, Jerry. I've crossed over. As Jesus said, it only takes a mustard seed of faith to move a mountain. Maybe I just have that mustard seed at this point. Maybe guys like Eckhart Tolle have three seeds worth of whatever it is we have."

"Who the hell is Eckhart Tolle?" Jerry interjected.

"He's a spiritual teacher, look him up," Vogel said. "The point is, there are a lot more seeds to be accessed. This is where we're evolving next. Do you understand what I'm talking about?"

"Not a clue," Jerry said. "But if violent death is part of the equation, I don't think many people are going to sign up."

"There's no reason to run from danger or death," Vogel said. "We're going to be here until the job is done and then we'll 'return to the source,' as Lao-tzu put it. Or in the words of Diogenes, the great Cynic philosopher, when he was asked, 'What is the difference between life and death?' he answered, 'No difference.' The next question: 'Well then, why do you remain in this life?' His answer, 'Because there is no difference.'"

Jerry looked at Vogel skeptically. Was he serious about all this?

"I'll tell you the secret," Vogel said. "If you treat the spiritual as physical and the physical as spiritual, you'll come much closer to reality than any religious teaching out there."

"I have no idea what that means," Jerry said.

"You don't have to take my word for any of this. You can give it a try. Are you ready?" Vogel asked.

"Ready for what?"

"For the experiment."

"What, here?" Jerry said. The tables around them had cleared out in the pre-lunch lull. They were out of earshot of their next nearest neighbors and the din of table prep by the busboys gave them their own bubble of privacy.

"I'm not sure I want to," Jerry said.

"Just relax," Vogel said. "You're here to evaluate my case. Isn't that true?"

"Well, yes, but—"

"This is the one and only way to do that," Vogel said. "Now give me my day in court. It's a very simple exercise. Close your eyes."

Looking around first, Jerry reassured himself of the privy of his environs and only then complied.

"Okay, now I want you to take your awareness into your feet," Vogel said.

"What does that mean?"

"Imagine your feet. Feel them, from the inside."

Jerry did as directed and waited a moment. He didn't feel anything except discomfort at having to do such a ridiculous thing in the middle of a Cracker Barrel restaurant. "Okay."

"What do you feel?"

"What do you mean, what do I feel? I don't feel anything." Except ridiculous, he didn't include.

"Give it a minute."

A minute? This minute will be the longest of my life, Jerry thought. "This is stupid."

"Just humor me," Vogel said. "Are you feeling anything yet?"

Jerry concentrated as hard as he could, hoping that would bring this painful indignity to a swifter end. And then he did start to feel something as he realized that his toenails needed clipping, hoping the next step in the experiment would not be to take off his shoes and socks.

"It's kind of like that feeling when your arm falls asleep and then the blood rushes back into it."

"A tingling sensation?"

"Yes." And it was just as uncomfortable as that. Jerry hoped the experiment would end soon. He couldn't take much more of this.

"Okay, good," Vogel said speaking slowly just above a whisper. "That's all it really takes. Everything stems from this. 'A little yeast leavens the whole lump of dough.' This is you...being. Not doing, not thinking—it has nothing to do with rationality—just being. This is your soul, the life that you are, which animates your body. Shifting the sense of who you are from the virtual world of mind to this—whatever you want to call this: soul, consciousness, being, love (it feels like the embodiment of love), joy (the joy of being, our natural state)—it's the great secret of life. As mundane as this may seem to you now, it's a profound experience, just concentrating your awareness on your body. It's the sum total of all the religions. Now do the same thing with your ankles."

"My ankles."

"Yes."

Jerry complied but a panic was starting to set in. This shift from mind to being was very disorienting. In an instant, he sensed that all he had worked for in his life would come to nothing if he kept this up. That mind might be nothing. And if mind was nothing, what advantage did he have? It felt like death, the death of his self.

Even with the panic vying for his full attention, Jerry could feel his ankles almost immediately. “Okay,” he said.

“Now work your way up to your calves,” Vogel instructed. “Tell me when you can feel them.”

Jerry tried to comply, feeling his calves, but before he, himself, knew what was happening, he had opened his eyes and slammed his hand on the wooden table. “Enough!”

Brad didn’t react at all. Neither man spoke for a moment. Jerry looked around and saw that the patrons at the far end of the dining room had looked his way, and when his eyes met theirs, they went back to their own conversations.

After a moment more, he noticed the check on the table and picked it up and read through it. “I’m going to go pay,” he said and he got up and walked to the register, and when he had paid, he went out and waited by the car.

When Vogel came out a few minutes later, Jerry was leaning against the Bimmer, his hands in his pockets. Vogel had Jerry’s jacket in hand.

“You forgot this,” Vogel said.

“Didn’t want to blow my exit,” Jerry quipped.

They didn’t talk throughout the short drive back to Vogel’s house. Once in the driveway, Vogel said, “That’s a very common reaction. The mind doesn’t take well to being undermined by being.”

Jerry got out and then so did Vogel. “Good luck with your lawsuit,” Jerry said.

“Thanks.”

“Good to see you again.”

“You, too.”

Jerry got into his Cherokee and drove away.

Chapter 5

A few minutes later, as he was driving back to his mother's house, Jerry's cell phone went off. It was the COS's ringtone.

"Christ almighty," Jerry said. "Hello."

"You work fast," the COS said.

"Meaning?"

"Pattie tells me you have something on Obamacare."

"Oh, uh, it didn't pan out," Jerry said, knowing this wasn't going to fly. "It's just some crackpot who doesn't want to pay his taxes."

Jerry's honest opinion? Now? After talking to Vogel? His case was legit. It would indeed gain some traction with Republican voters and the national media. Without question, it would be much better to get in the game before the opening tip off than to hope to call the shots from the sidelines.

But Jerry's unnerving interaction with Brad Vogel—the new Brad Vogel—made him want to run like hell and never look back. He had experienced being for the first time. There was actually something to him that wasn't thinking, wasn't rational. It was like the Ghost of Christmas Past. In an instant, in that damned experiment, Vogel had opened his eyes to a world he'd never seen before, a vision that destabilized the world in which he had lived his whole life. Damn that Vogel.

And damn that Pattie too, Jerry thought. Why in the hell did she have to open her fat mouth?

"Nonsense," the COS said. "If he's a crackpot, then you've got to see to it that he pulls it together."

"Patty is an intern and you're not an attorney," Jerry said. "It's my professional assessment that this is not worth pursuing, and that's the end of the matter."

The COS grumbled something and hung up. Jerry looked at the phone before throwing it at the floorboard.

* * *

"Why did you have to say anything?" Jerry complained. "Who told you to say anything? I didn't tell you to say anything!"

Pattie was part of that old world that Vogel had somehow, inexplicably taken from him the moment Jerry began to feel his own feet from the inside. He could sense that. He didn't know how or why, but he knew it deep in his soul like he knew his own name. And Pattie, herself, had been the agent of that destruction!

"I, I, I—" was all the Georgetown-trained lawyer could muster under the withering tirade.

"You don't talk to the COS, I talk to the COS, you got that?"

"I wasn't really talking to the COS," Pattie said, holding the phone a few inches from her ear. "I ran into him a few minutes after I got off the phone with you. It was an offhanded comment. Just making conversation and he started grilling me and immediately got on the phone with the Speaker."

"Christ Almighty," Jerry said, pacing the floor back at his mother's house, in her bedroom, the only place, to his frustration, where he could find enough bars to call Washington.

"You have no idea what you've gotten me into," he said before clicking off.

His mom had been on her way out when he rolled back in around lunchtime. Now, after talking to Vogel, the COS and Pattie, his chest hurt like hell. He didn't want to think anymore about Brad Vogel, so he headed out to the barn to shovel a little hay. Farm work, as much as he detested it, always had a way of clearing his mind.

Just as he reached the barn, a Kentucky State Police cruiser turned into the drive. In his anger, Jerry quelled a groan. "This is all I need right now." The loan trooper proceeded slowly up to the edge of the barnyard and eased to a stop. Though he was wearing civilian work clothes—flannel shirt, jeans, a barn jacket—the must-be trooper took his time getting out of the cruiser in that same practiced manner as when he was about to ruin someone's day with a ticket.

"Hi, Eric," Jerry said, with as much chipper in his voice he could muster under the circumstances of the day, and the presence of his brother. "Good to see you."

"Cut the crap, Jerry. What are you doin' here?"

Here we go, Jerry thought. Same ol' same ol'. He just didn't get it. Offer to get a guy one little six-figure job in the Department of Homeland Security and he makes out like you're the crookedest bureaucrat the world has ever seen—self-righteous bastard. Just the latest thing for him to get his nose out of joint about, nothing new.

"Just came by to see Mom for a few days," Jerry said, maintaining decorum, turning his disgust further in on himself.

"I'm surprised the gov'ment can function without you. Prob'ly have another shutdown pretty soon, won't they? What are you doin' near the barn?"

"Mom asked me to put some hay out for—"

"You don't need to worry your pretty little head about that. I'll take care of it. Just like I've taken care of everything else around here."

"Fine," Jerry said. "That's just fine with me."

Eric brushed passed his brother and went into the barn, leaving Jerry standing in the barnyard dust, shaking his head. He looked at his watch. One-thirty.

Maybe he'd drive around, see his cousins. It was always nice to see them. *They* were proud of him. In summer, he would roll up in his Cherokee and invariably find one of them in a field somewhere, mowing or tending a fence, and they'd always stop whatever they were doing and talk for as long as he sat there idling, the land and the cattle weren't going anywhere. The conversation would meander along aimlessly until finally there would be a pleasant pause in the conversation, with all hands staring out at the horizon. Greetings would be exchanged, a parting jocular potshot at Washington, DC, would be proffered with a smile and Jerry would drive on, watching them in his rearview mirror as they slowly got back to work.

But in winter, they were much harder to find. And it looked like it was about to rain. "I bet one of *them* would take a six-figure government job," Jerry mumbled as he turned to head back into the house, wondering if his mom had left him something for lunch.

* * *

After his conversation with the COS—a few angry hours after—Jerry decided it would be better to move on this proactively. The COS would inevitably stew in his own juices, as the saying goes, until he called Jerry back to twist his arm until he cried uncle. In the meantime, maybe he could find something that would make even the COS realize this course of action was imprudent. And if not, it would look better to say he had reconsidered working with Vogel all on his own.

It was seven-thirty that evening and dark by the time Jerry had convinced himself to return to Brad Vogel's house. The man had the highest-tech phone money could buy but he seemed disinclined to answer it.

As he approached the house, Jerry could already see and hear why: outside, the street was lined with cars, and inside, Vogel sat Jesus-like in his leather chair in the midst of an attentive flock that surrounded him on three sides, chairs pulled from the kitchen and dining room to accommodate most of them, with a couple seated Indian-style on the authentic Persian carpet. The overfilled living room radiated heat when Jerry stepped up on the porch and pressed his face against the screen to announce his arrival. The audience couldn't help but crane in his direction when Vogel waved him in even as he continued to speak: "You've often heard the phrase, 'You can't legislate morality,' right? But there's a difference between law and morality. Don't drink—that's morality. It applies only to how the person lives his life. Don't drink and drive—that's a law. It's an attempt to protect other people from that same person's unconscious behavior."

Vogel paused, looking from one person to the next, allowing his audience a moment to absorb what to him was simple and what to them, by the looks of them, must have been like an alien language.

"We need laws to protect people from the unconsciousness of others, but we don't need morality. We don't need any additional set of rules to tell people how they should live their lives, whether that moral code come from the clergy or the likes of Lady Gaga."

That drew a laugh even from Jerry.

"And there are a lot of extraneous moral tenants coming from both, I assure you. There are two problems with moral codes. First, they don't work. They are completely ineffective in changing a person's behavior. Second, moral codes vary depending upon the assumptions on which they're based." He paused again...this was important. "So how do you pick one over another?"

"Pick the one that comes from God," someone said.

"But the Muslims say theirs comes from God," Vogel countered. "So do the Christians. What then?"

After an ensuing silence, Vogel said, "I'm afraid it's up to each individual to decide what to do and what not to do, and that decision can only be made in any given moment, not ahead of time. I'll explain how in just a moment."

Shifting his weight from one foot to the other to wait ou Vogel's talk, head down, hands in pockets, Jerry surprise himself by thinking that at least this should be interesting.

"Morality has its roots in Aristotelian philosophy. It's about judgment. It's about rationality. Contrary to the prevailing viewpoint of our day, rationality—thinking—is only a very limited aspect of the totality of consciousness. It holds only a limited place, which is the production of laborsaving devices and communication, like we're doing now, and that's it. As the *Tao te Ching* says,

> If a country is governed wisely,
> its inhabitants will be content.
> They enjoy the labor of their hands
> and don't waste time inventing
> laborsaving machines.

"Think about that for a minute. Think about the mad rush of technology we see in the world today. It bespeaks a lack of contentedness, doesn't it? Do these things add to our peace? If you're at peace, do you really care about the next iPhone Apple puts out? At any rate, this is the realm of rationality. For higher questions of life, rationality has nothing whatsoever to say to us. So the very concept of morality—which is the application of rationality—thinking—to the question of what we should do, or how we should live—is irrational.

"That's why Jesus taught us not to judge. He taught us not to apply rationality to the higher questions of life. He taught, in essence, to reject the concept of morality."

Jesus rejected morality? Jerry looked around at the gathering. Would they get this? And if they did were they buying into it? Living rooms in London, Kentucky, were not generally known as places, like Parisian cafés, where high-level philosophy was discussed.

"Actually, the concept of morality was the upstart," Vogel continued. "Aristotle came three hundred years before Jesus and told people in essence to judge everything—that's what rationality means. Jesus advocated a return to an *earlier* way of life, before the infection of Aristotelian thought—that is to say, the application of rationality to all aspects of life—had taken root in the Judaism of his day. So what did Jesus advise should replace morality to answer the questions, 'What should we do and how should we live?' Maybe you can guess it. Anybody? What was that earlier way?"

After a long pause with no takers, Jerry heard himself say, "Love." Here he went again, speaking up when he probably shouldn't have. The group whipped their heads around again to stare at the latecomer.

From where he sat, Vogel looked up at Jerry, standing just inside the front door, and smiled. "That's right."

"I've been to church," Jerry said, and the group snickered. Only then did he recognize one of Brad's following to be the plump receptionist from the law office he had visited that morning, when she smiled up at him from the couch, his gold star for answering correctly.

"Love," Vogel repeated. "Love versus rationality. Love

versus morality. This is big, this is very big."

Vogel paused again for emphasis. Fabulous, Jerry thought. Nicely done. He was good at this.

"But what does that mean, exactly? What is love and what is rationality in this context? Well, here's the short answer: love is a feeling, rationality is a thought. This is such an important point that I want you to repeat that back to me."

Vogel was smiling when he said this. He was kidding, but all including Jerry complied. "Love is a feeling, rationality is a thought."

"Good," Vogel said. "I have you well trained." Some chuckled, some smiled, some remained straight-faced, attempting to zero in on what Vogel was telling them. "A thought is of the mind—that virtual space, the original computer, where nothing is real. A feeling is of the body. It's real. And here's the real key to all this: feelings and thoughts are connected. To understand how they're connected, we have to do a little reverse engineering. There's a simple progression we have to follow to get back to those feelings. We start with words. What are words? Words are attempts to express ideas, right?"

Agreement all around.

"Ok, now what are ideas?" Without waiting for an answer, which wasn't on its way anyhow, Vogel said, "Ideas are attempts to rationalize feelings. In other words, you have a feeling in your gut about something, some aspect of life, and you want to put that into words to express it in rational terms to someone else—communication, one of the two legitimate applications of rationality. All right?

"Now the rather obvious next question would be: where does the feeling come from?" He waited again to let the question resonate for a moment. "It comes from a connectedness to all that is, to the Universe, with a capital U. Our bodies are receivers. Antennae, if you will. Learn to rely on the feelings that come in. These feelings are the root, so to speak, the root from which most people are completely cut off."

Jerry shrugged internally. He could buy off on all of that without a problem.

"So getting back to Jesus," Vogel said. "We're going to bring this whole discussion full circle. We're going to close the gate, as it were. Let's remember the experiment we start off every meeting with, where we take our awareness into our bodies."

Ah, yes, the experiment, Jerry thought. He knew it well. He had a feeling this was all coming back around to the experiment. Jerry tried not to register any discomfort on his face, allowing his mind to wander back to the Uncle Hershel's breakfast he had had, rather than that experiment. He wondered if this would forever taint his appetite for the Cracker Barrel.

"From that experiment we can feel the nature of the universe—that it is benevolent, right?" When he got back blank stares, Vogel said, "What would a benevolent reality feel like?"

"Good."

"Yeah, good."

"And that's how it feels, right? When you're in direct contact with the reality that is your body?" Vogel shifted in his chair. "This is why it's an experiment. Don't take anyone else's word for it. Do it for yourself and decide what reality feels like for yourselves. If reality *feels* good, as you say, then it must *be* good. Peaceful, blissful, joyful. This is what Jesus means when he talks about love."

Jerry shook his head. If he was lost, these people were way lost. But maybe Vogel had it in him to bring it all together in a big finish. If he could do that for this group—and for Jerry—he might just have what it took after all to make it on a bigger stage. He might be just what the Speaker ordered. This was the finale, Jerry could sense it.

"We started off talking about morality and how it wasn't necessary, right?" Vogel said. "Now we've gotten all the way back there. Jesus came about three hundred years after Aristotle. It would take another three hundred years before the next sage came along to deepen our understanding of Love. That was a guy named Augustine. He was the Bishop of a place called Hippo, which is located in modern-day Algeria. He pointed out that the familiar phrase from the

Gospel of John, 'God is love,' necessarily also means that love...is...God...Huh? Think about that...He expands on this in his most famous sermon, in which he explains exactly what we've been talking about. That there is no need for a top-down morality to be imposed upon people. The better way is to 'love and do what you will.' In other words, tune into the Universe through your bodies to figure out what to do, how to live. In modern terms, we might say, 'Be conscious and do what you will.' When you're fully conscious, you are aware that the nature of the universe—the nature of reality—is what? Benevolent, peaceful, joyful, blissful? Or in a word...love."

Vogel's own sermon was complete. But it appeared he wanted to leave them with one last flurry, just in case this proved to be the last time he would ever get to address them.

"Be conscious of the signals coming into your body at any given moment. This is how we know what to do and how to live. Pay attention to the feelings in your body at all times. This is how God communicates with us. Ok, enough of my ramblings," he concluded. "Next time we'll talk about the Münchhausen Trilemma. It's a philosophical concept that's been known and suppressed since at least the third century. Look it up on Wikipedia for our next meeting. And also let's finish up with *Zen and the Art of Motorcycle Maintenance*, okay?"

* * *

It took a while for the group to file out. Little clusters remained until, one by one, people donned outerwear and migrated toward the door and out into the night in groups. Vogel fielded questions amiably from the more earnest participants. Jerry chitchatted politely with the receptionist until enough time had elapsed for her to leave.

When the last of them sallied forth into the night, Vogel said, "Welcome back."

"I didn't mean to interrupt your—"

"Don't be silly," Vogel said. "It's good to see you." He was clearly pleased, which made Jerry uncomfortable. Vogel seemed to be getting the wrong idea from his reappearance.

But what was the right idea?

"Do you like cigars?"

"Cigars?" Jerry said.

"Yeah, cigars."

The question caught Jerry off guard. "Yes," he finally said. "I like cigars." Brad stepped into his bedroom and Jerry felt the need to fill the momentary silence with chatter. "I have to say that I'm pretty spoiled, though. It's kind of a dirty little secret that Cuban cigars are almost as plentiful in DC as they are in Havana. I haven't had one in a while, but . . ."

Vogel reemerged with a humidor made of cherry wood in hand. It was open to reveal an array of brands: Punch, Montecristo, Romeo y Julieta, Cohiba. Jerry's hand felt irresistibly drawn to a Cohiba, a torpedo, and he ran it under his nose for a good sniff. Vogel held out a cutter and Jerry took it and snipped off the end at an angle.

Vogel placed the humidor on the coffee table and went to the kitchen.

"I haven't had one of these in a while," Jerry shouted between puffs as he lit up.

"I know," Vogel shouted back. "I don't often get a chance myself. It's no fun smoking them alone."

He came back with a bottle of Hennessy Cognac in one hand and two snifters, the stems between his fingers, in the other.

"You strike me as a Cognac man," Vogel said.

"What am I, a hip-hop mogul?" Jerry took the bottle. "XO, very nice."

"I've had it for a long time." He popped the cork on the half-full bottle and poured a little into each of the snifters.

Vogel took his and raised it in toast. "Here's to Cuba and France," he said.

"Here, here."

They took a sip and both sat down and Vogel began preparing his smoke of choice, a Punch panatela. A pleasant quiet hovered between them along with the blue smoke. It was a little too pleasant for Jerry. He felt the need to chase it away.

"You talk a lot about Jesus," he said. "So is this a

Christian thing you're into? Or . . ."

Brad finished lighting his smoke. "It's what they know," he finally said. "A point of departure. It's in all religions, and all religions sooner or later pervert it through the infection of rationality until it's unrecognizable."

"I see," Jerry said, his cigar clinched lightly in his teeth, though in actuality he did not see, which once more gave him pause regarding his presence here in Brad Vogel's home. It wouldn't be good for him personally to encourage any kind of proselytizing, nor would it be good for the mission. "Listen, Brad, you're kind of killing the fatted calf here, and I appreciate that, but—"

"Well, it isn't every day you meet up with old friends down in these parts," Vogel said, pretending a country accent as he turned his cigar before the flame of the match and puffed.

Another silence ensued.

"Good folks," Vogel said after a while, bringing the conversation back. "One of them wanted to talk to me about a personal issue. Next time, he came back with a friend and pretty soon it was a regular thing. They have no idea what I'm talking about, but I think they're drawn to—I don't know what you would call it—my spirit, I guess? My vibe? Maybe that's what you're experiencing, too."

"Actually, Brad—"

"You know," Vogel interrupted, and then he took a puff and let it out and looked up into the smoke. "The reaction you had to the exercise, the experiment, isn't at all uncommon. The mind very quickly realizes that its power will be usurped if the exercise is allowed to continue. So it shuts it down. The mind likes to feel like it's in charge, that it's in control. The exercise demonstrates that it isn't."

"Yes, well," Jerry said, cutting Vogel short. "Be that...as it may, that's really not why I came back."

Vogel paused and then smiled. "Okay," he said. He seemed to be playing along, as if to say, *Sure it isn't*, which got under Jerry's skin a little. "Then why *have* you come back?"

"Marching orders," Jerry said. "You're going to need help

with your lawsuit and I'm going to be the one to give it to you."

Vogel shifted in his seat, crossed his legs. "What kind of help? The legal aspect is pretty straightforward. I'm pretty sure I can handle that."

"But you're not really all that interested in the legal aspect," Jerry said. "You're also going to need publicity, image crafting, damage control. That's where I come in."

"I will have all the resources of the Speaker of the House at my disposal," Vogel said. "Is that it?"

"Unofficially, yes," Jerry said. "It's pretty simple, really. Not much real reporting gets done anymore. What you do is, we have a publicity firm put out a press release. It's like rats to the cheese. After that, we get a conservative think tank to do a quick study on your constitutional challenge, Fox News picks it up. Pretty soon you're making the rounds on all the talk shows."

"I'm not sure I'm ready for that kind of scrutiny," Vogel admitted. "I've gotten a few calls today. Reuters, Associated Press. Haven't returned any of them."

"Then why'd you file the suit?" Jerry said, momentarily peeved. Then he recalled Vogel's mystical assertions in their first encounter about not knowing why he had filed the suit and not judging himself and so forth. "I know, I know, it wasn't up to you." Jerry sat back against the arm of the couch and kicked his legs up. "The Speaker can never be implicated in any of this, that's very important."

"But you're on his staff," Vogel countered.

Jerry held out his hands. "We're old law school buddies. I'm on an unofficial mission to help out a friend in his hour of need."

"But I only knew you through Mouchie," Vogel said. "Are you sure they're going to buy that?"

Jerry smiled, getting the *Seinfeld* reference. He was glad his old friend could maintain a sense of humor through this. That would make this exercise a little less painful.

"Mouchie's dead," Jerry said through teeth clenched around his stogie, the perfect comeback. "Nobody needs to know the nature of our relationship back then. Besides, we had some good times. Sure, we weren't housemates or anything, but remember that trip to South Carolina after we took the bar? What was it, ten of us? That'll play." Jerry swirled his snifter, holding the bowl in his palm. "That'll definitely play."

"So what does the Speaker get out of it?" Vogel asked. "Unofficially. He's clear on the narrowness of the exception we're carving out, on the off chance I'm successful."

Jerry paused. "To be honest, Brad, I doubt the Speaker knows anything about it, at this point. His Chief of Staff will likely call all the shots. The COS says run it to ground, that's what we do."

"Plausible deniability."

"That would be the technical term for it."

Jerry sat back and tried to puff a few smoke rings into the air, eventually achieving success.

Vogel said, "Are you starting to see what I'm talking about? Do you see how the world is? You have to admit it's uncanny how this has worked out so far. You...here...just at this moment?"

"The COS has a good feel for these things. But I'm not going to lie. I'm not a big fan of all this stuff."

Vogel sat up to twirl the end of his cigar in the ashtray. "Even better," he said, a big smile finally creasing his face. "Who knows why things happen? All of this could be about just one person. You never know."

"Sometimes you do," Jerry said. "If the one person you're referring to is me, then it ain't. I'm just a foot soldier. A grunt. I do what I'm told for the cause."

"We'll see," Vogel said.

Cigar clinched once again in his teeth, Jerry said, "Yes, we will." He sipped and puffed in the dim lamplight. The cognac was beginning to have its warming effect. This was the first real pause he'd taken since he couldn't remember when.

Vogel looked at the white ash at the end of his cigar and let a few moments pass in silence. "Doesn't feel right."

"What's that?"

"I said it doesn't feel right. That's how we know what to do at any given moment, by feel. This doesn't feel right. Your offer's very generous but I'm going to pass on it. I'm going to go it alone."

At first Jerry was nonplussed. Competitive by nature, when he went in for the hard sell, he hated to come up empty. On the other hand, he didn't want to do this, and this was his out. Yet oddly, he felt both relief and fear at the same time.

"Then what more is there to say? You've got to go with your gut."

With promises to keep in touch and thanks for the booze and the cigar, Jerry was quickly on his way before Vogel could change his mind. He finished his cigar on the way home.

Chapter 6

For Jerry, duty called, not so much externally as internally. The time off—as it were—wasn't helping. His heart irregularities, but for a brief respite the previous afternoon, were back on again, and he was quickly over dealing with his brother, Eric, who had made a point of sticking around until Jerry got back that evening.

More than that, the things that Vogel had said were getting inside Jerry's head more than his brother ever could, causing his mind to race even more than it normally did—and causing Jerry to notice its racing—causing in turn copious loss of sleep. If he wasn't going to get any sleep in sleepy little London, Kentucky, what was the point of being there? He kissed his mom the next morning, dutifully stopped by the Speaker's Cincinnati office in the afternoon, had an early dinner out with the fam on the way to the airport and was back at work in DC the following morning.

"He doesn't want our help," Jerry told the COS.

"Even better," the COS responded. "It's not like we need his approval to do what we need to do."

"No," Jerry said. "Suppose not."

If they were in it unofficially, better to deal with Vogel at arm's length, more deniability for the Speaker. No problem here, Jerry thought, as long as I don't have to deal with Brad Vogel directly.

Jerry put the wheels in motion. The press releases were on the street within a day. He also called a couple of trusted reporter friends to give them information on background about the lawsuit.

But nothing in DC is ever completely on background. And one Senator Mack McCormick didn't get to where he was without plenty of deployed tentacles. The Senator mentioned the Vogel case to Jerry a day later at a cocktail party, a quiet one-way conversation.

"Jerry, nice to see you here," McCormick said. The two

men found themselves back to back at the center of the room. It was a nice spread put on by a shale oil drilling conglomerate. The Speaker had already come and gone.

Jerry had just gotten out of a conversation with a stray liberal staffer who had somehow wandered in. "It's almost Pynchonian," she had said about something or other. Jerry had never read anything by Thomas Pynchon, but nonetheless knew enough to include the phrase "rampant paranoia" in his response. When the staffer, a nice looking Asian woman, looked at him funny, Jerry got out of the conversation with: "More wine?" And that's when he bumped into McCormick.

"You know me, Senator," Jerry said, nibbling from a handful of peanuts in one hand, a highball of bourbon in the other. "Free drinks, I'm there."

Truth was, he wasn't going to show up for this one until he found out that Tim Hanrahan was going to attend. There he was, working the other side of the room, pocket hanky in place. Pattie was right, the pocket hanky was pretentious for a guy of his station. Sure, his family was rich, but he needed to realize his place in the pecking order on the job. He wished Pattie hadn't mentioned anything about Tim Hanrahan.

The Senator was getting a little stooped as he got older. Jerry had a couple of inches on him and dominated him with his girth. And yet the Senator seemed to overwhelm him in some indefinable way. That's why he was the Senator and he the staffer, Jerry guessed.

"Shouldn't you be down in London looking after your friend?" the Senator tossed out glibly. "Mr. Vogel, isn't it?"

Jerry was about to pop another peanut into his mouth. "Vogel?" he managed to repeat. The Senator smiled up at him. Jerry quickly regrouped. "Vogel…the name rings a bell. . ."

"My office, 8:30 tomorrow morning," Senator McCormick said and he was already beginning to drift away, other interests lining up to get his attention.

"You mean Jim Wiedemann," Jerry said. "You want to talk to the COS."

Senator McCormick said with a chuckle, "Everybody knows you're the brains of that outfit, Jerry. My office, eight-thirty."

Jerry now stood in the middle of the room alone. Nobody was interested in his opinion on shale oil extraction. He migrated to the table with the large bowl of cocktail peanuts and began funneling more of them into his mouth. Terror always made him hungrier.

He saw pocket hanky over there, who presently raised his dimpled chin toward Jerry in salute. Man, that was a nice suit, blue and a little luminescent. He looked down at his own charcoal gray with chalk pinstripes, holding his stomach in with his free hand to have a better look down his leg. When he lifted it, he noticed a palm print of peanut dust where his hand had been and he brushed it away.

There had been a time when he, too, had invested in his attire, buying a handful of five-hundred dollar suits before he had the money to afford them. That three-button get up Hanrahan was wearing cost as much as all those had combined, probably. Come to think of it, this might be one of those suits. Jerry looked inside at the label on the pocket: a Macy's house brand. No, it wasn't, he was relieved to discover. But of course it wasn't. No tailor could let a suit out that much. He'd let himself go a little.

Even so, if that rich little upstart thought he could waltz in here and take whatever job he wanted, he was in for a rude awakening.

He held out his leg one more time to get a gander at the hollows at the back. Maybe he could at least iron out the creases behind his knees once in a while....

And what did McCormick want with him? The implication was that he should come alone to that meeting. He shoveled another handful of peanuts into his cakehole then knocked back the watery bourbon to wash them down.

* * *

After the party, Jerry stopped by Pattie's apartment to discuss this strange interaction with Senator McCormick. Usually, such late-night consultation requests were simply a cover for sexual advances—they kept Jerry from ever having to define the relationship—but not this time. He had always been on the best of terms with the man, but there had been something sinister in Senator McCormick's demeanor somehow. Something cautionary.

"It's just been a while, that's all," Jerry said. He sat naked, covered to the waist by the bedclothes.

"That usually makes it go more quickly," Pattie said. "Not . . ." She gestured dismissively toward Jerry's lap as she got up and walked naked to the bathroom. Jerry watched her. She was a little overweight, but she had a pretty face, she was young, and she was nice. That was usually enough.

"You didn't have to confiscate my pills," Jerry said.

"I don't want you dying on me. What a nice scandal that would be."

He pulled the pink comforter up to his chest as he listened to the faint tinkling sound. "The COS felt the same way," he said, not loud enough to be heard.

"You have peanut breath, by the way."

"Peanut breath?" Jerry said. "That's not objectionable."

"You don't want to take your other pills, you don't get to take those."

"It's just stress. The doctor said so."

"It's just stress now, but with cholesterol like that you can't take chances."

Jerry set his jaw and shook his head, though there was no one in the room to see. He just couldn't take all those pills.

Pattie returned, terrycloth bathrobe cinched tightly, and plunked herself down at the foot of the double bed.

"Maybe you're having some misgivings," she said.

"No, no," Jerry said, patting her knee.

"It's only natural," Pattie said.

"It isn't that," Jerry said, though perhaps to an extent it was. It always was. That's what made him enjoy it at first, it's illicitness, but something had changed and he didn't wish to draw the line of that something back to Brad Vogel.

"I don't get it," he said. "Why would anyone care about this lawsuit? Especially Senator McCormick?"

"You care about it," Pattie said. "It's all you seem to be

able to talk about since you got back."

"What am I missing?"

"No clue," Pattie said, exhaling heavily. "You're exhausting me, Riggs."

"Should I go back down there for the next six months or more while the case wends its way through the courts?"

"And leave Hanrahan in charge again? I'd watch that if I were you."

"Tim?" Jerry dismissed. "He couldn't manage the legal affairs of the Speaker of his own house, let alone . . ." Momentarily drawn out of his revelry about the Senator, Jerry looked up at Pattie as if noticing her for the first time. Why did she have to keep bringing up Tim Hanrahan?

"If you say so."

"I don't know," Jerry said, back on the Senator, as Pattie got up and left the room. "I don't get it. I just don't get it."

* * *

"Jerry Riggs is here," the Senator's male assistant announced.

"Send him in," Senator McCormick said, continuing to read.

Jerry appeared in the doorway and the Senator looked up as if his presence were a total surprise. "Jerry," he said, giving him the politician's smile. "Come in."

"Morning, Senator," Jerry said.

Senator McCormick waved him over to the desk without getting up. He was sitting with legs crossed in shirt and tie. His suit coat hung on the rack by the door. His socks were black and to his knees beneath his charcoal pinstripe pant leg, a pure Kentucky gentleman.

"Now what in the hell is the Speaker doing mixed up with a . . ." he searched for just the right word "...a disturbed individual like your old friend Bradley Vogel?"

"I'm not quite sure what you're talking about, Senator," Jerry said. "I've heard about the District Court case filed by a law school acquaintance, of course, but we have nothing to do with it. We're watching it from afar just like everyone else. And my legal analysis of it is that it won't help us bring down Obamacare."

The Senator pulled a think dossier around to the edge of his desk and opened it. On top was a black and white paper copy of a photo of Jerry standing at Vogel's front door. The Senator flipped that over and the next item was one of Jerry's anonymous press releases.

Holy shit, were the only words that popped into Jerry's head. He remembered the scraggly guy with the haunting blue eyes in the Monte Carlo he had seen on Vogel's street, the guy who had almost hit him as he drove by. Could it have been him who snapped this photo? He did seem to be looking awfully hard at the houses. No, no, it couldn't have been. He didn't look the type at all. It couldn't have been him...could it?

Jerry swallowed hard. He didn't bother with further denials, explanations or apologies.

"So this is the route they're taking, is it?" he said plainly. "He's disturbed. You're going to discredit him by challenging his sanity, right off the bat?"

"I'm doing no such thing," Senator McCormick said. "I'm simply summarizing the information I've seen so far on the matter. Have you taken a look at his District Court brief?" The Senator gestured toward the document he'd been reading when Jerry came in.

"I've read it."

"Then wouldn't you agree that the man who wrote that would have to be insane?"

"Many people who have maintained deeply-held religious or spiritual beliefs have been called insane down through the years." Jerry couldn't help but defend Vogel when pressed, though he didn't disagree, and had made the same argument to himself repeatedly since returning from London. "The point is, these are his views, his values, and the First Amendment protects them."

"Be that as it may," the Senator countered, "there are political realities to be taken into account here. If the Speaker gets mixed up in all this, he may not be Speaker much longer. These views are extreme."

Jerry was well aware of the dangers and political sensitivities. Always great for a Congressman, those sensitivities went into hyper-mode at any of the leadership positions, and especially so for the Speaker of the House, the individual just two steps from the Presidency. The Democrats could make a lot of hay over the Speaker throwing his full weight behind anyone their media branded a lunatic. It's why he and the COS had made sure to incorporate a goodly amount of plausible deniability into their schemes. And it's why Jerry had to quell another hard swallow as he attempted to reposition the Senator. He was already beginning to feel a little isolated, a little out there on his own.

"That's why you're going to do all you can, Senator, to make sure that connection is never made."

"Come again," the Senator said. "I'm not following you."

"As a good Republican," Jerry continued, "you ought to be in this guy's corner too. Anyone who takes down Obamacare, even a little bit, ought to be a friend of yours. But he isn't. Why? Because Populous Healthcare is in your backyard." And you're in their back pocket, Jerry thought but didn't say. "Now, as long as the Speaker is out there preaching the party line, you have political cover."

"Cover for what?"

"I've been around a while now, Senator. I know how the Senate works. No one is more effective in working behind the scenes than you are. You were as responsible for getting Obamacare through the Senate as Obama, himself. Maybe more so. Without you it dies in committee."

The Senator could not completely suppress a self-satisfied smirk.

"You need the Speaker to cover your six with the base. He goes, you'll go with him eventually. Two thousand fourteen ain't that far away and you know they're going to bring in the big guns. You never know, they may get George Clooney to run against you. Not to mention a potential Tea Party challenge in the primary."

The Senator got up, thrust his hands into his pockets and looked out through the window behind his desk at the Mall.

"You know, I always liked you, Jerry." The words sounded menacing. "We need to get you back into the fold, back into the Commonwealth where you belong. What's a Kentucky boy like you doing working for an Ohioan, anyway?"

"Is that a job offer?" Jerry asked, smiling.

"That's right." The Senator turned to prove his veracity.

"No can do," Jerry said. "I have warrants." He stood up to get a better view, himself. "What I can't figure out is why your constituents even care about this little constitutional challenge in the first place. They won't see a dime in lost revenue. As you say, these views are extreme and specific to one person."

The Senator stood momentarily considering Jerry's words, and then his own. "I don't know," he finally said. "I honestly don't know."

McCormick turned to his desk, found a magenta pack of Post-it notes and scribbled something on the top one, plucked it from the stack and showed it to Jerry:

They will kill him.

When Jerry had read the note, McCormick took a lighter from the open drawer, lit the note on fire and dropped it into the marble ashtray, a nod to the tobacco farmers of his state, that sat, clean as a whistle but nonetheless defiant, on his desk.

"You can't be serious," Jerry said.

"This is something you have to take my word for."

"Which 'they' are we talking about here?"

The Senator waited in silence for the flame to burn out and then sat down. He wasn't prepared to answer.

"Over this?" Jerry said, still unable to believe. Once again, Jerry saw visions of Republicans and others flocking in droves to a church of Vogel's creation to keep from having to buy health insurance, completely thwarting the intent of Obamacare, sending its budget so far into the red that it would have to be abandoned. Maybe that's what was in the minds of the senator and his backers too. "What do they think? That he's going to start the, the, the Anti-Obamacare Church of Christ or something and everybody's going to join to keep from paying the individual mandate?"

"That would certainly be enough," McCormick said, but his expression reflected uncertainty. There was even more to it than that—much more—but the Senator didn't seem to know what it was, himself. "It's a multibillion dollar industry," the Senator concluded. "They are taking this challenge very seriously, that's all I can tell you. If you care about your friend, you'll get him to drop this case. Tell him we'll pay his mandate for him. Do whatever it takes but get him to drop that case."

Jerry still had a hard time believing what the Senator was telling him—and not telling him. But he was here, in the man's office. If this were some kind of a bluff, he would have passed it on through one of his cronies first. Senator McCormick was not a man given to histrionics or hyperbole. And there was that dossier, which included surveillance—surveillance!—of him at Vogel's door. Who in their right mind would cover the cost of that? They—whoever they were—were taking this seriously, all right.

"He's not going to do it," Jerry finally said. "He's one of those people who isn't afraid to go the distance."

"Then as a practical matter, Mr. Riggs," the Senator said, "I would distance myself from the situation, if I were you. The Speaker too. When a grenade goes off, what is it they say? Duck and cover?"

* * *

"You don't say," the Speaker's Chief of Staff took the news well. His braces held his woolen pants to the lower contours of his paunch as he stood diminutively, surveying his substantial desk. He looked as if he should have been puffing on a pipe just then, but he didn't actually smoke a pipe.

"He wouldn't even say the words out loud," Jerry continued. Jerry himself had whispered them close by the COS's ear. "He wrote it out on a Post-it note." For emphasis Jerry added, "Then he burned it in an ashtray! They've got surveillance and everything."

His heart was giving him fits again.

"Unusual," the COS said. He was not easily rattled by the prospect of death. Late in his army career, he had been involved in some capacity, which remained classified, or so he said, with the Highway of Death in the First Gulf War.

"This two-bit challenge just isn't worth all that, from a political perspective," Jerry argued, though his gut told him otherwise, a position his head was having a hard time coming around to. "I'm with Senator McCormick. We need to stay away."

"That's the Senate, my boy. They're more pragmatic. This is the House. We're zealots, true believers."

"This case is nothing."

"To the contrary," the COS said. "This means you're on to something. I don't know what it is yet and neither do you. You're a scout, my boy. You've made contact with the enemy. You've found a weak spot in his line. Now it's time to drive the armor through the gap."

"So we're taking this seriously?"

"Oh, yes."

Jerry had seen the political implications of Vogel's case himself from the beginning, with its potential to burrow a tiny hole into the Obamacare dam, one that might one day effect an all out breach of it. Yet his personal resistance to the philosophy—a resistance born in the Cracker Barrel restaurant no less—remained.

Jerry shook his head. "All right. I guess I better give him a call, try to warn him."

"You're not planning to pass along this information over the phone are you?" The COS mouthed the letters NSA.

"Come on, COS," Jerry said. "It wasn't satellite surveillance, for Christ's sake."

"Democracies are fragile things."

"Who'll run the shop while I'm gone? I thought you had a problem with me being away just a week. This could take a lot longer that that."

"I got over it," the COS said. "Hanrahan's been doing a fine job in your absence."

"Hanrahan?" Pattie was right. "Now wait just a minute."

The paranoia was setting in. Maybe the COS was simply trying to get him out of the office. Maybe he knew something about Pattie and him. And the office politics of politics could be political in the extreme.

"Your job is secure," the COS said. "This is a more

important mission than you apparently realize."

Now, why would the COS say *that*? 'Your job is secure'? Sure, that's what Jerry was thinking but apparently so was the COS!

After a little more discussion about covering a couple of key cases while he was away, Jerry left the COS's office feeling like he was on a conveyor belt over which he had no control. Taxpayer dollars got him back to Cincinnati that evening and he was snug in his old bed at his mother's farmhouse by that night.

But even at that, Jerry was too late. The events of which Senator McCormick had prophesied had already been set in motion...

Chapter 7

"Riggs." Jerry, fast asleep, picked up and answered his cell phone in practiced manner. He had gotten to the point where he could carry on entire conversations without waking up. Funny thing was, he'd long since realized that he gave much better answers that way.

"Your friend's house is on fire."

Jerry recognized the voice. "Eric?"

He had no idea where he was. Without opening his eyes, he tried to recall his movements. Was he in his apartment in Arlington? At home in Cincinnati? Had he fallen asleep in Pattie's bed? That gave him a jolt and he sat up. "Where the hell am I?"

Jerry looked around the room. Old Little League trophies out of reach on the high up shelf, a couple of model hotrods on the dresser, an ancient Farrah Fawcett poster, already vintage when he'd gotten it second hand, still on the wall...Had his life just been a bad dream? Was he a teenager again? He felt from within the corpulence of his body stressing the bedsprings. No, unfortunately he was not. It dawned on him that the Farrah poster was probably worth some money...he'd had good taste as a kid. Why didn't his mother turn this room into a billiards parlor or something?

"Your buddy's nowhere to be found," Eric said. "You better get him over there."

"Vogel?" Jerry said. "You're talking about Brad Vogel?"

"I'm on patrol near Corbin," Eric said. "I'm about 20 minutes out."

"Wait a second," Jerry heard himself saying. "How do you know I know Brad Vogel?"

He was having one of those moments again, asking the better question in his sleep. Eric couldn't have known that Jerry and Vogel had gone to law school together, and shouldn't have known that they had gotten reacquainted earlier in the week. And yet somehow he did know. Jerry remembered the surveillance photo he'd seen in Senator McCormick's file the previous day. Could there be a connection? Anything was possible at this point, he figured.

Only when the line went dead did Jerry wake up fully. He recalled his very pertinent question, and also that Eric had not seen fit to answer it. Jerry got dressed and got on the road in short order, his attitude growing sunnier and sunnier the closer he got to London.

He had no idea why he was almost gleeful at the idea that Vogel's house was on fire, yet he joyfully drove his Cherokee on through the night. The game was afoot. "God help me," he mumbled. "I do love it so." Maybe that's why he and the COS got on so well. Jerry mused that he would have made a great military man, himself—except for the discipline, of course. The mission, though, he was all about the mission. Loved the mission.

As he drove at high speed, Jerry made the call he had planned to make the following morning en route. And to his shock, Vogel actually answered. He hadn't answered during the day but dead of night he picks right up. Vogel was a strange bird. "Where are you?"

"At a friend's house," Vogel said. "Why?"

"You might want to meet me at your place," Jerry replied.

"Why?"

"From what I hear, it's a fireball."

After processing for a moment, Vogel said, "Can you pick me up?" He gave the address. Jerry knew exactly where it was.

When he got to the house, a woman a few years older than Vogel, her long blonde hair mussed, stood at the doorway with a concerned look on her face.

After a minute or so of driving, Vogel was the first to speak. "Look, I'm not a priest, all right?"

Even Jerry could feel the judgmental vibe he was giving off.

"You just have to be careful, that's all," Jerry said. "They're going to use anything they can against you."

Jerry had to admit it was more than that, though. He

wanted to hold Vogel to a higher standard, a Judeo-Christian moral standard he didn't live by himself and didn't realize meant anything to him except in a political sense. Deep down he was hoping to believe in Vogel, but if he cavorted with women in the same way that Jerry, himself, did, well...how was that any different?

"It doesn't work like that," Vogel said. "If you spend any time with me at all, you'll find that I'm the least moral person you know."

"Then what was all that talk about Jesus and the Bible last time I was here?"

"Jesus is one thing, the moral code that modern Christianity has fashioned in his name is quite another. We need laws to protect people from the unconsciousness of others, but beyond that a top-down, enforced morality doesn't work. In fact, it's counterproductive."

"You can't legislate morality," Jerry said, recalling Vogel's talk from a couple of night ago.

"'Judge not, lest you be judged.' That was Jesus' way of putting it. You can't have morality without judgment."

Given the circumstances of the second coming of their re-acquaintance, Jerry let the thread of the conversation drop. Vogel seemed upset, as anyone would be. The blaze was in sight over the trees. A moment later and Jerry pulled up behind a fire truck, red lights flashing, mixing with the yellow glow from the house. Vogel let out a heavy breath and got out. His shirt was untucked beneath his coat, and his hair was messed up. Jerry got out too and came around.

"How are you feeling now about the Speaker's office getting involved?" Jerry asked. He stood side by side with Vogel, their faces illuminated by the flames.

"Better," Vogel said, dazed.

"You want to tell me what this is all about?" Eric said, coming up beside them, now three faces in line, like Mount Rushmore minus one, staring at the flames as the firemen did their work. The detached garage was more engulfed than the house. Jerry surmised from the fact that Vogel had needed a ride and the look on his face as he stared at the garage, rather than the house, that his beloved little convertible was behind that green-painted wooden door.

"Why don't you go sit in the car," Jerry said to Vogel, handing him the keys to his Cherokee. Vogel took them and turned to go.

"Just a minute," Eric said. Vogel stopped and looked at the trooper. "Did you have any insurance?"

"On the car," Vogel said.

"This wasn't your place? You rented?"

"Yes. I also had insurance on my laptop."

"Ok," Eric said, releasing Vogel.

When Vogel had gotten into the Cherokee and started up the engine from the passenger side, Eric said, "What's he into? Drugs?" He had the same chip on his shoulder with his brother that he always had.

"No, no, nothing like that," Jerry said.

"This kind of thing only happens around here when there's a meth lab involved."

"He filed a lawsuit in Federal District Court that big healthcare seems to be concerned about."

Eric's eyes widened with surprise. "Yes, I would say they seem to be extremely concerned about it."

"I don't understand it, myself," Jerry admitted.

"'Big healthcare, huh?" Eric said with a smirk.

"Yeah."

"Look here," Eric said, turning on Jerry. "I don't know what kind of shit you're mixed up with but you keep it outta my backyard, you hear?"

"I don't have anything to do with this," Jerry said, incredulous.

"Oh you don't, huh? You just show up out of the blue again for the second time in a week and you expect me to believe you had nothing to do with this?"

"I'm your brother, Eric! You know me. You know I wouldn't have anything to do with—"

"Oh, I know you, all right."

"And how did you know to call me just now?" Jerry countered. "About this?" He motioned toward the house, now partially on fire, partially ruined by water. "There's no way you should have known about my connection to him."

"You don't come to town without a reason," Eric said. "It's called proactive police work."

Jerry started to say something else, but stopped. He knew it wouldn't do any good. Eric was probably afraid he was going to get written out of the will or some other such nonsense and used his police network to keep tabs on his brother.

"Are you through?" Jerry finally said. "Are we done? 'Cause I gotta get him outta here."

Eric looked at Vogel sitting in the Cherokee. He looked at Jerry. Other police and firefighters were beginning to gather, along with a small group of gawking neighbors.

"Yeah, get him outta here," Eric said.

Jerry got in the car, already running and warm. "We'll stay the night at my mom's place," he said to Vogel, who sat staring straight ahead. "She has plenty of room. Then we'll head up north to my house until we can get this sorted out."

* * *

Jerry called ahead and got his mother up. She had coffee brewing by the time they got there.

"I'm sorry to get you out of bed in the middle of the night like this, Mrs. Riggs," Vogel said.

"That's what neighbors is for, at a time like this," she said. "I'm just so sorry to hear about your loss. Come in, sit down. Let me fix you some breakfast."

"Ma, it's the middle of the night," Jerry said. He noticed a couple of prescription bottles on the counter by the sink and put them away in the cabinet before Vogel noticed them.

Vogel sat down at the kitchen table as if that was just what he needed to do. Mrs. Riggs poured him a cup of coffee and placed it in front of him.

"Eric's room is ready," she said. "The sheets is clean."

"I don't think I'll be doing any sleeping," Vogel said.

"Too keyed up, prob'ly," Mrs. Riggs said.

Jerry thought about it. He was tired but he was unlikely to sleep either. "You know, I guess I could eat," he said.

Without waiting for an answer from Vogel, which was not forthcoming at any rate, Mrs. Riggs busied herself about the stove.

No one was talking so Mrs. Riggs filled the air: "I was going to get up in a hour or so, anyway," she said. "These doctors have got me like a hamster on a wheel, takin' pills early in the morning and last thing at night."

"Brad probably doesn't want to hear about that right now, Ma," Jerry said, smiling sheepishly at Vogel, who managed a kindly expression. This wasn't the time for a discussion about prescription drugs. He had his own wounds to dress at the moment.

Once the breakfast was prepared and Jerry and Vogel were in the middle of eating, Mrs. Riggs wiped down the stove and took a deep breath. "I'll let you boys alone," she said. "Just leave ever'thing in the sink. I'll get it in the morning."

"Get a little more sleep, Ma," Jerry said.

"I'll lay down a while," she said. "I doubt if I'll sleep."

"Thanks again, Mrs. Riggs," Vogel said. "Eggs and bacon are just what I needed."

"Comfort food," she said. "That's understandable at a time like this."

The silence hung in the air along with the aroma of bacon and coffee.

In a few minutes, Vogel took his dishes to the sink and began cleaning them off. Following his lead, Jerry handed in his plate, saucer, cup and fork and found a tea towel in a drawer and was prepared to dry. Vogel searched in the cabinet nearest the sink for some dishwashing liquid and found only a cupboard full of pills.

"Wow," he said, spontaneously, then he closed the door and continued his search, finding the desired detergent beneath the sink.

"Even I can see that's too much," Jerry said.

"That's what's happening these days," Vogel said. "Once you start down that path, that's all you can do really. 'You have a pain? Pay no attention to that, here take this pill. That pill causes discomfort? We have a pill for that too.'

They're hell-bent on proving that life is possible without consciousness."

"Consciousness," Jerry repeated.

"Body consciousness," Vogel said as he washed a plate and handed it to Jerry. "Which is also consciousness of all that is, the Universal."

Jerry frowned and shook his head.

"If you'd just give it a try, you'd know what I'm talking about," Vogel said. "Body consciousness will heal you and keep you healthy. They don't want anybody to know about that." There was a momentary silence. "That's what spirituality is. That's what it is and that's all it is."

"I'm not so sure I can go that far," Jerry said. "But where do you start weaning her off of it?"

"I'm sure she's lived her whole life like that," Vogel said. He shrugged as he handed a wet cup to Jerry for drying. "You know, it's funny. The oldest man in the world at the time, a man in Montana named Walter Breuning—he died a couple of years back—credited his longevity to eating only two meals a day and never taking anything stronger than aspirin. That's body consciousness in action. He's the oldest man in the world and the advice he chose to give was eat only two meals a day and take nothing stronger than aspirin. Think about that."

Jerry did think about that.

"Then there's the case of Richard Overton. At 106 years old, he's the oldest living American veteran. His secret to longevity: a slug of whiskey in his morning coffee and twelve cigars a day. I'm telling you, Jerry, they don't have it right."

When the dishes were done, Vogel drained the sink and then paused, looking hard at Jerry.

"What?" Jerry said, the damp tea towel over his shoulder.

"Why are you here?" Vogel asked. "Now. Just at the right time."

"A little late, actually," Jerry said. "I came to warn you."

"Warn me?"

"Somebody's been keeping a pretty close eye on you lately. And we had it on good authority that something like this might happen. And now it has. We've got to get you out of here."

"What, like a safe house or something?"

"I'm not sure we need to go that far," Jerry theorized. "It's not like they can send out a sniper or anything like that. It would have to look like an accident. Now that they've messed up once, it's going to be hard to arrange a second attack and no one take notice."

"Geez," Vogel said.

"This is big time," Jerry said. "But I think we'll be okay if we can just get you out of your routine."

"Yeah, okay," Vogel said, leaning against the sink, looking at the floor. "I can get one of my colleagues to take over my cases. That shouldn't be a problem."

"We'll drive up to my place in the morning, regroup from there."

* * *

The sunlight streamed in the window of Jerry's boyhood room around nine o'clock that morning, as it always had, give or take a few minutes depending on the season. Why had it awakened him? He was dead tired. He rolled over and then he heard again what he had not realized he had heard the first time, the quick blip of a siren. He got out of bed and looked out into the barnyard. It was his brother, Eric, standing in full regalia beside his trooper-mobile in the cold, hissing daylight.

Digestion of the bacon and eggs the previous night had been just what both Brad and Vogel had needed to make them sleepy again. Jerry pulled on his trousers and stepped into his shoes.

In the kitchen, his mother was reading the newspaper. "Tell 'eem to stop that," she said as Jerry grabbed his jacket.

"What's going on?" he said, pulling the door closed behind him. He walked all the way out to the car before the answer was forthcoming.

"Turns out your friend has a few enemies around town," Eric said.

"Enemies," Jerry repeated, still waking up.

"I thought that sounded more likely than your

cockamamie 'big hospital' theory."

"Big healthcare," Jerry said.

"You know as well as I do that burnin' people out isn't all that uncommon in these parts," Eric said.

"What sort of enemies?" Jerry asked, stealing a glance back at the house to make sure Vogel wasn't up, and gauging whether he might be in earshot if he were.

"Sleeping with the ex-wife of one fella, for one," Eric said. "The family of another woman who he told to go off her medication, for another."

Sleeping with somebody's ex-wife...come on. As Pattie had said about Hanrahan's pocket hanky, get real. But telling people to go off meds...Shit, that *was* worrisome. It was an aspect of this whole crazy philosophy that Jerry hadn't consciously contemplated. People start going off their medications, they start dying and some prosecutor somewhere can trace that back to Vogel, suddenly bringing down Obamacare isn't looking like so much fun anymore. Bringing down the Republican Party would be the more likely scenario at that point.

"What happened?"

"She nearly died before they got her back to the emergency room. Another guy went off his psych meds on account of your friend's advice. We've had a problem with him ever since."

Psych meds too, Jerry thought. Oh, boy. Now we're not only looking at the prospect of somebody dying, we're also looking at the possibility of some guy going postal on Vogel's watch, too. All the most recent mass shootings blazed across Jerry's mind's eye.

"Arson?" Jerry asked after the psych patient's criminal history.

"Not up to this point, no."

"Anything else?"

"If it was some kind of corporate black ops thing, they did a hell of a job making it look like just another good old-fashion burn out, that's for sure."

"All right, all right," Jerry said. "I get your point."

"I'm not sure you do," Eric said. "We don't need this shit

around here. So why don't you just pack up your shit and your friend and head back to Cincinnati and Washington, DC, and leave us the hell alone?"

Jerry was fully awake now and he had had enough. "What is your problem, Eric?"

"You want to know what my problem is?" Eric said, looking down on his older brother. "I'll tell you what my problem is. You. You're my problem. You're wasting your life."

"Wasting my life? Are you kidding me? I'm working for the third most powerful man in the country here. What are you talking about, wasting my life?"

"You ought to *be* that guy," Eric said. "Not his lackey runnin' errands for him all over godforsaken Laurel County, Kentucky."

"This old saw again, Eric? Come on, man, you've got to move on."

"Ma and Pop spent every dime they had to send you out of state to the University of Virginia, 'til there wasn't nothing left for anybody else—"

"You didn't have the grades!" Jerry said. "They could have gotten loans for you, but you didn't have the grades."

"—nothin' left for anybody else except EKU."

"That was perfect for you," Jerry said. "They have a great law enforcement program. You love your job. What are you complaining about?"

"Then you partied your ass off in Charlottesville, barely graduated. You had to come back here to go to law school 'cause you couldn't get in nowhere else. Now that's a fact!"

Jerry had to admit, that *was* a fact. If his LSAT score hadn't been so high, he would have landed at Chase, in Northern Kentucky, the worst law school in the state—which may have led him right to where he was today anyway, as a matter of fact, working for the Speaker, whose office was situated just across the Ohio River from Chase in Cincinnati anyway, which got him thinking...

"You could have gone to an Ivy League school if you'd applied yourself, been running this state, like Bill Clinton did over in Arkansas."

Jolted from his reverie by the comparison to a Democrat, Jerry said, “Now that’s a low blow. And I know for a fact that Bill Clinton did his fair share of partying.”

Disgusted, Eric took off his trooper cap and flipped it into the front passenger seat.

“You don’t understand, Eric. It’s not about brains. The Speaker would be the first to tell you he’s no rocket scientist. It takes a certain kind of constitution. I just don’t have that. I never did.”

It was Eric’s turn to turn reflective.

“I knew what the expectations were for me growing up,” Jerry continued. “Can’t you see that was too much pressure on me? Which didn’t help the situation, let me tell you.”

Eric looked across the yard at the barn as if he’d lost interest in the discussion. The overnight shift seemed to take its toll on him all at once and he sat down in the driver’s seat of his Crown Vic.

“Why are we talking about this now?” Jerry said. “This is ancient history. And you’ve got a crime to solve...or something.”

Eric shook his head, still a little disgusted. “I’m going to get home and get some sleep.”

“Let me know if you hear anything else,” Jerry said.

Jerry stepped away from the car as Eric eased it back and then forward toward the gate.

Chapter 8

“This is a small town, Brad,” Jerry said. “Everybody knows everything about everybody. You can’t just roll in here and start ogling the local wildlife and not expect to ruffle some feathers.”

“It wasn’t like that,” Vogel said. “I had been here a year before I started seeing Amy.”

“Doesn’t matter. You’re a foreigner as far as they’re concerned.”

Jerry had waited until they were on the road before he hit Vogel with Eric’s accusations. He didn’t want his mother to hear anything. When he did finally start in, Jerry began with the least controversial of the three, the one that involved a woman, because Vogel’s continued interest in women just didn’t compute for him.

“‘Seeing Amy’? What exactly does that mean?”

Vogel shook his head and looked out the window at the passing trees. “You have this impression of me that just isn’t accurate,” he said. “I’m not a priest.”

“No, more like a guru,” Jerry retorted.

“Same thing. I’m not a priest or a guru. In fact, I’m the least moral person you know.”

“That’s what you keep saying.” Vogel didn’t respond. After a moment, Jerry continued his interrogation: “You told some other woman to go off her medication and she nearly died.”

“I never told anybody to go off medication,” Vogel said. “I would never do that. That’s a whole unconscious system they’ve got going there. But if you’re unconscious yourself, you have no other option but to submit to that barbarity—cutting you open, plying you with potions and pills.”

“You have to admit that it might be pretty tempting for someone to believe they’ve achieved total karma or whatever and stop taking everything to prove they have faith.”

“That’s just it,” Vogel said, now more animated. “There is

no faith. Anytime anyone asks you to have faith in something, you should run like hell because that person doesn't know what the hell they're talking about. Body consciousness is a way to *know*."

"But that can be taken out of context," Jerry said.

Vogel shook his head and the corners of his mouth turned up in resignation that perhaps this conversation was pointless. "That's just another aspect of their control," he said. "The threat of liability if anything should happen as a result of the misapplication of these 'dangerous' ideas. Do you realize that medical error is the second leading cause of death in this country? Think about that. But no one ever says stay away from hospitals because of it. What if—just what if—what I'm describing really is the way the world is?"

"What if," Jerry repeated.

"I can't control what anyone else does or thinks," Vogel said. "But body consciousness doesn't require faith. It's one of the three true experiments that we can do to know the nature of the universe. It doesn't require any faith and it doesn't require anyone to go off of medication to practice. You can and should do them at the same time."

"Three experiments?" Jerry asked. "What are the other two?"

Vogel said, "You won't even do the first one. Now you want to know about the other two?"

Jerry was getting under Vogel's skin, pressing buttons with precision. At a deeply unconscious level, Jerry made a note of that and filed it away for future use as needed. He wanted to know about those other two experiments, but he didn't want Vogel to know that.

"Does all this go for the psych guy too?" Jerry asked.

"What psych guy?"

"Eric says that there was a guy who went off his psych meds and they've had nothing but trouble with him ever since."

"I don't know anything about that," Vogel said. "But it's the same thing. Think about what so-called psych meds do. 'Hi, we're the pharmaceutical companies. We make the pills that allow you to get back to work so you can buy our pills.'

They don't solve the underlying spiritual issue. The focus on the past that's causing the depression. The focus on the future that's causing the anxiety, or whatever other symptom they're experiencing. And then the drugs create their own side effects that the pharmaceutical companies and the psychologists then get to treat at great profit to themselves."

"It's all just that simple, huh?" Jerry said.

"You don't have to believe a word I'm saying," Vogel said. "Just go into your body and find out what it tells you."

Jerry broke off this line of questioning. It was going nowhere. Next thing you know, Vogel will have me closing my eyes and feeling my feet, Jerry thought. No thank you. I'm not up for that right now. If this was experiment one, maybe he didn't want to know what those other two were, after all. It was probably Big Healthcare that had burned out Vogel anyway, he decided consequently. So no use talking about these other possibilities...

* * *

"So you're against all judgment, huh?" Jerry said.

"Judgment is rationality," Vogel said. "Yes, no. Right, wrong. Good, bad—"

"Good, evil?" Jerry interjected, pushing the cart. Vogel walked along beside him, grabbing needed items as they passed them.

"Same thing. Its role is limited to the creation of laborsaving devices and communication. Beyond that, rationality or judgment has nothing to say to us about the deeper questions of life. That was an invention of Aristotle: to separate out the rational function from overall consciousness and then apply it to spiritual questions. The Jews—the Pharisees and the Sadducees, for example, if you remember your Vacation Bible School lessons—had taken that and run with it. Judaism had been infected with materialism, what I call Aristotelianism. Jesus' ministry was all about combating that, returning to the original law-based roots of the Jewish people, as opposed to the morality-based religion that had developed. Before Aristotle there was really no such thing as religion. There was only consciousness and law."

"Consciousness," Jerry repeated. "Consciousness of what?"

"Best to leave that blank," Vogel said. "But if you must have a word, you could use any number of them: consciousness of God, soul, inner-body, love, all that is, the Universal, Universal Intelligence. The list goes on and on. At different times, different words have been in vogue. The problem is people get fixated on the word, then the spirit gets institutionalized and that kills it."

Vogel had muddled through the morning, borrowing stuff from Jerry. But just like any victim of a house fire, the first stop was Wal-Mart to pick up as many necessities as he could absorb. They stopped at the London location before hitting the road to Cincinnati. Jerry had access to a Republican slush fund that was coming in handy.

Vogel had taken it all quite stoically, which seemed just right. It was certainly consistent with his stated philosophy. He still had his expensive watch and his iPhone (and now a Wal-Mart universal charger), and all his data was backed up in the cloud. Everything else was lost.

"Wait a second," Jerry said. "What about the Greek pantheon of gods? You know, Zeus and Apollo and Athena and all that. Wasn't that a religion?"

"Ah," Vogel said, stopping his forward progress in the middle of the busy toiletries aisle. "Astute question, my friend."

Really? Jerry thought. Maybe I'm not as dumb as I feel when I'm talking to this guy.

"Think about those Greek gods. And the Romans were exactly the same only with different names. Weren't they just humans with superpowers? Greek and Roman mythology wasn't a religion as we know it today. But rather, it was simply a way to describe human nature. A way of describing the way life is. There was no top-down morality involved in it whatsoever. That came later, with Aristotle as its chief architect."

"Hmm," Jerry said. "I hadn't ever looked at it like that."

Vogel continued: "The ancient mind rallied around a

concept called *arête.* It's a Greek word that means an all-pervasive excellence in every aspect of life. Put another way, it means quality. The ancients and the pre-Socratic philosophers didn't even use a word like 'God' as a placeholder. It was too big for that—unknowable, uncontainable by words and ideas. It was Aristotle who dumbed it down and separated it out as a mere concept.

Jerry tried to come up with an intelligent response but couldn't come up with anything. He chalked it up to the Wal-Mart effect.

"You know, it's fascinating how all this lines up. The ancient Jews looked at it the same way. They wouldn't even say or write out the word they used for God. It was considered blasphemous to reduce the unknowable infinite to a word or a concept. It was all in all. Of course, we're talking about western civilization here. In the east it's completely different. In general, they get what I'm talking about, although there has been a tendency toward rationalization there too. They've turned Buddha into a god, for example. That doesn't make any sense, does it?"

Jerry shook his head and had to laugh. "Where do you get all this?"

All he got by way of answer was a shrug of the shoulders, and with that they started moving again.

They pulled into the checkout line. A couple of packs of underwear, some T-shirts, a pair of jeans, toiletries—the slush fund could handle all that. Oh geez, Jerry thought, it was going to get expensive replacing Vogel's suits.

"You have renter's insurance, right?"

"Don't believe in insurance," Vogel said. "Only what the law requires."

"But you have insurance on your laptop," Jerry said.

Vogel smiled as he lifted shaving cream and razors on to the conveyer belt. "Nobody's perfect." He finished emptying the cart. They stood back and let the cashier do her work.

"But the thing to consider here is that with consciousness, there are no rules," Vogel continued, still on the insurance question. "Connectedness to the Universal means that you do whatever you do based on a feeling at any given moment. Like if you felt you were about to have an accident, for example, so you felt moved to buy insurance. Even a rule to buy or not to buy insurance would be an aspect of personal morality."

"When did you buy it?" Jerry asked.

"A few months ago when I bought the computer," Vogel said. "I also have the full package on the car. I've had that all along. I didn't really even think about it back when I bought it. And as it turned out...I needed it."

"The Universal steered you in the right direction."

"Perhaps so, although I bought it before my awakening began. The Universal is always there, though. It's just a matter of us awakening to it, or to put it in negative terms our level of resistance to it."

* * *

The ride up from London to Cincinnati encompassed a little over two hours of driving time. But the duo had also pulled off the interstate in Georgetown, just north of Lexington, for their second breakfast of the day, courtesy of the Waffle House, adding thirty additional minutes.

"Well," Jerry said in response to something Vogel had said, "having one's house firebombed is never pleasant . . ."

Vogel bobbed his head as he concentrated on his plate.

"But on the bright side: fewer bills." Jerry took a bite and swallowed. "Look at us, we're free as birds, man. With Republican money backing us," Jerry knew better than to speak directly of the slush fund, "we can do whatever we want."

"I'm seeing now, as if for the first time, that Republicanism has its perks."

Vogel was being ironic. That was good to see. The weight of the burnout was beginning to lift from his shoulders.

Finding in his vast repertoire the perfect *Seinfeld* quote for this exact moment, Jerry said, "'Don't you remember, we always talked about how cool it would be to have a van and just drive?'" That image on the show was one of two buddies alone together, out on the open road.

"'We were ten,'" Vogel responded on cue even though his mouth was full.

Jerry smiled. Vogel had nailed it. Boy, he just couldn't imagine the Brad Vogel he knew from law school ever getting *Seinfeld* references. And that juxtaposition made his comebacks all the more funny. He was still pretty straight-laced and serious when it came to his philosophical mumbo-jumbo. But there was a humanity in him, too. Maybe this wasn't going to be so bad, Jerry thought.

"Lloyd Braun," he said.

"What's that?" Vogel said, wiping up egg yolk with buttered toast for the second time in ten hours.

"That's who you remind me of: Lloyd Braun. I have this theory that you can find the perfect *Seinfeld* character to fit every personality. You're Lloyd Braun."

"The first Lloyd Braun or the second?" Vogel said.

"Very nice," Jerry responded. "You know your *Seinfeld.* The first Lloyd Braun was debonair. The second was post crackup." Jerry thought for a moment. "It's both. Because of your story. A hybrid."

"I guess I can accept that," Vogel said. "You equate what happened to me with a nervous breakdown."

"In a way," Jerry said. "But let's not take this too literally. It's a sitcom. What about me?"

"You're definitely a George," Vogel said, without missing a beat.

"George!"

"If I'm in any way a secondary Lloyd Braun, then you're a perfect George."

"No way I'm a George," Jerry said.

"What, you think you're a Jerry because you have the same name?"

"Well, now that you mention it . . ."

"No way you're a Jerry," Vogel said. "You're lucky I didn't say Newman. "

"Serenity now!" Jerry said, still unconvinced he was a George.

"You know," Vogel said, "I do know my *Seinfeld* very well. I have the entire DVD box set of the series." He stopped, remembering the fire. "Make that *had* the entire set. Anyway, I've been watching it intently for years—still do—

looking for something in it, some meaning that I just know is hidden there. And you know what I just recently found out?"

"What's that?"

"Remember that experiment I tried to get you to do? Jerry Seinfeld has practiced meditation his entire adult life," Vogel said. "Forty years."

"Is that right?" Jerry said. "But is he master of his domain? That's the real question."

"One of my favorite writers, Eckhart Tolle, wrote about how TV can be beneficial. He talked about a show about 'nothing in particular' demonstrating the futility and stupidity of the ego. I've always thought he was talking about *Seinfeld*, the show about nothing." Brad took a sip of coffee. "I'm not so sure about Larry David. *Curb Your Enthusiasm* is just as funny as *Seinfeld*, maybe funnier. But it seems to lack that...how would you say it...that transcendent element. It's not something you can watch over and over like *Seinfeld*. Once you've seen an episode, that's pretty much it. At least that's how it is for me."

"Yeah, yeah, I see what you mean." Jerry had stopped listening for the moment. Something about what Brad had said had gotten him thinking about something else, something far afield. He had remembered the line about people thinking Jerry Seinfeld was gay because he was in his thirties, he was thin and he was neat.

"Listen, Brad, there's just one thing about staying at my house. Nicole is kind of a neat freak."

"That's no problem," Vogel said, "I certainly know how to be tidy." He was alluding to the OCD issues he had developed. "But if this is an imposition in any way—"

"No, no, no," Jerry responded. "Are you kidding me? It's no imposition at all. You should see this place. It's like the Taj Mahal. It's huge, way more house than we need, and more than we can afford, to be honest. We have not one but two guest rooms, if you can believe that. We don't need that much house, to tell you the truth, but Nicole—how can I put this—she has a need to impress people."

"This may not be the best fit," Vogel said.

"She'll be fine," Jerry said. "You just have to keep things in order."

Vogel said. "I know my place didn't show it when you were there, but I can do it. I actually make a conscious effort these days to let things go a little, to be honest." Vogel paused again. "She's not going to like me, you know."

"Come on," Jerry said. "She'll remember you from back in the day. That'll give you something to talk about."

Vogel weighed his response for a moment. "She'll remember me, all right." He weighed some more. "I should probably tell you at this point that Nicole and I went out briefly."

"You're kidding," Jerry said. He couldn't see Nicole going for the old Vogel. He could imagine her going for the new Vogel even less. And with that comparison in his mind, there was some illumination as to what Vogel was getting at. "So what," Jerry said. "A lot of people were dating a lot of people back then. You didn't . . ."

"No," Vogel quickly answered. "Certainly not. It was like one date. It was a real power struggle between us. She was like the Republican me."

"And you were like the Democrat her," Jerry said, his eyes lighting up at the observation. "I can see that."

"And now," Vogel said, leaving the implication unspoken. "She's not going to like me one bit."

Jerry shrugged as he took another bite. "Nicole's a nice person," Jerry said. Vogel nodded his agreement. "She wouldn't deny help to a friend in need."

He smiled uncertainly at Vogel, who *wasn't* Nicole's friend, truth be told. And Jerry now got completely what Vogel was saying. This new Vogel would represent a complete failure in her eyes, just as the latest Jerry represented—at best—a partial failure. Vogel could be right, Jerry thought, this could be a blood-in-the-water situation we're about to swim into.

"You know," Vogel said. "If you ever get a chance to meet Jerry Seinfeld in person, you already have an in to strike up a conversation. 'You have the same first name...Jerry.'"

With a mouthful of eggs, Jerry responded, "'Oh, that'll

intrigue him.'"

* * *

Jerry gave the nanny the night off, and instead of the dinner Nicole had instructed her to feed the girls, he gave Sarah Grace and Sophia their choice of restaurants.

"McDonalds!" they both said in uneven unison, jumping up and down.

"You see how easy it is to brainwash people?" Vogel whispered to Brad. "That's what advertisement is, it's brainwashing. And McDonald's starts young and gets their multi-million-dollar advertising budget's money's worth."

"We can go anywhere you want to go and you choose McDonald's?" Jerry chided. He loved McDonalds, himself, and the girls were exploiting knowledge of that information. But he knew there would be hell to pay if Nicole got wind of it, and he wasn't going to need any more hell-paying going on with Brad Vogel in tow.

"McDonald's!" in closer unison came the reply.

"What's wrong with you two!"

With great effort, Jerry finally got them off their first choice, nudging them ever so slightly up the food chain to O'Charley's, luring them with remembrances of great chicken tenders, the only food they ever seemed to eat.

* * *

When Nicole arrived home later that evening, she took one look at Brad Vogel and decided: *He can't stay here.* Vogel knew it the moment it happened, and truth be told, so did Jerry. Though he could read her thoughts as plainly as if they were written in a comic book thought bubble beside her head, Jerry fought the understanding, remaining in denial for as long as he could.

Jerry and Vogel were seated on opposite ends of the couch while the girls played on the floor in front of the TV. They had just gotten back from eating out and they were all feeling pretty good. It was at that moment that Nicole came home after her evening with the girls playing doubles at the country club, presenting herself at the door to the family room, still glowing from exercise. She waited for someone to notice her.

"This is what I'm talking about," Vogel said when a commercial came on during *Jeopardy*, warning of the dangers of lime disease. "The advertisers here have spent a lot of money on this so-called public service announcement, but you have to ask yourself, 'What are they selling?' And the answer is lime disease. They're planting that fear in the subconscious minds of impressionable people and thereby expanding their markets. Best to at least turn down the sound on advertising, especially advertising that has to do with any aspect of healthcare, so-called. If not turn off the TV altogether."

"Nicole," Jerry said, finally noticing her arrival. "Did you get my text?" When she didn't respond, he said, "You remember Brad Vogel from law school."

"Hello, Brad," she said stiffly. "Don't get up." But Vogel was already up. "Could I have a word with you, Jerry?"

When they had removed themselves to the kitchen, Jerry said, "I tried to call but—"

"He is not staying here," Nicole said. "I've got a family to run. Carrie said you gave her the night off?"

"What's the big deal?" Jerry said. "We've got the room."

"So you just breeze back into town for the second time in three days and you run into one of your law school buddies and you decide, 'Hey, why don't we head up to Cinci and see what Nicole and Sophia and Sarah Grace are doing'? 'Hey, I've got a great idea, why don't you spend the night, it'll be like old times'?"

"No, no, it's nothing like that," Jerry protested.

"Is there a problem at work again?" Nicole pressed. "Have you been drinking?"

"Haven't had a drop," he said, now resigned to enduring this latest barrage.

"Because if you lose your job, that's it, we're sunk. I can barely keep things together as it is."

Jerry began to feel pain in his chest again and it distracted him momentarily because it had been a while since he had felt that.

"Are you listening to me?" Nicole said.

"Look," Jerry responded. "The guy just got burned out of

his house, okay? He needs a place to stay for a day or two until we can figure things out."

That took Nicole by surprise. One penciled in eyebrow lifted. "Burned out? What does that mean?"

Jerry shrugged, not wishing to elaborate, realizing the trap into which he had just fallen.

"Did he leave a frying pan on the stove? Did he leave his curling iron on? I want to know what happened, Jerry?"

He gave in: "We don't know."

"Oh, so your buddy there gets burned out down in London, Kentucky, burnout capital of the world—"

"Why does everybody keep saying that?"

"—and you decide it's a good idea to bring him up to stay with your wife and daughters for a few days? Is that what you thought, Jerry? Because let me tell you something: that ain't happening."

Jerry blew out a deep breath and endured. He remembered the diatribe he had absorbed from his brother that morning and wished he could head back to O'Charley's and order another two or three entrees and another dessert because that had been the most fun he had had in a long while, just him and the girls and his friend, hanging out, having a good time.

"And what was that bullshit he was talking when I walked in about lime disease and advertising? I don't need that kind of nutjob around the girls, okay? It's advertising and business and the best healthcare system in the world that pays the bills in this country, and if he doesn't like it, he ought to pack up and move to Iran."

As withering as this assault was, along with the usual smattering of defense of the American way, Jerry simply checked out, thinking back to when they had met, in law school at a Young Republicans meeting. Nicole had graduated but never took the bar, opting instead for domestic bliss with his-truly, Jerry Riggs.

Nicole went back to the family room. "Come on, girls. It's time to start getting ready for bed." Sensing the usual discord between Mommy and Daddy, this time in the presence of a non-relative guest, a completely unfamiliar situation, none of the usual protests ensued. The girls got up dutifully and preceded their mother out of the room and down the hall. "And I'll need you to take the herbie down to the curb. Tomorrow is garbage pick up. That's normally Carrie's job."

"No problem," Jerry said.

When Nicole was gone, Vogel said, "I'm sensing that didn't go well."

"No, it didn't," Jerry said. "No, it didn't."

After a moment spent staring at the hardwood floor, Jerry went into the kitchen and out through the back door, down on to the patio and out through the wooden gate. He wheeled the garbage receptacle down the path around the garage, on to the driveway.

In his peripheral vision, more sensing than seeing, a dome light in a minivan two houses down went dark. Could have been anything or anybody, but somehow he knew that it wasn't. Jerry was sufficiently preoccupied with the fight he had just had with his wife that the occurrence didn't register with him right away. He deposited the herbie at the curb before it clicked, and by then he was cognizant and aware enough not to react by looking directly at the minivan.

He was being watched. His house was being watched. More precisely, someone was keeping an eye on Vogel.

It was fear that alerted him, only then did rationality come. Holy shit! he thought, and then: Of course! Why didn't I realize this earlier? Someone had thought enough of Vogel and his lawsuit to burn down his house. Did I think they were going to just sit back when that proved unsuccessful? Have they been bird-dogging us all the way up from London? How did one respond to a surveillance detail with murder on its mind? Jerry hated to admit it, but maybe Nicole was right. How could he have been so naïve? He needed to get them away from his house as quickly as he could, and under no circumstance could Nicole ever find out about this.

He took stock of the situation. There was his Cherokee parked in plain sight in the driveway. He had not pulled it into the garage. That seemed good.

He stood there at the curb, hands in pockets, looking up at the cold, starry sky, appearing for all the world like a man nearing the end of a long day, his last chore complete, wondering what it was all for, what it was all about (and maybe he was that man, too).

He gave the minivan owner enough time to either start up the engine if he was leaving, or to exit the vehicle if he was staying. Neither option transpired.

Head down, Jerry strolled pensively back up the driveway and around the house. By the time he reached the back door, he knew what to do.

"Pack your stuff," he said to Vogel, who sat in the family room right where Jerry had left him a few moments earlier. The remote rested on the arm of the couch. The TV was on but the sound was muted. A commercial was running.

"I never unpacked," Vogel said.

"You didn't?"

"No, it's still in the back of the truck."

"It is?" Jerry thought for a moment. "That's good."

"Why? What's going on?"

"Someone's out there," Jerry said. "Watching the house."

"Are you sure?"

"Pretty sure," Jerry said. "I'm not swearing. I don't want to swear." Jerry put some more thought into it. "Here's what you do." He thought some more. "I'm going to pack a few things and then I'm going to go out to the truck like I'm leaving you behind. You come out—no coat—and we'll chitchat for a minute or two, like you wanted to tell me one more thing before I leave. That way, they see for sure that you're not with me, understand?"

"Got it."

"Then you go back inside, grab your coat and head out the back. One house over, there's a chain link fence at the back of the yard. You hop the fence, go out through the gate and I'll meet you on the other side. Simple but effective. They'll stay here thinking you're inside, we'll be home free, and Nicole can get her knickers out of a wad—maybe."

"Where are we going?" Vogel asked.

"We're going to pay a visit on an old law school friend," Jerry said.

"Oh, yeah?" Vogel said. "Which one?"

"Orlando Broxton," Jerry said. "He got a little upset when I didn't stop in last time I was in Lexington. Looks like we're going to be making up for lost time now."

Vogel stood with his hands in his pockets. He frowned but didn't say anything.

"Wait in the bushes on the other side until I flash my lights. And whatever you do, don't use your cell phone." Jerry remembered the COS's admonition about NSA. Vogel was a threat to bring down Obamacare. Who knew who was trying to bring down Vogel? "We don't know who these people are yet."

"Why would I do that?" Vogel said.

"I don't know," Jerry said, aware that perhaps he was over thinking things. "You might get over there, it might take longer than you expect and so you call and say, 'Hey Jerr, what's taking so long?'"

"I'm not going to do that," Vogel said.

"You might."

"I won't."

Chapter 9

Whistling a tune ("Side by Side"), Jerry strolled out to the Cherokee first, placed his grip in the back seat and then started up the vehicle. In a flourish, he went back inside as if he had forgotten something and emerged a minute later carrying a pair of black socks. He got in and put the car in gear and began backing out, just as Vogel came out the front door, arms crossed as the cold hit him.

Vogel leaned in and Jerry said, "Can you see the black minivan two houses down?"

Vogel looked through the tinted windows of the Cherokee. "Yeah, I see it."

"Anybody in there?"

Vogel studied. "I don't know. Maybe."

"Look harder."

"It's too far away," he said. "I can't tell."

Jerry frowned. "All right, that's enough."

Vogel hustled back inside and Jerry backed down the driveway and drove off in the opposite direction from where sat the minivan. He drove slowly to give Vogel enough time to execute his part of the plan; but neither did he wish to tip off the guy (or guys) in the minivan by going too slowly.

Down the street several houses and around a strategically significant bend in the road stood the stop sign. Jerry couldn't quite decide if he could take credit for consciously remembering that feature of the topography and how it might figure into his plan's execution, but the fact remained that he was no longer in view of the minivan. Nevertheless, he quelled a reflex to flick on the right turn signal. The red glow in the near total darkness on that horizon, no street lights near enough to dissipate it, might tip them off, for if he were actually leaving the neighborhood, he would have been by all rights moving forward through that four-way stop.

Just relax, Jerry told himself as he eased around the

corner and drove the width of two large houses and their postage-stamp lots to the next street, where he turned right. You're over thinking things again. What could possibly go wrong now?

He let the Cherokee coast. Finally warm, it had just dropped down out of high idle. When the right stretch of houses was in sight, he scanned the house-side bushes for Vogel, but he couldn't make him out anywhere. Jerry flashed his lights one time. Vogel emerged from just where Jerry had been looking and jogged toward the car, opened the passenger door and got in.

"Not bad," Jerry said.

"There was a dog in that backyard," Vogel said.

"Snowball? He's usually not out this time of night."

"He bit me on the ankle," Vogel said, checking the mark. Jerry turned on the dome light to assist.

"Snowball bit you? You're kidding."

"He was on me before I knew what was happening."

"He locked on to your ankle 'like it was a soup bone,'" Jerry said. "I'm sure he has all his shots."

He flicked out the light and checked the rearview. There were headlights behind them, back at the beginning of the street. This side of the block had a sweeping bend in it, too.

"It didn't draw blood," Vogel said. "I guess it just scared me more than anything."

"You're on a bad roll," Jerry said. "House fire, now getting bitten by Snowball." He sped up. Vogel rolled his pants leg down and now noticed Jerry's preoccupation and took a look behind, himself.

"Is that them?" Vogel asked.

"I don't know."

"I think it is," Vogel said after careful study.

"You know what this means, don't you?" Jerry said. "They're not following you...They're following me."

Jerry didn't bother to stop at the stop sign. The Cherokee cornered well, this time to the right. Vogel held on tightly and then in the straightaway belatedly strapped himself in.

"Can we lose 'em?" Vogel asked.

Jerry said, "I'm a Republican, remember? This baby's got

the biggest engine they make."

He slalomed through the parked cars, down a few blocks and out of the neighborhood via an alternate exit point. By the time they reached the nearest arterial highway, those lights, whether they had belonged to the minivan in question or not, where no longer behind them. The two men breathed a relieved sigh. When they reached I75 south, they figured they were home free.

Until they reached Florence.

Beneath the large high-up highway lights not far across the Ohio River bridge, Vogel could get a good look at the vehicles to the rear, almost as if it were high noon.

"I think they're still with us," Vogel said. "They're back there pretty far, but I think that's them."

Jerry checked the rearview mirror. "Are you sure? A lot of black minivans on the road."

"Pretty sure," Vogel said.

Jerry shook his head. "Damn it!" He thought for a moment. "I think I've got some binoculars back there somewhere."

"Yeah, I saw them earlier," Vogel said.

"Can you shimmy back and get them?"

Vogel complied while Jerry kept a watchful eye on the mirrors.

"Camo," Vogel said, sliding into his seat. "Nice. You a hunter?"

"As a Republican and coming from the country, I feel the need to make the effort. To be honest, I don't really enjoy it. Although, once you get past the getting up at unreasonably early hours, the boredom, the bone-chilling cold, the blood and the near-death experiences at the hands of your drunken fellow hunters, it's really not that bad."

"Not to mention having to spray yourself with deer urine," Vogel said. "What's the plan?"

"I'm going to pull over just past the next exit," Jerry said, "so they can't turn off. They'll have to go by us. You try to get a read on the license plate."

"I'll try," Vogel said. "What if they pull up behind us?"

"Then I'll take off like a frightened schoolgirl, of course,"

Jerry said, adding flatly, "I'm not *that* brave."

Just past the Florence Mall exit, Jerry said, "Tell me when they're past the turn off." They were still in an urbanized stretch of highway, part of the greater Cincinnati area, and thankful for it. Jerry had no desire to attempt this maneuver on any of the long swaths of countryside that lay immediately ahead, surrounded by nothing but night-black hills and jagged limestone cliffs, angry where the road had been cut through them.

After a moment, Vogel said, "Now," and Jerry edged to the shoulder and slowed to a stop. Vogel tried to get a bead on the minivan as it sped by, picking up steam when the driver saw the trap that had been laid.

"Five, five, two, three," Vogel said. "'Price of honor."

"'Price of honor'?" Jerry repeated. "What's that?"

"That was the motto at the bottom of the plate," Vogel said. "I couldn't see which state is was from."

"Five, five, two, three? That was the whole thing?"

"I think so," Vogel said. "Seemed like some kind of official plate."

"Yeah," Jerry agreed, "yeah," a little hopped up on the adrenalin rush the maneuver had triggered.

He thought for another few seconds, then threw the Cherokee into reverse, draped his arm over the back of Vogel's seat and began backing down the shoulder as car after car whizzed by on his left, some of them laying on their horns.

"What are you doing?" Vogel said.

"We're taking back roads from here on out," Jerry said. "Looks like we'll be getting to Orlando's place a little later than expected."

* * *

An hour or so of silent drive time later, the glow of Vogel's iPhone lit up his face in blue in the dark of Kentucky Highway 27 South, just as they passed the sign for Falmouth.

"Turn that thing off," Jerry said. "That's probably how they're tracking us."

"Right," Vogel said. "Sorry."

After a moment, Jerry said, "Aaa, screw it," and he whipped out his own iPhone. "I'm lost anyway." He dialed up GPS. Vogel clicked his phone back on and began Googling license plates.

After several minutes of clicking, he said, "Looks like 'Price of Honor' is the slogan they put at the bottom of New Jersey law enforcement vehicles. There was probably an "LE" on that plate I didn't pick up. Look." He showed the picture he'd found in Google Images.

"New Jersey law enforcement. Weird." And ominous, Jerry thought but didn't say. "I'll get my brother to look into it."

* * *

"You told me to stop in or else," Jerry said. "Well, I'm stoppin' in. . ." Jerry held out his hands and smiled as if he were a Vaudevillian.

"I didn't mean at one-thirty in the mo'nin, now," Orlando said, holding his robe together. He stood on the wraparound porch in his bare feet, reeking of Bourbon. He'd had a few and fallen asleep on the couch in his office, or so he said. Otherwise, he might not have responded to the bell. "Couldn't you have at least called?"

"And let NSA know where we were going?" Jerry said. "That would have put you in a very precarious position. I didn't want to do that to you."

"NSA?" Orlando looked out at Vogel, who waited patiently in the car.

"I don't know, maybe," Jerry said, a little-to-a-lot punchy after little sleep the night before and a drive he wasn't expecting and a surveillance unit on his tail he didn't need. "Look can we stay here or not? You don't use the third floor of this behemoth. You won't even know we're here."

Broxton's mid19th century home had a Bluegrass Trust plaque beside the door. It sat facing the up-and-coming business district a couple of streets over, where trendy restaurants and night spots managed newfound prosperity. Its back was to the hood behind it—his bread and butter—with easy access to his first-floor office through the rear entrance. He and his wife lived on the sprawling second floor.

"Yeah, all right," Orlando answered. "How long are we talkin'?"

"The District Court should make it's ruling within a month."

"A month?"

"Six weeks at the most," Jerry said, waving Vogel in. "That should give us enough time to get to the bottom of who burned down his house."

"Burned dow . . ." Orlando said, the word dropping off in incredulity. "The old lady's not gonna like this."

"I would think she would enjoy spending a little time with some of her own kind," Jerry said.

"Hi, Orlando," Vogel said when he arrived on the porch. He handed Jerry his grip and held on to his own.

Orlando scrutinized Vogel's countenance for a moment and found it sufficiently contrite that he finally responded with, "Hey, Brad. Sorry to hear about your house."

"Thanks," Vogel said, following Orlando and Jerry through the front door.

"Those are the stairs," Orlando said, pointing to a massive back-and-forth set done in dark wood with period floral carpeting running up the middle. "We don't use the third floor 'cause it's haunted. But you're welcome to it. Just dust the sheets off a little before you get under 'em. You're not getting' fresh linens tonight."

When Orlando had cloistered himself behind the door to the second floor, Jerry said with a deep relaxing breath, "I think we're finally in for some high living." And he found his last gasp of energy to bound excitedly up the stairs ahead of Vogel.

* * *

"Did you ever read *Moby Dick*?" Vogel said.

"No," Jerry said, uncomfortable to be chitchatting like this under the circumstances.

"This is how it starts out," Vogel said. "The narrator, Ishmael, rents a room in a hotel and the room is already occupied by a Polynesian guy named Queequeg. They end up going on the whaling ship together."

"Well, if this were a novel, we'd be in good company, I

guess," Jerry said, his back to Vogel, who lay with his arms akimbo behind his head.

"Some modern critics have tried to read a homosexual storyline into the novel because of that scene," Vogel mused, "but—"

"Thank...you," Jerry said. Vogel bringing up the elephant in the room did nothing for his comfort level. "Let's just try to get some sleep."

"Right," Vogel said.

At least the bed was large. When they got up to the third floor, Jerry hurried expectantly to each of the closed doors along the hallway, opening one, closing it, opening the next, closing it. He found them mostly unfurnished with only one bed in one of the rooms. Attached to that room was a fully functional, fully stocked bathroom with a standup shower and towels in a small armoire. They would make it work. He figured Orlando had conceived this circumstance as a very funny prank, or at least just desserts for having woken him in the middle of the night, and recollected that he might have noticed a smirk on Orlando's face as he closed the door on the second floor. Or maybe his old buddy Orlando was too drunk to remember or care that there was just one bed up there. And it would take the radiator a good little while to heat up the room even enough to sleep.

Whatever. Jerry's discomfort in the situation was just enough to keep him from falling dead away, which by all rights he should have done when his head hit the pillow. He was too agitated again, too keyed up.

Minutes passed. He knew Vogel wasn't asleep either. "Doesn't any of this bother you?" he said.

"What, you mean having my house burned down, losing all my stuff, being chased through Ohio and Kentucky by New Jersey police and now sleeping in the same bed with my new best friend?" Vogel said. "Naahhhh."

Jerry chuckled. "When you put it that way, it doesn't sound quite so bad."

"We don't live life," Vogel said. "Life lives us. When you come to grips with that reality, you become a little detached, an observer rather than a full-on participant. And from that angle, it's generally more amusing than stressful."

"Just waiting around to see what happens next," Jerry said.

"There was a famous spiritual teacher named Jiddu Krishnamurti. He asked his followers once if they wanted to know his secret. They said yes, of course, and he said simply, 'I don't mind what happens.'"

Jerry chewed on the profundity of that for a moment. Then his mind went back upon the day.

"You were right about Nicole not liking you," he said.

"Because I used to be just like her," Vogel said. "Now I'm like the opposite of her. I knew she would see it as a repudiation."

"Didn't take her long," Jerry said. "I really don't get her mentality. Maybe it was because I grew up in the country where that sort of stuff doesn't matter as much."

"Some egos try to extend themselves or make themselves seem more important or more stable through identification with material things, material wealth. That's what Nicole's doing. She doesn't feel like she's enough just by herself. She's attempting to justify her existence through the accumulation of the trappings of wealth. I used to be like that, too."

"We're not wealthy at all," Jerry said. "We have a negative net worth, in fact. She doesn't seem to get that. There seems to be no connection in her mind between the money she spends and our financial situation...at all. And she's a very intelligent woman. She did as well as either one of us in law school. You remember that."

"It doesn't have to make sense," Vogel said. "That brings us back to judgment and why you have to eliminate it from your life for all but the most mundane tasks. Because anything—absolutely anything—can be justified by rationality, depending on what your assumptions are. And almost everyone's assumptions are completely unconscious, which allows them to be completely crazy. Begin with crazy assumptions and where will you end up?"

"With crazy conclusions," Jerry said.

"Some people, for example, attach illnesses to their egos

to attempt to give themselves a sense of self-worth. They attempt to derive a sense of uniqueness or specialness from the belief that they are the sufferer of this or that illness. And the more exotic the illness, the more special they feel."

"I have an aunt like that," Jerry said. Sleep was coming on and he was slipping into that unguarded phase just before tumbling into unconsciousness. For the moment, he was no longer critically evaluating what Vogel had to say, which was a dangerous place to be. "She wants to tell you all about her MS every chance she gets. Talking about it seems like the only source of joy in her life."

"That's it," Vogel said. "That's exactly it. Mind is a virtual space, a blackboard on which anything can be written. Nicole has some unconscious assumption that the more stuff you have, the better person you are. If you asked her if that's really true, she would probably say, 'Of course not.' But it's unconscious thoughts that control us, not conscious ones."

"I wonder what my ego has written on it," Jerry may have said. He wasn't sure. And Vogel was wise enough not to answer that question. Or maybe he did. Jerry wasn't sure and didn't care and a moment later he was asleep.

Chapter 10

"Is the coast clear?" Jerry asked.

Orlando was seated behind the desk in his office.

"The old lady's at work, if that's what you mean," Orlando said. "We're DINKs. Dual income, no kids." This wasn't quite true. Orlando still had a couple of kids he paid child support for but they lived with their baby-mama. "I ain't no dummy. I sends her out to make some dough. Some years she makes more than I do."

Presently, a young blonde woman brought a cup of coffee and placed it on Orlando's desk. "Thanks, Jessica," Orlando said.

"You're welcome."

When she was gone, Orlando said, "The old lady knows she can be replaced," with a wry grin, meaning the old lady wouldn't be replaced anytime soon. "Don't worry, though. I explained your predicament in round terms to her. She's cool with you stayin' here—for a few days."

"Gotcha," Jerry said.

"Is NSA still on your tail?" Orlando was looking at his computer. He had seen it all in his day—or if not all, then most—and was not the least concerned about the NSA.

The first thing that Jerry had done upon waking was to open the little door on to the little third-floor balcony. Years of green paint made the opening a bit sticky. With the bright morning sunlight and the bareness of the trees, he could see a good way down the street in both directions, and sure enough there was the black minivan a few houses away on the east end of the avenue. He pulled the door closed, thought for a minute and then got in the shower.

"It seems so," he said.

"Maybe these will help," Orlando said. "He opened a lower drawer and pulled out a handful of cheap cell phones along with their chargers all in a tangle. "A client just brought 'em in last week. They should have some life left in 'em. Use 'em a couple of times, then throw 'em away."

Jerry stood over Orlando's desk. He picked one up, turned it over in his hand then put it down. "Will we be implicated in a murder or something? A drive-by?"

Orlando smiled. "Hey, I gots to get the po-po off my guy's tail some way."

"Seems like you're talking way more ethnic than you used to, these days," Jerry said. "Is that the way you talk to the judges?"

"I just do that with you because I know deep down it pisses you off," Orlando said. "I useth the queen's English in cou't. If you need to get our friend off the grid, let me know. I know of a good safe house here and there that will do the trick. It won't be as pleasant a stay as this, mind you. He won't like it one bit. But won't nobody find a brother in one of these places. Not even NSA."

"Really?" Jerry said. "Right here in little old Lexington?"

"You better believe it," Orlando said.

"Good to know," Jerry said. "I'll keep it in mind. Is that today's paper?"

"Have at it," Orlando said, handing it over. "I get it hardcopy for the waiting room. I read it myself on line. Coffee's in the kitchen."

"I don't guess Jessica—"

"That's just for me, and only part-time at that. Have whatever you like in there. Make eggs and bacon if you want to."

"Morning." Vogel entered the open space of Broxton's office, his hair still wet from the shower. He was wearing his Wal-Mart jeans with a fresh T-shirt and sweater.

"Hey, Brad," Orlando said.

"Thanks for the heads up on the sleeping arrangements, by the way," Jerry said to Orlando.

"When I was growing up in DE-troit, we would have slept six in a bed like that if we had it, which we didn't. So I don't want to hear it. You boys go in the kitchen. I got a client coming in a few minutes, the paying kind."

Jerry rolled up the paper, then looked around for where the kitchen might be. A couple of twists and turns in the direction of Jessica's closed door and he found it, Vogel in tow.

Vogel found a couple of coffee cups and filled them. Jerry sat down at the table.

"You want some of this?" Jerry said.

"I never read it," Vogel said.

"Too much negativity for you, I would imagine," Jerry said, with a renewed sense of disdain after a good night's sleep.

"Cuts into my meditation time," Vogel said.

Jerry wasn't sure if Vogel was joking, but he had already gotten to the point that he was afraid to ask for clarification, even though his natural inclination was to keep conversations going when he could. For with each seemingly innocuous aspect of the minutia of daily life, Vogel managed to propound another aspect of a worldview that destabilized him just a little bit. It was like there was a crack running through the plaster of the walls of his house and Vogel was walking around inside with heavy feet.

Jerry spread the paper out on the table, just the way his mother had done the previous morning down in London. He wanted to drop it, but he couldn't. It was almost as if he just wanted to find out what Vogel was going to say next. "So how do you stay informed?" he asked.

"I don't," Vogel said. "I avoid staying 'informed.'" He enunciated the words to indicate his own disdain for the idea. "What you call staying informed, I call indoctrination, brainwashing. Just about everything written in the paper or talked about on TV is geared toward making sure you believe in the solidity of the material world, which is a religious belief."

"You don't believe in the...'solidity of the material world'?"

"Nope, it's an illusion," Vogel said, pulling out a chair and sitting down. "But the scientific community, what I like to refer to as the high priests of the Science religion, are hell-bent on proving otherwise, that the material world is real. Have you ever heard of the Large Hadron Collider?"

"Yes, of course," Jerry said. "Because I stay informed." He rattled the paper as he turned the page before laying it out on the table again. "It's run by CERN in Switzerland."

"Beneath the France-Switzerland border," Vogel said. "The governments of the world are pumping billions of tax dollars into that massive underground complex and it has only one purpose."

"And what's that?"

"To prove that matter is real," Vogel answered. "Science, the state religion throughout most of the world, hasn't been able to prove this simple yet crucial tenant of their religious belief system, and it never will. The whole process entails crashing atoms into each other as they race around this massive underground ring cooled to as near absolute zero as they can get until atoms break apart. Then they're supposedly studying the particles that result with all sorts of computers and calculations. But it's no different from the Oracle at Delphi. Why? Because you have to *believe* that their results are telling you what they pretend they are telling you. You have to have faith, in other words. Every so often a story comes out that the discovery of the 'God Boson' is right around the corner. They'll do another one of their so-called experiments and then they'll get in a room and oo and ah about the results of their machinations of the data and how close they are to proving . . ." Seeing that he had Jerry's rapt attention, Vogel stopped.

"Proving what?" Jerry said.

"That the world exists," Vogel said, smiling. "Can you believe it? All this money and all these scientists cloister themselves underground, just like the Catholic cardinals when they're choosing a Pope, and all to prove something so simple, and so easily disproven."

The hugeness of Vogel's claim was completely lost on Jerry. "Another one of your three experiments?" he said.

"That's right," Vogel said. "The third experiment."

"And what's the third experiment?" Jerry pressed, stopping his perusal of the paper and looking straight at Vogel.

"The third experiment is to do the first two experiments for a while and see if your world changes. If it does, then the world couldn't possibly be as material as they say it is, could it?"

Jerry considered the hypothesis, staring out into space for a moment. "Wait, what's the second one?" When Vogel looked a little annoyed, Jerry said, "I think I've earned the right to know." For emphasis, he held the paper out and turned the page with great deliberation. "Don't you?" he added, staring at Vogel with raised eyebrows.

Vogel shook his head. "The second experiment has to do with negativity in the body. Take any minor ailment you might have, whether it be a headache or a bruise, or a minor cut or a cold—"

"Got it."

"Take your awareness into the area of discomfort and see what happens. See for yourself whether it has any impact at all and if so, is that impact positive or negative? By this experiment, you can know for yourself the impact of consciousness upon negativity."

Jerry looked up into the air. "So I take my awareness into my body every day, like we did at the Cracker Barrel—"

"Experiment one."

"—then, if I have any physical problems, I concentrate my awareness there to presumably heal it—"

"That's right. Experiment two."

"—I do that for six months or a year and then look up and see if that has had a positive impact on my world."

"Right."

"If it has," Jerry concluded, "one would be hard pressed to believe that the world is anything other that a dream...because...such things can only happen in a dream."

"Right."

"There's no way that feeling my body from the inside and concentrating my awareness on a physical malady should have any impact whatsoever on my exterior world if that world is material . . ."

"Right."

"...and separate from that consciousness of mine. If it's all just rocks floating in space, as you say, governed by cause and effect, all the causes of which have already happened. That application of consciousness isn't a cause in the material world as any scientist would ever understand it."

"You got it," Vogel said. "You're smarter than I give you credit for."

"That's not bad, actually."

"Thank you."

"Was that so hard?" Jerry said. "Now please feel free to return to your diatribe on the non-materiality of the universe already in progress."

"All right," Vogel said. "Now think about it: matter, even by so-called scientific measurements, is mostly space. Relatively speaking, there are huge distances between atoms, and huge distances between parts of each atom. Then there are huge distances between the parts of the parts of the atoms. Now they're trying to get down to one infinitesimal little piece that they can hang their collective hat on and say, 'Ok, this little piece exists for sure.' And they just can't do it. Because it isn't real. It's an illusion. But everything they say is designed to confuse this crucial fact that they've already discovered. All their language has the pretense of concreteness about it. But remember, all language is metaphor, keep that in mind. They're like creationists who simply will never admit the first thing about evolution even though it's staring them in the face. They're very paternal in their explanations, these scientists. Very religious. Because so-called Science is simply the latest mythology that they're preaching. I invite you to read anything out there through this lens and tell me how it comes across to you. It's simply a religion that you've been indoctrinated to believe in."

"Yeah," Jerry said, now reading again. "Evolution." The word distracted him and he lost track of Vogel's main point. "What's your take on that?"

"The problem with evolution is that Science only believes in the neutrality of the universe. They believe—faith, remember—that genetic mutation has to take place randomly. But it's impossible to get to our level of sophistication randomly. So what they do is simply expand the timeline of their mythology in hopes of convincing people that given enough time, the universe could have produced the human eye, the human brain simply through random mutation—which it couldn't, it's impossible."

"Um hm," Jerry said, already reading again. He had applied himself to the subject of philosophy for as long as he cared to for the day, and maybe for the week, and was now distracted by the weather forecast—turning a little colder with a twenty percent chance of snow.

"This level of sophistication becomes much, much more likely once you're willing to admit that the nature of the universe is not neutral but positive. You can prove this to yourself through one of the three experiments, by the way, the one I showed you."

"Is that right?"

The Cracker Barrel Experiment. Jerry decided to rename it Uncle Hershel's Theorem. That had a better ring. It did feel good, though, Jerry remembered, a little too good. If he allowed himself to feel that blissful on a regular basis...He stopped reading for a moment. There went that crack in his walls again. A little connection between body and soul was made. Jerry shook it off and went back to reading.

"This is to say," Vogel continued, "that the nature of the universe is to go from one state to a higher state, not the other way around as Science supposes. It goes from nothing to something, for example, when the world came into existence. Or from sickness to heath. Or from inorganic material to organic material. Or from amoeba to crustacean, or whatever, right on up to human life, which is the highest life form because it's able to become aware of its own awareness. Consciousness becoming aware of itself. God becoming aware of Itself in form."

"Uh, huh."

"Now religious folk, on the other hand, reject the notion of evolution too because they have a misconception about what God is. They believe God is this other entity outside the world of form, when in actuality 'God' *is* this transformative nature of the universe, so to speak, which is in all form."

"Right." Jerry picked up the paper to turn the page.

"And of course, if the so-called material world is an

illusion—which you can prove to yourself through the third experiment, if you're ever inclined to give it a try—it would adhere to the nature of the consciousness that dreamed it up, which is the consciousness that is in us. Which you might call the Consciousness of God. Or you might even call it God. But try not to get fixated on the words or the ideas—that's rationality. There is no reason to come to a conclusion on any of it, which is judgment. You have to just let all of this wash over you and then go inside yourself to understand it all."

Jerry looked at Vogel around the side of the outstretched newspaper for a moment, his eyes pinched in concentrated observation of his friend. Then he shook his head, as if to wake himself back into reality—illusion or not—and stuck his nose back into the paper. "That's dynamite," Jerry responded. "One thing I know isn't an illusion is that minivan parked down the street."

Vogel got up from the table and looked into the refrigerator. "I've had so much breakfast food these last couple of days," he said. "I would love...yes!" He eyed some cold cuts at the back. "A turkey sandwich."

"A turkey sandwich at this hour of the day?" Jerry said. "You *are* controversial."

"I eat what my body tells me to eat, Jerry. And right now...turkey sandwich."

"Are you not at all concerned about these guys from New Jersey?" Jerry asked.

"Well," Vogel said finding white bread in the cupboard. "If they know where we are, we also know where they are, right?"

Jerry thought for a moment. "Yes, I guess that's true. It's the old Mexican standoff." He thought about it some more, staring out into space in the direction of the light coming from the back door. "You know what? I'll take them on a nice little goose chase back down to London a little later. I foresee myself getting bored sitting here all day."

"London, Kentucky, is no cure for boredom," Vogel said, with hope of an invite in his voice. "I wouldn't mind seeing Amy, though."

"*Fletch*, right?" Jerry said.

"What?"

"'Utah's not exactly a cure for boredom'?" Jerry said.

"Utah?"

"Too obscure, never mind," Jerry said. "You better stay here. We better not bring Amy into this for the time being."

* * *

"Here," Jerry said. He handed Vogel a hundred bucks in twenties.

"What's this for?"

Jerry held his finger to his lips. "Shhh. It's from the slush fund. Don't worry about it."

"I have money in the bank," Vogel said, handing the folded bills back to Jerry.

"Trust me," Jerry said. "This pit is bottomless. You need to reserve your own funds because we don't know how long we're going to be on the lam, you know what I mean?"

After a couple of rounds of protest, Vogel reluctantly pocketed the money.

Vogel, of course, knew his way around Lexington. He would head downtown a little later, when he'd finished his meditation, for something to eat, a very pleasant walk with eateries in either direction from Orlando Broxton's manse. He said he would head west to the new restaurants down on Jefferson Street, rather than into the heart of downtown where he was sure to run into old acquaintances from Lexington's legal establishment roaming the streets between the courthouses, the government offices and the bars. Jerry agreed that was a good idea.

When Jerry was preparing to leave, Orlando gave Vogel a key to the back door so he could come and go from there. It would add an extra block of walking, through the hood, but it would probably throw off the New Jersey bloodhounds, at least for a while.

"Take a look down the block before you set out," Jerry said. "Based on what they did up in Cinci, I suspect these guys will be following me down to London."

"Following *you*?" Orlando said. Jerry and Vogel had apprised him to a certain degree on the salient features of the back-story that had led them to his door the previous night. “Why would they be following you?”

“I don’t know,” Jerry said, putting on his jacket. “But that’s what this little jaunt south is intended to find out.”

Chapter 11

With a good bit of glee, Jerry kept smiling up into his rearview mirror. He had driven off in the opposite direction down Orlando's street and turned without waiting for the minivan. They would catch up, just as they had in Cinci. So he glanced back, expecting at any moment to see the black minivan trailing him. All the way out to I75...nothing. But they would catch up—of course they would.

There were long stretches of I75 south that would have made it impossible for those guys to remain unobserved beneath the clouded winter sun. Conditions were perfect for observation: no glare, no haze. Jerry, frankly, loved solemn days like these, especially when he wasn't ensconced within Fortress DC.

That thought made him think about Pattie, his intern and lover back in the nation's capital. He was glad the COS's communications blackout gave him an excuse not to call her. Too distracting. He was on a mission. He had real work to do here.

Seeing nothing behind him through Berea, Jerry gave up looking back, believing they would just show up at his final destination, just as they had that morning at Orlando's house—they had their secret tracking methods. Then with his brother as trusted protection, he would turn the spotlight on them. It was the perfect plan and only required a tiny bit of cooperation from the boys from Jersey to bring it to fruition.

* * *

How could Eric be such a trusting sort in his line of business? Jerry thought as he strolled through his brother's unlocked front door. Probably a dangerous thing to do, he realized as he did it each time he stopped by his brother's place over the years, what with his sibling perpetually packing heat and perpetually angry with him.

There were his keys! Time to return a favor. Jerry picked

them up and went back out to the cruiser parked in the driveway, left there the better to deter the criminal element in the neighborhood.

Blip, blip. He hit the siren. After a few minutes, nothing. He hit it again. Blip, blip, just as Eric had done a couple of mornings before. Now it was mid-afternoon. Neighbors appeared in doorways next door and across the street.

Finally, one of the plastic slats of the blinds in a front window dipped, and an angry blue eye peered through. Jerry thought he could hear cursing emanating through the brick walls but he was probably just imagining it.

Eric came to the front door. “Thanks a lot, asshole,” he said, glaring at Jerry. “Worked the overnight last night. Just got to sleep.”

“Pretty funny, ain’t it?” Jerry said, following Eric back into the house. “Got anything on Brad’s house fire yet?”

“You couldn’t have just called about that?” Eric said as he lay down on the couch, still in his boxers and white T-shirt. Jerry kept an eye out for the minivan through the picture window, first one way down the street and then the other.

“NSA, my friend,” Jerry said. “You can never be too careful. They’re probably listening to us now.”

“NSA?” Eric repeated. “Get real.”

“You never know,” Jerry said. “Well?”

“Got nothin’,” Eric said, eyes closed. “Arson specialist came down from Frankfort yesterday. He said they weren’t trying to scare him, they were trying to kill him. A couple of out-of-towners poking around asking questions about your buddy.”

“See, what did I tell you?” Jerry said. “That’s NSA.”

“Vague descriptions. We’ll never find those boys.”

“What would you say if I told you I already have?” Jerry said.

Eric opened his eyes as Jerry dropped a piece of paper on to his chest. He sat up to read it.

“What’s this?”

“It’s the plate number of the minivan that’s been on our tail since we left London yesterday.”

“No shit,” Eric said. “’LE’,” he read from the tag. “Law

enforcement?"

"New Jersey."

"No shit," he repeated.

"Can they do that?" Jerry asked.

"Some sort of surveillance unit," Eric said. "They can cross state lines. They'd have to check in with Frankfort. State–federal joint op, maybe. New Jersey's a little far away for that sort of thing, though. Ohio, Tennessee, maybe. I'll check it out. If it's legit, we'll find them."

"You won't have to find them," Jerry said. "They should be here any minute. So you might want to put on your little outfit."

"I'm not getting back into uniform," Eric said. "If they show up, I'll call somebody."

"I don't want anybody else handling this," Jerry said. "Only you."

"I'm flattered," Eric said. "But—"

"This guy's trying to bring down Obamacare, Eric. My boss has me on cell phone lock down. I got state troopers from New Jersey following me. *Capish*?"

Eric didn't respond. He was too tired to process this information.

"Nobody but you."

* * *

After fifteen minutes or so, Jerry pulled up a chair and watched the front window from a seated position. Another half-hour and Eric began to snore. A few minutes after that and he was sure the minivan had stayed with Vogel. But how? Why? It had been a mistake to leave Vogel alone. They may have taken this opportunity to make their move. He was in danger.

"Eric...Eric.... Eric!"

"What?" Eric said, trying to turn over. "Stop waking me up."

"They didn't show," Jerry said.

"What a shock. I'll look into it tomorrow."

"No," Jerry said, shaking him. "Today. We gotta do it today. Right now."

Eric sat up enough to push him away. "What is your

problem!"

"Come on, man. This is police work. No time for sleep. This lead will go cold."

* * *

Eric made the call. As soon as he had given the license plate number to the proper bureau in Frankfort, Jerry called his brother a peach and got back on the road.

Next stop was Vogel's office to pick up his phone messages. The plump receptionist frowned with deep worry the moment Jerry had crossed the office threshold. "Is Brad okay?" she asked as she handed him a stack of message slips.

"He's fine," Jerry assured her, though he felt the need to get on the road north again quickly, himself.

Still, he hoped to work some of his magic with her, as he had the last time he'd been to that office. Jerry stood there awkwardly, forcing as charming a smile as he could muster. Nothing doing this time, so he said goodbye and left.

Once back on I75 north, the chest pains began again. He was tempted to break radio silence to check his own messages, even taking his cold iPhone out of his pocket and staring at it for a moment. Maybe the doctor's office had called, maybe the tests had come back. But with unusual military discipline—and also because he didn't want to know the results—he finally decided to put the phone back into his shirt pocket and tough out the pain by thinking of something—anything—else.

No time to pull over this time. He needed to get back. It had been a mistake to leave Vogel alone. The mission, that was it, that would distract him. Get Vogel to the courthouse on time. Bring down Obamacare. If they got to him, the cause of action would be moot. The case would be closed and no one would ever hear about Vogel's weird ideas again. The Speaker was desperate if he thought this was going to do any good.

Then again, maybe the Speaker had never heard of Vogels' weird ideas. Maybe this was simply the COS's way of getting him out of the office so Hanrahan could take over. Who needs a sick legal advisor on his staff anyway?

Maybe the COS knew about Pattie.

Jerry's internal monologue became more and more negative, which had the secondary effect of taking him further and further away from his body, away from his heart pain, which had the tertiary effect of causing even more damage to the heart muscle. But he no longer felt the heart pain and so began to think he was feeling better, when in fact he simply wasn't feeling at all.

Then he got to thinking about Brad and his weird ideas again. The whole thing seemed so perfect, it all fit together so well, a veritable impregnable fortress of anti-medical conviction. Boy, Jerry wished he could come up with one argument—just one!—that would bring those walls crashing down.

And what if he were able to come up with that one argument, what then? He'd be left holding the bag with some kook that had the potential to bring down him, the COS, the Speaker and maybe even the Republican Party (assuming it needed anybody else's help for that), and a heart that needed its arteries replaced with the veins presently in his legs. But that was the way of things, to tear things down, and better to do it now before anyone was the wiser about any of it.

He thought like this for only a moment more before it came to him, like a soap bubble in his brain, blown there from the great beyond. "Of course!" he said. "What about children!"

Jerry put the peddle to the medal and was back in Lexington in record time.

* * *

"What about children?" Jerry asked accusingly upon arrival at Orlando's house, forgetful at least for the moment to concern himself that Vogel was safe and sound. Vogel was sitting in Orlando's quiet waiting room, leafing through an architectural magazine. Jerry handed him his stack of phone messages.

It was evening by the time he got back. Orlando was out. Jerry had said hello to Orlando's peroxide wife, Heather, who had greeted him at the door. She seemed genuinely happy to have houseguests.

"What about them?" Vogel said.

"What about children who get sick?" Jerry pursued.

"Ah," Vogel said, putting aside his phone messages. "Yes, that's a tough one."

"Ah ha," Jerry said. "Just as I suspected."

"Because it isn't my experience," Vogel continued. "I wasn't sick as a child and I've never had children. It's an important question, though. One I've thought about and meditated on many times, myself."

Oh, no, Jerry thought. He's going to have an answer.

"Remember that we're all one thing," Vogel said. "One consciousness. So if one of us dies at five or two or in childbirth, nothing is really lost. That consciousness returns to the source. None of us are here for very long, either, whether it's five years or fifty or one hundred. To paraphrase Mark Twain, we're all going to spend a lot more time dead than we were ever alive. It's only when we view these individual life forms, these consciousnesses, as extensions of our own egos that they cause suffering. Yes, you or I will feel empathy for a parent that has lost a child. But that situation only causes *them* suffering—over and above the pain of it—because it's *their* child who has gotten sick or died. Children get sick and die all the time and it causes no grief for those parents, or for you and me."

Jerry thought of his own kids, the twins, and could understand rationally what Vogel was saying, but he was having a hard time imagining how he might not be grief-stricken if anything happened to either one of them. No, he just couldn't do it. "That's how it is when you're a parent," Jerry said. "And I wouldn't want to change that, not for anything in the world."

"That's understandable," Vogel said. "But you would *have* to change that if it happened. After a period of mourning, you would have to let go of it or the grief would kill you too. And that does happen to people."

Jerry wanted to change the subject now.

"But to get back to your main question," Vogel continued. "You're really wondering why they get sick in the first place."

"Yes," Jerry agreed, though he was already a little bewildered about his main question and what the point of this exchange was, if he were honest about it.

"We all inherit traits from our parents," Vogel said. "Why would we not also inherit spiritual traits along with physical characteristics? This has been called 'original sin' in the Christian tradition. It's an aspect of karma, I think, in the Hindu religion. I might be tempted to call this 'spiritual DNA.' And if we treat the physical as spiritual and the spiritual as physical, when we're talking about spiritual versus physical characteristics, aren't we talking about one and the same thing? Parents are perhaps passing down these spiritual traits to their children, which are then reflected in their children's physical bodies, as well as their own in some way. And remember, the so-called physical world isn't real. It's an illusion. A reflection of one's inner state."

"Ok, ok," Jerry said. Spiritual DNA. Inheriting spiritual traits in the same way that physical traits are inherited. Jerry felt himself squirming inside his skin. He shifted from one foot to the other, then went to look out the large front window at the beautiful old house on the other side of the street. Maybe we don't start off pure. Maybe we're behind the eight ball from the beginning.

"But again, this isn't my experience," Vogel said. "So while I might share these thoughts with a parent, I wouldn't ask them to believe any of this. They still have to go inside their own bodies to find the answers. And so do the children. Parents should teach their children to go inside their bodies at the earliest opportunity, that much I'm sure of."

Jerry was thinking about his own kids. Would they get any of this? Yes, maybe they would. Sarah Grace, would anyway. Not so much Sophia, who took more after her mother. Twins were an interesting phenomenon: so much alike and yet they had such distinct personalities.

Now that he thought about it, he got the same vibe from the twins that he got around Vogel, in a way. Less so as they got older. The idea bothered him.

"All words are metaphors," Vogel went on. "At this point in human history, we're using words to describe the world as solid and real—the terms of the Science religion. We've got to change our language to use words that point us in the direction of the world as illusion, lacking in solidity. If we do that, no telling where future generations will take it. Not only will they be able to heal themselves at will, they will be able to do anything—absolutely anything—they can imagine. Our current lexicon is tending in the other direction. It's all about future generations, as far as I'm concerned."

"All right, all right," Jerry said, almost angry that he had brought it up.

"You asked," Vogel said. He seemed bemused, which only served to upset Jerry a little more.

"Where's Snooki and The Situation?"

"Snooki and The Situation?" Vogel repeated.

"*Jersey Shore*?" Jerry said. "Maybe you've heard of it? It's a TV show?" Vogel was struck dumb. "Never mind. Where's the minivan? It isn't out there."

Leafing through his messages, Vogel said, "The London Fox affiliate called me. And the Herald-Leader." He looked up at Jerry and thought a moment. "I got back about an hour ago. The van wasn't there."

"Huh . . .That's interesting." Jerry looked at his watch. "Maybe they went to get dinner. Which reminds me, we need to take our kind hosts out for a nice meal, courtesy of the slush fund. Where's Orlando?"

* * *

They imposed upon Heather to locate Orlando. When told of the plan, Orlando said, "Well, as long as you're buying, let's go to Le Deauville. It's all you can eat mussels night."

"Mussels," Jerry said. "Nice. Look at you!"

"I takes a break from chicken and ribs occasionally," Orlando responded, with his ubiquitous Cheshire grin.

* * *

They all ordered the mussels. Jerry couldn't believe it. Sure, he, Vogel and Orlando were up to the challenge, but Heather too? He was really impressed with that. She was a gamer, up for anything it seemed, not nearly so high maintenance as she appeared. Okay, so she only drank water while everyone else had a bottle or two Kronenbourg 1664. She was holding it together pretty well, physically speaking. If that's what it took, Jerry considered, more power to her.

The restaurant ended up making money on her since she only consumed the one helping of Thai-style mussels. But of course, they had given it all back and then some by the time Jerry ordered his forth helping of the ebony shells, not to mention Orlando's three, all of them Diablo—there would be hell to pay later, he confided, but he just couldn't stay away from the hot stuff. With Vogel's' two servings, the restaurant broke about even. And the platter of *pommes frites* in the middle of the table was refilled a couple of times to boot.

The four of them sat near the front door. "They open these walls up during the summer," Orlando said. "It's real nice. You ever spend much time down here?"

"Out of my price range during law school," Jerry reminded him, the only time he would ever have had occasion to frequent the place.

"Um hmm," Orlando said. He knocked back a couple of quick vodka cocktails, whereupon Heather had tsk-tsked him with a smile, whereupon Orlando ordered one more. "It's real nice in summer," he repeated.

The effects of the alcohol aside, Orlando finally seemed to take a moment to enjoy the fact that two old law school acquaintances were in town and staying at his house, now that the initial crisis had passed and all involved had come to tacitly accept the presence of New Jersey law enforcement personnel in their lives. He and Heather sat beside each other, but Orlando sat back, almost lounging, talking only to Jerry, while Heather and Vogel, after initial getting-to-know-you formalities, really seemed to take to each other.

Jerry had had a couple of cocktails, himself, and so he wasn't really following their conversation, coming in and out of it, talking to Orlando most of the time, but there seemed to be some common cause there with Vogel's spiritual views. Yes, now Jerry could see it. Heather was kind of new-age-y, wasn't she? She also had to be pretty liberal to be with Orlando.

"She would never tell you, herself," Orlando said a little dreamily, "but our Heather is a published author."

"Oh, really?" Vogel said.

"Um hmm."

"I just self-published it about a year and a half ago," Heather said. "Just a resume builder, really,"

"That's interesting," Vogel said. "What's it about?"

"It's about how Hurricane Katrina changed the way nonprofits operate. It's called, *Katrina: Her Aftermath for Non-Profit Organizations.*" As Jerry and Vogel cooed appreciatively, Heather said, "You can find it on Amazon if you're interested in that sort of thing."

And then she changed the subject back to a prior thread, seeming a little uncomfortable with the limelight trained in her direction. "So your law case isn't against Obamacare, *per se*, then," she said, touching Vogel's arm as she said it.

"No, Vogel said. "It has nothing to do with the policy implications of the law whatsoever."

"Oh, okay," she said. "You scared me for a minute." She smiled across the table at Orlando, who was talking to Jerry about a lucrative personal injury case he had recently lost.

"When the estate decided to intervene," Orland was saying, "that was it. We were out of the case. I stood to make a hundred grand, and you know what the saddest part is? That fool ended up missing the filing deadline and that lady got nothing, not a penny on her claim."

"You're kidding me," Jerry said.

"Um hmm," Orlando said, still a little despondent, although the case had slipped through his fingertips more than a year before.

Heather was saying to Vogel, "Because I'm all about the mind, body, spirit connection. I'm with you there one hundred percent."

Vogel said, "I was just looking for a way to somehow—what's the word I'm looking for—dramatize, I guess you would say, this contrast between where we're going in the world with how it could be, you know what I mean? It's the contrast between consciousness and rationality."

"I know exactly what you mean," Heather said.

"Or more accurately, how the world really is," Vogel clarified. "And I thought, 'Hey, I'm an attorney, why not file a constitutional challenge?' Something just clicked and I knew this was something I had to do."

"Wow," Heather said. "That's really amazing. What's your take on Eckhart Tolle?"

"I'm a fan," Vogel said.

"The pain-body and the ego," Heather said. "Where does one end and the other begin?"

"Ah," Vogel said. "That's an interesting question. The pain-body is stored up negativity. It's either negativity you were born with—in Christian theology this is called original sin—or it was negativity you experienced earlier in life, maybe when you were too young to know how to properly deal with it, to process it out. Some people never learn how to do that."

"How do you get rid of it?" Heather asked.

"By feeling it," Vogel said. "As simple as that. I'd like to say that I've processed all of mine out but that wouldn't be quite true. It rears its ugly head every once in a while. And by realizing what's happening, each time it does I'm able to fully feel it and that way dissolve a little bit more of it each time. You see, the key to understanding the pain-body is that it's a big overreaction triggered by something small, some insignificant connection to the past that would go unnoticed by anyone else."

"Maybe if you gave me an example," Heather said.

"That can be a little personal, don't you think?" Vogel said, drawing back his head for effect, Jerry noticed.

"Oh, I'm sorry," Heather said.

"I'm only teasing," Vogel said, and Heather laughed and touched his arm again. "Back when I was still in the big time, like Jerry and Orlando here . . ."

Jerry said, "Get outta here." Orlando didn't say anything. He was a little tuned out by then.

"It used to really push my buttons whenever anyone would try to speak for me. You know, do the talking for me. That was *my* job, right?"

"Okay," Heather said. "Pressing buttons. I understand what you're talking about now."

"I used to get really upset. It gave me something of a reputation, but it also burned a bridge or two. That's a part of the pain-body too. It can be very disruptive."

Ah, yes! Jerry thought. He remembered this about Vogel. Even professors, if he thought they were putting words in his mouth, he would shoot them down remorselessly. He was usually right, too. But it cost him and most of his classmates knew it. He was up for the Editor-in-Chief position on the Kentucky Law Journal, the most prestigious the law school put out, but that was a faculty decision and he didn't get the job. Rachel Washington got it, though Vogel was probably a little more qualified. It didn't hurt her prospects that Rachel was African-American, either. Vogel could not afford that little down tick in his résumé and it cost him the job.

"And this was something from your childhood?" Heather asked.

"You know, I've never really been able to match it up with anything in particular," Vogel said. "It must have been something I was born with. It still happens from time to time. The difference now, though, is it doesn't ever completely take me over. There's always some objectivity there, and because of that awareness it gets a little weaker each time. And now, the universe somehow manages to turn those situations to my advantage in the long run."

"Really," Heather said. "That's interesting."

"Maybe it always did, in a way, and I just didn't recognize it before. I don't know." Vogel held out his hands, something had come to him. "Perfect segue. Now, take what we've just said about the pain-body and apply that to physical maladies."

"Really," Heather said. "Okay."

"Pain is pain," Vogel said. "It doesn't matter if it's so-called psychological pain like we've been discussing, or physical pain. It all happens in the body. And it all has the same root in unconscious negative thoughts. It starts out as the one and if you ignore your body's warnings, it ends up as the other."

"That's fascinating," Heather said, looking down, thinking it through.

"And the problem with modern medicine is that it completely ignores the spiritual roots of disease."

* * *

When the meal was sufficiently over, Heather was ready to go, but Orlando wanted to hang around and have one or two more. They had taken Jerry's Cherokee—Jerry watching in the rearview mirror all the way for the minivan to show up while maintaining pleasant conversation—though Le Deauville was only a few blocks east of Orlando's house.

"Here," Jerry said, handing Vogel his keys. "Take the lady home. We'll call a cab. We're going to need one, anyway."

Perhaps they should have stayed together, but both Jerry and Orlando had already had too much to drink to think clearly, Vogel had no fear and Heather was in the dark about the entirety of the intrigue.

When Vogel and Heather had gone, Orlando and Jerry remained at their table beside the bar inside the authentic French brasserie, with its black and white tiled floor and dull green shuttered windows that looked—beautifully—like something out of a *Pink Panther* cartoon background. In summer, as Orlando mentioned, the walls folded up, giving way to open-air breezes, but in winter, the place was shut up and pleasantly stuffy, fragrant from Provencal dishes and haute cuisine.

Orlando said, "Brad's gotten weird."

Whenever Jerry was in a diminished state, as when falling asleep or as now when somewhat inebriated, he was more open to Vogel's ideas and felt the need to defend them. "I don't know about weird," he said. "I'm starting to think he may be on to something. I'll tell you this: he's more likeable than he ever was in law school."

"He is more likeable," Orlando agreed. "I'll give you that. But all this meditation and self-healing. Come on, man."

"He doesn't ever talk about it unless someone else brings it up. Heather was peppering him with questions."

"She's all about that New Age bullshit," Orlando said. "Thank God he's joined the priesthood. Otherwise, it might have been a mistake to let the old lady go home with him. Back in the day, now, he used to pull some wool, if you know what I'm sayin'."

"I don't think it's like that," Jerry said. "I don't think Brad's a priest. That may have been what got him in trouble down in London. They don't cotton to carpetbaggers from the north coming down and scooping up the local talent."

Orlando swirled the ice in his vodka. "You don't say." He swirled it some more. "He is a handsome man, no question about it." He added with a smirk, "No homo."

Jerry didn't quite know why he had added that last bit. "I didn't think you were...homo," he said.

Orlando closed his eyes and shook his head. "It's just something we say to be funny. Though we probably shouldn't."

"What, a politically correct thing?"

"Yeah," Orlando said, finishing his drink. "Maybe we should get going. I don't want to give him too much time to work his New Age voodoo on the old lady. That would be on me."

Jerry paid the bill, which gave Orlando a minute to go outside and smoke a cigarette. When Jerry got there, he said, "Wanna walk?"

"Yeah, let's walk," Orlando agreed.

It took them about fifteen minutes. Orlando smoked another cigarette en route, the cold temperature just offset by the mild briskness of the walking. It felt good.

When they got to Orlando's block, Jerry said, "Hold up." From there he could see where the minivan had been parked, but it wasn't there anymore. "It's gone."

"Maybe it was never there," Orlando said.

"No, it was there," Jerry said. They continued walking and passed by the spot where it had been. Jerry slowed, looking for evidence around the Subaru that had taken the minivan's place.

"Maybe it was all in your imagination," Orlando suggested.

"No, it was there," Jerry repeated. "Maybe I spooked them by talking to Eric. Which means they really were New Jersey police."

"And doin' somethin' they weren't supposed to be doin'," Orlando said.

Jerry looked at Orlando. "That's right."

Chapter 12

Tap, tap, tap.

Jerry heard it from the third floor. Then he listened more closely. There it was: the chimes of the doorbell. It didn't ring up on the third floor for some reason. A moment later, it came again in the same sequence: tap, tap, tap, followed by chimes. Heather was gone but where was Orlando? Maybe he'd gone out too.

Jerry had slept late with nothing particular to do that day and too much to drink the night before. He and Vogel had gotten up and had coffee and eaten and otherwise tried to keep themselves out of Orlando's way. Jerry didn't know what to do next and his heart was giving him fits, so he read the paper and took advantage of the down time. When he heard the insistent knocking on the door and the repeated chimes of the bell coming through the floorboards, he thought maybe he was about to find out what came next. He went down to answer the door.

"Blinker?" Jerry said, pushing back the curtain on the sidelight. He opened it. "Blinker, what are you doing here?" Jerry was dumbfounded. Blinker was one of the administrative aides in the Speaker's Cincinnati office.

"Hi, Jerry," Blinker said. "The COS sent me over. He wants to speak with you."

"What?" Jerry said.

"He wants to talk to you."

"Why? Where?" Jerry felt as if he'd been caught by his mother with a girl in his room. This was weird. He couldn't get his mind around what Blinker was doing there at the front door to Orlando's house. He had never mentioned where he was to anybody, not even the COS.

"He's at Cheapside," Blinker said. "He wants me to bring you there. Jerry looked behind Blinker. Sure enough, there sat one of the official black Chevy Suburbans from the Speaker's vehicle pool.

Jerry looked down at what he was wearing, wash khakis and a chambray shirt, and up toward Vogel. He was up there meditating or something. He would never know he was gone, if that's all the COS wanted to do was talk . . .

"Yeah, okay," Jerry said at length, and he grabbed his jacket and followed Blinker out to the truck.

* * *

"COS, what are you doing here?" Jerry said.

"I'm having a bourbon," the COS responded, holding his hi-ball glass up as proof. He was seated at the elbow of the bar and Jerry pulled out the high wooden chair on the other side of it and sat down. His back to the plate glass window, Jerry looked around the bustling traditional bar, thick with the standard lunch crowd of suited lawyers and others serviced by young tattooed and pierced waitresses scurrying in and out of the wait-station at the back. Beyond that was the backroom and the closed-up patio. It was simply surreal to see the COS here.

"You know, I never drink bourbon except when I'm in Kentucky?" The COS had taken off a blazer and tie and left them in the Suburban. Jerry had noticed them hanging in the back of the truck when he'd gotten into it. Blinker had pulled up in the loading zone right outside, where he let Jerry out. That's where he'd let the COS out first, Jerry assumed, right outside the front door. No need for over-garments. The COS knew how to drink.

"You don't say."

"The minute I cross the river, I start to taste it."

"The 'Car Strangled Banner'," Jerry said. The local moniker for the Brent Spence Bridge. "What is that?"

"That's Papp," the COS said, taking a sip, then squinting.

"Pappy Van Winkle?" Jerry asked.

The COS nodded. "Hard to find outside of Kentucky. You can drink Beam anywhere."

The COS *did* know how to drink. "Twenty-three?"

"Fifteen."

"Still...." To the bartender: "I'll have the same...since you're buying. What is that, twenty bucks a pop?"

"It's nine," the bartender confirmed. "It costs more outside

Kentucky. Aftermarket."

"I may have two," Jerry said, warming up to this strange turn of events. "I need a good smoke with this. Shoulda brought Vogel."

"You know, they used to sell slaves right out there?" the COS said. "One of the biggest slave markets in the South. I think there's a historical plaque out there about it. Abraham Lincoln is even said to have witnessed it. His wife came from just up the road here. Changed his view of the world."

"I lived here for three years during law school," Jerry said. "I'm well aware of the history."

"Indeed," the COS said, taking another sip and squinting as it warmed his gullet. "Indeed." He seemed to become contemplative for a moment as he felt the ghosts of tortured humans nearby.

"So what are you doing here?" Jerry repeated.

"I had to check in on the district office," the COS said. "Thought I'd come down and pay you a visit."

"When was the last time you 'checked in on the district office'?" The COS didn't answer. "And how did you know where I was?"

"The bond of war is a strong one, my boy," he finally uttered. "As you might imagine, many in the warring trade often find themselves in the policing business upon return to civilian life. I have two such colleagues who happen to be proud natives of the Garden State. We were on the ground together during the First Gulf War."

The black minivan. "It was you," Jerry said. "You were behind it."

"When I heard about the house fire, I did a little digging. We are not without our own intelligence resources, as you know."

Jerry took his first sip, now that the ice had melted a little. "Oh, that is good," he said, and he squinted as the COS had. "And what you found wasn't good, so you called in a favor."

"It isn't unusual for a surveillance team to track suspects into other states," the COS said.

"But when my brother started making official inquiries . . ."

"I had forgotten you brother's occupation," the COS said. "Even if I had remembered, I'm not sure I would have made that connection." He took another sip, another squint. "Getting old."

"You couldn't have told me?" Jerry said.

"Better you didn't know."

"What about the FBI? If you've got something, wouldn't they be interested? This is a major crime we're talking about."

The COS shook his head. "Executive branch."

"Executive branch?" Jerry repeated. "What, like the President? You think Obama and his men are in on this? You think this goes all the way to the top?"

He couldn't believe what he was hearing, but the COS was not one to speak out of turn, he was not one to not do his homework. The only thing he could think about was how Nixon had sicced the IRS on his political enemies and how his own tax returns probably wouldn't stand up to such scrutiny.

The COS laid a firm hand on Jerry's arm to get him to quiet down. There were spaces on either side of them and a din that gave them their own bubble of privacy. Nevertheless...

"Obamacare is a multi-billion-dollar proposition," the COS said quietly nearby Jerry's ear. "There are some who stand to gain profits that haven't been seen since the Gilded Age. On the level of Vanderbilt and Carnegie, dwarfing the likes of Gates and Buffett. Your friend has something—I don't know what it is—for which they have very little tolerance."

The COS paused to allow that to sink in and to take another sip. Jerry did likewise.

The COS continued confidentially: "They wanted to eliminate him before his case picked up steam. They failed, which is rare. Your friend is very lucky, because they can try that maybe once more without anyone taking notice. Now, you have a little time. These types of operations require a great deal of planning. It won't be a drive-by shooting. It's got to look like an accident this time. I suggest you get him underground as soon as possible."

"An accident," Jerry repeated. And he tried to remember some controversial figure who had recently died under circumstances where foul play was "not suspected." There seemed to have been a few that had gotten his attention, that had made him think at the time that the natural death seemed just a little too natural, a little too convenient. With time and resources, it probably wouldn't be all that difficult to fool the Lexington coroner's office, especially if there were no reason for them to look very hard. And he seemed to recall a doctor's wife in California who couldn't have possibly hanged herself in the manner described, and yet the police had quickly closed their case. A little money greasing the right palms could make all the difference, and whoever was after Vogel had plenty of that to go around.

"And what about your detachment from Jersey?" Jerry asked.

"They're off the job," the COS said. "I need you to call off your brother as soon as possible."

"I'll call him now," Jerry said, reaching for his phone. The COS stayed his hand. "NSA again?" Jerry complained. "Do you know how difficult life is without this thing?"

"Use it at your own peril," the COS said. "We're behind your efforts one hundred percent but realize that you're officially on your own going forward."

"I thought I was on my own before," Jerry said.

He was going to have to make a call at some point. He needed to know the results of the tests run on his heart, didn't he? Maybe he could use Orlando's office phone. Maybe landlines were more difficult to track. Or one of his throwaway phones.

"That's not something you can see anywhere else," the COS said. Two young women in riding helmets, barn coats, sweaters and riding pants were tying up horses outside the plate glass window, their rosy cheeks puffing fog from their mouths. Presently, they entered the restaurant and began to undress, unbuttoning jackets, shaking out hair.

"We're not going underground," Jerry said, his next move

dawning on him. "That's just what they want us to do. Oh no, we're taking this to the streets. We're going to get too big to fail. Or in this case, too famous to eliminate."

With resolve, Jerry stood up behind his chair. "I gotta get going." He put on his jacket and then reached for his glass of bourbon. "But I'm not wasting this." He tilted it back and drained it.

"That's high octane," the COS said. "It's for sipping."

"I'm five-ten, two-fifty," Jerry said. "I think I can absorb it."

* * *

"Have you called Fox back yet?" Jerry asked. He found Vogel in the kitchen.

"Not yet," Vogel said.

"Call 'em. And the Herald-Leader, too."

"Did something happen?" Vogel asked.

"It's time for your fifteen minutes of fame, my friend," Jerry said. And that fifteen minutes might just save your life, he thought but didn't say. "Where's Orlando?"

"He has court this afternoon," Vogel said.

"Perfect," Jerry went to Orlando's office and sat down behind his desk. Vogel followed. "Would you mind giving me a little privacy? I need to make a phone call. Hopefully, landlines aren't as easily traced."

"It's the same if you're calling a cell phone," Vogel said, skulking out of the room.

"Good point," Jerry said, holding the handset. "I know: I'll call dispatch. They'll get a message to him." He thought some more. "But what's that number? Man, this is hard." He looked up at Vogel, who remained hangdog at the office door.

"I don't know if I'm ready for this," Vogel said. "Especially TV. Something about it."

"A crisis of conscience?" Jerry said. "You?" Vogel didn't respond. "That's just stage fright. Give me a few minutes. We'll talk about it."

Vogel left. Jerry checked Orlando's computer. It was on, no password required. He Googled the London police station, called the number, asked for dispatch.

"Can you put me through to Eric Riggs? This is his brother. It's important."

After a few moments on hold, the twangy woman came back on the line. "He's not responding, sir. Would you lack to leave a message or a number where you can be reached?"

"Damn it!" Jerry said, covering the receiver. He thought for a moment what message he might leave.

"Sir?"

"No," Jerry finally said. "No message." He hung up. He would have to go down there again. Another hour down and back. Funny, in DC he wouldn't think twice about an hour-long commute, but here in Kentucky an hour took you from one world to another.

The test results...did he really want to know what there were? Jerry sat looking at the phone, at the computer. Back at the phone. He picked up the receiver, then returned it to its cradle.

"Lunch."

* * *

After raiding the icebox for nearly all it contained, Jerry returned to Orlando's desk. Feeling a bit better with his belly full, he Googled the phone number for the doctor's office, then thought about it for another moment before finally taking the plunge.

"Mr. Riggs," the woman said. "We've been trying to get in touch with you. The doctor needs to speak with you. It may take him a few minutes to get him to the phone. Don't hang up."

This can't be good, Jerry thought. What would Vogel say about this? He would probably say they were icing him, softening him up so he would accept their pronouncements. Let him sit there stewing in his own fears until the doctor came on the line. At that point, Jerry would be near tears with anxiety, prepared to do whatever the doctor dictated.

On the other hand, maybe the doctor was just busy...as doctors tend to be.

And this music. Was there some subliminal message hidden in the doleful instrumentation? Or was it simply stock Muzak that came with the phone system?

Beads of sweat pushed their way to the surface of his forehead, Jerry could feel it. He mopped his brow with the fingertips of his free hand, then looked at the moisture they had accumulated.

"Mr. Riggs?" It was the doctor this time. After some amiable chitchat, he said, "Looks like you have significant blockage, and more concerning, you might have some weakening of the aortic valve, maybe some leakage there. We need to get you checked in as soon as possible...." And, "We may be able to treat this with a stint. We can put that in place with a heart catheterization procedure. If that proves unsuccessful, you may need surgery. But lets try the least invasive procedure first...." And, "Please don't worry, but we need to get you in as soon as possible."

Jerry couldn't absorb it all and what he did absorb may not have been accurate. "So bottom line, doc, what might happen if I don't do what you're telling me?"

There was a pause as if the doctor had never heard this question before, never even considered it. "Well, this condition can lead to your basic heart attack," he finally said.

Jerry was all right until the doctor said the words heart attack. His chest heaved in and out. He was at the funeral again, beside the casket with his mom, his dad's lifeless face painted up like a ventriloquist dummy.

"I gotta think about this," Jerry said. "This is a big decision."

"I understand." But there was something in the doctor's tone that sounded as if he didn't understand. Was this just Vogel's paranoia coming through? How could the doctor not understand that he would have to think about letting someone cut him open, exposing all his vital organs? It didn't make sense. And lurking in the unconscious recesses of Jerry's mind were the mistakes other doctors had made that had killed his dad on the operating table. Jerry was just about to blow, asking the doctor where he got off acting like God, etc., etc., when the doctor, perhaps sensing the rising emotion, said he had to go and got off the phone.

"Mr. Riggs?" the woman was back. "Can we go ahead and get you scheduled for a hospital visit?" She was apparently a pediatric nurse, Jerry thought, because she was talking to him like he was a child.

"I'm not in DC right now," he said. "I'll call you when I get back." The woman was talking as he hung up the phone.

Jerry stood up and stalked about the office. Why had he made that call? He felt fine before he'd talked to that doctor. And the woman was even worse. He could hear the concern in her voice. The fear. She was translating it to him on the doctor's behalf. She was the acolyte, the doctor the high priest.... This was Vogel talking, and now he was pissed at him, too.

He got up and went to the stairs, taking them gingerly one by one. Before that conversation, he'd never made any effort to avoid over exertion. But now the doctor had given him a "condition," his state was now defined and he felt some internal need to act in accordance with that new label.

Worst of all, it was Vogel's fault for having made him aware of this marketing technique of the healthcare industry, how they grow their markets, as Vogel had described it. You give a person a "condition" and it's natural human psychology—unconscious psychology—for them to then live up to that label. That's what Vogel had said.

"Well, I'm not falling for it," Jerry grumbled. "That's for damn sure." But he continued to take the stairs one by one. Was it better to know about all of this? Or would ignorance have been more blissful? Jerry couldn't decide.

Chapter 13

"What's with you?" Vogel said. He was sitting on the bed looking like he had been meditating. Jerry sat down in the rocking chair by the window to rest. It was perfectly situation for a peaceful gaze out the high up window across the budless trees and the neighborhood rooftops. It creaked sturdily when he sat down in it. He wondered why Vogel didn't use it for his own meditation. It was old, possibly antique, and felt as if it had always been a part of this nineteenth-century abode. The light from the window was bright. Jerry basked in its warmth.

"Nothing's with me," he said. Vogel didn't buy that. He moved to the edge of the bed to study his subject more closely. "Don't worry about me," Jerry said. "What about this stage fright?"

Vogel broke off his examination of Jerry, stood up and looked out the window. "I don't think it's that," he said. "It's just that I've always been so healthy. Oh sure, I've had little things here and there, but nothing major."

A complaint like this? Now? What were the odds? Jerry thought. "What the hell are you talking about?"

Vogel sat down on the bed again and leaned in to press his point. "I know this stuff works. I've proven it to myself. But . . ."

"But what?"

"But I've never had to use it to heal anything big," Vogel admitted. "I've always been as healthy as a horse, as the saying goes. How is that going to look?"

"You had that infection on your leg. What about that?" Jerry was feeling some sort of pressure, but wasn't yet sure why.

"Oh, you were right about that," Vogel said dismissively, pulling up his pants leg. The infection was completely healed, perhaps with just a slight pinkness that was only visible because Jerry knew where to look. "It was going to heal on its own anyway."

"Not necessarily," Jerry argued. "Those can need antibiotics sometimes."

"Trust me, I know all about needing antibiotics," Vogel said.

"There you go," Jerry said. "That's something, isn't it?"

"I don't think it's enough," Vogel said, standing up, pacing to the other side of the room and back. "But it's not like I can will a disease on myself and then use consciousness to make it go away. Consciousness is the most powerful stuff in the universe. Consciousness is what we are. Once you tap into that to eliminate the negativity, it keeps you health—"

"Well, what do you expect me to do about it?" Jerry said looking squarely at Vogel, then sullenly back out the window.

Vogel, taken aback, said, "I don't expect you to do anything about it." Jerry's ill will, and the silence, hung in the air between the two men. "That's why I'm a little concerned, that's all," Vogel finally said.

Jerry took a deep breath. "Look, I'm sorry. I . . ."

He looked up at Vogel, weighing what he wanted to tell him about his "condition." He almost came right out with it, figuring the telling of it might do him some good, might provide him with some relief. On the other hand, he had no desire to be Vogel's guinea pig, either. Still, his distaste for and fear of Vogel's way of thinking were presently running head on into the more deeply-seated, mostly unconscious fear of doctors and operations and the medical profession in general since his father's botched surgery—and neither was giving an inch.

"So you haven't had any physical maladies whatsoever since your..."

"Not really, no," Vogel said. "Nothing of any significance."

Jerry picked up on something, an uncertainty in Vogel. "What?" he said.

"The only thing that has given me any pause since my awakening turned out to be a case of indigestion. This was down in London, not all that long ago. The only thing I had to eat that night was some chili from the deli at the grocery. After I ate it, I began to feel really bad, like something was really wrong. I even considered going to the emergency room, that's how bad I felt. Because years ago, I used to get so sick with that sort of thing that I couldn't stop throwing up. I'd have to take Phenergen to stop the dry heaves."

"That's pleasant," Jerry said.

"Sorry, but you wanted to know," Vogel said.

"So what happened?"

"Nothing happened. I decided I had to practice what I preached. I laid down and took my awareness into my stomach."

"And?"

"And it ended up just being a case of indigestion. No vomiting, no diarrhea, nothing. I fell asleep and woke up the next morning. I've wondered if it was something much more serious that I was able to heal ever since."

"You could have had the container tested," Jerry suggested. "If you were serious about it."

"I actually thought about that, but as soon as I ate it I threw away the container. And as it happened the next day was trash day. By the time I thought about it, that bag was long gone."

"Stool sample?"

"Yeah," Vogel said smiling. "I wasn't willing to go that far."

Normally, Jerry would have picked right up on the humor value of the anecdote. The story had done nothing to calm his fears, though. He couldn't believe he was prepared by it to ask the next question.

"Why don't you just tell me how you do it," Jerry said calmly.

"How I do it? How I do what?"

"How you...heal . . ." Jerry swallowed, completely at odds with his own suggestion. "How you heal yourself."

"Well," Vogel said, alighting at the foot of the bed again. "Like I said, the short answer is that I take my awareness into the part of my body that needs healing. That's what pain is for, to draw your awareness to a particular place. Consciousness—that is to say your own awareness—is an extremely powerful force, but not many people realize that because it seems commonplace to them. How could their own consciousness be anything of any significance at all? They don't know who they are, in other words. They don't know *what* they are? So instead of taking their awareness intensely into the area of the pain, they simply run to the so-called medical professionals or the pharmaceutical companies and say, 'Please solve this problem for me.' It's a missed opportunity to gain understanding into the nature of things. This happens due to thousands of years of brainwashing." Vogel got off his roll and looked at Jerry and saw that for a change he was still listening, so he continued. "And the doctors and pharmacists are happy to respond, telling them essentially, 'Pay no attention to what's going on below your neck, it's of no interest to you. Stay up there in the virtual world of mind. We'll take care of you.' See what I mean?"

"So you just take your awareness into the area where the pain is," Jerry said.

"You know, I've told people this before, people who had life-threatening issues. I've told them they don't have to change anything about their medical regimen. They don't have to stop taking their drugs. Just do this in addition to that. And they still wouldn't do it. You know why? Because their egos wouldn't let them. It sits perched at the top of their being like a gargoyle, keeping people from simply feeling their bodies, because it knows that the first move into the body is the end of the ego. It will begin to die. And it has convinced the person's consciousness that death of the ego is death of the consciousness. Which isn't true. It's the death of a dependence on rationality and the beginning of real life."

Jerry took in a deep breath and let it out. You ask a simple question..."Ok, you've lost me again."

"Doesn't matter," Vogel said. "Going into the body in any way will begin to open your eyes. Like we started to do at the Cracker Barrel. That's the only way you'll understand what I'm talking about. You want to give that another try?"

"Just tell me about the healing aspect," Jerry said,

unwilling to try the simple procedure again.

Vogel shook his head, smiling. "It never ceases to amaze me how hard it is for people to go into their bodies. This is why it has been said that the initial step requires a divine touch to get people to do it. But after that, it's pretty much automatic. It happens by itself."

"JUST! . . .Tell me about the healing thing, okay?" Jerry said. Boy he could feel that one. "Just tell me about that. You take your attention into the place where the pain is, right? Is that it?"

Jerry could see that Vogel was taken aback again. He couldn't seem to figure out where this was coming from. "Okay," Vogel said. "Just relax." He was keeping a watchful eye on Jerry as he spoke. "The trick is to make that area feel good even as it feels bad. Joy is a physical phenomenon. You feel joy in your physical form. So is peace. You feel peace, which is the absence of negativity, in your body. And joy grows out of peace. This is your natural state of being. But where there's pain, you have to feel that pain as intensely as you can and find out what it has to tell you. Because all pain is from the pain-body, which is negativity lodged in your inner-body, or soul as you might prefer to call it."

He was getting going now, so he took his eye off Jerry. That was a relief.

"You might also call the pain-body 'the flesh' or 'sin nature,' terms for it from the Christian tradition. The world is an illusion and the first aspect of that illusion is your physical form. If there is pain in your body, that's merely a reflection of your soul and its attached negativity. So you have to figure out what it is that has caused that reflection. It's something in your soul. Something in your psychology, if you will. Surround the pain with peace, so to speak—another way to say this is to allow the pain to be there without judgment, realizing that it won't kill you—and joy will arise out of the peace even as you feel the pain, and then the pain will reveal its cause."

"Sin, in other words," Jerry said. "The pain is caused by sin."

"The pain is caused by unconsciousness. It's an unconscious thought that's causing the pain, and your inability to feel the pain causes it to accumulate, and that accumulation eventually turns into disease. Feeling the pain as intensely as you can and surrounding it with intensely felt joy will bring that unconscious thought into consciousness, at which point you can dispense with it, because it will be such a ridiculous thought, you'll wonder how you ever thought that thought in the first place. But you did think it at one point in the past, perhaps when you were very young and unable to fully evaluate what was going through your mind, and you thought it over and over again so many times that your mind made it unconscious so it could concentrate on other things. Conscious thoughts can't control us, only unconscious thoughts can."

"This is too much," Jerry said, backing off the edge of the chair and rocking a little. "I can't get any of this."

"No one can," Vogel said. "That's why you have to start small. You have to start by going into your body little by little. That process will reveal everything to you as you can handle it. Your body will teach you everything you need to know. That's what it's there for."

"I haven't got time for that," Jerry said, belatedly wondering if Vogel might have understood what he really meant.

Vogel looked up at Jerry, studying him. He said, "There is only now."

"That's right," Jerry said. "And right now, I have to get back down to London." He made no move to get up, however. He was too comfortable there in that old rocker.

"London? What for?"

"I have to talk to Eric again." Jerry didn't want to divulge to Vogel any of the details about the Jersey boys or the COS's visit to the Bluegrass. Everything was on a need-to-know basis, and he wasn't sure Vogel needed to know. "See where things are going."

"Yeah, all right," Vogel said, a little suspicious. "Mind if I tag along?"

The conversation about his heart and how to heal it had

made Jerry very tired. It hit him all at once. He looked at Vogel—it's his life we're talking about here. He needed to give him the option, though he knew what the answer would be.

Jerry shook his head, Vogel couldn't go with him to London. "To be honest," he said, "I think it may be time for you to go underground. Just for a little while. Orlando has the contacts to do it." When Vogel stiffened at the suggestion, Jerry added. "Look, I have it on good authority that they may take another shot at you."

Vogel took that in for a moment. It hadn't thrown him, but he seemed well aware of the gravity of Jerry's statement. "I'm not afraid to die," he said.

"What would be the point of that?" Jerry countered.

"Do you want to know what happened that night? The night of the fire? I got a call about eleven o'clock. I put on my shirt, pants, jacket and I left out the back door, through the neighbor's yard, three blocks over. Just like we did up at your place in Cincinnati."

"A backdoor man," Jerry added. "A booty call."

"They must have been watching, but they never would have seen me go out the back. It's a pain to get that garage door open. Plus it's better if no one in that small town sees my Bimmer parked in front of Amy's house."

"Especially her crazy ex."

"Right."

"So a piece of ass saved your life."

"It's not like that, exactly," Vogel mildly protested. "But for the conscious person, there are no rules. If I'm supposed to make it, I will. If not, I'll be happy to experience the next phase."

"Yeah, well, there's also collateral damage to consider," Jerry said. "I'm sure your landlord was none too happy to have his house destroyed."

Conceding the point with a shrug, Vogel said, "That reminds me: insurance has been most accommodating. My new wheels are coming soon. I'll be out of everybody's way once I get mobile."

"Probably a good idea to stay off the cell phone," Jerry

said.

"I borrowed one of Orlando's throwaways," he said.

"Good luck with the police interrogation to follow," Jerry said. "Are you sure I can't talk you into going to one of Orlando's safe houses?"

"I'll be fine," Vogel said. "I'll lay low."

When it was clear Vogel's mind wasn't going to change, Jerry said, "Suit yourself. I'll probably sleep at my mom's house tonight."

Jerry remained seated in the chair by the window for a moment longer, staring out into the overcast sky. He was tired and he began thinking again about children and sickness. He didn't want to go there again, that was for sure. But he wasn't quite ready to hit the road again down to London, either.

"I suppose you have an answer for abortion, too," he said.

"What's that?" Vogel said. When Jerry didn't even look his way, Vogel said, "Oh." After another pause, he said, "So, you're trying to make this as complicated and controversial as possible, is that it? I don't think that's a rock you want to look under just yet."

Jerry shifted in his chair but didn't respond. He felt like he might have had his friend with this point, but now he wasn't so sure he wanted to prove him wrong.

"I don't believe in medical treatment, first of all," Vogel said. "So that would kind of take care of the issue for me. I mean, you know...if I were a woman. Which of course, isn't my experience."

"It's a healthcare issue," Jerry said. "You're going to have to address this question at some point."

Vogel went inside himself for a moment, Jerry could sense that. "Perhaps healthcare shouldn't interfere in the birth process at all. Perhaps keeping the weak ones alive is just another way that modern medicine creates income streams for itself. While at the same time terminating perfectly health babies? Interesting pattern, to say the least."

"But what do you do about it?" Jerry said. "You said yourself that laws are in place to protect people from the unconsciousness of others."

"You're paying more attention than I thought," Vogel said. "But again, I'm not a lawmaker. That has to do with where we draw the line between the mother's right to autonomy and the child's right to life. That isn't my experience; I simply don't know. Where and how far government can go, that's the issue. That's more your bailiwick than mine."

"But you vote," Jerry said. "This is why I got involved in politics. It's where the rubber meets the road. It's all well and good to have these high-minded philosophies, but at some point somebody's got to make a decision."

"Do they?" Vogel said.

"You're damn right, they do,"

"But that's the crux of the matter, isn't it?" Vogel said. "It's the difference in approach to life between rationality and consciousness."

Jerry, as usual, at this point was mystified.

"The person with the rational approach feels compelled to come up with an answer to this conundrum. I don't. When it comes time to vote, I simply look inside myself, thereby connecting with the Universal, and pull the lever that feels best."

"Sounds like a copout to me," Jerry grumbled under his breath as Vogel reloaded.

"I will say that to terminate a pregnancy is one of the most unconscious acts a person—a woman—can perpetrate. But I don't think you'll wring much controversy out of that statement. The vast majority of pro-choice advocates would certainly agree. The creation of human consciousness is the greatest miracle and benefit one can bestow upon the world. It's the manifestation of consciousness into form, the only potential for consciousness to become conscious of itself in the entire universe."

"They may agree," Jerry said, closing his eyes and recoiling his head in response to Vogel's cosmic description of childbirth. "But I'm not sure they would put it in quite those terms. So you agree then with the Pro-Life position?"

"Maybe it's best left up to the women," Vogel said. "It's their experience. They have a way of sorting these things out."

"Leave it to the womenfolk," Jerry said.

"The women are actually in charge," Vogel said. "Always have been, always will be. Their ways are not our ways. But they're in charge not by becoming men—we certainly don't need any more of that—but while remaining women, that's the yin and the yang of it. The universe is a loving mother, not a stern father."

"God is a woman, in other words."

"So to speak," Vogel said. "'Know the male, but keep to the female,' says the *Tao te Ching*. The sooner you learn that, the better off your marriage will be."

Par for the course, Jerry thought. This was all he needed. He pursed his lips in resignation. "So we're on to my marriage now," he said. "How did that happen?" Thinking about Nicole brought him a little further down, if there was, in fact, further down to go.

"I can also tell you that none of this matters very much," Vogel said, returning to Jerry's original question. "It's not the big concern that people think it is. If the world is an illusion and we are all one consciousness, nothing is lost. Consciousness will return to the source. Consciousness will make more babies, and will continue to be born into the world of form. Consciousness can't be stopped."

The conversation had outstripped Jerry's depth. He sat hunched over a little, preparing to leave, beaten again. "Unconscious people, as you call them, producing fewer babies may not be such a bad thing, either."

"Consciousness has three options in its choice for parenthood," Vogel said. "Conscious, unconscious and rational. By far the worst choice of the three is rational. It's the rational mothers—not the unconscious—that are most willing to abort their children. Ponder that self-correcting little aspect of the whole thing."

Wow. Jerry had to think about that one for a moment, along with its implications. He wasn't Catholic, he was Methodist—neither was Vogel, he was a Lutheran by birth—but maybe it was the Catholic lobby that caused abortion and the wider issue of birth control in general to be inextricably linked in his mind. Copious use of birth control was dictated by a rational impulse to wait until one was "ready" for children. Vogel would certainly agree with that assessment, but he wouldn't consider it such a good thing. As he thought about it, Jerry might have disagreed with him before he actually had kids. Now that he had them, he knew that no one was ever "ready" for children. Irrationality or unconsciousness always had to play some role in the mating process or no children would ever be born—ever—and the species would die. Yeah, Jerry kinda got that. This marked a discrepancy in Vogel's behavior.

"You use birth control with Amy, don't you?" Jerry said.

"Hey, what Amy does is her business," Vogel said raising his hands. Jerry laughed, the quiet kind that comes out through the nose. When Vogel made a joke it was always a little funnier because it was so unexpected. "Isn't it funny that the people who have the most sex tend to have the fewest children? I've applied a lot of rationality to sexuality in my time."

"Tell me about it," Jerry said. The more they discussed this stuff, the more he found himself missing Sarah Grace and Sophia.

"On the other side of the equation," Vogel said, returning to the earlier discussion, "it's an egoic attachment to morality that leads some people to be so vitriolic in their opposition to abortion. That's a purely rational approach too. I say promote consciousness and leave it at that."

Jerry nodded. He was still thinking about his kids.

"What about you?" Vogel asked. "Do you tow the party line?"

Jerry let out a deep breath. "I'm not so sure, anymore," he said. "And that's not *my* experience." He thought a moment more, and said, "From a governance perspective, though, I've always thought that *Roe v. Wade* was a mistake. If you leave it to the states—as the pre-Roe state of the law did—it's easier to make more people happy. With twenty-five prolife states twenty-five prochoice states," he waited a beat for the vision of that reality to sink in, "it would be pretty easy to get abortions for every woman who wanted one while allowing prolife folks to live in states with laws that fit their views."

"Pragmatism," Vogel said.

"Politically," Jerry went on, "it's been a boon for Republicans. Without this wedge issue, we lose all the Catholics and will never have the slightest chance with the Hispanic vote." He thought some more about it without looking up. He was on autopilot now, politics his lifeblood. "Big mistake for the Dems."

"If I were to ever run for office," Vogel said. "Governor, let's say, or President. I would tell people that I don't hold any opinions about abortion or gay rights or any other subject, and that my method would be to simply go inside myself when an opportunity to act presented itself, and that's how I would decide what to do—or not to do, as the case may be."

"You're not likely to win the election, I'm afraid," Jerry responded offhandedly, without really thinking about it.

"I'm not likely to run, either," Vogel said.

"That sounds like the perfect waffle," Jerry said. "A non-answer with a high-sounding rationale."

Inside, Jerry was ridiculing the approach...until he realized what he was saying. Most politicians use non-answers to direct questions to *hide* their real views until they get elected. Then they pull the levers of power in support of those views, or at least that's what most voters think. But what if you had a guy—Vogel, for example—whose philosophy was never to hold any opinion at all? If the voters believed him, this could be political genius.

"The perfect waffle," Jerry said aloud again.

And maybe this happened more often than Jerry had previously considered. He would have to go back in his extensive political memory banks and reevaluate all those non-answers politicians seem to give. Maybe they really didn't hold as many opinions as he had always assumed. Maybe it was possible not to be so opinionated...Maybe that's the way people at the top really functioned...Maybe they weren't so soulless and Machiavellian as he and other keen political observers had always accused them of being. Perhaps they simply responded in any given moment to this higher consciousness that Vogel was describing. Could this be the difference between Jerry and guys like the Speaker and Senator McCormick? The lone difference? Had Vogel stumbled upon what Jerry had been trying to comprehend for so many years now? Was this the Holy Grail of political life?

"This *is* the perfect waffle," Jerry said. "I've been searching for it all my life."

In an instant his view of his friend had shifted from bewildered trust to something akin to suspicion for this discovered, accidental political acumen—this was his backyard, not Vogel's. The implications of the stuff Vogel talked about most certainly ranged far and wide.

Chapter 14

All the way down to London, Jerry tried to take his awareness into his body, just as Vogel had explained, but he just couldn't do it. It was like his body was an impregnable fortress, with thick stone walls. Cannonballs would have bounced off of it. He would try to feel anything below the neck—hands, feet, anything—but he kept going back into his thoughts. He turned the radio off.

What the hell am I doing? he asked himself. Modern medicine could handle this just fine. Pop's situation was malpractice. But for that experience, he could move right into this heart catheter procedure. His life would be extended. It works out just fine much more often than the opposite, right? That's what he needed to do. That's where he needed to expend his psychic capital, on overcoming his unnatural fear of medicine.

Still...what Vogel was suggesting was free. Why not try it?

He turned the radio back on. He'd been listening to AM newstalk, on a station now out of range. He switched over to FM and pressed the search button. It landed on the unmistakable ranting of the Beastie Boys who were standing up for the perhaps quasi-constitutional right to party. Man, Jerry remembered that album, *License to Ill.* It came out in 1986. He was fifteen. His dad had made him "turn that noise off." Pop enjoyed country (and western, as he would call it), especially the older stuff, and could tolerate rock and roll, but rap was nothing he was prepared to accommodate. Jerry had listened to it for weeks under his big set of headphones.

Aaah, Pop, he thought, wearing a wistful expression.

Eric, and others like him who always intended to stick around London, listed to country music: Garth Brooks, George Strait, Clint Black. But not Jerry and his friends. They were going places. Classic rock suited their tastes, Led Zeppelin, The Who, more Led Zeppelin. But in 1986, Jerry's inclinations took a momentary turn toward rap with the Beasties. His ship was righted not long after, along with most everyone else's.

Maybe Vogel was right. It seemed our society had, indeed, taken a turn for the worse if we now imputed to ourselves a "license to ill." Vogel would say that an M.D. degree is a license to ill. Jerry smiled, amused at the thought, until he looked up and saw the billboard Vogel had pointed out that first day: "All Saints Hospital – Your Doctors for Life." The woman in the owlish glasses seemed sinister now. He was at the edge of London.

His heart was hurting again. Or was that his imagination? He was beginning to wonder what was real.

* * *

Jerry waited in his Cherokee in front of the restaurant. He had stopped by Eric's house first. This time he found nobody home and the front door locked. Perhaps he had taught his brother a lesson on his last visit. Unwilling to wait, he cruised down to the police station.

The policewoman working the window had been helpful. She had gotten through to Eric via dispatch this time. Eric had told Jerry to meet him at Sonny's Barbeque. He was just about to have his dinner. That was fine by Jerry. He still wasn't sure how he was going to explain the New Jersey connection in such a way as to get Eric to back off, while at the same time leaving the COS and his military connection out of it.

Sonny's. Should he really bc cating this stuff anymore? It was the first such thought he could ever remember entertaining. Sonny's had a renowned salad bar, didn't they?

Salad bar? Oh, god! What have I become!

* * *

"Turn it off? What do you mean, turn it off?"

Jerry had had every intention of ordering the salad bar, but when the waitress apprised him of the all-you-can-eat pulled pork option, his resolve folded up its tents.

"Just call them back and tell them the situation has been resolved," Jerry said, his mouth full.

"It don't work like that," Eric said. "Once you put the wheels in motion, they don't stop. The inquiry goes out and it comes back through channels. There's a reason for it. They could have been on a legitimate top secret surveillance detail—"

"They weren't."

"—and the New Jersey state police will be very careful about letting out any information. It may take weeks or months before they get back to us."

"I guess that's something," Jerry said. "Look, these guys are friends of a friend, okay? They were doing him a favor in looking out for me. There's a good chance they'll be fired unless we can get that inquiry shut down."

"They won't get fired," Eric said.

"Misappropriation of government vehicles?" Jerry advised. "Of government funds for gas money? Not to mention the payroll expense, overtime? What they were doing was completely illegal."

"They won't get fired," Eric repeated. "Yelled at prob'ly. Happens all the time for one reason or another. It's easy to cover their tails on something like that."

"Well, even so," Jerry said. "I would appreciate it if you would do what you can about withdrawing the request."

Eric picked something from a back tooth. "Yeah, all right. I'll see what I can do."

"Anything new on the investigation?" Jerry asked.

"We had exactly one lead, and now you're asking me to shut it down. If it was as high level as you claim, we're never going to find these guys. If it was an old-fashion burn out, somebody'll brag about it sooner or later."

Eric's cell phone went off. He checked the number and answered it. "Riggs." He listened for a moment, said he'd be there in fifteen minutes and hung up. "Speaking of which," he said to Jerry, handing him the check.

"This is on me, I guess," Jerry said. "That's fair. Speaking of what?"

"They picked up Crace."

"And Crace is...?"

"Shamus Crace," Eric said, sliding out and adjusting his

holster. "The crazy ex."

"His name is Shamus Crace?" Jerry said.

"They still got names like that up in the mountains," Eric said. "Guess he forgot something when he lit out of here."

* * *

"Shamus Crace," Jerry said as he observed the interrogation through the two-way mirror. "That's the perfect name for a guy like him."

"I reckon," Eric agreed. He was still working a toothpick from Sonny's.

The detective in shirt and tie, a young guy with short blond hair, was asking all the routine questions, all business. Only then did Jerry get a look at the man's eyes when he looked up. They were those same ice-blue eyes he'd caught a glimpse of in that Monte Carlo in front of Vogel's house on that first day, the one that almost hit him.

"Hey, wait a second," Jerry said. "I've seen that guy."

"Oh, yeah?" Eric said. "Whereabouts?"

Jerry looked at Eric. "On the street in front of Vogel's house, three days before the fire."

"Make's sense," Eric said. "He's been keeping tabs on her for years. Him too since he's been in the picture. He was casing the place."

"Must have been," Jerry agreed. "I drove by a couple of times myself, just to make sure Vogel was up and around before popping in. I saw this guy twice, coming and going. I thought he was just heading into town for cigs and coming back, but . . ."

Eric calculated for a moment. "That may be enough to get him charged," he said.

"Oh, no," Jerry said. "I can't get involved like that."

"Sure you can. You've got to now. We'll get a lineup going."

"That's not going to work," Jerry said, thinking quickly. "You've already shown me the guy. A lineup will be of no value at all. And with me as the investigating officer's brother? That won't make it past the preliminary hearing."

"So you're fine with just letting him walk, then?" Eric said.

"I'm not so sure he did it," Jerry said.

"Your big healthcare theory again?" Eric said without emotion. "Lieutenant'll eat me alive for bringing you back here."

"Don't tell him," Jerry said. "I won't."

"Damn lawyers." Eric walked away, "You can show yourself out."

Jerry watched for a moment longer. He couldn't see Vogel's girlfriend with this guy. They had clearly been on different trajectories for a good long while, her moving up, him sliding down, way down.

He turned up the speaker and listened in for a moment.

"Where you been the last few days, Mr. Crace?" the detective asked.

"I don't know what business that is of yours," Crace said. "Are you charging me with a crime? If not, then you cain't hold me here. I know it and you know it."

"Where've you been?" the detective asked again calmly, without even looking up. It appeared, even to Crace, that the detective didn't really want to be there, that for him this was just another day at the office and that he would outlast his competition.

So Crace gave up this insignificant skirmish. "Been working up at a horse farm in Versailles," he said, pronouncing the name of the town properly as it is spelled. Jerry was well aware of the place just outside Lexington, with some of the lushest digs for horses anywhere in the world.

"Which one?" the detective asked. When the answer wasn't immediately forthcoming, the detective repeated, "Which one, Mr. Crace?"

This one took a little more thinking on Shamus Crace's part, a little more calculation. Jerry could almost see the smoke coming from his tufted ears. When he finally appeared to decide that the ratio of incriminating information to uselessness of resistance was in his favor, he said, "Stedwell."

Stedwell. Jerry knew the place, or knew of it, hard not to. It was the thirty-five-hundred-acre jewel in the crown of the international stud operation owned by the Sultan of Brunei's brother, or half-brother, or cousin—something like that. He was the deputy ruler (or something like that) of the Sultanate, Sheikh Akmed Ben Vereen. Okay, it wasn't Ben Vereen.

Not many outside the Bluegrass realized that Middle Eastern petrol dollars, with their penchant for seeking out the best money can buy in every aspect of life, had bought up a fair chunk of central Kentucky, the best farmland the world had to offer. Arab sheiks were now just another ordinary feature of the landscape, like white plank and dry stone fencing.

Stedwell, huh? So Shamus Crace has been working for the Deputy Sultan of Brunei, has he? Sounds like something to do...

* * *

Jerry stopped by his mom's place before heading back to Lexington. He meant for it to be just a quick pop-in, but it didn't turn out that way. He found her sitting in front of the TV. He sat and watched it with her. When she asked him what brought him back to London so much these days, he said, "What, I can't come down to watch Fox News with my mom, anymore?"

"You don't want to say," she said. "I get it."

A commercial about diabetes came on and Jerry couldn't help but notice it now. The remote was on the table between them. He picked it up and turned off the sound.

"Ever' one of these commercials nowadays has to do with gettin' old," she said.

"You old folks are the only ones a-watchin', I reckon," Jerry said. When Neil Cavuto came back on, he hit the button a second time.

They sat in silence, watching for a while. It was pleasant and Jerry remembered his dad sitting in that very chair almost every evening of his life, it seemed like.

At that moment, the house phone rang. Mrs. Riggs got up and answered it. "It's for you," she said.

After a beat of anxiety in which Jerry asked himself who might have tracked him down here, he got up and went to the old phone on the wall in the kitchen, the one he'd answered a thousand times before. How strange it was, with its ergonomic cup to the ear and microphone directly in front of his mouth. Some things were indeed better in days past.

"Hello?" he said. And the sound quality was far better, wasn't it? People used to be able to talk at the same time. The move from duplex to simplex communications in cell phones had taken its toll on a good old-fashioned telephone argument, that was for sure. He thought of Nicole. And with that thought, Jerry found himself growing a little pugnacious as he awaited a response.

"It's Brad."

"Brad, what are you doing calling me?" he said. "We still need to be careful."

"Land line to land line," Vogel said. "I'm calling from Orlando's office."

"I guess that's all right," Jerry said. "How'd you get this number?"

"I'm not without investigative resources," Vogel said. "I called my office for my messages. London still has a phone book, you know. I also called the TV station down there, as you suggested. They've got a news program at noon, apparently. They want me on it."

"When?"

"Day after tomorrow. I gotta tell you, Jerry, I'm pretty nervous."

"This is just what you need. No time to think about it. It's like a minor league game down here in London. You can work out your shtick before you hit the national stage." The wheels of Jerry's mind began to turn. "You'll need a new suit," he said. "I'll be back later tonight, we can take care of everything."

"I'm already on that," Vogel said. "My new car will be ready this afternoon."

Jerry was about to hang up, when Vogel said, "You got a call from your intern back in DC, a Pattie Dugan."

She, too, was not without her own investigative prowess. "Thanks," Jerry said as nonchalantly as he could. "I'll try to give her a call."

He hung up the phone and came back into the living room and sat down.

"You leavin' again?" Mrs. Riggs said.

"What?" Jerry said, lost in his thoughts. "No, no. That was Brad."

"I know," she said. "He said hello when I answered."

"He did?" Jerry said. "Yes, of course he did. He's that kind of guy. He's coming down here day after tomorrow. He's going to be on the midday news show on Fox."

"About the far?" Mrs. Riggs asked.

"About the fire?" Jerry repeated, momentarily forgetting. "The fire. No, it's not about the fire. It's about a lawsuit he filed in federal court. That's what I'm down here advising him about, actually."

"That little girlfriend of yours from high school is the host of that show," Mrs. Riggs said.

"What—Lisa?" Jerry said. "That was junior high and she was never my girlfriend."

He knew that Lisa Posey had become a reporter after college but he had long since lost track of her. It would likely make for an interesting dynamic the next day, nonetheless. She did have a crush on him all those years ago, but all Jerry had ever done was ignore her. In hindsight, perhaps that had been a mistake. He thought of Nicole again. Maybe Eric was right. His life could have been a whole lot simpler if he'd stayed in London, married Lisa, worked his way up to governor eventually. Instead, he had made it as complicated and stressful as possible.

This brought his thoughts back to Pattie. What was she doing calling him? Was it work related? Or extracurricular? He could give her a call from the house phone, but it was ironic: they had always eschewed communications over government lines for the same paranoid reason he was afraid to call her now on a cell phone now. One never knew who was listening.

Jerry was prepared to admit to himself that these precautions were beginning to feel a little silly and that perhaps they were his psychology's way of obtaining a little isolation from a life that was running him into the ground, psychologically as well as physically. Maybe Vogel was right. Maybe the two were inextricably linked. And maybe life had a way of bringing situations along that are just what you need. Two weeks ago he never would have dreamed he would be where he was right now.

"Hey, Ma," Jerry said. "Do you ever remember hearing about an outbreak of some sort of food-related sickness around here. Botulism or salmonella, E. coli, something like that in the last year or two?"

"Goodness gracious, yes," Mrs. Riggs said.

"You do!"

"Course, I do. I'm surprised you didn't hear about it up there in Washington."

"When was this?" He sat up in his seat, facing his mother.

"Oh," she said thinking. "Must a been back a year or so ago, I reckon. I must a mentioned it to you."

"No, I don't think you did."

"Two little girls died. Nearly shut down the groc'ry for good."

"You're kidding me!" Thinking, thinking. "Chili from the deli, right?"

"I say little girls, but they was in their twenties, I think," she said. "From the deli. I don't know if it was chili."

"But how could he not have heard about this?" Jerry said aloud. Because Vogel avoids all news, that's how.

"Who?"

"How could *I* not have heard about this? Ma, how far back do your newspapers go?" He got up to look in the back corner where she always kept them neatly stacked. "Oh, no!" he said. "You're throwing them all out now?"

"I moved 'em to the garage a long time ago," she said.

"Oh, right," Jerry said, walking down the hall to the garage.

"They prob'ly go back that far."

"About a year or so ago?"

"Maybe a little more than that. Now they may not all be there. I use 'em for startin' a far and cleaning and such."

Jerry switched on the light. There they sat in two pristine

stacks, a chronicle of all that had happened in London, more or less. He leafed through them. They were in close to chronological order. It was cold in the garage. This was going to take a while and may even prove to be fruitless.

"Well," he said, hands on hips. "What else do I have to do?" And he got to work.

* * *

Botulism had been the culprit. It had entered through the grocery's in-house brand chili sauce, causing the deaths of two unrelated female victims in London, and was linked to 4 other deaths around the country. Hundreds had fallen ill, with graphic, longstanding symptoms.

Jerry thought for a moment. Sure, Vogel could have survived a case of botulism. But reducing it to a simple case of indigestion?

And why hadn't Vogel heard about it? There must have been talk. Jerry did the calculation...That would have been around the time he arrived here, not long after his firing from Brackman-Hollis. He probably didn't know anybody then. He didn't read the newspaper. No TV. And no one would have gone out of their way to let him know, not a stranger here in London-town.

"Kinda spooky," Jerry said to himself.

"What's spooky?"

Jerry jumped out of his skin. "Ma!"

"It's cold," she said. "Looks like the weather's turned again. Close that door."

That's just what his heart needed, a nice little jolt. Maybe it was time for him to take his medicine—Vogel's medicine. He resolved to go into his bedroom and sit there on the bed, just as he had seen Vogel doing at Orlando's house.

But as he passed the TV and his dad's chair, he found himself asking, "What's for supper?" sitting down and watching the news.

Chapter 15

Jerry was still a little concerned for Vogel's safety, but at the same time he didn't relish the idea of sharing a bed with him if he didn't have to, and it was the latter concern that won out. At the last minute, Jerry decided to stay the night in London. When he arrived back at Broxton Manor the next morning, Vogel sat safe and sound in the kitchen, eating country ham and biscuits. One of Orlando's clients had had a wake for a relative the night before. Too much food had come in, so they sent him home with a heaping plate.

"You wiry guys can eat whatever you want," Jerry said. "It pisses me off."

"You eat whatever you want," Vogel said.

Jerry, standing in front of Vogel, held out his hands. "But as you can see, I ain't wiry."

He took a plate from the draining basket and heaped six of the meat-filled biscuits on it. Noticing that Vogel only had two, and noticing that Vogel noticed, Jerry shrugged and took to eating.

"You know, the only difference between you and me when it comes to food?" Vogel said. "I see that empty, hungry feeling as my normal state."

"I hate it," Jerry said with his mouth full.

"You hate it," Vogel repeated. "That judgment causes suffering, which in turn magnifies that hungry feeling...so you eat more. Then, in an effort to get your attention, your body gets bigger, because the material world is merely—"

"I know, I know," Jerry said. "The material world is merely a reflection of my inner state."

"So you have been listening." Vogel took a moment to chew and swallow, then he opened his second biscuit and squirted mustard on the ham. "Eat consciously. Realize any time you're eating—and afterward—exactly how the ingestion of that food makes you feel." He took another bite.

"Diet is about eighty percent of it. Exercise, about twenty percent. The trick with exercise is not to do too much. If you do too much, then you get too hungry and eat too much. You don't get anywhere. Just do what you feel like doing."

"Isn't that how people get fat?" Jerry asked. "By doing what they feel like doing?"

"That's a myth," Vogel said. "Again, the problem is rationality, and it cuts both ways. When someone is overweight, their rational element overrides their bodies, telling them not to exercise, in reaction to some fear that they have. Maybe a guy has a fear of poverty, so he decides not to take time away from work to look after his body."

"Or maybe he's just lazy," Jerry said.

"The lazy person is stuck in his head, too. They're cut off from their bodies. It's a physical manifestation of depression. But did you also know that elite athletes have a shorter lifespan than the general population?"

"Get outta here," Jerry said, picking up another biscuit.

"Sixty-seven years," Vogel said. "And that's because they have the ability to override their bodies' natural balance to force them to exercise much more than is healthy for them. To be the healthiest, then, the best approach is to simply do as much or as little as you feel like doing. Never override your body's natural inclinations regarding exercise, Jerry." He took another bite and with a full mouth said, "That's the only weight loss advice anyone will ever need."

"I don't remember asking for any weight loss advice," Jerry said. "What, do you get out of bed every morning in pontification mode?"

"You're the one who brought it up," Vogel said. "Now, the sex addict is just the opposite of the overeater. He sees that full feeling as something to be avoided. This is all unconscious, of course. But it's that full feeling that would pull him along like lift in a winded sail, so to speak, if he would let it out sparingly."

Jerry didn't recall bringing *that* up. He wondered if he might be gaining some additional insight into his friend's past personal history, the kind men of his own ilk are not wont to discuss openly. "But even the best sails are in need of trim from time to time," he said, hoping the humor would relieve the awkwardness he felt.

"Well played, my dear fellow," Vogel responded in his best upper crust accent. "But only enough to keep you moving forward at best speed."

"No problem on that score," Jerry said. "I'm about as full as you get right now."

"And you see?" Vogel said, standing up to pour a second cup of coffee. "There is movement in your life. Things are happening."

Nope, humor hadn't done the trick. And now for a change of subject . . .

"They picked up Shamus Crace," Jerry said.

Vogel closed his eyes and shook his head, a slight wince of pain creasing the space between his eyebrows. "You want some?" he asked, avoiding the new subject, holding out the coffee pot.

Jerry nodded. "Your fly in the ointment, is he? Your thorn in the flesh."

"That's a good way of putting it," Vogel agreed, handing Jerry a mug and sitting down.

"He's been working over in Versailles at Stedwell Racing." Vogel cocked his head and frowned. "Yeah, *that* Stedwell Racing."

"Sultan of something or other," Vogel said.

"Right," Jerry said. "Now here's what we're going to do. We're going to get you all gussied up like you're some big hotshot looking to avail yourself of the Sultan's stud services for one of your prizewinning brood mares. You can pull it off. I'll be your flunky assistant."

"No, no," Vogel said. "I'm off that. I've renounced the trappings of wealth, as it were."

"It isn't real," Jerry said. "It's for the investigation."

"I don't know," Vogel said, with real concern wrinkling his otherwise taught features. "And besides, I haven't got the...*accoutrement.*" He used the French pronunciation, whether to lighten the mood with humor or because that's the way he always said it, Jerry wasn't quite sure.

"Come on," he prodded. "You can't visit the Bluegrass

State without a visit to a horse farm. It's...what's the word I'm looking for?"

"Obligatory?"

"Right, it's obligatory," Jerry repeated. "You can pull this off. We'll go down to Graves-Cox and get you everything you need. We gotta start building up your suit collection, anyway."

"Shouldn't we leave the investigation to—you know—the professional investigators? Like your brother? He didn't seem like the kind of guy who would cotton to amateur sleuths getting in his way."

"Naaa," Jerry said, drawing it out to accommodate a get-outta-here wave. "He's perfectly fine with it." Or what he doesn't know won't hurt him...or something. "Believe me, he's not that professional. Besides, what could possibly go wrong? Come on, let's get going."

* * *

Vogel let out a low moan of pleasure as they approached the display case full of cufflinks. He stroked the glass affectionately. "I've got a thing about French cuffs," he said. "It's starting to come back, I can feel it."

He had already been fitted for his suit. He'd breezed by the gentleman manning the shop, back to the rack that might as well have been marked "Most Expensive." He put off the little man by asking if this was all he had. When the answer came back in the affirmative, with a pained expression, holding out a black worsted wool size forty with yellow loops across the shoulders, Vogel said, "This'll have to do."

On his way to the suits, Vogel appeared to consciously avoid this display case. Now Jerry was beginning to understand why.

"And I'll take a pair of the black Ferragamos you have back there, size eleven and a half."

"Don't you want to try them on?" Jerry asked.

"Jerry, please," Vogel said with a bit of a condescending smile. "I think I know what size I wear in Salvatore Ferragamo shoes."

When the impressed shopkeeper passed through the

curtain, Vogel said, "I can feel it all coming back. Ego, you know?"

"I can see that," Jerry said. Vogel was still very self-assured these days, but it wasn't off-putting like it was back in law school. Not until now.

"You're the one who wanted to do this," Vogel said. "This is what it takes."

"What, you mean you're acting?" Jerry said.

"Half yes, half no," Vogel said. "I don't want to do this for too long. I feel like I'll be right back where I started. There's certainly nothing wrong with being drawn to the best in every aspect of life when that's a reflection of who you are, a reflection of your inner space, your soul. But when the trappings of wealth are used merely as an extension of your ego, that's an altogether different story. It's just another manifestation of the fallacy of putting any faith at all in the concreteness of the so-called material world, 'where moth and rust doth corrupt.' It's painful. It's what led ultimately to OCD symptoms for me when it all began slipping away. I don't ever want to go back there again."

"Will there be anything else, sir?" The shopkeeper was back with the shoes.

"I'll take these cufflinks," Vogel said, pointing to a gold and pearl set, expensive but not the most expensive.

Jerry swallowed hard, careful not to react in any noticeable way. He remembered now that he was a little afraid of this Vogel.

The man located a box at the back of the display case and placed it on top. "Will that be cash or charge, sir?"

Jerry reached into his pocket for his wad of Republican bills. Vogel stayed Jerry's hand and froze him in place with a look that quickly and efficiently communicated just how gauche cash was.

"I'm going to need this tailored while we wait," Vogel said, looking down, thumbing through his wallet.

"While..." the man said. "While you wait?"

"That's right. There's been a fire and I have a very important meeting this afternoon. So as you can see, I'll need to wear it out. What did you think? That I'm the kind of person who normally wears clothes from Wal-Mart?"

"Certainly not," the man responded. "Unfortunately . . ."

Vogel produced a black credit card from his wallet and casually tapped it on the glass as the man stammered. This time Jerry couldn't help but manifest the same eye-popping expression as the poor suit salesman.

"Where can we have it delivered, sir?"

Brad was happy to provide Orlando Broxton's address, a suitably upscale locale, an address to impress.

When the man had gone back behind the curtain again, Vogel was the first to speak. "If you want to spend your cash, you can buy me that pen."

Jerry looked at it. "Six hundred dollars!"

"What if we get out there, Jerry, and I have to write something down? If I reach into my coat and pull out a Bic, how's that going to look? Every detail has to be right with these guys."

"And the credit card?" Jerry asked.

"What can I tell you? I'm good with money. You'll have to pay me back, of course. I don't maintain a balance on this thing." Before Jerry could protest, Vogel said, "This was your idea, remember? If we're going to do it, we've got to do it right."

* * *

Jerry put the extravagant expenditures out of his head and began to enjoy the ride, quite literally. He flexed his fingers around the leather grips of the steering wheel.

"In what other city with a population less than five hundred thousand can you rent a Range Rover at the airport?" Jerry asked. "But what else are the queen's men going to drive, right? Who knows, maybe that's just urban legend that she buys all her horses here."

Vogel didn't say anything. He was fully in character now, with his tight-fitting suit, his black Tom Ford sunglasses and that vintage tweed overcoat he'd dug up. While they waited on the tailoring, Vogel took Jerry to a consignment shop he knew about where rich folks left all their old clothes. There he found this thing, which, according to Vogel, was just the thing. "You don't want to look too perfect," he had said, digging through the stacks. "It makes people look twice, and we don't want that." Jerry had to admit that Vogel was right: he still looked rich. Maybe very rich.

When the suit arrived at Orlando's house, they drove straight to the airport, where they rented the necessary driving accessory.

"I could have gone for the Jaguar," Jerry prattle on. "But this is cool, too."

"You want the Range Rover," Vogel said. "It's still a farm."

"Yeah, you're right," Jerry said.

"In one thousand feet, turn left and you will have arrived at your destination," advised the feminine voice accented in British. Unbeknownst to the Global Positioning System, they had arrived at their destination a while ago. All around them was the rolling bluegrass pastureland of Stedwell Farm, lush even in the yellow deadness of winter.

Jerry pulled up to the gate and lowered the glass to press the button on the intercom. From the stone entrance through the bare trees, he could make out the barns in the distance—if you could call them barns. They were big and painted in rich pewter blue and dove white and housed millions of dollars on the hoof in clean, horsey opulence.

"Yes?"

"Mr. Bradley Vogel," Jerry said. They had decided there was no point in making up names. "We have an appointment."

"I'm sorry, sir, but he's not on the list."

"That's unusual," Jerry said. "We called last week. He's in from Maryland just for the day."

There was a delay while the security guard took a peek at Jerry through the lens on the intercom. Then the surveillance camera up on the gate whirred and repositioned itself to take a look at the vehicle and its other occupant.

"The sheikh won't be able to see you, I'm afraid."

"That won't be necessary," Jerry said. "We had an appoint with someone else, a Mr. Crace. Shamus Crace. He was going to show us around the operation."

After a full minute, the gate opened. Jerry looked at Vogel and shrugged.

* * *

"Yep, they're still barns," Jerry said, stepping out of the Range Rover, onto the rubberized pavements. He took in a deep breath and let it out. "I love the smell of manure in the morning."

Vogel stepped around to Jerry's side of the vehicle. One hand in the pocket of his tweed overcoat, he was looking at his Breitling watch. "Yes, it is still morning," he confirmed.

Jerry, in his off-the-rack civil-servant-wear, looked just right, too. In his standard blue pinstripes and grey wool coat, longer and less stylish than Vogel's, he might have been a local agent of some sort assigned the task of squiring the rich out-of-towner around for the day.

A man in a quilted Stedwell barncoat approached. "Good afternoon, gentlemen," he said. Handshakes complete, he said, "George Dawkins. Shamus isn't here, right now."

"That's quite all right," Jerry spoke up. "We don't even know the man, really. That's just the name we were given."

"You were given Shamus's name?" the man asked. He was spry and in charge, not quite a jockey type. He was too big to be a jockey, but not by much.

"Does that surprise you?" Jerry asked.

"A little," the man said amiably. "He hasn't worked here all that long." Vogel shifted impatiently and the man said, "But who knows?" with a smile. "I just work here. Let me show you around."

Most of the stallions were turned out to the paddocks surrounding the barns. There were a few standing in their stalls, with feedbags containing specific grain regimens for each, as prescribed by the manager in consultation with the veterinarian, Dawkins explained. The oak floors that ran down the middle of the barn between the stalls were squeaky clean, the way the humans liked them. Inside the stalls, the horses got their way with strewn hay and the softness of earth.

The mares were housed in a separate barn in which every light in the place and then some was on as bright as it would go.

"What's with all the lights?" Jerry asked.

George Dawkins' smile dissolved into something a little less amiable and a little more wary.

Before Dawkins had gathered himself to explain, Vogel said, "It's to bring on the estrous cycle early. It's triggered by the photoperiod—the longer days later in the year. If they wait for it to occur naturally in the spring or summer, the offspring will have to wait an extra year to race." And to Dawkins, "He's not in the business. Shall we take a look at the breeding shed?"

George Dawkins' smile returned. "Yes, sir," he said. "This way."

When the little man was out of earshot, Jerry said, "What the hell is an estrous cycle?"

"Heat," Vogel said. "The mares going into heat."

"How the hell did you know that?"

"Googled it," Vogel said, holding up his iPhone. "You have to look like you know what you're doing."

"You're supposed to stay off that thing."

Dawkins was waiting inside the breeding shed. "We do both live cover here, as you can see, and artificial insemination."

The thunderous naying of the aroused stallion echoed around the metal building. The mare presently nickered a response while the man holding her reins held her in place, whispering to her to keep the thousand-pound beast calm.

"Have a seat," Dawkins said. "If you have any questions, let me know."

He directed Jerry and Vogel to the small gallery, and then walked around the ring to the other side of the shed. Just as they were about to sit down, an Arabic man who could only have been the Sheikh entered from a door on the far side of the building. He was laughing and joking with another man, both of them in suits, and had two security men flanking them. The Sheikh and his companion sat down in a smaller, more opulent gallery that looked like a couple of thrones.

"And there's your smoking gun," Vogel whispered, as he

scrambled to put his sunglasses back on. "That's Bill Pennington,"

Jerry had gone into the gallery first and he noticed that Vogel was doing his best to keep Jerry's wider body in the line of sight between this fellow, Pennington, and himself.

"Who's Bill Pennington?"

"Keep you voice down, for heaven sake," Vogel said.

"He can't hear anything," Jerry said. "The acoustics in here are terrible."

"He's Populous Healthcare," was all Vogel would divulge. "I'm going to wait in the car. Give me the keys."

Jerry handed him the keys and then watched as Vogel turned up the collar of his overcoat and hustled out of the shed. When Jerry looked back into the center of the ring, the live cover operation had begun. His head recoiled reflexively. "I could have gone all day without seeing that."

Sure that both these wealthy men were used to having eyes on them, Jerry glanced up at the Sheikh and his companion, Bill Pennington. He stood up and pretended to watch the goings on in the ring—oh, god—and then casually sidled to his left, attempting to get himself into earshot without anybody noticing.

"She's a fine mare," the Sheikh said. "They make a nice couple." The man chuckled. Another Arabic man came in—seemed like a butler type—and reminded the Sheikh about his next appointment. The Sheikh made his apologies and rose to leave.

"Will we see you at the fundraiser tonight?" Pennington asked. "Black tie. You get to dress up..." He held out his hands like that would sweeten the deal.

"I'm sorry, Bill," the Sheikh said. His accent was very light. "I can't make it. I have to fly to New York this evening."

"But Sheikh," Pennington said, drawing out the title in mock complaint. Jerry got the impression that the Sheikh had promised to attend and was now reneging.

The Sheikh laughed. "I'll send Omar, here."

"Fine," Pennington said. "So long as you send your checkbook with him."

"Where is it?" Omar asked.

"Buffalo Trace distillery over in Frankfort. Eight o'clock."

* * *

"Who is John Galt?" Jerry said. The Range Rover was toasty warm. Vogel sat in the passenger seat, looking a little concerned.

"John Galt?"

"Haven't you read Ayn Rand?" Jerry asked. "*Atlas Shrugged*? Required reading for Republicans. Never mind. Who is Bill Pennington?"

"He's the president of Populous Healthcare," Vogel said.

"The President? You're shitting me."

"At least he was a few years back. He and Paul Brackman—"

"Of Brackman-Hollis, your old firm?"

"—are golfing buddies. I've met him many times. Even worked on some litigation for him a few times. He's loaded. Runs the company for sport, not for money."

Jerry thought for a moment, trying to fit together the pieces of the puzzle he now saw before him.

"So Shamus Crace winds up working for one of the buddies of the President of Populous Healthcare," Jerry said, thinking out loud. "Who just happens to be an Arab sheikh."

"There are no mistakes when it comes to consciousness," Vogel said. "Maybe we're here at just this moment for a reason."

"Maybe it's just a coincidence." Jerry asked, "Are there coincidences in consciousness?"

"Good question," Vogel said.

"What, you don't know everything? I'm surprised."

"I'm just a few steps ahead of you, my friend. Nothing more."

Vogel ducked down in his seat. Jerry looked around. Pennington was coming out of the barn. He got into a black limousine and his bodyguard, one of the security detail from inside the breeding shed, doubled as his driver.

"There he goes," Jerry said. "You can sit up now. Take it easy, man. He didn't recognize you, anyway."

"Then what's up with those guys?"

Jerry looked back toward the barn. A small cadre of Arabic men, headed by the Sheikh's bodyguard, were stalking in their direction.

"Maybe they just want to ask us politely to leave?"

Jerry looked at Vogel. Vogel looked at Jerry.

"It doesn't take five men to do that." Vogel said. He looked back toward the departing limousine. Jerry knew what he had in mind. "Gun it!"

The Range Rover lurched back and then forward on Jerry's command. Soon he was sailing down the exit ramp in hot pursuit.

"This thing has pretty good pick up. Nothing like my Cherokee, but it's decent."

The long, tree lined avenue provided enough length to make up the distance just as the gate swung open. "Come on, come on," Jerry said, willing the engine to churn out more speed. He was nearly tailgating as the limo squeezed through the opening. Nearly, but not quite.

"Oh, boy," Jerry said as the gate began to close. "This is going to be . . ." His thought was interrupted by the grating of metal on metal.

"That's gonna leave a mark," Vogel said.

But the fun was yet to come. Jerry did his best to brake and slalom to the right—as the gate was closing in that direction—to keep out of the ditch at the left side of the road. He just managed to do so, only to look up and see a truck—not quite an eighteen-wheeler, but close enough—bearing down upon them with significant speed and not much distance to work with.

"This road is desolate most of the time," Jerry pushed through his set jaw. "I get a washer and dryer delivery man."

He managed to shift the weight of the great boat of a vehicle in the opposite direction without capsizing, but now they were careening toward the drainage ditch on the right-hand side of the road."

"It's gonna take a miracle," he muttered, gathering all his strength and personal balance to walk the tightrope that was the crest of the roadside ditch, just long enough to wait out the ship's righting moment to point it back on to asphalt, all to the welcome music of the truck's blaring horn. He pulled to a stop to gather his wits.

"Holy crap, that was close," he said, catching his breath.

Looking back where they had come, Vogel said, "We better get moving."

Jerry looked back, too. The gate was opening again. He started going. The limo was nowhere in sight. Jerry recalled that it had gone left out of the gate and had probably seen nothing of the ensuing drama.

At the end of the road, Jerry ignored the stop sign and turned left as soon as he saw that the coast was clear. He opened her up on that slender straight ribbon of asphalt through the rolling hills of dead bluegrass.

Jerry said, "Maybe there's no such thing as coincidences."

"What do you mean?" Vogel said.

"Pennington's going to be at a black-tie event at Buffalo Trace Distillery tonight. You're going to join him."

"What would I want to do a dern fool thing like that for?" Vogel said.

"Sometimes the best defense is a good offense," Jerry responded. "Think about it. If he has nothing to do with any of this, you're just an old acquaintance saying hello. If he does have something to do with it, you're sending him a message. You're telling him that you know what he's up to."

"But I don't know what he's up to."

"But he doesn't know that you don't know. See what I mean?"

Vogel thought about that for a moment. "We don't have tickets."

"Where there's money, there are Republicans," Jerry said. "We'll get tickets. All we need now is to score some tuxedos and we'll be all set."

"Tuxes?" Vogel said, looking up. He was edgy again, like when he got an eyeful of the cufflinks. "Oh, boy."

"Sure, we gotta have a night out in tuxes," Jerry said. He glanced over at Vogel, who was drumming his fingers on his knee, and tried to conceal a devious smile. "Look at it this way, Brad. When all of this is said and done, if they want to make a movie about our lives, then we'll want to get the best actors to play us, right?" Vogel stopped drumming and looked over at Jerry. "If you want to get the best actors, then you've got to give them a tuxedo scene. Otherwise, they're not happy. I'm thinking Men's Warehouse."

"Surely you jest," Vogel said in an I-wouldn't-be-caught-dead tone of voice.

"You know of something better?"

"Geno's Formal Affair, Southland Drive," Vogel said. "Let's ride."

"Geno's? Are you kidding me? That's where kids go for the prom. They'll have us suited up in powder blue with ruffled shirts and platform shoes."

"Yes, but they have a tailor in the back, a little guy from Naples named Angelo. You pay him a little, he can take what they've got on the rack and make you think it's an Armani, complete with labels. He's got a connection back to the old country."

"Ah, the Camorra," Jerry said, knowingly.

"No, the Chinese," Vogel corrected. "All the knockoff shops are Chinese now."

"Hey, doesn't any of that interfere with, you know, the new Vogel?"

He shrugged. "You seem to think this is important. I hope Angelo's still around. I haven't needed his services in a few years. He really seems to enjoy airing out his craft."

"Hey, I noticed you never had to whip out that pen," Jerry said, hoping they could return it.

"There's still time," Vogel said.

Chapter 16

Jerry pointed to the dented fender and broken taillight on the Range Rover as he handed the keys to the Valet. "This happened last time I was here."

The kid in the red jacket didn't get the reference. When he was gone, Jerry said, "*Beverly Hills Cop*?"

"That's a pretty old movie," Vogel said, straightening his jacket.

"Oh god," Jerry said. "I've become my parents. Well...not *my* parents. But somebody's parents."

Jerry adjusted his cuff so the onyx cufflinks were prominently displayed. Angelo's tailoring was a little tight in the legs, as was the fashion, or so Jerry was told, but he otherwise felt like a million bucks. Maybe old Vogel had something here. I could get used to this, Jerry thought. Maybe one day I'll froth at the mouth at the sight of a houndstooth overcoat. Never seen anything like it.

The aroma of the mash bill, the sour scent of steeping malted barley, corn and rye, was in the air. Jerry breathed it in. "Can you smell that? Wonder what they're making? Old Charter? Smells like Old Charter." He sniffed again. "Or maybe McAfee's. I don't smell any wheat."

"I doubt very seriously that your bourbon pallet is that refined," Vogel said as they mounted the wooden steps to the wraparound porch, complete with rocking chairs. "I'm too nervous to smell anything right now."

The reception hall, surrounded by the nineteenth-century plant and warehouses of the sprawling distillery, was built to look like a huge log cabin, rustic and well suited to the place. It was lit festively inside and out, and through the windows, Jerry and Vogel could see the mingling, well-dressed partygoers, a little stiff but appearing to enjoy themselves, with drinks in hand and jazz music from a live trio playing from the other side of the large room. The music was out of place—it should have been a bluegrass band.

But it suited this particular group of donors and that's what counted, not authenticity.

"Oh, come on," Jerry said. "You can smell that. Anyone could smell that."

"All right, all right, I can smell it."

"What's there to be nervous about," Jerry said. "No one expects you to be here. This is a sneak attack. He's the one who should be nervous."

"If it's a sneak attack, how could he be nervous? He doesn't know anything about it."

"All right, all right, take it easy." Jerry held up his iPhone in front of the barcode scanner. The young beauty at the reception podium smiled and handed both men packets. "Mr. Riggs, Mr. Vogel, welcome. Bidding will end in about an hour."

"Thank you," Jerry said. "Where is Mr. Pennington?"

"I'm not sure," the woman said hesitantly. "There's his wife, though."

She pointed to an even younger beauty on a small stage in front of the roaring fireplace.

As they passed into the room, Jerry said, "That's Mrs. Pennington?"

"Mrs. Pennington number four, I guess," Vogel said.

"She's twelve," Jerry said. "Jeez, these old, rich guys.... Where do I sign up?"

"Never met her," Vogel said. "He was still on number three when I knew him."

Jerry looked at the packet. "Ah man, there was a tour of the distillery earlier. I would have enjoyed that."

"Prosperous Healthcare Cancer Research Fund Drive?" Vogel was reading his packet too. "You've taken us right into the lion's den."

"That's right, baby," Jerry said. "Carcinoma, melanoma, Hodgkin's. They're all represented here, my friend." Jerry was taking sardonic pleasure from watching Vogel's skin crawl at the prospect of raising money to feed the healthcare beast he so abhorred.

"Hodgkin's?" Vogel said.

"That's a type of cancer, isn't it?"

Vogel just shook his head with eyebrows raised, the remark undeserving of a response. “Pennington will likely breeze in when they hand out the awards, kiss his new wife inappropriately to scandalize all these older women and then breeze out—if he shows up at all.”

“He’ll be here,” Jerry said. “I could hear it in his voice. This is his pet project.” He stopped at one of the silent auction items, a platinum bracelet with a flowery description attached to it. Letting out a whistle, he said, “The bidding on this one started at ten grand.” Eying a set of gold cufflinks at the next table, he took Vogel by the arm and turned him in the direction of the bar. “Don’t get any ideas about bidding,” he said. “The slush fund is tapped out.”

“Let me just take a look,” Vogel said, craning his neck to see the cufflinks.

Once they were sufficiently out of range of the merchandise, Jerry let go of Vogel’s arm and the latter proceeded to straighten his attire, while Jerry took a moment, drink in hand, to survey the crowd.

Dresses: black. All except for Mrs. Pennington the fourth. As the queen of the ball, she got to wear whatever she wanted and she went with a rich green. And man, was it smokin’. Slinky-sexy, without revealing anything, and with an unmistakable quality to it—translation: big bucks for a one-off from some fashion designer Jerry had probably never even heard of—the only one that came to mind was Wang, just because he liked the sound of it. And Gautier, but that was from *Seinfeld*: “I think maybe you’re flattering yourself. That manikin is wearing a twelve hundred dollar Gautier dress.” Jerry quelled his carnal thoughts, he was on a mission here.

Tuxedos: black too. And not a bowtie to be found. Vogel had gone with the long tie and tried to convince Jerry to do the same, but he wasn’t having it. He held his ground firmly: “I’ve got to have a bowtie with a tuxedo,” he had said. And stubbornly, he refused to shift his position now, even in reaction to the sea of long ties before him. I will not be a slave to fashion, he thought, shoving his hands into the pockets of his satin-side-striped trousers.

"Do you think there are any tats under any of these evening gowns?" he asked.

"Without a doubt," Vogel said. "All that glitters is not gold." Vogel set his chin as he gazed out across the see of gold, and diamonds, and pearls...real...pearls. "That's what I keep telling myself, anyway."

The bar was in an adjoining room. To the left, one of the Buffalo Trace tour guides was giving a demonstration. They would later learn that his name was Freddie and that he was a third-generation employee of the oldest bourbon distillery in the world, depending on how one counts. "All right, clap your hands together. Now smell your hands. What do they smell like?" The answer came back corn. "That's how you can tell what the distillate is made of."

Jerry ordered up a couple of bourbons. "This will help you relax," he said. When they had both taken their first sips, he said, "So who do you think they'll get to play us?"

"What are you talking about?" Vogel said.

"In the movie about all this?" Jerry said. "Who will they get to play us? Come on, loosen up."

Vogel studied Jerry for a moment. "Paul Giamatti."

Jerry took a step back. His mouth hung open a little as he thought about it. He hadn't considered him, but was flattered. "He's one of my favorite actors. Believable, with a sense of raw honesty. I'll take it." He took another sip and took a good look at Vogel. "For you, I'm going with Clooney."

"Get outta here," Vogel said.

"I'm serious," Jerry said. "You're both good looking guys. And there's the Kentucky connection there. Did you know that he may be running for Senate next year against Mack McCormick?"

"Really," Vogel said.

"I was talking to Mack, himself, about it just the other day, in fact." Jerry wasn't sure why he felt the urge to get this particular rumor going. He had heard nothing specific, though it was clear the Dems would pull out all the stops to unseat McCormick, a long shot no matter who they put up against him. "Wouldn't be surprised," he said a little nervously, just to fill the air. "Mack, the Knife. Old Mackie's back in town . . ."

Something told him he shouldn't have mentioned the Senator's name. His Post-it note flashed again before Jerry's eyes: "They will kill him." He looked around. Were these the "they" he was referring to? He had tried to warn Jerry off, but was McCormick friend or foe? That was the question. It didn't necessarily matter, though, he was the boss, or more accurately one of two bosses. The trick to staying afloat in Washington as a civil servant, Jerry had long since learned, was to keep all of the bosses happy, not just the one you worked for. That was the political reality of the situation, a reality that Jerry had chosen to defy. And why had he chosen thusly? Jerry wasn't quite sure. It seemed circumstances had conspired to make a very irrational choice the only logical option. Or maybe like the proverbial frog in the cooking pot, he was boiling himself by degrees.

He looked past Vogel to Freddie, the tour guide, who was still giving his demonstration. He was an older gentleman, completely bald, of indeterminate mixed race. The story of his family history in these parts would be at least as interesting as the lesson on bourbon he was presenting, but Jerry had just enough sense not to ask him about it. Life couldn't have been easy for Freddie, and yet there was a twinkle in his eye, a depth about him. His customers, all very rich and very white, were clearly drawn to him and he to them.

"This guy's good," Jerry said. "There's something about him."

"It's his spirit," Vogel said, turning to take a look. "His vibe."

"That's what it always comes down to with you, isn't it?" Jerry said. Freddie's pupils were just then thanking him and leaving the schoolhouse. "Shall we?"

Vogel shrugged and Jerry put a five-dollar bill on the bar and said, "Good evening, my friend."

* * *

They had not quite gotten their money's worth from Freddie when they heard something of a commotion in the other room. The band stopped playing and someone made a short announcement they couldn't make out.

Jerry looked at Vogel, both men wondering what it was all about. Jerry went to the entrance into the main room. He had been right that he should not have mentioned Mack McCormick's name, for there he stood, side by side with one William Pennington III. Jerry rushed back to the bar and picked up his welcome package. Leafing through it, he found what he was looking for.

"Oh, man," he said. "He's the freaking guest of honor." What a stupid mistake.

"Who is?" Vogel said.

"Excuse us," Jerry said to Freddie. He took Vogel by the arm and escorted him out of earshot. "Look, Brad, I think it's time we aborted this mission."

"Abort the mission?" Vogel said. "Why?" When Jerry couldn't immediately find the right words to explain it all, Vogel said, "No, I think you may have been right. I'm just an old friend stopping by to say hello, that's all. We have our tickets. We have every right to be here. I'm not afraid of these people."

"This is the bourbon talking, my friend," Jerry said. He looked back toward the main room, then at Vogel again. "We'll never get anywhere near either of them," Jerry said. "You know that."

If they attempted a full frontal assault on Pennington, the Senator would see them and nod his head and a couple of bodyguards would come out of nowhere to divert them back out of range. That's how it worked. Jerry had seen it go down dozens of times with the Speaker. There would be no negative photo ops happening if anyone could help it. Then there would be hell to pay with the Senator and the COS and maybe the Speaker himself afterwards.

"You're Chief Counsel to the Speaker of the United States House of Representatives," Vogel said. "The man who is third in line to the Presidency...act like it."

"You don't understand," Jerry said. "That's the problem. The Speaker can't be implicated in any of this. Working behind the scenes is one thing. Confrontation is quite another."

"They already know you're here," Vogel countered. "Your name is on the guest list. You signed in."

"But there's no indication that we're here together," Jerry said. "McCormick is the one guy who can connect those dots. If he sees you, then he might go looking. Don't you see?" Jerry now held Vogel by both his shoulders, trying to talk sense into him. "He puts the Speaker together with all this, Pennington brings the full weight of the healthcare media machine to bear and soon he isn't Speaker anymore. And he may not even be a Congressman, for that matter."

But Vogel was now locked on. What did he care about the Speaker of the House? He wasn't going to be dissuaded. His jaw was set.

"Okay, well, there he is," Jerry said with resignation, letting go of Vogel and gesturing toward the main room. "Now's the time. I'm going to wait for you on the lanai."

He went back to Freddie, who was already giving his spiel again. "Excuse me. Is there a back way out of here?" Freddie pointed and Jerry made his escape out to the wraparound porch.

* * *

He had been out there for a couple of minutes when he got the bright idea to have the valet bring the Range Rover around. Before he could execute his new plan, however, he heard a soothing voice from behind.

"What are you doing here, Jerry?"

Jerry got that porn shop feeling again, sleazy and truant.

"Senator," he said, turning around. McCormick was wearing a traditional tux with a black vest. "Good to see you again. I'm glad to see someone else still sports the bowtie. Now to me, it isn't a tuxedo without a bowtie. Oh sure, you see all these celebrities on the Academy Awards wearing the long tie, but in my view nothing says formality like the bowtie. Of course, when you put it together with a seersucker suit and saddle oxford shoes for Derby Day, that's another story. But then again, it's not a black tie on those occasions, is it? It's more colorful and maybe that's the real difference, not the style of tie but the color—" The

Senator's jowls were already taking on a pinkish hue in the chilly breeze. "As the guest of honor, shouldn't you be inside?"

The Senator strolled up beside Jerry with hands in pockets. "We have a few minutes yet," he said. He looked out into the darkness at the warehouse across the road and hiked one foot up on the varnished log railing.

"What, do you have us on some sort of a watch list or something?" Jerry asked.

The Senator smiled, laughing a little to himself. "This was a mistake," he said. "A bad move. You're out of your depth here."

"You're right about that," Jerry said. He loosened up, now that everything he had feared had come to pass. He took in and let out a deep breath and sat down on the log railing, crossed his arms over his stomach. "I still don't see what all the fuss is about. I mean, it's one little lawsuit that will pertain to one little person. Yes, it is possible that at some point, people might claim some fraternity with Brad Vogel's views to get out of buying health insurance, but even that can't account for it all." Jerry broke off and studied McCormick's face closely. "You don't get it either, do you?"

"This is beyond the range of us mere mortals to understand," McCormick said, still smiling a little. "But he knows...Your friend? Mr. Vogel? He's pulling on a thread that has the potential to unravel the whole sweater. None of us can afford for that to happen—that's the piece that I understand. Now, just you go home and forget all about this. And tell your friend here to do the same." He nodded toward the main entrance.

Jerry turned to see Vogel escorted by two men in tuxedos, part of the security detail, glorified bouncers, but not the brawny type. These guys were smallish with lean physiques, more the kind who were well versed in Krav Maga and carried sophisticated weaponry under their jackets.

"A fuss, indeed," Jerry said.

"Escort these gentlemen to their car," the Senator said. "And treat them gently. We're on the same team, after all."

Senator McCormick was already walking away in the

direction from which he had come, hands still in pockets, whistling a tune Jerry didn't recognize.

"Come on, let's go," the blonde security guard said.

Jerry looked around. The valets had—wisely—made themselves scarce. "We'll need our keys," Jerry demanded. Their dark-haired captor jingled Jerry's wad, complete with two security devices, one for the Range Rover, the other for his Cherokee. To Vogel: "Looks like they thought of everything."

That was rather foolish, Jerry thought, giving up his keys like that, and their car. What if someone decided to strap a bomb to the engine? That wouldn't be any problem at all, would it? The senator was right, they were out of their depth, way out, and wading further out into an undertow.

But the COS had said they wouldn't do it like that. It would have to look like an accident. Jerry clung to that hope as they marched stiffly along in front of the senator's bodyguards...or were they Pennington's? The COS was never wrong, not about things like this.

They passed the guard shack. The light was on but no one was home. "Never here when you need them," Jerry quipped. No one seemed to be amused.

When they reached the Range Rover, silvery in the bright moonlight, Jerry turned back for the keys.

He got instead a sucker punch to the solar-plexus. As he tumbled in agony to the pavement, he heard Vogel receive the same treatment from the other guy.

As he writhed, Jerry thought the roundhouse to the breadbasket was beneath these martial artists. It lacked imagination. But Jerry lacked both the breath and the concentration, a result of the searing pain radiating in waves throughout his body, to say so.

Instead, he managed to choke out: "The senator told you to go easy on us," belatedly realizing that such an ejaculation would likely warrant a kick of some variety, which was indeed forthcoming, and again unimaginative. But quite honestly, Jerry had to admit, it was the perfect compliment to the haymaker.

"We don't work for the senator," whoever was doing the

kicking said. "He works for us." With that, someone dropped the keys from above, causing the oversensitive alarm on the luxury vehicle to add the mix the perfect audible representation of the pain both men were feeling at that moment in time.

Jerry reached out for the keys and pressed the appropriate button so they could at least lie there on the wet, cold blacktop in peace while they waited out the pain.

A good minute later, Jerry said, "I think he jostled my liver."

"Yeah," was all Vogel could muster. But at least he was still alive.

Jerry rolled out of the fetal position and on to his back. He turned his head to look under the car. "What if they put a bomb under there?"

"It might put us out of our misery," Vogel said. He was the first to stagger toward the vertical. But then again, he hadn't endured that extra kick, had he? And he could only make it to one knee at that. "We've tried it your way. Now we're going to try it my way."

"*Your* way?" Jerry said. "And what's that?"

"We're going to shout it from the rooftops," Vogel said.

Jerry thought about that for a moment, anything to distract himself from the pain was welcome. "What? You mean we're going to get too big to fail? Too famous to rub out? Is that what you mean?"

"That's exactly what I mean," Vogel said. "That's all I ever really want to do anyway."

"That was my idea," Jerry protested, sitting up.

"No, your idea was 'the best defense is a good offense,'" Vogel said.

"But that was only after they found Crace. And it seemed like a good idea at the time."

"Well, it wasn't and we're going back to the original strategy," Vogel said.

"*My* original strategy," Jerry said. Vogel was up now.

"Fine, your original strategy."

"Speaking of which, thankfully, they saw fit not to alter our faces. You're going to be on TV tomorrow."

Vogel struggled to his feet. He steadied himself with a hand on the Range Rover. "Hey, you know what I just realized?" he said.

"What's that?"

"I just saw Arnie Brackman in there," he said, staring back into his memory.

"Arnold Brackman of Brackman-Hollis?" Jerry said, still seated on the pavement. Vogel's old law firm.

"Yes," Vogel said. "Yes. I was a little distracted by the bouncers on each arm but it was him. I can see him plain as day."

"What, you think they're part of all this?" Jerry said. Vogel helped him to his feet.

"Oh they're a part of this, all right," Vogel said, dusting Jerry off a little and then walking around to the other side of the vehicle still in recollection mode. "A big part."

* * *

"The federal government self-insures," Jerry said. "Let's say this was official business. If I rented a car, I don't get the insurance because if I have a wreck the government pays for it. Did you know that?"

"No, I didn't know that," Vogel said.

Jerry's bowtie was hanging open and both men looked a little odd standing at the rental counter inside Bluegrass Field terminal in their battered tuxedos. Behind them, a small group of former passengers awaited their luggage around one of the two carousels.

"At some point, the bean counters decided it cost less in the long run to pay for the damage than to buy the insurance."

"That's interesting," Vogel said, perhaps not really meaning it.

Presently, the attendant was back. "I'm sorry, Mr. Riggs but the insurance provided by that particular credit card only covers damages of up to a thousand dollars on luxury vehicles."

Jerry looked at her confounded for a moment. "But that's ridiculous. What difference does it make why type of car it is?"

"I quite agree with you, sir. Perhaps they're attempting to dissuade you from renting high-end automobiles, which historically are much more expensive to repair, thereby limiting their exposure. Be that as it may, sir, as you can see, the Terms and Conditions clearly state that—"

"And besides," Jerry insisted, "that's nothing but a scratch. A thousand dollars should easily cover it."

"The preliminary estimate on the damage is nearly eight thousand dollars, sir."

"Eight thousand dollars!" She placed the estimate on the counter and Jerry reviewed it with alarm. "There's no way I'm paying this."

The officious woman said, "You have the right to arbitration on the claim, sir. Now if you will just sign here, acknowledging your receipt of the estimate . . ."

Jerry looked at the woman long and hard. "You sound like a lawyer." He looked at Vogel. "There's no way I'm paying eight thousand dollars for a scratch."

Finally, he relented, searching his pockets. Before the attendant could produce a pen, Vogel held out his brand new S.T. Dupont Elysee writing instrument.

"Oh, that's cute," Jerry said.

When the woman went to the back to make a copy for Jerry's records, Vogel said, "Remember that *Seinfeld* episode where Jerry gets the rental car and George wrecks it, so his credit card insurance wouldn't cover it?"

"Your whole business is based on other drivers,'" Jerry quoted, snatching his copy of the estimate from the woman as he walked away. "Yeah, I remember it."

"Remarkably similar, don't you think?" Vogel said with a smile, following along behind.

Chapter 17

"Jerry Riggs, as I live and breathe."

"Lisa Posey," Jerry said. "As *I* live and breathe."

"It's not Posey anymore, it's Amburgy, which tells me you haven't been watching the news."

She was a statuesque blonde, Jerry's age. Could she have made it in a larger market? Jerry asked himself as he smiled. Maybe she could have. But she seemed more like a grade school music teacher. She didn't have that hard edge he'd come to expect in TV people over the years in Washington.

"Well, I've been out of town," Jerry said, uncomfortable that he wasn't wearing a suit. This situation called for a suit but he had neglected to bag one up and toss it in the back of the Cherokee, as was his habit, to guard against just such an occasion as this. These situations were always popping up in his line of work.

"Yes, I know," she said. "You are talked about at each high school reunion. Fondly, of course."

"I don't have a suit with me," Jerry said. "I'm just here in an unofficial capacity. This is Brad Vogel."

"Nice to meet you," Vogel said, shaking her hand.

"He's an old law school chum. I'm here for moral support while I'm home visiting my mom."

"How's she doing?" Lisa asked, apprehensively.

"She's fine," Jerry said.

"We're all getting to that age when our parents...well, you know how that goes." She stopped short. She would have known about his dad, Jerry realized.

"Yeah," Jerry said. "I know how it is."

"Mr. Vogel, a pleasure. It's going to be a few minutes into the show before we bring you on. No need to be nervous. Not all that many people are watching."

"Okay," Vogel said.

"And anybody who takes a swipe at Obamacare will be

well received by my audience, believe me."

Vogel said, "It's not exactly a swipe at Obamacare, to tell you the—"

"Brad, please," Jerry said, noticing Lisa's Republican brow quickly tensing up. To Lisa, "Trust me, it's a swipe at Obamacare."

"No, it isn't," Vogel said, in his first hint of testiness since Jerry had become reacquainted with him. "It isn't a swipe at anything."

Jerry chalked it up to nerves. When Vogel looked down to pick some lint off his lapel, Jerry mouthed the words, "Yes, it is," to Amburgy.

Nodding to Jerry, she continued, "So, I'll just ask you a few questions about your background as an attorney, how you came to London, and then a question or two about the lawsuit, and that will be it. This isn't going to be *60 Minutes* or anything like that, okay?" Vogel nodded. "So just relax and talk about your case. What questions do you have for me?"

"No questions," Vogel said.

"I can tell the engineer and he can put your website on the screen," she said.

Jerry and Vogel looked at each other. Vogel said, "No website."

"No website?" Amburgy said, surprised.

"It's still in development," Jerry lied. "We're not quite ready to go live."

"Oh," she said. "Okay, well . . ."

When Amburgy was out of earshot, Jerry said, "Why do you have to be such a stick in the mud?"

"I'm a little nervous, that's all," Vogel said.

"Yeah, well you gotta play the game." Looking around, Jerry saw what he was after. "They've got a nice pastry spread. I'm going to take a swipe at that."

"You didn't eat breakfast, either?"

"I had a huge breakfast. But when I get nervous, I eat."

"I thought you said . . ." But Jerry had departed the pattern. "...there was nothing to be nervous about."

* * *

They were sitting alone in what sufficed as the green room just off the sound stage. Vogel sipped from a bottle of water. Jerry knew he had to be quiet now, to allow Vogel time to collect himself. But that wasn't a good look for Jerry. Introspection made him very uncomfortable in the best of circumstances. Now it only made him think of his heart.

"You remember when you told me about that time you had indigestion?" he said.

"What about it?"

"When was that exactly?"

Vogel thought it out aloud for a moment and then concluded when it must have been. The dates lined up perfectly with the stories Jerry had found in the paper.

"That was when you first got to London."

"Yeah."

"You probably didn't know anybody here yet."

"Probably not," Vogel said. "Can we talk about this later?"

Jerry crossed his arms and legs as he nodded.

* * *

She had introduced Vogel as a member of the London bar association, originally from Louisville. He'd graduated third in his law school class at the University of Kentucky and had practiced at the prestigious statewide firm of Brackman-Hollis.

"What made you want to leave the big city and come down to the country?" Lisa Amburgy asked with a smile.

From the wings, Jerry had his eye on her. It wasn't a hardball question, merely introductory. It was clear she had no idea Vogel had been fired and had come to London as a last resort.

Vogel wasn't ready for the question. He sat stiffly under the bright lights, his new grey suit riding up on his collar. "Well, I uh, I don't know," he said. "I guess you could say it was a move that was forced upon me, to a certain extent."

"No," Jerry squelched through pinched lips. Oh well, that's what this was for, working out the kinks with few people watching. But Jerry was more keyed up than he had expected. Maybe it was the sugar rush from the Danish.

He shifted his attention back to Amburgy, who was now

aware that this wasn't likely to go well. She looked at the paper she held in her hand. There was a moment of dead air and then:

"If I understand your lawsuit correctly," she probed, "Obamacare conflicts with your religious beliefs."

"Well, no," Vogel said. "I don't have any religious beliefs. I don't even believe in having religious beliefs or any kind, in fact."

"No," Jerry muffled again. "No, no, no." This was the one thing he could not say and expect his case to go forward. The one tack he could not take. Vogel was such a smart guy. How could he not realize this!

"You don't?" Amburgy looked at her notes and back at Vogel. And then at Jerry. All Jerry could do was shrug.

"Science is the real religion. My position is the real science."

Oh, god! This would all soon be over before it got out of the starting gate if Jerry didn't speak up. Neither the old nor the new Vogel would like that very much, but what can I do? He's blowing it!

Something inside took over. Jerry migrated apologetically up to the chair beside Vogel. Lisa Amburgy managed to roll with it.

"If I may," Jerry said, staring awkwardly into the camera, feeling for the chair behind him, into which he then sat.

"Why not?" Amburgy said, with a sweeping gesture that said now she had seen it all. "This is Jerry Riggs. He's a native son of London. Advisor to the Speaker of the U.S. House of Representatives. Welcome to the program."

She was aware, Jerry quickly surmised, of the newsworthiness of this unexpected turn of events, and by her introduction now so was Jerry. But it was too late to turn back. He'd crossed his Rubicon.

Vogel beside him was giving off heat, he was so upset. Jerry didn't dare look in his direction. "I don't mean to interrupt," he continued.

"You're welcome here anytime, Jerry," Amburgy said.

"I'm sorry I'm not wearing a suit," he began. "But what my good friend, Brad, here is trying to say is that he maintains a belief system that is impacted by the individual mandate contained in the Affordable Care Act, better known as Obamacare, which requires him to buy health insurance when he doesn't believe in doing so."

"It's not a belief system," Vogel said, steam rising.

"It may not be to you," Jerry said, "but legally speaking, it is."

"No, it isn't," Vogel said.

This was getting out of hand. Jerry was about to withdraw. He was about to put up his hands and bow his head a little before backing away from the stage slowly. He looked at Amburgy for some relief. She was sitting back, arms crossed, eyebrows pitched, and by that Jerry knew he would not be leaving here with his dignity. In for a dime, in for a dollar, he thought, let's make a little noise. Somehow, at a deeply unconscious level, he knew just which buttons to push, just which intonation would do the trick.

"Yes, it is!" he said, going all in, letting himself get lost in the moment, maybe for the first time ever in his life. And what a time to do it! "You say so in your brief to the U.S. District Court!"

"There you have all the time in the world to explain your position," Vogel countered. "Here we have just a couple of minutes to explain all this and I don't think it will be helpful to a TV audience to tell them that in a legal sense it's a belief system when in the vernacular it's actually the opposite."

Lisa Amburgy put her finger to her throat and was about to give the cameraman the signal to cut to commercial, but thought better of it with a sly smile. She gave him the sign to keep rolling instead.

"Your opponents will have a field day with that, you idiot!"

"What are you, Bud Abbott?"

"What, you're stealing my *Seinfeld* references now?"

"I haven't got any opponents."

"You will soon enough. Ever heard of the Attorney General of the United States?"

It wasn't clear (even going to the video tape later) who pushed whom first, but the confrontation came to fisticuffs as all the tension of the previous few days had finally come to a head.

"You can't push me!" Jerry said.

"I didn't start this," Vogel said, taking Jerry by the collar with what seemed like wiry superhuman strength, especially given Jerry's present girth. "But I'm going to finish it!" He forced Jerry off stage, knocking a chair over in the process.

Only then did Lisa Amburgy give the sign to cut to commercial. The engineer came out of the booth to help the cameraman separate the two feuding men. Others came running in as if a silent alarm had been sounded. In fact, the broadcast had been running live on televisions throughout the building and people wanted to see the train wreck in person.

Everyone involved seemed upset until Lisa Amburgy stepped down off the stage and between her two guests. As if confronted by their mother, Jerry and Vogel broke off what remained of their verbal engagement. The moment quickly passed. With assurances given, all the bystanders backed away and returned to their normal lives, already in progress.

She gave the nod to the engineer, who hurried back to the booth.

"Gees, I'm sorry, Lisa," Jerry said, straightening his sweater.

"Don't be," she said smiling. "We haven't had TV this entertaining in London in...well, ever. The engineer has probably already posted the raw video to YouTube."

"YouTube," both men muttered in different tones.

"I wouldn't be surprised to see this one go viral."

"Listen, Lisa," Jerry said, the depth of the *kimshee* he was in well before him.

"Gotta run," Lisa said. "I'm back on. Great to see you, Jerry." He noticed a twinkle in her eye. Revenge is, indeed, a dish best served cold.

She returned to the stage. Someone had straightened the chairs. Jerry watched for a moment as Lisa introduced her next guest, a local beekeeper—who had had the wisdom to remain in the green room for the duration of the melee—as if nothing had happened. After a moment, Jerry looked around for Vogel, but Vogel was gone.

Jerry went out through the security doors into the lobby. Through the large windows, he could see Vogel in the parking lot getting into what must have been his new car. Orlando had taken him to pick it up that morning and then he had driven separately down to London. Without hurrying, Jerry went passenger-side just as Vogel backed out and to the left.

Seeing Jerry, Vogel pressed the button to lower the front window and waited for him to say something. Spontaneously, both men began to chuckle.

"What the hell was that!" Jerry said.

"I don't know," Vogel said, still not come down from his agitated state.

"It actually felt kinda good," Jerry said, then he thought back to his junior high school days. "Guess I shouldn't have ignored Lisa back in the day." He thought about that for a moment, then turned his attention back to Vogel. "That wasn't very...enlightened of you, though."

"I guess my pain-body came out. I thought I was past that by now. Guess not."

Jerry shook his head. "I have no idea what you just said."

"It's how I used to be," Vogel said. "There's still some accumulated pain in there. Each time it comes out, though, a little more of it gets dissolved, simply through consciousness of it. Not judgment. I don't judge myself anymore. Only awareness."

"We're in deep doo-doo."

Vogel shrugged. "We'll see. That's what I've been trying to tell you: with consciousness there are no rules. Good may come of it yet."

"Well," Jerry said, considering, "sorry for pressing your buttons. Something just took hold of me. It's like I couldn't do anything else."

"Don't worry about it," Vogel said. "That's the way the pain-body works. I press your buttons, you press mine, and both of the dragons get fed. Unless you break that cycle through awareness."

Jerry nodded, though Vogel might as well have been speaking a foreign language. "Where you headed?"

"I need to stop by the office," Vogel said. "Then later this afternoon I'm going over to Amy's."

"Don't stay there," Jerry advised. "For her sake. Eric's still working the case. Come on back to Lexington until he finds something."

"And what?" Vogel said, smiling. "Sleep with you?"

"We'll buy Orlando another bed with Republican money," Jerry said. "Top of the line. We'll put it in one of the other rooms. We'll call it the Lincoln Bedroom. Orlando'll get a kick out of it. What do you say?" Vogel shrugged. Jerry looked down and around at the car. "These your new wheels?" It was a late model Honda Accord. "Kind of a step down."

"Insurance covered it after depreciation," Vogel said. "I thought it would blend in better down here," he said, meaning on the street in front of Amy's house.

"In that case, you should have bought a Ford or a Chevy. They still believe in buying Amur'can down here."

Jerry thought about the botulism incident one more time. Part of him wanted to bring it up, part of him wanted to withhold the "exculpatory" information. Instead, he said, "We gotta get to work on that website. Don't worry, I know a guy. He'll get us up and running in no time."

He tapped the roof twice and then backed away as Vogel rolled gently out of the parking lot and down the street.

Chapter 18

"Well, sir," Jerry said. "It's gone viral!" He came down the stairs the next morning, holding his iPhone in front of his face. With this kind of publicity, he was no longer paranoid. Not even the NSA could withstand this level of public scrutiny.

"You gotta be shittin' me," Orlando said. When Jerry brought up the short video clip on his desktop computer, Orlando reviewed it. "You guys look like idiots."

"Maybe so," Jerry said. "But it got the word out."

"In no small degree thanks to Fox affiliates all over the country," Orlando said. "I think you staged all this."

"I wish I could take credit," Jerry said. "But something just seemed to take over. I can't explain it." Jerry saw himself for the first time on a larger screen. "Am I really that fat?"

"They say the camera adds fifty pounds," Orlando said with a mean-spirited smile. "Thanks for the bed, by the way."

The Temperpedic Jerry had bought and paid for out of the slush fund had been delivered late the previous evening. He had slept in it that night in one of the third floor bedrooms he now called his own.

"You're welcome," Jerry said.

"What's all the fuss about?" Vogel said, coming down the stairs in what had now become command central for this Republican onslaught on healthcare, much to the chagrin of the property owner.

"Orlando thinks we staged this," Jerry said. "And look, there in the notes. They let us put a link to our new website, which isn't the best on the net yet, but it's a start."

"I knew ya'll was in cahoots," Orlando said, talking about Fox. "That proves it."

Jerry tapped his phone to watch the clip one more time when it vibrated. He'd gotten a text message.

"Oh, shit," he said. When someone asked what was up, he informed them: "I've been recalled to DC."

* * *

Jerry sat on the couch in the outer office, waiting for the COS's door to open, the view still dark outside the office windows. Something in the vibe told him he couldn't just walk right in, as was his habit. He'd stopped at Krispy Kreme on the way in from his apartment in Arlington, but somehow he felt hungry again.

He had tried to get the 411 from Pattie the evening before, but she didn't know anything. She kept saying they needed to talk, but Jerry was in no mood to get all relationship-y. He'd gotten on the next plane out of Lexington, connecting in Charlotte.

After the COS had iced him for fifteen minutes, Jerry found himself standing at as close to attention as he knew how to stand in front of the desk. A noticeable lack of verbal niceties filled the dead air before the COS started in on the litany he had recalled Jerry to discuss.

"A nine hundred dollar H. Freeman suit?" Jerry lifted his gaze just long enough to see that the COS was reading from some sort of hardcopy accounting report. "A six-hundred-dollar S.T. DuPont Elysee Ballpoint Pen?"

Jerry briefly weighed his response before instinct kicked in. "Well, what if he had needed to write something down in front of rich people?"

"A two-hundred dollar Range Rover rental, and its eight thousand dollar repair?"

"That repair was inflated," Jerry countered. "They are not going to get away with that, that's my vow to you!" He held up both index fingers in pledge. And then the oddness of the COS's objections finally struck him. "Wait a minute," he said lowering the fingers. "How do you even know about these things? It's supposed to be a slush fund, for crying out loud!"

"Keep your voice down!" the COS scolded. "You were supposed to stay out of the picture." He dropped the report in the middle of his desk, the only item on it that was askew.

He had not invited Jerry to sit down. But why did he feel compelled to remain standing there in front of the COS's desk? The last time he had been there, he'd been lying on the couch with chest pains. Jerry remembered his heart momentarily but he didn't have time for that right now.

"I guess I got caught up in the moment," Jerry said. "It seemed to me he was ruining everything."

The COS stood thinking for a moment. He shook his head with a grimace and then thought a moment more. "Now is the time when you decide to take a leave of absence," he said.

"Leave of absence," Jerry repeated. His normal flippancy abandoned him. His mouth went dry.

"Spend more time with your family, that sort of thing."

Jerry blew out a deep breath. "Temporary?"

"Wait and see if all this blows over."

"Paid or unpaid?"

"If you don't think this is in their sights," the COS said, "think again. The President's press secretary mentioned it in his afternoon briefing with a good deal of jocularity—implicating the Speaker. We've already fielded questions about it. We said that you were on a leave of absence, helping an old friend. We're simply making that official. And back dating it, of course."

"Of course," Jerry said. Like a secret agent, duty-bound to bite down on a cyanide capsule should he fall into enemy hands, he knew the drill.

He had gotten back to Reagan Airport late the previous night and exhausted. Consequently, he had not seen the news—and perhaps that was by choice—but he was not surprised about the press secretary's comments.

"You have the fund to get you through for a while. Use it sparingly." The COS emphasized the word. "If the case turns out well, we'll see what we can do."

"You expect me to keep working on this?" Jerry said.

"I don't see any other way," the COS said. "Do you?"

* * *

"This a bad time?"

Pattie stood at the door to Jerry's office. He had a

cardboard box at his feet and he was tossing personal items into it. He nudged it with his foot out of view and bellied up to the desk.

Patty closed the door and sat down. "I know you've been busy and everything, but I really need to talk to you before you hear it from someone else."

Jerry thought he was numb at that point, but he could feel his heart doing flip-flops again.

"I've been offered a job at a firm in New York," she said. "My last day is at the end of the week."

The relief was overwhelming. He didn't need anymore changes to the structure of his life just then. But a move to New York? He could handle that.

"That's great news," he said with a smile and he stood up to give her a hug. "Congratulations."

"Thanks," Pattie said. They sat down on the couch. "The COS didn't fire you, did he?"

"Still on the case," Jerry said truthfully. "You saw the video?"

"Me and a million of my closest friends." Patty searched for something to say. "It's an interesting case, though."

"Maybe that's what it takes to get the word out these days," Jerry said.

"Absolutely," Pattie said. "Sometimes things are weird like that. It's a new digital age." She made a funny gesture, which was unlike her, and laughed a little nervously.

"So NYC's just a short hop away, right?" Jerry said.

"Absolutely," Pattie repeated. "I'm a little nervous about the move, to tell you the truth."

"I'll come help you get set up."

"Really?"

"Absolutely."

"I thought you might be upset," Pattie said, tucking her hair behind her ear, a nervous habit. "This can work, right?"

Sure, it could work, Jerry thought. He gave her a kiss on the forehead and she left happy.

Absolutely.

* * *

"And don't think I don't know about your little friend in DC," Nicole said.

Jerry couldn't help but come clean about what had happened with his job. It was evening before he could get home. By the time he made it to Dulles, no direct flights to Cincinnati were left. He had to stew in Atlanta for a couple of hours to boot.

"How long have you been holding on to these?" he asked, looking at the divorce papers he held in his hands.

"A while," Nicole said with no outward reactive indicators, but with seething pent-up emotion—plenty of seething, Jerry noticed. More than usual. "Just waiting for the right time, and this is definitely the right time."

He wasn't shocked. He wasn't surprised at all. In fact, something inside him knew this was going to happen. And he wanted to get home as quickly as he could so he could *make* it happen as soon as possible. He found himself utterly detached from this tableau, and observing only his detachment, which didn't suit Nicole at all.

"How can you just stand there and watch eleven years of marriage go down the tubes?" she said, forcing a tear to the corner of her eye.

Jerry didn't know how he could do that, himself, but he could. Pattie's new job in New York City was more destabilizing than this. While he certainly had his misgivings about that relationship, it was a far cry from this: he realized then that he affirmatively hated Nicole.

"I'm going to go kiss the girls goodbye," he said.

That part was a blur. He patted them on their heads as a sort of blessing, kissed them, hugged them, all very much as usual, then he found himself driving once again down to Lexington.

As he drove, Jerry realized that his emotions were not that cut and dried. His feelings for Nicole were intimately and irrevocably tied to his love for his twin daughters. He couldn't keep himself from crying. It had been hard to see them before leaving—this only registered in his consciousness in hindsight, and so he hadn't let on. This was just the standard business trip, as far as they were concerned.

It wouldn't be long before Nicole would let them know what was going on, though. It wouldn't be long before she began to shape their perceptions against him and toward her. It was in the nature of things. There was nothing he could do about it. Vogel was right, women really did run the show.

He thought about Vogel. He had been the catalyst. As painful and disorienting as all of this was, Jerry couldn't hold that against him. There was something inevitable and right about what was happening—he understood that—even as it was unbelievably painful.

Chapter 19

"Brad Vogel and his attorney, Jerry Riggs, have filed a constitutional challenge to the Affordable Care Act's individual mandate, which requires the payment of a penalty for anyone who doesn't have health insurance. That's not strictly why they're here today, however. Take a look.

Jerry sat beside Vogel on the NBC soundstage inside Rockefeller Center. Outside the windows, a crowd was craning and mooning in morning cold so deep their collective breath rose like iron was being smelted. Jerry sat slightly angled toward Vogel, positioned that way once the producer understood their present dynamic. This was Vogel's show, Jerry was there in support.

The *Today* show played just five seconds of the video from their Fox appearance in London, the part where Vogel lifted Jerry by the collar and forced him off stage. It looked to Jerry like they sped up the clip ever so slightly to make it even funnier.

"So have you guys kissed and made up yet?"

"Well, Matt," Jerry began. "It wasn't really like that at all. We were never really upset with each other."

Both men wore suits for this interview, Jerry in his hard-edged Republican blue and red tie, Vogel in a softer pink pattern, more subtly independent than Democratic.

"So the whole thing was staged to get the word out? Is that it?"

Vogel piped up. "No, it wasn't staged. Not by us, anyway. When you're in the moment, you're plugged into the Universal, so to speak. The Universal compelled me to file the lawsuit. The Universal compelled us both to react the way we did on live TV. And here we are on the *Today* show with a great opportunity to explain how life is to millions of people."

"I see," Matt said.

"You must understand that. You would never have gotten to where you are in life without this kind of intuition working for you."

"Don't drag me into this," Matt said with a smile.

Vogel had certainly improved his shtick over the course of the dozen or so interviews he'd sat for the last few days leading up to this *Today* show appearance. He'd been to the left coast and back again, making hay while the sun shone, but this was your big boy. Jerry was happy to sit back and watch Vogel do his thing.

And it was working. The website was improving day by day. With hits in the six digits every day too, there was real interest out there in anything that would get people around Obamacare and its individual mandate.

And he, himself, would be back in Republican good graces in no time, Jerry figured. Back in the fold. And back in his old job.

"Isn't this your standard religious objection to medical treatment, though? Like the Christian Science aversion to blood transfusions?"

"For legal purposes," Vogel answered, "this is what we call a deeply held conviction, akin to a religious belief. But for non-lawyers, this isn't religion at all. It's the opposite of religion. In fact, religion, including the Science religion, as I call it, is on one side, I am on the other. Science is the state religion, just like Christianity used to be. Just like Islam is in other parts of the world. It's probably your religion too, Matt, although I'm sure you don't see it that way. To prove my point, think of all the things you must have unshakeable faith in to believe in Science. You don't actually do experiments yourself, do you?"

"No."

"You believe your high priests, the Scientists, when they tell you about their studies and experiments. And then for your pastoral care, you go to your doctors."

"That brings us back to the nuts and bolts of why you don't believe you need healthcare at all. Explain that."

"First of all, I'm not suggesting that anyone else doesn't need healthcare. I'm only representing myself in this regard.

The healthcare system is a barbaric effort to extend the lives of unconscious people. They cook this so-called disease, they poison that one, hack out another. My contention is that through consciousness, people are perfectly capable of healing themselves and keeping themselves healthy. But if you're an unconscious person, the healthcare system is all you have."

"And how do you know which camp you belong to?" Matt asked.

"By going into your body," Vogel responded with a smile. "Your body knows all. In fact, don't believe anything I say. Don't believe anything anyone says. Anyone who asks you to believe doesn't know what he or she is talking about. Spend time in your body and it will show you the way."

"Why do I find that so hard to grasp?" Matt said.

"Because of twenty-three hundred years of brainwashing," Vogel said. "You've been told so many times from so many trusted sources that the world is a random place, governed by cause and effect—two contentions that cannot both be true at the same time, by the way, and in fact are both false—that you can't believe that the world is any other way. That in fact it is benevolent, and that the so-called real world is actually an illusion. You've probably never consciously spent any time in your body, but you must have done so unconsciously to a great extent, which is the source of your great personal success. What we're trying to get to is consciousness of consciousness."

Vogel knew now to smile at the confounding nature of the things he was saying, Jerry observed.

"This is all cosmic stuff," Matt said. "Fascinating. But unfortunately we're out of time. The website is up on the screen if you're interested in finding out more. Gentlemen, thank you for being here. This is *Today* on NBC."

When the red light went dark on the camera, Matt said, "Thanks, guys, great job." When a woman came to retouch his makeup, he shooed her away. "This is interesting stuff. I think you may be on to something. You know, they give me these cards...The blood transfusion thing—that's interesting."

"Ah," Vogel said. "That's a line of cases based on the principle of *parens patriae*. Translated from Latin, that means 'father of the country.' In other words, the state is the ultimate guardian for individuals under a disability. In those cases, minors—"

The guy with the clipboard wordlessly imposed himself between the conversing parties. Vogel got the hint and stood up to follow Jerry away from the lights.

"But as you can see," Vogel concluded, "I'm not a minor."

"It's a sound-bite world," Matt said, turning to take in hand his next set of index cards.

"They're already hitting you with the Christian Science cases." Jerry said, as they were led away. "You handled that well, I thought."

* * *

"When was the last time you were in New York?"

Vogel didn't answer. He had ear buds implanted. No telling what he was listening to, or to whom he was talking. The *Today* show had put them up in a nice enough hotel, a two-bedroom suite, but all Vogel wanted to do was sit in it and answer questions on his blog. He was like a man possessed.

Jerry had negotiated an extra night, at least in part to see the sights, but riding up to the top of the Statue of Liberty by himself didn't really seem like all that much fun. So he grabbed a slice of pizza on the street (okay, three slices) and walked around Midtown for a while and then came back and had a drink at the hotel bar.

"I'm having dinner with a friend this evening," he said. "So you'll be on your own tonight."

Vogel, noticing Jerry finally, pulled one of the buds from his ear. "What's that?"

"I said I'm having dinner with a friend of mine tonight, so you'll be on your own."

"No problem," Vogel said. "I'll probably just have room service."

Jerry nodded and wasn't going to say anything more, but as Vogel began putting the buds back in his ears, he said, "Don't you want to go see the Empire State Building or something?"

"I feel like I need to get all this down in the blog before I forget it," Vogel answered. "While it's still fresh. This and a hundred other things. You know, I always kind of wanted to write a book, but it just didn't seem immediate enough. It wasn't in the moment like this is."

Jerry nodded again.

"Feels like I'm racing against the clock."

* * *

Jerry observed himself sitting across the table from Pattie. They were together in New York—it was a little surreal. On his way over by taxi, he had been excited about what the evening might hold. He imagined himself being led back to her little apartment—in his imaginings it was located in Soho or Greenwich Village—where unopened boxes remained strewn hither and thither. Now seeing her, radiant with youth and possibility, he felt more apprehensive.

"'What a Difference a Day Makes,'" Jerry said.

"Actually, it's been a week exactly," Pattie quipped.

"It's the song," Jerry said, pointing toward the ceiling. It was playing quietly from the restaurant's sound system. Coincidence? You be the judge, Jerry thought.

The linen napkin lay across his lap, though he had wanted to tuck it into his collar. He'd kept his suit and tie on—the clothes make the man, after all—and now he was glad he did. Pattie had come straight from work. He use the napkin to dab at his lips, the way he knew he was supposed to, before taking a sip of water.

"...and I'm loving it so far. The firm has the whole moving thing wired."

"Well, this ain't their first rodeo, is it?" Jerry said, remembering another song.

"I know, right? I've even lost a few pounds in the process."

"Eat," Jerry said. "You're skin and bones."

Pattie was talking now but Jerry had no idea what she was saying. He felt fat...and bald. He was just some fat, balding guy with no job, and—where did he live now? He guessed he technically lived with his mother, although he still had the apartment in Arlington. What would he need with that, now that he had no reason to be in DC?

Pattie was just a kid on her way up. Even Vogel had found his *raison d'être* in the blog Jerry had caused to be created for him. Meanwhile Jerry, himself, had officially become George Costanza. Vogel had been right, he was a perfect George.

Pattie already knew the best restaurants in town. She ordered something froufrou, gourmet. All Jerry wanted was a Delmonico steak. And to be honest, he wanted two of them. He knew where this was going with Pattie. Did he really have to play it out? She hadn't wanted to do this, he could tell by her hurried response on the phone, and she was eating in a hurry too. She had already become a New Yorker. She had a whole new life now, one of which Jerry could not be a part.

"How's the case going?" she said between bites.

"We have the hearing coming up in a few weeks," Jerry said. "We think that one will go our way, of course. Van Doren was a Bush appointee. I'm hoping he'll render his opinion quickly so I can get my job back."

Jerry winced internally. He'd forgotten he'd left that out of the conversation last time they'd spoken.

She held her fork at bay. "But—"

"I *am* technically still on the case," Jerry said. He knew the issue for Pattie would be the lie, not the job, not his predicament. "The COS said when all this blows over, I'd be back. It's just a leave of absence."

Pattie's wrinkled forehead mirrored Jerry's own concern. God, what am I doing! He beat himself up a little more. Am I running my life into the ground on purpose?

"Piece o' cake," she said. Upbeat. Positive. That's where her life was right now. Jerry...not so much.

"Yeah, well," he said. "These guys are appointed for life, remember. That tends to give them a mind of their own. Which would be the first time for this guy. I'm hoping he doesn't pick this case to test the waters of free thinking."

Pattie didn't say anything more about it. She let the subject die of its own momentum, which wasn't a good sign.

Later, after some small talk to cleanse the pallet, Jerry figured he might as well go the distance here. He said, "Nicole and I are getting a divorce."

"Oh, no," she said, her brow furrowed again. "I'm so sorry."

"Well, you know," Jerry said. "It's been coming for a long time. You know that better than anybody."

"Yeah," she said. "But you always hate it, especially for the kids, you know?"

"I know," he said. He dismissed his feelings for the twins as quickly as he could, pushing them down, holding them down. "Anyway, this kind of clears the way for, you know, you and me, if . . ."

She took the linen napkin from her lap and dabbed at her mouth. There was food left on her plate—expensive food—but she wasn't going to eat any more of it. She said, "Look, Jerry, you're a nice guy, but . . ."

No conversation that begins that way is going to end well.

* * *

"I can take that for you."

The Hispanic man in the green and beige waiter's jacket and matching pants waiting outside the hotel room seemed startled at Jerry's appearance, but then again everyone in New York seems startled, and after that annoyed or angry. Jerry took the small tray with a covered plate from him, figuring Vogel must have ordered the room service he had considered earlier.

"Thank you," the man said in English accented only by the city.

It was a trick to take the tray and insert the credit card door key simultaneously. By the time Jerry had put the tray down on the ledge inside the room and thrust his hand into his pocket for a few bucks for the tip, the man was gone.

Jerry shrugged it off and closed the door. He lifted the lid on the plate: plain cheeseburger, the cheese oozing, and French fries, the hand-cut kind with the skin still on them, and at a place like this probably seasoned with sea salt. He had just eaten way too much, how could he be hungry again?

"Brad?" Jerry said, still holding the domed metal plate cover. No answer. The fries were plentiful—he could easily take a few without anyone noticing. Jerry leaned further into the room and looked around for good measure. "Anybody home?"

There on the small table in the center of the common area sat the remains of a very similar plate of cheeseburger and fries. Jerry walked over to the table and picked up one of the cold fries and examined it before tossing it back on the plate.

Curious. No way Vogel ordered up a second meal. He wasn't that kind of a guy. That's more me than him, Jerry realized. He went into his bedroom, picked up the phone and made a call.

"Room service," the woman answered.

"This is Mr. Riggs in room 312. Was an order placed for this room a little while ago?"

"Jes, sir."

"A cheeseburger and fries?" Jerry asked.

"Jes, sir."

"But only one order, right? No one ordered two plates of cheeseburger and fries, did they?"

"You want another cheeseburger and French fry?" the woman asked.

"No," Jerry said. "Well, yes, actually, I would. But that's not my purpose here." Jerry thought for a moment. He wasn't going to be able to get this woman to understand what he was after. "Never mind," he said. "Forget we every had this conversation." He thanked her and hung up.

Jerry went into the other room and studied the stainless steel plate cover. He looked at the door, thrusting his hands into his pockets. His face formed a pained smile—something wasn't right. No one in New York ever walked away from a tip. So far, that fellow in the hallway had been the first...ever.

Beneath the ledge on which the plate and tray sat, the ubiquitous brass trashcan stood empty but for the pristine white plastic liner. Jerry removed the lid, picked up the plate and was about to angle the cheeseburger into it, when he hesitated.

He picked up the cheeseburger and studied it, all juicy and melted together like a McDonald's quarter-pounder. He crouched down beside the trashcan, willing himself to let go of the burger, reminding himself that there was a good chance it might be poisoned—no reason to take that risk. There was food aplenty in the Big Apple, with everything open twenty-four/seven.

Good chance? Might? He sounded like Vogel describing an advertisement about a medical study. What that really means, Vogel would say, is that they actually have no more clue after the study than before they had undertaken it.

It was at that moment that the door clicked and opened, freezing Jerry fearfully in place.

It was Vogel, wearing a hotel robe and slippers—and a smirk—his hair slicked back and wet, looking every bit the part of the more debonair first Lloyd Braun.

"What are you doing? Eating out of the garbage? Boy, you *have* become George Costanza."

"Very funny," Jerry said. He dropped the cheeseburger and then dumped the French fries into the can after it.

"What are you doing?" Vogel said.

Jerry didn't want to admit his paranoia. The kitchen, in a place this big, had probably just made a mistake and sent up two of the same order. "I, uh, saw what you had for dinner and thought it looked pretty good, but, uh, now I'm not hungry anymore."

"You? Not hungry?"

"Uh, yeah, yeah," Jerry said. "It just went away. That can happen."

As Vogel proceeded into his bedroom, Jerry sat down on the couch, flipped on the TV. He navigated around the dial. The piped-in noise of news, reality shows and a couple of porn options passed over him like raw sewage.

"I had to get some exercise," Vogel said. "I was going stir crazy."

"You remembered to bring swimming trucks?"

"Gym shorts," Vogel said coming back into the common area. "They worked. Got a lining and everything. What's with you?"

"What's with me?" Jerry said, forcing a smile. "Nothing's with me. I'm good old Jerr'. Always on top of the world."

"Okay." Vogel stood over Jerry, studying him. "This is about a girl, isn't it?"

"What makes you say that?"

"You have lipstick on your cheek."

Jerry stood up and went into the bathroom. He wiped the pink substance from his face. Had she done that on purpose? No, no, of course not. He had walked her outside and put her into a taxi. It was dark and she was in a hurry.

"It was just a friendly peck from an old friend," Jerry said from the bathroom.

"I'm sure it was," Vogel agreed. He sat down on the bed and checked his laptop.

Jerry looked at the bags under his eyes, his beard, which needed a trim. It was no wonder she didn't want to have anything to do with him anymore.

"You know," Vogel said, raising his voice to cover the distance from his bedroom to Jerry's bathroom. "If we stopped right now, I would be perfectly fine with that."

Jerry was looking at his tongue—why was it so white and mossy? He was about to take a swig from the little bottle of green hotel mouthwash, hoping that would help. As he struggled to remove the cellophane wrap that tamper-proofed the cap, Vogel's words registered with him. He looked again in the mirror at his own eyes, with the dark rings that half encircled them to determine his own reaction: yes, on top of all he's been through this evening, by the looks of this poor wretch, this new turn of events *is* very concerning to him.

Jerry came to the door of Vogel's bedroom and tried his best to remain calm, to appear casual. "Wha-what do you mean?"

"The case," Vogel said. "I've already accomplished everything I really wanted to accomplish. You could get back to Washington, where you could 'continue to do the work of the American people,' as they say."

"Yeah, well, let's just see it through to the District Court ruling, then we can see where we go from there."

"This is interesting," Vogel said.

"What is?"

"Got an email from Amanda."

"Amanda?"

"The secretary at the office. You met her. She scans in all my mail now and sends it to me."

"That's smart."

"The American Healthcare Insurance Providers Association has filed a motion to join the feds in opposition to my petition."

"Really," Jerry said. "I guess they don't think Eric Holder will take us seriously enough."

"The AHIPA is Populous Healthcare's lobbying arm," Vogel said, looking up and giving Jerry a bland look. "It's fully funded by Populous."

"Let me take a look at that," Jerry said. Vogel turned his laptop toward Jerry to facilitate. It was Attorney-General Eric Holder's responsibility to answer Vogel's constitutional challenge, but others could file Amicus Curiae briefs as "Friends of the Court" to aid the presiding judge in making his decision. And if they had standing, a particular person or entity could even intervene or join a case in opposition to the challenge. A nonprofit political arm of the healthcare Industry would certainly have the necessary interest in a challenge to the Obamacare individual mandate requirement to be allowed into the case.

And if they had now decided to plead their cause to the courts, maybe they had also decided that choking the life force out of one Bradley Vogel was not strictly necessary after all. Maybe all the recent publicity had been effective. And maybe it was their little foray into William Pennington III's personal space that had done the trick.

"This could be a good sign," Jerry said. "Maybe Pennington and his goons have decided to go legit."

"Maybe so."

Then Jerry watched Vogel's visage turn dark. "What is it?"

"Guess who their attorneys are?"

Jerry waited but Vogel didn't seem able to form the words.

Instead he turned the computer screen toward Jerry. Bending down and squinting, Jerry read the signature block, "Brackman-Hollis," as Vogel began to squirm. "Well, well, well, your old firm."

"I told you they were wrapped up in this," Vogel said.

Is it my sadistic nature that allows me to appreciate the irony? Jerry wondered. Or is it simply that misery loves company? "'Of all the gin joints in all the towns in all the world, she walks into mine.'" he quoted from *Casablanca*.

Vogel looked up at him, but failed to admire the irony, himself. Then he looked down and opened the next attachment while Jerry watched.

The opening line read: "YOU ARE COMMANDED to appear at the time, date, and place set forth below to testify at a deposition to be taken in this civil action."

"They want to take your deposition," Jerry said. "That was fast."

Vogel stared out into the space in front of him for a moment—thinking of good times, Jerry facetiously imagined. He got up and walked to the window, looked down on the city.

"This is highly irregular in a case like this," Jerry said. "I don' think you're required to—"

"No, no," Vogel said. "Let them bring it. I don' t care."

Jerry said smiling: "That's the spirit." Vogel was back on board. That was a relief.

He wasn't quite sure why this turn of events caused his friend such discomfiture. This was, after all, part and parcel of why he'd filed the action in the first place. He wanted to take the fight to the healthcare industry. But the sight of him squirming brought something akin to joy to Jerry's heart. Misery loved company, indeed.

Jerry said, "Speaking of irregular. . ." The afternoon's pizza and the Delmonico steak already seemed lodged in his colon. He went into the bathroom and closed the door.

Chapter 20

"Do you see this?"

"Let the record reflect that the deponent if flipping the bird."

The court reporter at the end of the table couldn't completely suppress a giggle.

"I'm sorry," she whispered.

In response to a simple question asking for an accounting of his medical history, Vogel calmly held his middle finger six inches in front of the bald attorney's face. The three lawyers on the other side of the long cherry table—a table with which Vogel was quite familiar, and so he had remarked upon entering the Brackman-Hollis conference room—held themselves as coolly as they could, pretending not to be offended by their former colleague's antic. Jerry sat beside Vogel, admiring his chutzpa.

Vogel knew these three men personally but Jerry knew them only by type. They had introduced themselves cordially after a few minutes' wait in the marble-floored reception area. Larry Upton, a well known litigator, the one closely examining Vogel's middle finger, was the oldest. He played a lot of golf and had the tan and carcinoma scars on his bald pate to prove it. Larry was only brought in these days to make an impression. They probably flew him in from South Florida, by the looks of him, especially for the occasion. Vogel knew to go right after him and that's what he was doing.

Jay was the young punk, the hotshot to Larry's left. With his spread collar, fat tie knot, checked shirt and standard issue smirk, he looked like a smaller clone of Johnny Manziel, the Heisman trophy winning quarterback from Texas A&M who was everywhere in sports news for the last several months during the college football season. Manziel was apparently spawning a whole new generation of college-educated jerks who lacked the benefit of phenomenal athletic ability to get them by their present lack of circumspection. Jay was one of those, though he must have had some smarts to get him in at Brackman-Hollis. He might just as easily have had a rich daddy who knew Stallings Hollis, too. Jay would be the attorney handling the grunt work on the case.

On Larry's right was the attorney Vogel had called Stew. Dead eyes behind wire-rimmed glasses, he was Jay's boss, an administrative type, bland, there only as makeweight, Jerry figured. He seemed like the kind of guy to make a career out of repeating in similar but slightly different words what had just been said by someone else, whether judge, witness or colleague.

"Did you get that in the record?" Stew said presently. "That he's flipping the bird?" The court reporter nodded.

"That's a scar from a staph infection," Vogel said, withdrawing his hand. "After they operated on it, they gave me a long-term regimen of antibiotics. They said it was to build up antibodies in my blood. But all the while, unbeknownst to me, a gloom was building. A dark cloud hung over my head night and day, to the point where I was beginning to think about ending it all, committing suicide. One day—I'll never forget it—I was sitting at home on my couch. It was almost time for me to take my next pill. As I was contemplating suicide, I could feel the effects of the antibiotic wear off, like the last grains of sand falling through the narrow part of the hourglass. And the gloom disappeared at the same moment. I never took another one of those pills and I've been fine ever since. It was then that I began to understand the barbaric nature of the service your client provides."

"Did it work?" the bald attorney, Larry, of the shiny thousand-dollar suit and pinky ring asked.

"In a way, yes it did," Vogel said. "It got rid of the staph infection. But the question isn't *did* it work. It's *how* it works and *why*?"

"You take the pills and your staph infection goes away," the attorney responded. "Simple cause and effect. Or...am I missing something, Mr. Vogel?"

"There's no such thing as cause and effect," Vogel said, somewhat offhandedly, Jerry noted.

"Yes, but it's good enough for the courtroom," the attorney responded, then to put it in the form of a question in keeping with proper deposition format, he added belatedly, "Isn't that right?" He had a slight smile on his face.

That made Vogel sit up a little. Jerry watched the bald attorney closely. He seemed momentarily unsure of himself, his eyes wavering as if he'd divulged something he shouldn't have, looking down at his list of questions and then back to Vogel. Something had just happened but for the life of him Jerry couldn't figure out what it was.

Then he noticed Stew. His fish lips never seemed to change their expression, not even when he was talking. Until now. It was like in *The Matrix* when Neo sees a black cat walk by twice, revealing his world to be a virtual reality. Stew's fish lips altered their expression slightly, just slightly. Maybe Stew was just a computerized hologram. Beyond that, however, what had just transpired was much bigger than the moment had seemed to indicate. And then Vogel confirmed it.

"I think you've just told me everything I need to know," he said.

Wait a minute, wait a minute, wait a minute. Jerry wanted to ask the court reporter to read back that exchange, but he didn't have the guts to butt in. What had been said? 'No such thing as cause and effect'? And Upton had actually agreed with that? What was happening here? Were we living in some sort of Pynchonian reality where the forces of good and evil are configured around philosophical positions?

Of course, Jerry had never read a Thomas Pynchon novel, they were much too thick—he never read any novels, come to think of it. Who had the energy after reading legal briefs all day? But he had picked up a working knowledge of many such authors over the years. If he didn't, he would look like a rube in front of the Democrat intellectual set, and he couldn't have that. But even this much awareness was enough to clue Jerry in on the fact that a Thomas

Pynchon moment of the highest order had just transpired. No such thing as cause and effect? What, are you kidding me? This is a legal deposition, for crying out loud. There's no place for philosophy here.

Larry Upton ignored Vogel's comment, and then to parry, he went on the attack.

"And you have had other infections," the attorney said. "Isn't that right, Mr. Vogel?"

Vogel didn't answer that either, not right away. It appeared to Jerry that he was thrown a little for the first time in the questioning.

"I think you'll find that I don't embarrass very easily these days, Larry," Vogel finally said.

"Just answer the question, if you please, Mr. Vogel."

"I have availed myself of medical services in the past," Vogel answered. "But that was before my...transformation."

"Would you mind reading back the question posed?" Upton addressed himself to the court reporter.

"Read that back, if you would," Stew said.

"The question was: 'But you have had other infections, isn't that right?'"

"Yes, I've had other infections," Vogel answered.

"Have you ever had an STD, Mr. Vogel?" Larry asked. "A sexually-transmitted disease?"

"I object to this line of questioning," Jerry said, unable to keep quiet. "Irrelevant."

The Brackman-Hollis boys seemed satisfied, both with the question and with the fact that it had upset Jerry.

"Don't get excited," Vogel said. "Larry, Jay and Stew here just want me to understand that they have complete access to my entire medical record."

"Then I object on the grounds that it's a violation of the HIPAA statute," Jerry countered.

"Oldest trick in the book, eh, Larry?" Vogel said. "As our esteemed members of the bar are well aware, HIPAA has no enforcement provision."

HIPAA, the old Health Insurance Portability and Accountability Act, with its Privacy Rule that put all health records forever after on lock down. It was passed during the

Clinton administration, probably to keep President Clinton's record of multiple penicillin shots from ever seeing the light of day...Kinda like Vogel, it seemed. Now Jerry realized what was going on here. These damn Democrats can't seem to keep it in their pants. No enforcement provision, huh? Jerry didn't realize that...learn something new every day in this business.

"They can violate it smugly," Vogel continued, "as they are today, with no fear of reprisal. It gets some plaintiff's to lower their demands. But as I said, I don't embarrass easily these days."

"For the record," Larry said, "we have no such access to your medical files."

Stew added, "We don't have access to your medical record."

"Sure, you don't," Jerry said.

"But we did work with you for over two years," Larry said. "We know who you are."

"And you don't call that a conflict of interest?" Jerry asked.

"The client waived it," young Jay felt confident enough to offer as he straightened his bulky tie, but not his smirk.

"We know this is all just an act," Larry continued unperturbed by the exchange. "A publicity stunt. And we're not going to sit by and let you undercut the greatest healthcare system in the world. We're prepared to do whatever it takes to bring this unfortunate and ill-advised legal action to a swift close."

"You knew who I *was*, Larry," Vogel said. "You knew who I *was*."

Jerry watched Vogel as Upton attempted to stare him down. Stew and Jay began stacking papers and opening briefcases. They had done all they had come to the conference room to do. Vogel smiled a little. He seemed to be calculating whether to take one more crack at storming this citadel, even as the drawbridge seemed to be cranking shut.

"The body tries to get our attention," Vogel said. "In subtle ways, like appetites, for example, hunger pangs, even the simple breath. Or a sore throat or a cold, just trying to get us to get out of our heads and feel our bodies from the inside. If we don't listen, it raises the alarm with pain, as from depression or anxiety, to cause us to get help from someone who can point us in the right direction, from clergy or a psychologist. When that doesn't work, the body gives us actual physical symptoms that require medical treatment, hoping that the doctor will fix the problem and then send us back down the ladder to the clergy or the psychologist, who in turn will point us into our own bodies where we can solve our own problems and experience the peace and joy that are our natural states. The problem is, not the doctor nor the clergy nor the psychologist knows the first thing about this ladder, so they all keep us on as customers for as long as there's an income stream to exploit. You, Larry, Jay, Stew—of all people—are in the perfect position to observe this process, understand it and stop it."

"This deposition is over," Larry said, standing up, buttoned his suit coat.

Ignoring Larry's dramatics, Vogel sat back in his chair and looked out into space. "You know, now that I think about it, it wasn't exactly as I described. It didn't actually go away when I took the antibiotics. It came back several times until finally they put me on that long-term regimen that caused the 'suicidal ideations,' as they would have called them if I'd told anybody. Nothing happened after that for a good long while, but then the infection came back in altered form at the back of my head."

Jerry looked at Vogel and then up at baldy. He hadn't left yet. Usually, conventional wisdom dictated that a deposee give the shortest answers the deposer would permit and get out as soon as possible—but not always. Vogel seemed to want to get his licks in before these guys left the room. Jerry had to admit, there was a good chance Vogel would never get another face-to-face opportunity with his old colleagues again. And there was an even better chance that Vogel had been dismissed summarily by these same people without so much as a handshake, let alone an explanation. He could see how his friend might relish the moment to tell them off once and for all.

The deposee's attorney had the right to ask clarifying questions to set the record of the deposition straight, didn't he? Rolling with it, Jerry said, "Sit down. Now it's my turn."

With vitriol in his eyes—how one such as Larry Upton hated when his dramatic flourishes were upstaged—he sat down.

To Vogel: "So what are we talking about here?"

Vogel turned to show Jerry where he meant. "Here, around the edge."

Jerry looked closely at the horseshoe along the hairline and up by the ears Vogel had drawn. "I don't see anything."

"That's the point," Vogel said, "Nothing to see anymore. It was poetic justice, this ailment, to tell you the truth. The world is a reflection of our inner space, beginning with our physical bodies. Something so minor that ends up consuming all of your attention, with wounds that never heal. What could be more appropriate, under the circumstances? It's the life force in action. The mating process...as it were...is an involuntary function, just like digestion or circulation. When rationality is applied to it in any manner, the result will always be," he search a beat for the right word, "obsession."

Vogel leaned back, finished. Further circumstances were personal and would not be forthcoming, but based on Larry Upton's line of questioning, Jerry could surmise what they were. Vogel had led an oversexed lifestyle, everyone had always known that about him. Good-looking guy, maybe he'd taken his opportunities to the extreme somehow. And it was clear that Vogel's view was that his physical problems were in some way a result of that, spiritually speaking. That much was clear to Jerry. Filling the gap between the two, that was another story.

"That infection on your leg may have been the same thing," Jerry offered.

The guys on the other side looked confused. "What infection are we talking about?" Larry Upton asked.

"Yeah," Stew chimed in. "What infection?"

"He had a small infection on his leg a few weeks ago,"

Jerry said. “And it healed on its own.” To Vogel: “Continue.”

“May have been, and that may be the end of the story,” Vogel agreed. “When the infections first began to appear, my body would process them out. It was a little messy and I'd get slight flulike symptoms but that was it. Then on my finger, it grew fairly large before a doctor cut it out, after which I took those antibiotics for months on end. Later, when it appeared on the back of my head, my body kind of reached a standstill with it. It just sat there. It itched and the skin flaked. It looked like dandruff, but it wasn't.”

“That's when you went to see a doctor?” Jerry probed.

“By this time, I was well into my transformation,” Vogel said. “So I decided I wasn't going to see a doctor. I was going to try to heal it through consciousness alone.”

“Were you successful?” Jerry asked.

“No,” Vogel admitted.

“You weren't?” Jerry said. That wasn't the answer he was expecting. He glanced over at the Brackman-Hollis boys. What he got in return was either their best poker faces or they were about as lost as Jerry was.

A dull fear set in when Jerry realized he had actually held out some hope that Vogel had been right in his theories. But if Vogel couldn't even make it happen, what chance did Jerry, himself, have? His mouth got a little dry all of a sudden. There were glasses and a water jug in the middle of the table. As Vogel continued, Jerry availed himself of the amenity.

“I struggled with it for a long time,” Vogel said. “More than a year before I was willing to seek even the most modest of help with it. It wasn't life threatening by any means, so I figured why not use my body as an experiment? But it itched like crazy and finally I couldn't stand it anymore.”

“So what'd you do?”

“I'm a big believer in affirmations,” Vogel said. “So I decided to try it on the back of my head. I said, ‘I shall have itch-free skin by such and such a date,’ which was a week or so later.”

“After a year, you didn't give yourself much time,” Jerry said.

"Right," Vogel said. "And that was the point, really. It's just as easy for the Universal to respond to your spoken words of creation in a week as a year. It's just as easy for it to bring you a million dollars as a hundred."

"If you say so," Jerry said reflexively, as if this were just another of their private discussions. He looked across the table and only then did he get where Vogel was going with all this. He would give them his new age philosophy in a fire hose dose and watch them squirm. His strategy was having the desired effect. They looked like three eels in business suits over there. If they actually thought before that Vogel was putting on an act, they couldn't possibly believe that now. And in the same vein as their old buddy Orlando Broxton, this was not the type of audience that could sit and listen to this kind of preaching for very long.

"So what happened?"

"It was as if the Universal possessed my body," Vogel said. "I found myself watching as I looked up the condition on the internet. The treatment I found involved washing daily with a surgical scrub that kills staph. You can buy it over the counter at any drug store. I was already aware of this treatment. A doctor had told me about it long ago, at the beginning of this saga. But I wanted to remain pure, if you know what I mean. I wanted to do it through pure consciousness. So I resisted that until finally I couldn't take it anymore and I put the Universal on a deadline."

"And?"

"It worked," Vogel admitted.

"The surgical scrub," Jerry clarified.

"That in conjunction with consciousness," Vogel said. "Meditation during which I would concentrate my awareness in the area of concern. It didn't work completely, but I began making some headway. I knew I was on the right track. But as I said, it's not *that* it worked, it's how and why that's important." Now Vogel sat up and leaned into the table, holding his hands out in front of him as if he thought he might convert his old colleagues. "It works, and so did the antibiotics, by relieving fear." He allowed everyone, including Jerry, to process that for a moment.

"Fear gets down into the cells of your body. Down into the molecules and atoms, all the way out to the epidermis. When I used that surgical scrub and it began to relieve the symptoms, I understood how much fear I had of that staph infection. I could feel it, welled up at the back of my head. It was pain-body, plain and simple, understand?"

"Uh, well," Jerry said. "No, not exactly."

"Treat the physical as spiritual and the spiritual as physical," Vogel explained. "It's all the same thing and that proved it to me. I had only to dissolve the fear to rid myself of the staph infection. All physical pain, every bit of it, is caused by unconscious negative thoughts. When you concentrate your consciousness in the area where the pain is, it operates over time to bring the unconscious thought into consciousness, thereby curing the condition. What you resist persists, as they say. Don't resist what your body is telling you about your soul. Work *with* it to heal the soul and thereby clear up the physical condition."

Vogel sat back again. He had apparently given up on bringing the big guns of Brackman-Hollis into the fold.

"Resistance is the way of modern medicine. This is what they do—your clients. They're hell-bent on making sure that all of us remain cut off from our bodies, because that's their religion: consciousness is nothing, they—you—believe. And, not by coincidence, that's how they make their money. Resistance causes negativity that only exacerbates the illness. Awareness or consciousness—you might also call this love, internal love—does nothing of the sort. It doesn't judge the illness. It allows the illness to be there, and the soul learns from it."

Vogel was finished. There was a lull. That was actually pretty legit, Jerry considered. He had merely clarified his previous answer, and had done so to beneficial tactical effect. The Brackman-Hollis team didn't look quite so smug as it did just a few moments ago.

"Redirect, gentlemen?" Jerry asked cheerily.

Larry Upton now looked to Stew for confirmation. Fish lips gave an almost imperceptible shake of the head and now Upton got up and walked out, not so much for dramatic effect this time as in relief that the painful ordeal was over.

Stew, momentarily lost in his thoughts, remained behind. Then he moved in such a way as to indicate that he was about to speak. And since no one had spoken in a bit, the moment seem to be of some weight. Looking blandly at Vogel, he said, "Did you ever stop to think that maybe you have it backwards?"

What was he talking about? For the answer, Jerry looked to Vogel as if this were a tennis match, but he seemed just as confused.

"What do you mean?" Vogel asked.

But the enigmatic fish-lip smile never changed and Stew left the room without another word, leaving Jay behind to collect the gear.

Without his overlords in the room, and only a middle-aged court reporter for an audience, Jay lost the smirk and became more personable, and even ventured to strike up a conciliatory conversation to end the choreographed confrontation.

"This is all just part of the process," he said, snapping shut his portable file case.

"Beat it, punk," Jerry said, staring at him without getting up. "What, do you think you're Johnny Manziel or something with your fat tie knot and your checkered shirt? Let me tell you something, you're no Johnny Football. Now, get the hell outta here."

That brought the smirk back to Jay's face but it lacked authenticity this time around. The court reporter held her breath until he left the room and then she smiled appreciatively as she exhaled.

"Oh, I'm sorry about that," Jerry said, coming down a little.

"Loved every second of it," she said as she wheeled her equipment out of the room. "This must be some kind of a case."

When she had left, Jerry said. "It's some kind of a case, all right."

And the long room was still. Had they won or lost the

pitched battle? And would it matter? Would the things that had been said come back to haunt them or would they somehow save the day?

Vogel let out a deep breath. "'A prophet is not without honor, except in his own town,' I guess," he said staring out into the space in front of him.

Jerry waited to see if he would say anything else. "But this is Lexington," Jerry said. "You're from Louisville...not that there's anything wrong with that. "

No smile. Not even a nod of recognition at his trademark safety valve, Seinfeldian humor. Jerry filled the dead air: "Boy, I never would have believed they would—"

Vogel raised his hand and mouthed the word, "Bugged."

"Ah," Jerry said. He got up and moved to the blue-tinted window, looked down at the street. "Want a hotdog?"

"No, thanks."

"Sam's has the best hotdogs in town. Right down there. Come on. It'll cheer you up. Hotdogs always cheer me up."

Chapter 21

"That Stew seems like quite a sycophant," Jerry said.

"Baby Stewie?" Vogel said. "No, he's the only one of the three who really gets this. Stewart Granderson."

"Baby Stewie?"

"You wouldn't know it to look at him," Vogel said. "But he loves *Family Guy*. Or at least he mentioned something about the show one time and someone gave him the nickname and it stuck."

"I'm running all over the country like a maniac for nothing, meanwhile a guy called Baby Stewie is making five hundred grand a year."

"Give or take," Vogel said.

"You mean I'm right?" Jerry said. "I thought I was exaggerating."

It was a three-to-one ratio. Jerry ordered a slaw dog—that was like a salad—a Chicago dog was the main course, and a chili-cheese coney for dessert. Vogel ordered a plain hotdog, on to which he squeezed a thin line of yellow mustard, just to have something to eat.

"What was that about having it backwards?" Jerry asked.

"I don't know," Vogel said. "I don't know. They're the ones who have it backwards."

As Jerry finished off his slaw dog, Vogel turned pensive. The Brackman-Hollis gang had meant to put the fear of God into Vogel that his tawdry past would be revealed vis-à-vis the public display of his medical record should he wish to continue his impertinent constitutional challenge. That hadn't worked, but Vogel's resolve even in the best of time—like after the triumph that the *Today* show interview represented—was suspect. He was coming down now off the high alert that all depositions required. The last thing Jerry needed was more talk of pulling the plug on the litigation.

"I remembered how fearful I was, when it all started happening," Vogel said. He had finished his lone frankfurter and sat back with his legs crossed, looking out through the plate glass. “I thought I was going to have to deal with this stuff for the rest of my life. And not every antibiotic could kill it.”

“You’re talking about the staph infection,” Jerry filled in.

“It was only one antibiotic in particular that did the trick, and I felt such amazing relief when I found that one. But at that time of my life I was in no position to link up the fear in my mind with the ailment. So I suppressed the fear, stored it up as pain-body—at the back of my head—which would inevitably come back to haunt me later. And only later, when I used that surgical scrub, was I in a position to do that.” He looked at Jerry. “That’s what was going on there. My body was simply drawing my awareness to that pent up fear. Nothing more or less. Once you make the fear conscious, it goes away and then so does the condition.” With that, Vogel had stated his case succinctly. Even Jerry understood it. Now Vogel moved to the other side of the equation: “And don’t forget that the antibiotics have strong side effects.”

“Suicidal thoughts,” Jerry said.

“Not to mention the fact that it was only a matter of time before the bacteria built up a resistance to that one antibiotic that worked too,” Vogel said. “I’m using their metaphorical language now. Then I would have really been screwed. Neither of these factors commends their use one bit.”

“No,” Jerry agreed.

”I didn’t reach my goal with the scrub alone, so I set a new deadline a couple of weeks away. That’s when I discovered tea tree oil.”

“Tea tree oil?”

“It’s a natural oil that comes from a tree that grows in New Zealand. It kills even the toughest staph infections. What they call MRSA.” Vogel pronounced it as *mersa.* “It stands for Methicillin-resistant Staphylococcus aureus. It’s untreatable by modern antibiotics. It’s a big problem in hospitals because it runs rampant through them. It kills a lot of people. I have no idea if that’s the strain of staph that

I had but this ought to tell you something about our healthcare system, so called. Apparently, this tea tree oil kills MRSA, and yet you can find very little information about it. Why? Because it isn't patentable." He let Jerry think about that for a beat. "The company that comes up with an antibiotic that kills MRSA will realize windfall profits that haven't been seen since the AIDS antiviral drugs, because that drug will be patentable, and tea tree oil isn't. Wrap your mind around that one."

Vogel's words echoed those of the COS when he sat just a few doors up the street at Cheapside Bar—just a few doors up from where Jerry and Vogel sat right now at Sam's Hotdog Stand—concerning windfall profits.

Wow! Jerry thought, unconsciously scratching his own scalp. He's beating botulism, he's beating MRSA—which must be the case because he's apparently infection free at this point.

"I've heard of MRSA. Nasty business. I've never heard of tea tree oil."

"That's exactly what I mean," Vogel said. "So I used the tea tree oil. I used the surgical scrub and the combination did help, but it didn't cure it completely. Then again, the fastest way to cure something isn't necessarily the best. Who knows? Maybe the tea tree oil works by drawing consciousness into the area of concern. That's something they would never be able to understand."

"Guess not," Jerry said. "I wonder how you could test that."

"Look, we're not trying to avoid the modern world here," Vogel said, staying on point. He seemed to be working his way to something in his own mind by talking it out. "It's rationality that's the problem, not any particular pill. But something told me not to take those antibiotics. You see what I mean? That's consciousness, not rationality."

Vogel was struggling to find the right words when another tack came to him. He sat up and put his elbows on the table. "The moral of the story is, you can take antibiotics or what have you to relieve the fear that's actually causing the problem in the first place. But if the faith you have in them is based on a human ability to cure a physical disease, your confidence is misplaced, because you haven't gotten to the heart of the matter...pun intended."

Pun intended? What pun? Oh, how Jerry hated to miss a pun! But he wasn't about to ask.

Vogel said. "It's like the oldest man in the world said—the one I was telling you about who lived in North Dakota?" Jerry nodded. "You have to draw a line in the sand and not go past it to understand body consciousness, otherwise you're headed down their rabbit hole. He drew his line at taking nothing stronger than aspirin. I draw my line at natural topical remedies."

Jerry bobbed his head in agreement, now on to the chili cheese coney.

"It kind of feels good to think that maybe everything we need can be found in nature," Vogel said.

"As a dutiful Republican," Jerry quipped, trying to lighten Vogel's mood, "I'm duty bound to eschew the prod-ucts of nature whenever possible."

"You know, it's funny," Vogel said. He hadn't even heard Jerry. "Yes, I used all of these remedies, the strong soap, the tea tree oil. But it was kind of like they were just a cover for what was actually going on, because I knew the exact instant when that infection was healed. I could feel it the exact moment when the fearful unconscious thought was revealed. It was at *that* moment the infection was broken and I never needed to concern myself with it ever again. And the funniest part was that I can't even remember the thought that was causing that situation."

"You can't?"

"I know it was some kind of fear—my hackles were in constant high alert mode, is what is was, and awareness eventually dissolved that. But the specifics of it were so insignificant and silly that I couldn't tell you what that thought was to save my life. The point is, each time you see it work, it gives you more confidence that it will work the next time. I'd seen it work with the pain of anxiety, depression, OCD. Then I saw it work in what appeared to be a strictly physical malady. This is what I mean about knowing. Now I know absolutely how it all works."

Vogel stood up and took his leavings to the trash receptacle. Jerry finished his last bite, took a swallow of Coke and did likewise.

Once outside, Vogel took a deep breath of the bracing air. "If you don't get down to the underlying fear, whatever it is, and the behavior that the universe was reflecting back at you in the first place, it's going to come back in altered form until you get the message, like I did, that it's something like resentment or anger or regret—which are all just different aspects of fear—that's causing the problem." He bore down upon Jerry. "Because that's the stuff that the universe is actually made of. It's in the nature of the universe. Universal love. Diseased body reflects a diseased soul. How else are you going to recognize it? Recognition—awareness, consciousness—not judgment, brings change to the soul. You feel better."

Vogel straightened up and then started walking up the street in the direction of Orlando's house. It was a few blocks away.

"Car's this way," Jerry shouted.

"You were right," he said. "That hotdog did make me feel better. I feel like walking. See you back at the ranch."

"Brad," Jerry said before he got too far away. Vogel turned again. "What happened back there in the deposition when you were talking about cause and effect?"

Vogel stopped and without missing a beat he said, "We learned that they get all of this. Every bit of it. They know that they should be working to eliminate fear, rather than creating more of it, as they do through marketing and advertising. And they're scared to death that someone else has broken their code, again pun intended."

"I get that one," Jerry said. Vogel had been one of them, and he had broken their code in both senses of that word. The first pun still bothered him.

"It means that the healthcare industry is completely aware that my views are one hundred percent accurate and they suppress them at all costs because they're bad for business."

Jerry frowned. "But cause and effect? That's so basic. I mean—"

"There's no such thing as cause and effect." When Jerry held out his hands and shook his head, Vogel explained: "Walk it back all the way to the beginning. What was the first cause?"

Jerry did as directed. In an instant he was back at the big bang. What caused that? "God," he said. "God was the first cause."

Vogel held up a finger and smiled, triumphant. "There is no God in Aristotle's material world, the world of science." Jerry stood mouth agape, hoping a response might find its way out, but nothing came to him. Vogel said, "Does cause and effect hold any sway at all in a dream?"

Jerry thought for a moment. "No."

"In a dream, can two and two equal five?"

"Yes, I suppose so."

"Dreams are there to teach us the nature of reality," Vogel said, now bearing down upon Jerry once again. "Causality, logic, mathematical relationships—they're all tenants of a religion, nothing more." He pointed up at the big blue building towering over them, the place where Brackman-Hollis kept their offices. "And they know it."

It was cold but Jerry stood there pondering.

Vogel said, "To put it another way, any time you're treating the physical body, your dealing with symptoms, because the root of the problem is at a deeper level. This goes for the mind, too—psychology. A diseased body—or mind—represents a diseased soul." Vogel held his gloved hands together waist high, palms up. "You may have some success treating symptoms alone. But in the end, every individual has to make the connection between body and soul themselves, and that's obviously impossible if you deny that there is any such thing as a soul, or inner body. Not until we make that connection will health return. Not until I made that connection for myself, about my own diseased soul, did the infection heal completely. You can fix the body and not touch the soul. But heal the soul and the body will follow."

"But isn't that cause and effect?" Jerry asked.

"Not cause and effect," Vogel said. "Reflection. We replace the law of causation with the law of reflection. When we do that, the entire system reveals itself as a mirage. As the Hindus say, we are all merely ideas in the mind of a god."

Vogel nodded once and then stopped for a moment as if the pointed brevity of what he had just said had revealed something even to himself. He turned and began again his walk home in long confident strides.

Jerry couldn't get his mind off the first pun. If your faith is based on a human ability to cure a physical disease, it doesn't go to the heart of the matter...what had he meant by that? Matter...materiality...stuff of the universe...

He looked up. Vogel was already a good distance away...He got it.

"The heart of the matter is that matter doesn't really exist!" Jerry shouted after him.

Vogel smiled over his shoulder and waved.

Chapter 22

It wasn't long before the character assassination campaign began in earnest. With a billion-dollar industry backing the effort, the publicity machine had the ear of the media at every level. "Fired Healthcare Attorney Has Ax to Grind," was the *New York Times* headline. Anderson Cooper ran a piece in his Rediculist segment, stating, "This type of case could only come out of the backwoods of Kentucky." Jon Stuart took the same tack, running a piece with a British-accented reporter speaking over banjo music. In these stories and others, Vogel was not vilified, he wasn't pilloried. He was simply questioned as not quite right in the head for believing what he believed, mentally unstable, formerly suicidal, of questionable moral character.

Religious punditry was also utilized to point out that Vogel's views were not in line with orthodox Christianity. MSNBC could care less about Christian orthodoxy most of the time, unless it could be used as a wedge to divide the viewers of Fox News—anti-Obamacare folks on the one side, Christians on the other.

But this was to be expected from the liberal media. And yes, it was also true that the Fox News morning morons had weighed in, calling Vogel's views "whacky," but Jerry wrote that off in his mind. No one on either side of the aisle took those guys seriously. The more authoritative conservative commentators would rally to Vogel's cause, Jerry was sure of it.

In spite of all these efforts, the website continued to grow, as very few Christian contingents were willing to take their marching orders from MSNBC, and as people began to comprehend that Vogel's views might offer a very practical loophole for getting around Obamacare. As a result, Vogel was summoned to a number of mega-churches to explain his views. He accepted only one invitation, and that was from a church in Phoenix, where the pastor spoke from couches on a TV stage, Oprah-style, in front of a vast studio congregation.

This wasn't just *a* church, it was *The Church*, that's what the weekly Sunday broadcast was called, beamed out to millions of homes via its own cable channel. Pastor Clint Goforth could get away with such hubris because his show dominated its timeslot among its target demographic. Among Christians it was bigger than Oprah had ever been in her heyday. Even so, Vogel wouldn't have agreed to the requested appearance, except that Goforth had called him personally to use his charisma—as Vogel told it—to mesmerize him into doing what he thought better of.

Jerry tried to talk him out of it. Sure, they needed the Christian Right to get on board Vogel's train, but better to pick them off one by one through the secular media, driving them to the website for further information, rather than try to fly right into the teeth of the Christian orthodoxy beast. "He's going to take you down," Jerry argued after Vogel had already accepted the invitation. "What you're talking about isn't orthodox Christianity. You can't take this guy head on."

"It is as it is," Vogel said stoically as he got ready with Jerry at the hotel that morning. "There are no mistakes in consciousness."

They sat together in Vogel's Phoenix hotel room, Jerry on one bed, remote in hand, Vogel on the other. They had a few minutes before they had to leave for the church service.

Jerry was flipping around the dial and landed momentarily on *This Week with George Stephanopoulis*. After a moment, he said, "Hey, they're talking about us."

"Here we go," Vogel said.

It was the same ol' same ol' from the liberals, Stephanopoulis himself and Cokie Roberts. Then conservative pundit George Will spoke up. George Will, thought Jerry, now this guy's going to set the record straight.

"These views are extreme and dangerous," Will chimed in. "Only a very sick mind would hold out this kind of false hope to people. This has no traction in the Republican Party. The debate on the need for healthcare for every citizen is long over." His words echoed those of Senator McCormick.

Jerry swallowed hard and glanced over at Vogel. "I'll tell you who's an attractive man," he said, quoting Kramer to lighten the mood. "George Will...He has a clean look, scrubbed and shampooed...But I don't find him all that bright."

"Nothing like a good pat on the back to bolster one's confidence before a speaking engagement," Vogel said.

"Nobody really pays any attention to—" Jerry coughed and hesitated, "to...George Will." He changed the channel. "You know, it's not too late to back out."

"Yes, it is," said Vogel.

* * *

Jerry and Vogel were permitted to wait backstage during the opening segment, called "praise and worship," which was not televised.

"This is a lot like the *Today* show," Jerry said. He was uncomfortable and he could see that Vogel was, too. "The vibe here is nice," he said nervously. "A little too nice. It creeps me out." Looking around, he said, "This guy is going to take you down like a Christmas tree on New Year's Day."

Belatedly, Jerry noticed the effect his words were having on Vogel. He said: "But hey, what do I know? This guy's the Christian Oprah, right? Everybody loves the Reverend Clint Goforth—pastor to presidents." He held up his fists, backed by a wink, to bolster Vogel's confidence. Then looking around again, all Jerry could do was curl up his lips and shake his head with disdain, betraying his disingenuousness. And all Vogel could do was shake *his* head and let out a deep sigh of resignation concerning his friend's display of stupidity.

A man of about fifty dressed in an expensive suit came over and introduced himself as the Assistant Pastor for TV Operations. "Just relax," he said. "We're just here for a free exchange of ideas. Pastor Goforth will put you at ease immediately. It's one of his many gifts."

"Okay," Vogel said.

When the man turned to Jerry and offered his hand and

asked him his name, Jerry told him, then added, "I'm Brad's domestic partner."

The man was taken aback, as was Vogel. But just at that moment, a woman came from behind to inform the Assistant Pastor of some pressing TV business. He quickly hurried away, glancing nervously at Jerry.

Vogel said, "What the hell is wrong with you!"

"These guys creep me out," Jerry said.

"Don't be such an idiot!" Vogel said as he tried to catch up with the man. "He's not my domestic partner," Vogel veritably shouted at the back of the man's head, drawing stares from all around. Vogel returned to Jerry. "What did you have to say that for!"

"They take themselves way too seriously," Jerry said. "I don't like it."

"Yeah, well, you're not the one they're saying is unbalanced. I don' t need anymore bad press right now."

"All right, I'm sorry," Jerry said. "I'll find him and clear it up. Just concentrate on what you've got to do."

"Now you're doing something to help me," Vogel said.

"Again with the *Seinfeld*?" Jerry said.

* * *

"Not to be disagreeable on your home turf," Vogel said. "But I would say it *is* all about you."

This drew polite laughter from the audience, which in the darkness behind the bright lights Vogel could not see, and a humorous mock-wounded expression from Pastor Goforth, silver-haired and panning for the camera, that drew even more snickers. The Assistant Pastor had been right, Pastor Goforth had managed to put Vogel at ease. Jerry had never seen him so relaxed in one of these interviews.

He was sure, however, that Goforth was simply putting Vogel off his guard, awaiting just the right moment to put him in his place, theologically speaking, and that would spell the doom of their shared endeavor. The effects would snowball. The Christian Right would turn their noses up at the New Church of Vogel, the case would be dismissed—even judges appointed for life feel the weight of public pressure when it's unanimous—and Jerry would remain out on his ass, he just knew it.

"It's one hundred percent about you and about me and every single person in the world, because we're all one thing. We're all one consciousness."

"You're, of course referring to the first line of my new book, *Go Forth and Prosper*," the Pastor said, holding up a copy, conveniently located on the end table closest to him.

"I say that only for its shock value," Vogel said. "When you say, 'This isn't about you,' what you're actually referring to is the ego. And with that I can agree. Most people believe that's who they are, their ego. They're completely identified with it. But that's *not* who they are."

"A lot of this centers on definition of terms, doesn't it?" Pastor Goforth said. "When you're talking about the ego, what exactly are you referring to?"

"In Christian parlance, the term we would use would be 'the flesh,' or 'the sin nature.' But exactly what this is and how you identify it, and what you do about it once you find it, has been lost to modern Christianity for centuries. Christianity has chosen on the whole to emphasize its unique mythology—and by mythology, I don't mean fiction, I simply mean the supernatural aspect of the Bible story—rather than its spiritual aspect."

"Okay."

"And there's another term defined," Vogel said, smiling. "Of course, whenever you're trying to communicate, you're dealing with the rational. Communication is a rational process. It's one of the only two things rationality is good for: communication and the creation of laborsaving devices. What we're trying to get people to concentrate on—and where Jesus was trying to get people to focus their attention—is this greater realm of consciousness where all is and can be known. The definition of terms is an aspect of 'the academy,' as I like to call it. That's Aristotle, who is in fact, the anti-Christ in every sense of the word."

"Wow," Pastor Goforth said. "I've never heard that one before."

There were no snickers this time, Jerry noticed from the wings. Vogel had their rapt attention. The mention of the anti-Christ probably brought on visions of *The Omen Trilogy* and that precocious kid, Damian. It would probably make them feel better once they realized they wouldn't have to have 666 stamped on their hands or foreheads, seeing as Aristotle had already come and gone three hundred years before Jesus...if any of these people actually knew this historical fact...which Jerry was guessing they didn't. He wondered if churches removed page 666 from their hymnals the way hotels skipped the thirteenth floor.

Jerry had heard all this before: next would come the part about Aristotle's invention of the moral code by application of rationality—as opposed to consciousness—to the higher questions of life, and how this was antithetical to all that Jesus stood for. *Please don't say you're the least moral person you know*, Jerry willed toward Vogel. These people won't get that.

"Jesus said, 'Don't judge anything,' right?" Vogel asked.

"Right."

Vogel leaned forward, placing his hands lightly on his knees. "Aristotle came up with the scientific method, which tells you to judge everything. You can't get more 'anti' than that. Of course, Aristotle came before Jesus, so it might be more academically correct—notice the word 'academy' in there—to say that Jesus was the anti-Aristotle. Judgment of everything is the scientific method. Judgment, evaluation, determination, examination. That's what science is all about. Jesus came along at a time when these newfangled Greek ideas were still novel, just a few hundred years old at that point. His ministry was all about how rationality should be kept in its very limited place—communication and the creation of laborsaving devices—and should never be applied to the greater truths of life. That was a time when Greek thought had already completely infiltrated Jewish wisdom, turning it into a theology—you've heard of the Pharisees and the Sadducees."

"Of course."

"That's what that part of the Bible is all about. Jesus telling the Jews, 'Don't judge,' that is, don't apply rationality to the higher questions of life, while on the other hand the Pharisees and Sadducees had already incorporated Greek thought concerning the primacy of rationality into what had become the Jewish religion."

"This is fascinating."

"In fact," Vogel continued, "there was no such thing as religion before Aristotle. Aristotle was the first to separate out rationality from the higher questions of life, which he called Metaphysics. This made the idea of a religion possible. Before that, it was all one thing. There was one unified philosophy and the law of a people. But then, he went on to place rationality atop the whole structure—where consciousness had once ruled supreme—creating the concept of ethics."

"Now hold on a second," Pastor Goforth said, raising a hand. "Wasn't the Law of Moses an attempt at an ethical code of conduct?"

"Apart from the levitical law, which are about religious rites, no," Vogel said. "It was the law of a people. There's a difference. Law limits itself to the protection of people from the unconscious behavior of others. Don't drink and drive—that's a law. Don't drink—that's morality. Ethics or morality is an attempt to come to rational conclusions as to what is right and what is wrong. Jesus' ministry was about explaining to people why you can't get there from here, so to speak. And that's because rationality is always based on unconscious assumptions. And depending upon the assumptions one holds, anything can be proven through the application of rationality, that is to say logic."

"That's true," Goforth agreed.

* * *

Jerry had been wandering around the vast complex since the singing had commenced and found himself now in the glass-enclosed foyer at the back of the auditorium. He tuned out the audio of the broadcast through which he'd been monitoring Vogel's performance—with a wary ear on Goforth—playing there for anyone who needed to step out but didn't wish to miss a single pearl of Pastor Goforth's wisdom. There were video monitors showing the live feed too.

Jerry walked with his hands in his pockets toward the wall of windows and looked out at the flat landscape of asphalt and automobiles. It was nice to wear a summer-weight suit in the dead of winter, he admitted to himself.

In this moment of reflection, perhaps fostered by the sepulchral marble beneath his feet and the echo of far off footsteps, Jerry couldn't help but realize that his life was balanced precariously on the back of an unsteady wagon traveling rocky ground. What had happened? What goaded him into pressing forward at the beginning? He could hardly remember. At this point the only carrot dangling out there in front of him as he steered Vogel's cart now through the desert was the prospect of getting his old job back. Vogel's views, his experiments—especially the experiments—really got under Jerry's skin. But what could he do? He was hitched to them. Even so, if he got his job back, he would be on smooth pavement again on a road that might lead back to his old life somehow, the life he knew just before becoming reacquainted with Brad Vogel.

Beyond the parking lot, he imagined old people in golf carts, either on the links or inside gated communities moving from point to point, the turmoil of their working lives behind them. Jerry had never been to Arizona before. There was a peace here, a stillness.

He thought if he didn't get the job back, what were the chances he might find work out here? He would more likely have to return to Kentucky and use his law license in some capacity, a thought that didn't sit well, but Nicole wasn't about to let him off easy. She was sure to push for the lifestyle to which she had become accustomed, and that most likely meant the practice of law for him. No more of the trappings of power to which *he* had become accustomed....

Did Senator McCormick really mean it when he made me that job offer? What were his exact words? He had asked what I was doing working for an Ohioan, that he needed to get me back into the Kentucky fold. I had asked him point blank at the time if that was a job offer and the Senator had replied in the affirmative. He was trying to buy me off. That didn't really register with me at the time but that's what he was doing. And what did I say? I played it off, telling him I had outstanding warrants and couldn't set foot in the Commonwealth for fear of getting picked up and thrown in jail. I wouldn't say that now, would I? Boy, I really had some guts back then. Not now. Of course, that was just before Mack the Knife wrote, "They will kill him," on a Post-it note and then burned same in ashtray.

Jerry shook that thought off. He didn't want to think about that now...here. This place lent itself to contemplation. The senator's warning meant he should remain ever vigilant on Vogel's behalf, but the fact was, Jerry just wasn't in the mood. This was looking more and more like a marathon and less and less like the sprint Jerry had hoped it would be, and he was finding that he just couldn't be on all the time.

That was a job offer, all right, Jerry thought. But now my stock is down. I've got to get it back up again any way I can, only then will I have options....

He found himself below one of the video monitors and he tuned back into the show.

* * *

"Ok, now the sixty-four thousand dollar question," Pastor Goforth said. "I'm showing my age with that one. How do you get by without morality? Without a moral code?"

"You've heard the old saying, 'You can't legislate morality,' right?"

"Yes, and we don't like to hear that," Goforth admitted, shifting a little in his seat.

"You can't do it in government and you can't do it in churches, because it doesn't work. Unconscious thoughts always come along and make us do, as Paul put it, the very thing we hate. But what exactly do we do about that? On this, Paul seems pretty vague until you change a few words. 'Sin living in me,' we change to 'Unconscious thoughts control me.' And, 'Walk not after the flesh, but after the Spirit," we change to, 'Don't allow unconscious thoughts to control my behavior by, instead, living consciously.'"

"We're not big on changing words around," Goforth said,

leaning away and eying the audience cautiously. "Especially when they come from the *Bible*."

"I understand," Vogel said. "But words, through overuse and misuse often pick up a lot of baggage over time. The words lose meaning because people think they know what the originator meant. Sometimes when you substitute a different word it gives us a better understanding of what the speaker might have been trying to communicate. In this case, we've turned what Paul was talking about into a mystical otherworldly experience, one beyond human understanding. But perhaps he was actually talking about something much more practical that all of us can easily access and practice if we're shown how."

"Perhaps," Goforth conceded. "But it still isn't computing for me."

* * *

An older man and woman emerged from the auditorium. "I'm happy with orthodox Christianity," the man said as his wife helped him adjust his jacket collar. "I like orthodox Christianity. I'm comfortable with orthodox Christianity. That ain't orthodox Christianity."

"It doesn't hurt to hear other points of view from time to time, Harold," the wife said. As they passed Jerry, the man nodded in stride, then held the glass door open for his wife. "Let's go get some pancakes," she said. "That will make you feel better."

And so it begins, Jerry thought. Someone sticking up for the good old Christian religion as we now know it. Next, it would be Goforth's turn. Any minute now, the doors would fly open and people would stream out the exits once Pastor Goforth listens to as much of Vogel's philosophy as he can stand and then pronounces his views heretical.

In that instant, Jerry became more conflicted than he had ever been. If Vogel went down in flames at Goforth's hands, that would very likely mean the end of his publicity campaign to win the hearts and minds of the people. The media—both conservative and liberal—had already closed ranks against him, now if the upper echelon of the Christian right did the same, Vogel would be relegated to a backwater movement, like, like—I don't know—like homeschoolers, no bigger than a trickle. His website would slow to a trickle too. Of course, that would likely mean Jerry would never get his old job back.

On the other hand, it would let Jerry off the hook. He would never have to consider doing any of those experiments ever again. It would mean vindication for the life he had led up to this point—okay, that life was a bit of a mess at the moment, but still—and an authoritative repudiation of this fellow, Vogel, who seemed to think he had it all figured out. In a way, that would be sweet, wouldn't it? Although this guy had become a hell of a nice guy. Jerry had to admit that too.

And so, he was conflicted. And being conflicted, he gravitated toward sustenance. Not to mention the fact that Vogel would probably need some comfort food to help him get over the theological beating Goforth was about to give him, poor sap.

"Excuse me," he said, approaching the couple. The man was about to pass through the door behind his wife. "Did someone say pancakes?"

"Butterfield's," the man said. "Best in town."

"Butterfield's," Jerry repeated so he would remember it. "Thanks."

The man nodded and moved to go.

Jerry said, "You know, I'm surprised more people haven't left early."

The man stopped again and studied Jerry. "You new here?"

"Me? No," Jerry said, unsure why he had kept this conversation going. "I'm...friends with the speaker."

"Goforth?"

"No, the guest speaker."

The man seemed unsure whether Jerry was making fun of him or was simply a disloyal friend. Without further comment he continued on his way.

And that's when Jerry got it.

Of course! They had gotten to Goforth! That's what he, himself, would have done. They—the ubiquitous they!

Surely they could have found common cause with this man. He wants to champion orthodox Christianity. They needed Vogel taken down. He had to think about this. Jerry really had to think about this...

Republicans...It would have to have been Republicans. Conservative Republicans. Goforth wouldn't listen to Democrats, and might not even meet with them. A congressman or two, maybe even a senator—Mack McCormick, himself, perhaps—along with a fast talking lobbyist, flown into Phoenix from DC. They have dinner at a nice restaurant—but not too nice, they want to appear legit. They talk about how Vogel's views are New Age and weird and dangerous. They say, "Surely you realize that everybody needs health insurance, don't you?" Then they ask what they can do for him. Maybe help with a local zoning issue, or maybe it's immigration he's concerned about. Or maybe money. It wouldn't be money, Jerry considered. Goforth's books stayed at the top of the bestseller lists. They made millions.

Everybody needs more money.

Maybe they meant to kill Vogel figuratively, now that the firebombing of his home hadn't worked. The video monitor caught Jerry's eye.

* * *

"'God is love,' right?" Vogel was saying.

"Right," Goforth agreed.

As he tuned in again, Jerry couldn't imagine the segue that had gotten them here.

"That was John, the beloved apostle," Vogel said. "One of the early church fathers was a fellow named Augustine of Hippo, who was born about three hundred or so years after Jesus. Augustine was the first to point out that if the statement 'God is love' is true, then 'Love is God' must also be true."

Goforth was thinking. He was taking that in, and so was the audience.

"I'll give you a moment with that," Vogel said. Then after a brief pause, he went on: "At another point—in the book of Acts—the apostle Paul says, 'In him we live, and move, and have our being.'"

"Yes."

"In other words, God is reality, itself." Vogel paused again. "That's what that statement means, isn't it? That's a description of reality. Reality is where we live and move and have our being. That also, then, entails, logically speaking, that reality...is love. God is love is reality is God is love. God, love, reality—they're all words for the same thing. So then, at its heart, at its essence, a belief in God is a belief in the nature of reality, that it is love—that reality is benevolent, beneficent, positive, loving."

"Wow," Pastor Goforth said.

"This is in contradistinction to what the state religion—what I like to call the Religion of Science—would have you believe. Science would have you believe that the universe is a neutral place, coldly and randomly governed by the neutral laws of cause and effect—two opposite views that can't be true at the same time, mind you."

"Powerful," Goforth said.

"This may be easy for you to swallow," Vogel said. "But the next question may not be. And that is, where does modern Christianity fit into this spectrum?"

"Give it to me straight, doc," Goforth said.

"This is where another one of the church fathers, as they're called, comes in. This time it was in the 1200s when a fellow named Thomas Aquinas married up the philosophy of Jesus—'don't judge anything'—with the philosophy of Aristotle—'judge everything.' In effect, he brought the anti-Christ, philosophically speaking, right into the sanctuary. Again, here we are, attempting to synthesize two diametrically opposed philosophies, and that's logically impossible. But this melding of opposites was eventually accepted by the Catholic Church as orthodoxy and it was never questioned by Protestantism. In essence, Christianity was co-opted just as Judaism had been prior to Jesus' ministry. The same is true of Islam today as well. All the western religions are in the same boat. They're trying to hold on to one without letting go of the other. It can't be done."

Here we go, Jerry thought. This is where Goforth lowers the boom.

Instead, Goforth said, "You're right," holding up his hand and throwing back his head just a tick in his characteristic way. And he paused a little for effect. "You're right, I'm not quite following you when you say holding on to one without letting go of the other."

Jerry swallowed hard. This guy knew good television. He knew drama. He was building up to something, that was for sure, toying with his audience, giving them a good show by delaying the inevitable.

Vogel backed up a little, both physically and figuratively as he went at the issue from a slightly different angle. "Jesus said, 'Don't judge.'"

"Yes."

"But you judge all the time." Goforth's face screwed up, but Vogel kept going. "Christians are known for applying their own strict moral code to themselves and everyone else."

Stunned silence.

"This is only the most obvious example. But what Jesus was talking about was even more radical. 'Don't judge' means don't live your life rationally. That sounds crazy to you, doesn't it?"

"Well, frankly, yes. It does."

"That's because of centuries of brainwashing," Vogel said. "You think that the opposite of rationality is irrationality."

"Isn't it?" Goforth said.

"In this context, the opposite of rationality is consciousness. Consciousness is what's necessary to solve any situation, not rationality or judgment. Rationality is only a tiny sliver of overall consciousness, yet Aristotle raised it to the top of the philosophical food chain. So technically speaking, they're not opposites. Rationality is a subset of overall consciousness. Jesus sought to bring rationality back down to its rightful place as a subset of consciousness by teaching us not to judge.

"Consciousness, not rationality, is the power of the Universe. God is Love is Reality...is Consciousness. We're talking about living consciously versus living rationally. That sounds a little better, doesn't it? Simple awareness is all that's needed to solve any problem, improve any situation, including health issues—not thinking. We've all been brainwashed to believe that it's nothing, but in fact consciousness is the power of the universe—and that's what we are. Imagine that! That's what Jesus' ministry was trying to help us understand, but it's been lost through thousands of years of unconsciousness both within the church and without.

"And to bring it all back around and tie it up with a nice little bow," Vogel said with a smile, "the natural bi-product of rationality is ethics."

"We come back around to ethics," Goforth said.

"This is why some Christians have seen fit to view the Bible as a magic book," Vogel said.

Murmuring, not completely quelled by the producers, rendered from the audience. Though Goforth was engrossed in his conversation with Vogel, he took note of it, looking out at the congregation, squinting in the bright light, attempting to better gauge their mood. When Goforth then looked directly into the camera, Jerry thought Vogel's end was near.

"Ladies and gentlemen," Goforth said. "Mr. Vogel means no sacrilege in what he's saying. He's making a bigger point here."

"Yes, absolutely," Vogel responded. "The *Bible* isn't the problem. It's a holy book. Read it, meditate upon it, allow the wisdom in it to wash over and through you. But there's no place for using it as a weapon."

"Mmm," Goforth agreed. "We've said the same thing here many times. We certainly agree with you on that."

"This is what we're doing when we attempt to derive a set of ethics from it. 'These ethics come from God,' we are in effect saying, 'so our code of ethics is better than your code of ethics.' Without that divine claim, all ethics are equal, having been written on the black chalkboard of mind. This approach is unnecessary when you're grounded in your inner-body, your soul."

"By approach," Goforth said, "you're talking about the idea that the Bible is a moral code that trumps all others because it comes from God." Goforth frowned in concentration, once again fully engaged in what Vogel was saying.

"That's right," Vogel said. "You don't need that when everyone is determining what they should do in any given moment based on what their inner body is telling them to do. This is why the great spiritual teacher and former Catholic priest Justin Pitt has said, 'Wisdom is self-proving; it needs no canon.' That's because it's up to each and every one of us to go into the real world of our souls, our inner-bodies, where we can discover what to do and what not to do for ourselves, not from any top down ethic that's been imposed upon us, no matter how high sounding that ethic might be."

Goforth looked up at his director and nodded. "I'm aware of the time, ladies and gentlemen. For those of you who have pressing obligations, please feel free to slip out quietly. I want to keep going with this. I think we may be on to something here. The television broadcast of this service will be edited for time, of course, but we will have the full unedited interview on our website in the coming days. . ."

Chapter 23

The conversation when on for some time. Goforth even allowed Vogel to take his congregation through the first experiment, the one Jerry had suffered through at the Cracker Barrel in London. After that, Goforth had been as pliable as butter. Vogel could have asked him for anything short of devil worship and he would have complied. Jerry just didn't get it. Something wasn't adding up. Could his political antenna be that poorly tuned these days?

When it was all over, Goforth said a word of thanks to his guest, thanked his audience for their patience and thanked his Creator in benediction. From off camera someone said, "And we're out."

The red light on top of the camera went dark and production staff began milling here and there about the stage. A woman brought a glass of ice and a can of Diet Coke to the table beside Pastor Goforth's couch. He proceeded to pop the top and pour. The same setup then appeared beside Vogel but he didn't avail himself of it.

"You did real well," Goforth said, smiling at Vogel. He took a sip. "As you can probably tell, I'm fascinated by your perspective on things."

"I wasn't sure how you'd take to it," Vogel said. "It isn't something that should be threatening in anyway. My hope is that it might reinvigorate spiritually-minded people."

"I've come to a new perspective, myself," Goforth said. "But I've struggled to come up with just the right way to get into it. We may have made a start today."

Jerry emerged from the shadows. Vogel, noticing him, said, "This is Jerry Riggs. He's Chief Counsel to the Speaker of the U.S. House of Representatives."

Make that former Chief Counsel, Jerry thought as he mounted the steps to the stage and shook Goforth's hand, but he didn't offer the correction. Goforth didn't get up, too weary. His face tightened, though, Jerry noticed, at the introduction. "That was a heck of a show," he said.

Where he had been open just a moment before, Goforth was now noticeably tightlipped.

Perhaps noticing the new tension, Vogel said, "Jerry's been a tremendous help to me. I couldn't have gotten this far without him."

The endorsement did seem to help. By that, Jerry knew that his political antenna had picked up the right frequency after all. He squinched in beside Vogel on his couch and helped himself to his unopened beverage.

Addressing himself to Goforth, Jerry said, "Have you received any...overtures concerning this appearance?"

The auditorium was nearly empty but for the production crew, and there were only a couple of those left in earshot. Goforth took another sip. "I'm not sure what you mean," he said.

"About Brad's appearance on your show," Jerry pursued.

Vogel shot Jerry a questioning glance. "What are you getting at?"

"You have, haven't you?" Jerry said.

"Jerry," Vogel said.

Goforth calculated, looking toward the cameras. "You never know when these things are rolling," he said. "Come with me."

When he had gotten backstage, Goforth took off his suit coat and handed it to someone as he made his way through the worker bees to his dressing room. "I've got a plane to catch," he said over his shoulder. "Otherwise, I'd have you boys out to the ranch for Sunday supper. I say 'plane to catch,' but that's not really accurate anymore. People don't understand that when they want you to be in Schenectady for an ecumenical conference on Monday morning, followed by a TV appearance in L.A. the next day, you can't be waiting in Atlanta for three hours for a connecting flight. I used to fly my own plane but I gave that up when I turned sixty, just like the airline pilots have to. I've even given up the private jet. NetJets, only way to go. More economical and less of an image problem."

When they reached the dressing room, Goforth took off

his pants and hung them on a hanger, minding the crease dutifully.

"Should we wait outside?" Jerry asked.

"What's the matter?" Goforth said with a chuckle in his voice. "Haven't you ever seen an old man in his T-shirt and boxer *shorts* before?" He stressed "shorts" rather than "boxer," which made it sound a little funnier.

Neither Vogel nor Jerry knew quite how to respond. Then Goforth put on the robe that hung where he had just placed his pants. He sat down to remove the black knee socks from his spindly white legs and then turned toward the mirror to begin removing his make up.

"To answer your question," Goforth said, "a small cadre of well-meaning politicians who shall remain nameless did happen to pay me a visit a couple of weeks ago."

Vogel looked at Jerry, confused. With a frown combined with a quick shake of the head, Jerry waved him off; he would bring him up to speed later.

"Let's just say," Goforth said, aiming his reflected gaze squarely at Jerry as he continued to work, "that I'm an old and very rich man." He lowered his eyes again. "They had nothing I wanted or needed."

Finished with the cold cream, he rotated his chair and motioned for Vogel and Jerry to sit down on the couch behind them, which they did without looking away.

"And besides, we just don't treat our guests that way."

He paused for a moment and both Jerry and Vogel filled the air with statements of appreciative agreement until Goforth cut them off.

"Until they came to me, I'd never heard of your lawsuit or had any idea what it meant." He paused for a reflective moment and this time Jerry and Vogel knew to keep quiet. "As I said before, maybe it's my newly acquired wealth over the last few years, or maybe it's just age, but as I told you, I've come to see that there's something we're missing in the Christian community, and when I saw those old boys so..." he searched for the right words, "...intent on nipping this contagion in the bud—and I think those might have been their exact words—something inside me perked up, and all I could think about was hearing your side of the story." Goforth concluded with a smile, "Something about the Lord working in mysterious ways comes to mind."

"'His wonders to behold,'" Jerry said, staring out into the space between the three men. When he looked up, both Vogel and Goforth were staring at him with surprised expressions. He shrugged and explained, "My mom used to say that whenever anyone said, 'God works in mysterious ways.'"

"Sounds like you have a pretty good mama," Goforth said.

And then he had to get in the shower and get to the airport. Jerry and Vogel said their goodbyes and shuffled out to the hallway.

"Wow," Jerry said, a little mesmerized.

"What was that all about?" Vogel asked as they began to find their way out.

"I can't believe it," Jerry said. "It all makes perfect sense and that's what I thought had happened, but...I still can't believe it."

"Believe what?" Vogel said. "Tell me."

"Have you ever heard of Thomas Pynchon?"

Vogel wrinkled his forehead and thought for a moment. "Yeah."

"The contagion Goforth was talking about was you and your philosophy."

On the way to the car and in the car on the road, Jerry explained how Big Healthcare had come to Goforth in the hopes of procuring his cooperation in bumping Vogel off, theologically speaking, filling in gaps in his knowledge with unsubstantiated assumptions and speculation, which must have made it seem like he had a firmer grasp on what was going on than perhaps he did. But what the heck, it made the story more interesting.

Vogel was blown away. He thought he'd seen it all up to this point. Yet, he noted wryly, every time he thought that, the whole thing just ratcheted up to another level of weirdness. "It's like the texture of reality is changing before my eyes, you know?"

No, Jerry didn't know, not really. He was still completely

grounded in the apparent concreteness of the world. It was weird, though—he could certainly grasp that much.

Vogel seemed wired and exhausted at the same time. While Jerry drove, Vogel lounged back in his seat with his sunglasses on and Jerry might have thought he had fallen asleep but for his feet and hands which never stopped tapping, constant motion. He said all he wanted to do was to get to the blog and get his thoughts and feelings down in writing while they were still fresh.

Jerry had another idea. The conversation with Goforth had really buoyed his spirits. That old man had done Vogel a good turn. He had restored Jerry's faith in humanity, while at the same time reminding him that there were contrary forces at play here. Goforth had inspired Jerry to redouble his efforts if he needed to on behalf of his friend. This put him in a celebratory mode.

"And now for something completely different," he said, pulling the rented Lincoln to a stop in the midst of a strip mall.

"What's this?" Vogel asked.

"You'll see."

Chapter 24

"How'd you find out about this place?" Vogel said. "Hey, look. The ceiling looks like waffles. I didn't notice that when we came in."

"It's kitschy," Jerry said. "I have a pancake app."

"You've got iPancake?" Vogel said. "That's awesome. Like iToilet."

"*Seinfeld* reunion," Jerry said. "Nice. Lingonberry—who knew? Never had that before. You mind?"

"Go ahead."

Jerry took a small taste from the dollop of lingonberry sauce in the middle of Vogel's Swedish style griddlecakes.

"Mmm. Nice," Jerry said, returning to what was left of his banana-nut American-style variety. "I've got fruit here too? Huh? Very healthy?"

"I don't know about that," Vogel said.

"Well," Jerry said, choking down a large bite to clear his mouth to talk. "Nothing like pancakes and a yellow restaurant interior to keep the spirits flying high. That's what it's all about, right? You said so, yourself. That's basically your whole philosophy in a nutshell, isn't it?"

Vogel thought about it. "Yeah, kinda," he said, perhaps giving his simple friend the benefit of the doubt.

Jerry didn't care, he was feeling optimistic, like maybe, just maybe this all might work out in his favor after all.

Until Vogel said, "You know, this is it for me."

"What's it?"

"We've got the nonprofit set up, we have the website. We even have some donations starting to roll in . . ."

"What you need is a book," Jerry said. "Did you see how that guy, Goforth, did it? No telling how much that brings in every week. Just take the stuff from the website, have somebody put it all together for you. That's how they do that sort of thing. It's called ghostwriting."

"It would have to be somebody who gets it," Vogel said,

mouth full. "It couldn't be just anybody."

"What about Orlando's wife?" Brad said. "She's into this. You know she put a book out."

"Maybe," Vogel said. "But the lawsuit. It's become a distraction for me. I'm not feeling it anymore, you know what I mean?"

Here we go again, Jerry thought, and all his fears about his job and his family came rushing back in, just as if they had never left. What was it with this guy? After every triumph he wants to throw in the towel. He was going to have to talk Vogel down from the ledge once more, just the way he had in New York after the *Today* show interview.

The pancakes stopped working for Jerry. He put down his fork. "I'm sorry, no, I don't know what you mean."

"I don't think I'm feeling it anymore," Vogel said, looking inside himself now rather than at Jerry. "I'm really serious. If we lose, no appeal. I'm not even sure I won't withdraw the petition. I mean, it's all downhill from here, isn't it? What do we care what some judge thinks, right? We have everything to lose and very little to gain. That's when it's time to fold up your tents. That's what I've always told my clients. You have to be practical."

"Oh, no, no, no," Jerry said. "You are *not* withdrawing that petition." He punctuated his directive with an angry knuckle to the table, which drew Vogel out of himself, as well as involuntary glances from the tables around them.

"Well, with all due respect, Jerry, I appreciate all your help. But it's my case, I can do what I want with it. All I wanted was to get the word out about a way of life that can really make people's lives better. And we're doing that. The website and the chance to talk to people all over the country. It's surpassed all my expectations. I don't care anything about bringing down Obamacare, you know that."

"But don't you see? All these people are only interested in all of this crap because they think it's going to protect them from having to buy health insurance, thereby cutting Obamacare off at the knees. If you drop the lawsuit, you're out. They won't care about you anymore."

"That's not the way Goforth feels about," Vogel countered.

"He gets what I'm talking about. And he runs a nationwide mega-church. What about that?"

"I've lost my wife...my, my, my friend," Jerry sputtered, referring to Pattie, "because of this thing and now you're going to come along and give up? No way. We're staying in this thing until the bitter end or until I get my job back, whichever comes first!"

Vogel looked around. People were pretending not to notice, but now couldn't help but listen.

Leaning in, whispering, Vogel said, "What are you talking about?"

Jerry looked like he was going to cry, but then he started breathing heavily.

"What's the matter?"

"Nothing," Jerry said. "Just give me a minute. I'll be fine."

Trying to lighten the mood, Vogel said, "'I told you not to watch *Coronary Country* last night.'" When Jerry didn't bite, he said, "What is it?"

"Nothing," Jerry said. "Give me a minute."

Vogel looked on helplessly for a full minute, the dawning illumination deepening the creases between his eyes. "We've got to get you to a hospital."

"Yeah, right," Jerry said. "How's that going to look?"

"Who cares how it's going to look?" Vogel said. "How's it going to look if you don't? You can't do what I do, Jerry. It doesn't work that way. You're...completely unconscious. The hospital is your only option."

"No! No hospitals. No doctors. I just need to lay down, that's all."

Jerry got up and started toward the door. Vogel stood up too and pulled out a couple of twenties, left them on the table and followed Jerry out to the parking lot, where he took the keys to the rented Lincoln. He helped Jerry into the passenger seat and then got behind the wheel.

"Let me take you to a hospital."

"No!" Jerry said, fiddling with the seat controls. Momentarily, he got his seatback to recline. "Just...get me back to the hotel. This happens all the time. Nothing new. I just have to lay down, that's all. I'll be fine."

Vogel did as instructed. En route, he eyed Jerry and finally spoke up. "Don't avoid the pain," he said. "That's the worst thing you could do. Confront it. Feel it. Go directly into it."

Jerry didn't respond. He kept his eyes closed, but he was listening.

"The pain is one thing," Vogel said. "But resisting the pain is another. We might call this suffering. It adds exponentially to the pain, and the damage. Without resistance, you find that you can accept the pain, that it won't kill you. That way, you can go into it and allow it to teach you what it has to teach you."

Jerry had to admit that under Vogel's guidance he was able to calm down. But once the car stopped, he went back to his tried and true method of gutting it out.

"We are not dropping the petition," Jerry said, ambling toward the entrance to the hotel.

"All right, all right," Vogel said. "We're not dropping the petition."

* * *

The church had given each man his own room in a nice hotel. Their flight was leaving first thing in the morning. There had been some talk on the way to brunch about seeing the town. But after Jerry's coronary episode, he had taken to his bed and must have nodded off.

When he woke up, Vogel was sitting in the chair beside the bed, tapping on his laptop, probably dialed into his blog.

"You know, you shouldn't actually use that thing on your lap," Jerry said. "It'll roast your nads."

Vogel took that laptop off his lap and placed it on the table and reoriented his chair. "They posted the interview already," he said. "Tyler put the link on the blog already too. Getting a lot of questions."

"Great," Jerry said.

"Feeling better?"

"Like Captain Kangaroo said, a good long sleep can cure just about anything."

"I never heard him say that," Vogel said. "You want to tell

me about the job and the wife now?"

"What's to tell? Didn't like that I went on TV down in London."

"And the wife?"

"I was talking about the wife," Jerry said. "It didn't help that she knew I was shtuping the intern." Vogel didn't respond. Jerry knew he wouldn't—too judgmental. "That's over now, too."

At length, Vogel said, "Well, I guess we're just going to have to get you your job back." He closed up his laptop. "You want to go walking around? There's a massive pool out there, hot tub, swim-up bar. You should probably stay away from the hot tub, for more reasons than one."

"As I recall," Jerry said, "we didn't finish our brunch."

Chapter 25

The hearing in Federal District Court in London, Kentucky, was fast approaching. Meanwhile, Vogel had become something of a minor celebrity, especially so in his new hometown of London, a true Republican enclave. They decided to curtail their reality tour and return to that small town to prepare.

Vogel's law firm was most accommodating, providing office space, computers and all the clerical support they would need. They stayed at Jerry's mother's farm, although Vogel spent an ever-increasing amount of time at Amy's house—against Jerry's better judgment—an opposition Jerry fully acknowledged may have been based upon his own Judeo-Christian moral box, into which Vogel simply would never fit.

"They're going to throw *Lundman v. McKown* at you," Jerry said. "It's mentioned in the brief. They started making that case on the *Today* show, if you will recall. Matt talking about blood transfusions?"

A 1995 decision studied in virtually every law school across the country, *Lundman v. McKown* was a Minnesota Court of Appeals case that upheld the state's right to intervene in medical decisions concerning children over against a parent's right to the free exercise of her religion, in that case Christian Science. It wasn't a federal decision but since the Supreme Court had never decided such a case directly, it was generally considered to be the law of the land. In other words, most experts agreed that if the Supreme Court ever took such a case, the ruling in *Lundman* represented generally how it would rule.

If Vogel's case were ever struck down by a federal court, the ruling would likely be an extension of governmental prerogative to intervene in medical decisions, as described in the *Lundman* case, to not only include children but then also adults as well. In both Jerry's mind and Vogel's, this was an extremely unlikely outcome. But if *Vogel v. Sebelius* (named for Kathleen Sebelius, Secretary of the U.S. Department of Health and Human Services) were to ever be overruled by a federal court—i.e., if it were to be closed as the massive loophole around Obamacare that it had the potential to become—this would be exactly what the court would have to decide.

"Easily distinguishable," Vogel dismissed. "I'm an adult. I can make my own decisions about how and when to exercise my religion. And it's not a federal precedent. In fact, their inclusion of this case in their brief only serves to demonstrate that they have no leg to stand on and they know it."

"But that's how it's going to go down," Jerry said. "If it goes down."

This led into a recapitulation of Vogel's position that children come into the world unconscious—original sin, Jerry interjected, now sufficiently familiar with this part of the philosophy—and so recourse to the unconscious healthcare system, so called, set up to meet the needs of unconscious people, would probably be their only option. And he, as a parent, would have no qualms about doing just that, although he would insist that neither the doctor nor any of the other healthcare providers, so called, talk to the child while treating him or her. That's when it begins, this indoctrination into the concreteness of the material world and how their mythology is the way, the truth and the life. And he would have no issues about state-ordered inoculations, either. If the world is an illusion, those things won't cause any problems at all.

If it hurts, don't do it, is what Vogel would teach his kids. Because that's where it begins, with the shot in the arm and the poke of the finger. The children know we should not be doing these things, that's why they cry. But if mommy and daddy are standing there nodding their approval like it's some religious ceremony—and that's exactly what it is—what is the child to think? This is all part of the scheme to indoctrinate little junior.

Jerry remembered the tableau from his own childhood:

blood samples, vaccinations, that awful feeling of the tongue depressor at the back of his throat—he had hated them all and still did. Could his hatred of medical treatment predate his father's botched heart surgery? As he listened to Vogel's descriptions, Jerry thought that perhaps it did.

"They're also going to try to say that these aren't really my beliefs, based on my past medical treatment."

With a laugh, Jerry said, "Well, they would be wrong about that. I'll be your witness. I think you put that strategy to rest at the deposition."

"I'm not too worried about it. I'm not worried at all, in fact. I think we're going to win easily, at least in the early going. But I want to make a real statement. I want to make the difference between consciousness and rationality clear for all to see."

When Vogel stopped to ponder the notion, Jerry began to do likewise, but on an unrelated issue, as was often his wont during these prep sessions. And in hindsight, Jerry would imagine that maybe that was their real purpose, over and above the lawyerly need to think through any eventuality that might come to pass in the hearing—that by all accounts Vogel was likely to win no matter what.

Jerry could not remember such intellectual camaraderie, not since law school when he and some of his closest fellows would prepare for semester-ending exams and the conversations would ease into the more controversial aspects of the subjects at hand—state's rights, perhaps, or redistribution—the battle lines for these skirmishes generally drawn by party affiliation. These makeshift debates would halt their locomotive momentum well shy of fisticuffs as all felt the overwhelming restraint of the looming academic measure that actually mattered more than a whit, for which they had studied not a whit all semester long. Vogel had never been a party to any of these sessions. He was not in Jerry's circle of friends. But now Jerry wished he had been. He wished he had been, indeed.

"What about homosexuality?" Jerry asked.

"Homosexuality?" Vogel said, drawn out of his meditations on how he might distinguish rationality from consciousness. "Let's stick to the plot, shall we?"

"No, no," Jerry said. "It's going to come up sooner or later. It does for everybody these days. Now, I know you. You must have some sort of a position on it and it must be related somehow. Out with it."

"Too late in the day," Vogel protested. But when Jerry wouldn't have it, Vogel gave in. "First of all, that's not my experience, as you know. And that's where you should start with any intellectual discussion of issues that relate to the conduct of others. Because the real way to discern what we should do is to go inside ourselves, into the very molecules of our being, so to speak, the space between the atoms, and ask ourselves how we feel at any given moment. If there's anything you can't keep yourself from doing, don't run from the conduct in question. But rather, explore it and see how it makes you feel. And be honest about that. How you feel will always show you the way. Top-down morality simply doesn't work. It's completely ineffective."

"I think it's safe to say that your experience has actually been the opposite," Jerry offered.

"Indeed, sir," Vogel said. "But the opposite isn't as far away as you might think. Heterosexuality, bisexuality, homosexuality, these are all made up categories. They're ideas. They're not real. They don't exist except in the virtual space of mind. Whenever anyone tries to take on the characteristics of a category—whether it be homosexual, American, Republican, even male or female—they're moving further away from the truth of who they are rather than closer to it. They're attempting to add this feature to their egos to make themselves feel and appear to be more than they are."

"Like Nicole and material wealth," Jerry said, putting it together in his mind.

"Exactly," Vogel said. "She feels she needs a big house and a nice car to be somebody, just like I used to think. Or—who was it—your aunt? Whose ego attached unique illnesses to itself to feel more important. More alive."

"That's right," Jerry said.

"We move closer to the truth of who we are by shedding

these identities as we go through life until finally, instead of saying, 'I am heterosexual, I am Democrat, I am a man,' we can simply say, 'I am.'"

"I am," Jerry repeated.

"Doesn't that feel peaceful? Just to say that out loud like that?"

"I am," Jerry said again. "Yeah, a little, I guess."

"That's a good way to bring yourself back to the moment, just by saying, 'I am.' It feels good."

"I am," Jerry repeated.

Vogel now looked as if he wanted to get it all out, once and for all. He leaned into the table, his hands laced at his chin. "You know, for me it comes back to those gender roles we talked about before. You can have two people of opposite gender together in the same household, but if one of them is trying to be the other, what's the difference? If the woman is trying to be a man, or the man misunderstands that his role is to be in service to the feminine principle—we might also say feminine principal," Vogel spelled out the second version of the word, "—then there's no real difference between this scenario and a same-sex household, is there? Perhaps consciousness is trying to reflect this imbalance back to us, so that through awareness this critical balance will be restored. And it needs to be, because true femininity and true masculinity trump false femininity and false masculinity every time."

"That's a rather novel approach," Jerry said.

"Gay is actually a religion, my friend," Vogel said.

"Gay is a religion," Jerry repeated.

"That's right. It's a religion long suppressed that's finally getting the constitutional protection it and all religions deserve." When Jerry's expression registered incredulity, Vogel kept going, ticking off items on his fingers one by one: "It's practiced by heterosexuals just as much as homosexuals—lots of heteros just love it. Many people—perhaps most—who engage in what could be termed homosexual acts don't practice the Gay religion but go right on with their otherwise heterosexual lives. You have to make a public profession of faith—coming out, right?" Jerry reluctantly shrugged in agreement. "And you have to have faith in certain things. You have to believe, for example, as their High Priestess Lady Gaga has preached, that people are 'born this way,' right? That's an article of faith, not a fact. It's a belief."

"I guess," Jerry said, unconvinced.

"The Greeks and Romans had temples to gods like Eros and Aphrodite with sexual rites and temple prostitutes, didn't they?"

"I'm not sure, I wasn't there," Jerry said.

"How is the Gay religion any different from that? And that's all well and good, nothing to get excited or upset about. It's been around for eons, in other words. But the phenomenon can be easily explained when you stop to realize that we have a reproductive system, and that system is as involuntary as digestion or circulation."

Jerry recalled that Vogel had touched on this line of reasoning in the deposition, but he couldn't muster any more engagement about it, himself. Vogel had been right, it was too late in the day. He leaned back in his chair and waited for Vogel to finish.

"It's rationality—mostly unconscious rationality—that intervenes to give us all the variety in sexual activity that's so prevalent in our society today. We would all just mate like animals, otherwise, with very little fanfare about it."

Vogel was reinvigorated, clearly, by the topic, but finally looked outside himself to see that Jerry was not. Jerry assumed that what came next was an attempt to draw him back into the fray. "You're party is opposed to gay marriage, is it not?"

"Somewhat," was Jerry's guarded response.

"The better analysis of the issue, then, for your purposes would be under the First Amendment establishment clause—separation of church and state—rather than the equal protection clause of the Fourteenth Amendment."

"Is that right?" Jerry said.

"The government only supports opposite-sex *civil* marriages, not the religious ceremony, which isn't necessary and isn't always performed."

"Right."

"The government only supports these marriages because they're universally supported and because it's in the government's best interest to do so."

"Ok."

"Same-sex marriage isn't universally supported. That makes it simply a religious rite unique to the Gay religion, nothing more. Therefore, the establishment clause forbids the government from having anything to do with it."

"That, too, is a novel approach," Jerry said. Truth was, he hadn't really stayed with it. He was tired and Vogel's late burst of energy was making him more tired. Tilting his chair back, effectively done for the day, he said, "I am" again, listening to himself say it.

"You want to know the real crux of the matter?" Vogel said, leaning further into the table, when it was clear Jerry wasn't going to pick up on the political angle.

"'It's what I live for.'" Jerry gave it his best John Gielgud voice. "*Arthur*? Remember that one?"

"It's never the behavior that matters," Vogel said, ignoring Jerry's impersonation. "It's that the individual, him or herself, *believes* that the behavior makes them feel bad. That's the only reason anyone ever seeks out the advice of a so-called mental health professional, isn't it? Because they feel bad, right?"

"Guess so."

"Now, the solution that the proponents of the Science religion—the psychologists and the psychiatrists, by and large—have come up with is to simply tell these individuals—no matter what behavior we're talking about—that it *shouldn't* make them feel bad. That's the best they've come up with. If we're talking about homosexuality, they advise that there's nothing wrong with it, you were born that way, right?"

"Right," Jerry agreed. "Lady Gaga."

"But the reality is, the behavior doesn't actually make them feel bad. They feel bad—we feel bad, all of us have something—and that feeling bad drives all sorts of behaviors with all sorts of negative side effects and conesquences."

"Just like with the drugs," Jerry said. "The antibiotics."

"Just like with the antibiotics," Vogel agreed. "Once you go inside yourself and dissolve the *feeling bad*, then people become as boring—as lacking in drama—as...well, myself, for example."

Jerry let out a hearty laugh at that one. "Yes, you have become pretty boring in your old age, I have to admit."

"No need to judge anyone's behavior. Simply direct them inward and eventually the behaviors become healthy and peaceful and joyful and drama-free for the individual. And much less interesting to the casual observer."

"I am," Jerry said once more, and then he caught himself. He'd done it again. Vogel had taken the conversation into that uncomfortable place. End of discussion, Jerry wanted to say, but he steadied himself and thought again about the upcoming hearing. And maybe that little bit of "I am" consciousness he had experienced had elucidated his brain.

"Why don't you do that thing you do with the judge?" Jerry said.

"What thing?"

"You know, that little parlor trick you do when you get people to feel their feet and their hands."

"Yeah, right," Vogel said. "I'm going to do that with the judge."

In the moment that Vogel sat thinking about it, Jerry looked at the clock. They had been in a groove with this stuff all day long and it felt good. But now Jerry was tired. Maybe a little too tired. At the same time, he felt that pick-me-up that the realization that it's the weekend always brings...even when you've been put out of your eighty-hour-a-week job.

"I'm wiped," he said. "I'm getting out of here."

"Wait a minute." Vogel had gone inside himself again. "Why *not* do that exercise with the judge? That's a great idea."

"I was joking," Jerry said. "It's a terrible idea. If you try it, he's going to toss you in the lock up and throw away the key for a while."

"But if we keep arguing this rationally, eventually we're going to lose," Vogel said. "*That's* the philosophy. The exercise *is* the philosophy. That's the only way to demonstrate the difference. He's got to allow it."

"Bradley, courtrooms are bastions of rationality. That's what they're all about. There's no getting around that. He's not going to let you do it."

"Right," Vogel said. "Right. . ."

But Jerry could see that Vogel wasn't convinced. "Would you snap out of it already? I'm wiped. I'm getting out of here. You coming?"

"I'm heading to Amy's," Vogel said. "And you won't see me 'til Monday. We're driving down to Knoxville for the weekend."

"All right," Jerry said, with a little singsong of warning in his voice. He packed up his briefcase and was about to clear the doorway to the conference room. Vogel was still seated. "Have a good time."

"Uhh, Jerry?" Vogel said, stopping him.

"Yeah?"

"It's all about feeling good," Vogel said. "Inside. The better you feel inside, the better the world you perceive around you will be. Because the world around you, beginning with your physical body, is merely a reflection of that inner space. And if there's something in there that keeps you from feeling good—some negativity, that is to say pain—you have to root that out through awareness, or it's going to turn into an illness eventually."

"Okay," Jerry said. "Thanks. I'll remember that." He leaned toward the hallway again.

"Jerr?"

"Yeah." Jerry sighed.

"It doesn't matter if it's physical or emotional pain. Pain is pain. It's there to teach you something. Treat the physical as spiritual and the spiritual as physical. Because it's all the same thing. No difference. Just spend as much time feeling that pain as possible and eventually you can dissolve it. The unconscious thought that was causing the pain will give itself up to your consciousness and you'll be free to feel good all the time. Of course, there may be multiple sources of pain in there, but you'll feel a little better each time you resolve one of them. I like to think of it as inner posture, how you hold yourself inside your body. Keep one inner eye on your inner posture at all times. From time to time, take stock of your physical health. Is that not a perfect picture of the state of your soul, as well? As you become more aware, you'll see that it is."

"I got it," Jerry said. "Have a nice weekend."

"Just feel good, whatever it takes. If you can feel it, you can heal it. Conscious thoughts can't control you; only unconscious thoughts can do that."

"'Neither a borrower nor a lender be,' eh?" Jerry said.

Vogel smiled and tipped his head. He'd been caught out. "Nice reference. Shakespeare."

"*Gilligan's Island*, actually. Remember the one where the movie producer comes to the island and they do the musical version of *Hamlet*?"

"Right," Vogel said. "Maybe if you had sung it."

"While Tennessee might seem like another dimension, it's only a few minutes away. I'll see you on Monday."

Jerry was down the hall this time. "Jerry?"

"What!"

"Thanks," Vogel said. "For everything."

"'If you can feel it, you can heal it.' I like that, it's catchy." On his way out the door, Jerry said, "Make that the title of your book."

* * *

Why was Vogel telling him to feel good?

Jerry didn't reflect upon this question until he was in his Cherokee and well on his way home. He didn't feel good, now that Vogel had mentioned it, he didn't feel good at all. He felt...congested, all over, from head to toe, like every cell in his body hadn't taken the trash out in a week.

He stiffened, uneasy. And why was Vogel thanking him? Long overdue, of course, but why now? It was almost as if he were saying goodbye. Quickly Jerry began to tease out the possibilities. Vogel had talked about dropping the case many times. Maybe he had made up his mind to stay in

Knoxville. Maybe he and Amy were moving away from her crazy ex, starting a new life down in Tennessee. Or maybe he had only said they were going to Knoxville, and they were really traveling much farther afield, because if that's what was happening, if they were really moving away, a state line was no buffer for a guy like her Shamus Crace. Knoxville wasn't nearly far enough down the road.

Then again, maybe it wasn't Vogel who would be the one to leave. Guys like Vogel knew things. Maybe he knew how Jerry's heart problem would work out in the end. How else could it work out?

Jerry refused this thought entry into his consciousness. He left it where it always lurked, just below his awareness, where he could feed it with constant unnoticed negative thoughts, and from whence it could control his every behavior.

Jerry took out his cell phone and dialed up Vogel as he drove. He needed clarification. But he got no answer, as usual. With a shake of his head, he put the phone back in his shirt pocket and drove.

Gosh, it was a nice day. With his mind on Vogel's odd behavior, Jerry didn't notice that until he parked his Cherokee in his mother's barnyard. The sun was almost down and the sky was clear. It was supposed to be a nice weekend. Maybe he should drive on up to Cincinnati to see the girls. Jerry sat in his vehicle looking around at the chickens. His mother was inside, there was her Buick. He would put it in the garage for her a little later.

Maybe it was simple jealousy that made him want to stand between Amy and Vogel, rather than any protective concern vis-à-vis Shamus Crace. Jerry had met her only once. Seemed like a nice enough woman, attractive. He could certainly see what Vogel saw in her. A little older than Vogel but he didn't seem to want kids anyway, so what was the difference?

Jerry sat in his car, imagining them on their way down I75 toward Knoxville. It caused his heart some pain to think of it, but a good kind of pain, or so he thought, a motivational pain. It looked like so much fun, just the sort of fun he wanted to be having himself right about now.

He couldn't go see the girls. He just couldn't. Never mind that Nicole would throw a fit if he showed up without three days' warning. He couldn't face them in this state of utter failure.

He got out of the truck and went to the front door of the house and leaned in. "Ma?"

"In the kitchen," she said.

Jerry could smell the unmistakable aroma of meatloaf. He loved his mother's meatloaf. "I won't be home for dinner," he said.

"It's ready now if you want it."

"Sorry," he said. "I'll make it up to you."

He just couldn't sit at home with his mother on a Friday night either, not the way he was feeling. There was a little bar he knew about over in Corbin where you could get a decent cheeseburger and have a beer.

On the other hand, if it was ready now...

* * *

About a half hour later, Jerry was back in his Cherokee, heading down I75 toward Corbin, the only place he could get a drink in this otherwise dry county. There was a sign for Cumberland Falls. Maybe he'd drive on down there. Boy, wouldn't that be depressing this time of year? Nobody around, down among the barren trees, the rippling of the waters asking why he wasn't somewhere else and with his own kind, the other human beings.

"Nope, the home of Colonel Sanders it is," he said. He'd be in Corbin in about fifteen minutes.

Jerry had changed into a black sweater and jeans. He felt like this was what the local femininas would like to see him in. Heck, it had worked out well for Vogel around these parts. Maybe it could work out for him, too.

As he drove, Jerry remembered that he was still wearing his wedding band. He kept it in place for his mother's sake, thinking she might have noticed. He hadn't told her about the divorce yet. He couldn't bring himself to discuss it with her. He tugged at the band but his hands had gotten so fat that it wouldn't come off. He'd have to get some soap on it.

A few minutes later, he pulled into the parking lot of the watering hole he remembered. It was empty. He cruised up toward the door. A lease sign was in the window.

"All I want is a frickin' cheeseburger and a beer," he said, hitting the steering wheel. "Is that too much to ask?"

He let out a deep sigh then after a moment got back on Highway 25 and headed toward town. There was the Harlan Sanders Café, still open. He looked hard into the windows as he rolled by, looking for signs of the kind of life he was looking for. Nothing doing. It was, after all, just a glorified KFC with a little museum attached. He drove around downtown. Nothing cooking there either.

Well...he'd seen an Applebee's just past I75. He headed back that way to catch the last of the happy hour crowd. How depressing was this?

Chapter 26

The following morning, Jerry awoke to bright sunlight in his childhood bed. He'd had that cheeseburger, with bacon, along with a side of fries and three very tall beers. None of the local women wanted anything to do with him. Most of them were already teamed up and the others, in groups, kept to themselves. He ended up talking to the attractive bartender—his name was Mark—the whole night, and tipping him too much for the camaraderie.

There was still some coffee in the pot. It was still warm. His mother had not been gone long. There was a note asking him to do some chores for her. It closed with, "Always remember how much I love you." His mother didn't write such things normally.

What the hell? Jerry thought. Is she running off to Knoxville too? Or had she simply picked up on the mess his life had become?

This was just too weird. He drank the rest of the coffee while he read the paper, then he got dressed and went outside to the barn.

Jerry decided to start with the animals—give 'em a little extra food. No one had said the cows needed any supplemental feeding, though. Why his mother had mentioned it before, Jerry wasn't sure. There were sufficient round bales scattered around. He'd seen them on his drive-around when he'd gone out to see his cousins. Maybe she just thought he needed the exercise, or maybe she wanted to get rid of the square bales in the loft because they'd been there for a while. Whatever the reason, he felt like doing a little manual labor to clear his head and that's what came to mind. There was some concern as to the strength of his heart but it had been a while since he'd experienced any pain at all, and so long as he worked slowly, Jerry was sure that he would be just fine.

On the rack to the left of the sliding door, he found a pair of work gloves and put them on before mounting the ladder to the loft where the hay was stacked. Even the climb was an exertion, but he went slowly and it felt good. He was glad to have the gloves covering his milky white hands when he lifted the first bale by the string and manhandled it to the edge of the loft and then kicked it over the edge. He watched it explode on the concrete floor, just as he had done as a kid. That felt good too. When he'd done that three more times, he climbed down again and took a push broom and drove the hay out the back door. There he lifted it by the armfuls into the bunks. Some cattle standing nearby saw what he was doing and came over to get a jump on the competition.

When he had finished, he stood back for a moment and surveyed his handiwork. Eric wouldn't have approved of his methods, but the cows didn't seem to mind the extra dust in the hay and he had gotten some mind-clearing exercise out the deal. Not to mention the fun of seeing the bales explode when they hit the deck. He went back in and swept a little more of the dust away and then hung up the gloves.

His work complete, Jerry walked out of the barn toward the house and looked up at the pristine blue of the sky. After his bale-tossing enterprise and the sweeping and the lifting and more sweeping, he was perspiring. The cool breeze felt so good. He decided he was going to try to do something like that every day. Back in Cincinnati, maybe he would just go for a walk. Maybe he'd start going to the plush congressional gym back in DC. He was breathing heavily.

Then the pain hit him in the chest all at once. The episodes that came before had all been warning tremors. This was the earthquake. Jerry went down, first one knee, then the next, then face first into the dirt. In his peripheral vision, he saw the dust kick up in a soft gray plume. He could actually feel the sun on his neck.

As he went down, his first instinct was to reach for his cell phone. But he fumbled it. He saw it come to rest in front of his face. He reached for it.

No signal.

Behind him he could hear one of the chickens making her own casual investigation.

* * *

Jerry was a ten-year-old boy again. He was wearing a mask and snorkel and fins. He was swimming around peacefully underwater in the dark. He hadn't felt this good in years. He would have to go up for air soon. Up there. Up toward the light, he could see his heart beating.

There's no way I'm going up there, he thought. That's where the pain is. More pain than he had ever felt in his whole life—combined.

He was content to swim, down here, in the warm water. There was no pressure on him, either, to swim up there, take a breath. This was nice.

As he swam, Jerry's ten-year-old suspicion rose. Why didn't he need oxygen? He seemed to remember from his childhood an amazing breath control. He could stay under a lot longer back then, as he recalled, than he would ever dream of attempting these days. Even so, the pressure would mount little by little until he had to emerge like a rocket from the surface of the pool. He would pretend he was the flying saucer shot out of the submarine on *Voyage to the Bottom of the Sea.*

Then he understood what was happening. That regardless of the lack of pressure, he had only a few minutes to make his decision. That brain damage—at the very least—would ensue if he stayed down here much longer.

Maybe I'm good down here, he thought. This wasn't so bad, swimming around all day. Warm. Fingers pruny. His body little and perfect again. Maybe this was his version of heaven.

But it was awfully dark—and getting darker. He looked up toward his heart and saw that the window around it was closing. In the light that remained he looked around himself as he swam. There didn't seem to be any white escalators opening up for his convenience, and no other light source at all. That could only mean one thing...

He hesitated a moment longer. This really was a tough decision. He made one more circle around the tepid pool, the dimming sidelights flickering aqua and blue through the water. Flippers flipping, he adjusted his mask and snorkel. This was nice. He felt so good, his body devoid of any negativity at all. It was as if his father had never died. He felt only the pure joy of being. He stopped and looked up. If nothing else, he could use this as a reference point, a baseline toward which he would work all the rest of his days—if he had any more days—this was a promise he made to himself.

Oh, boy, little Jerry thought. I can't believe I'm doing this.

He swam up toward the light, toward the heart that as he drew closer he was happy to see was still beating faintly.

* * *

"God damn it!" Jerry said in his head, along with a string of evermore intense expletives. The pain was excruciating. He needed some relief. Could he go back down and swim a little while longer? No, he couldn't. Somehow he knew that as he gasped for air, his nose and mouth just above the rim of water around it.

What was it Vogel had said? Don't try to avoid the pain, but rather go into it.

Haven't I just done that?

Feel it as intensely as you can.

Isn't that what I'm doing now?

Jerry was panicking. The pain was too much. He was going to die, so with nothing to lose, inspiration came. Somebody give me a hand here. He focused his attention like a laser on his heart. He gave it all he had, pushing into the pain, just as if he were lowering his shoulder to break down a door, something he had never done before. He'd only seen it on TV.

And what do you know? He pushed through it! Oh, it was still there. It was as if it were surrounding him now. But the thing was, Vogel was right, this wasn't going to kill him. It couldn't kill him. In fact, he couldn't be killed. Oh, yes, death would come one day, but he couldn't be killed, not until it was time for that, and when the body was gone, he would somehow still be. Death is but a transition. Vogel was right, in pain there is great wisdom.

But he had more to do here. What else had Vogel told him?

Let the pain teach you.

Let the pain teach me, eh? Teach me what? All right, Jerry thought. What does this feel like? What's the meaning behind this feeling he'd held in his heart his entire life?

Fear.

Okay, but you have to have fear *of* something. Fear of what?

But all he could get was fear, that was as granular as he could go with it. And he began to think that an awareness of a generalized sense of fear just wasn't going to cut it. That to beat this thing, he needed to go deeper.

As Jerry thought this, the story of Peter, the disciple, who began to slip into the waves when he took his eyes off of Jesus as they walked together upon the water, came to him. There was his Vacation Bible School teacher, Mrs. Griggs. He hadn't thought of her in years.

And a moment later, the light of consciousness was extinguished.

* * *

The first thing Jerry noticed when he woke up was that his chest had been shaved.

"What the hell?" he said, looking down and then around.

His eyes focused on someone who was seated low beside his bed. As his mind cleared, he understood that it was his mother.

"What's happening?" he listened to himself say. "What's going on?"

"Thank you, Jesus," she said, standing up beside his bed. "You're in the hospital. Ever'thing's gonna be all right. You just rest."

There were lines going into his arm, which was restrained by a Velcro band. There were EKG monitors attached to his chest. He had a green oxygen line affixed to his nose, which he presently removed.

"No, no, no, not the hospital," he said. "Ma, you gotta get me out of here."

A nurse, having heard the commotion, entered the room.

"Please, Mr. Riggs, you have to leave that alone."

Jerry was tugging at the Velcro restraint. "They're going to do a zipper job on me! No zipper job!" He pushed the nurse away and she left. She was going to get help. He didn't have much time.

The nurse came back with a doctor and then another nurse. The doctor, wearing the same aqua-colored scrubs as the others, took command. "Mr. Riggs, you've had a tremendous trauma. Your heart muscle has all but given out. We're out of time here."

"My heart is better," Jerry said. "It's getting better."

The doctor shook his head and was about to remonstrate when Jerry saw his brother, Eric, the state trooper in his uniform, shading the doorway. "No zipper job!" Jerry said to Eric. "Don't let them operate. I'm in full command of my faculties and I refuse all medical treatment. Do you hear me? I refuse all medical treatment."

"Mr. Riggs," the doctor said as he worked, "your condition is irreversible."

"Do you see how they work?" Jerry said. "How they brainwash you from the moment you step in the door? They're trying to kill me! Where's Vogel? I need to speak to Brad Vogel. He's my attorney. Is he here?"

Jerry watched as his brother looked at their mother with alarm in his eyes. After a moment, Mrs. Riggs was the one to speak.

"We'll get 'im, honey. But right now, you have to rest."

The doctor was working on his intravenous line, while one of the nurses restrained Jerry, and the other attached a second Velcro restraint to his other arm. He could feel a sedative enter his bloodstream. He didn't have much time. He would have to make his case quickly.

To Eric, he said, "They did a full battery of tests on me up at Sibley in DC. Compare the data. I guarantee that my heart is getting better, not worse. They're trying to kill me, Eric. You've got to get me out of here."

"What was the doctor's name?" he heard someone say. Was it Eric who had asked? That would be a good sign if it was. The sedative was coming on fast though.

"Doctor Van Nostrand," was all Jerry could remember to say. "Doctor Van Nostrand, that was the guy. Doctor Van Nos...trand...."

* * *

When he woke up again, his head hurt like the dickens. It was mostly dark in the room. His hands were no longer restrained. There were no lines running into them. No oxygen.

He was alone but for a lone seated figure beside the bed, where his mother had sat. It was a man in uniform. A state trooper uniform. It took Jerry a few moments to recall where he was and all that had happened.

"Eric?"

"Eric's not here," the man said. "I work with your brother. Nothin' to worry about, pad'ner. We gotcha covered. Just get as much rest as you can."

"What time is it?"

"It's three thirty-eight in the morning," the trooper said.

The salient question Jerry didn't think to ask was, What day it was. He didn't try to figure it all out and soon he fell asleep again.

* * *

"They got Vogel," Eric said.

Jerry woke late the following morning. His mother had since replaced the overnight state trooper. After a few shared words, Eric had replaced her.

"What do you mean, they got him?" Jerry asked.

"He was gunned down outside a hotel in Knoxville," Eric confirmed. "He and his consort."

Jerry wasn't strong enough to handle the pain that this information by all rights should have generated, and at some level he knew it. He thrashed his head from side to side a couple of times, hoping the exertion might provide some avenue to channel the pain out of his body. Denial might also have been the way to go if anyone other than his brother had been the bearer of the news.

Jerry closed his eyes and said a little prayer. Help me, Brad. You gotta help me with this. *Allow the pain to be there,* was what came back from the ether. *Don't judge it, just allow it to be there.*

"Yeah, okay," Jerry said out loud. Then after a long pause, he opened his eyes and said to Eric, "The crazy ex? Shamus Crace?"

"He's the most likely suspect. We picked him up heading east. He's from over in Harlan. If he'd gotten up into those mountains, we'd never see his stupid ass again."

Jerry pulled in and let out a deep breath, imagining the city of Knoxville. About the same distance south of London as Lexington is north, it was a place he'd spent a fair amount of time in over the years growing up. He never should have let Vogel go there. He shook his head again and did as he had been told, allowing the pain to sit there on his shoulder like a gargoyle without judgment of it.

Jerry asked, "Are you sure about him?"

"Not one hundred percent, no," Eric said. "It coulda been a set up. He wouldn't shut up about being the fall guy. He was in the area. Says he was just keeping an eye on her, and that he never would have killed her too. Murder weapon was in the back of his Monte Carlo, though."

"Better post a guard at his cell," Jerry advised. "Jack Ruby will get him in prison and the case will be closed."

Eric didn't say anything. That probably wasn't going to happen. No resources for that sort of thing. It was only the personal connection that allowed a state trooper to be posted in Jerry's room.

"And the district court hearing?" Jerry asked.

"Talked to the lawyers in Vogel's office. It's supposed to be tomorrow. They say the case'll be dismissed without...."

Jerry nodded. "Yeah."

He looked out the window. The sun was bright and beaming in. On a distant hill he could see snow on the ground. He didn't want to think about all that he and Vogel had worked for, or about his job and what this might mean for his future employment.

He wasn't ready to know just yet about Nicole and the girls, either, and whether they had been informed and whether they were concerned or had visited. He needed to ease into all of this, his new reality.

"What about me?" Jerry asked. "No surgery, I see."

"It all seemed too neat, with Vogel gone," Eric said. "And all your talk about big healthcare. I told the doc if he didn't get all those lines out of you, he'd be charged with assault and spend a night in jail at the very least. That was enough to get him gone."

Jerry smiled. "Thanks."

"I hope you know what you're doing," Eric said. "If you die on me, they'll prob'ly take my badge."

"I'm not going to die," Jerry said. "I think I've finally figured out how to kick this thing."

"Daddy had heart problems," Eric said. "Stands to reason you would too. And me."

"You see," Jerry said, pointing. "That's just what they want you to think. They want you to think it's inevitable, because then it will be." He looked at his brother. There was a moment of meaning between them, maybe the first they'd shared since they were kids. "But what if it doesn't work that way? What if we all have a say in it?"

"What if it does work that way?" Eric said.

"That's what I'm going to find out for myself," Jerry said. "What else do we have to do while we're here?"

Hearing himself, Jerry thought: Yes, that's right. The thought brought inspiration and he knew now just what he would do in every detail, just as if he had thought long and hard about it throughout his long sleep. And maybe he had. Even dreams were beginning to come back to him now.

He found a pen and a pad of paper on the table beside his bed and began scribbling. "I need for you to do me a favor. I'm going to need something to read while I'm here." He looked up as he thought. "What was that guy's name? Ah yes, Eckhart Tolle." Vogel had shown him something with the name on it once, a blog post of his, that was it. "Get me everything you can find by this guy. What else? What else?" He thought a moment more. "He mentioned *Zen and the Art of Motorcycle Maintenance* at one point too, I think." He wrote that down, tore off the top sheet and handed it to Eric. "Would you mind running over to Books-a-Million in Corbin and picking these up for me? Mom can do it if you don't have time. I need those right away."

Eric looked at the sheet of paper as Jerry started scribbling again. “I need you to go over to Vogel’s office and tell them to file a motion to join,” he said as he wrote out the words. “I’m going to join Vogel’s case. He’s getting his day in court, if I have anything to say about it. They’re going to need to get that in by the close of business, so do that first. I’ll argue it tomorrow.”

“Are you sure you’re up to that?” Eric asked.

“I don’t know,” Jerry said. “We’ll see. One thing I do know, I can’t stay down like this.” Jerry allowed himself one more remembrance of Brad Vogel. “He was a good friend, one of the best friends I’ve ever had. I’m going to need to grieve, but my heart can’t take that right now. I’ve got to lift the spirits.” He looked back up at Eric. “Last but certainly not least, I’m going to need my laptop and the full DVD box set of *Seinfeld*. Can one of your buddies on the force pick that up for me at Wal-Mart?”

“By the way,” Eric said, nodding his agreement. “We couldn’t find a Dr. Van Nostrand anywhere in DC. We checked everywhere.”

“What are you talking about?” Jerry said, shifting uncomfortably in his bed. He knew the name, of course. It was one of Kramer’s alter egos.

“When they were putting you under, I asked you what your doctor’s name was in Washington and you said Dr. Van Nostrand.”

“Did I?” Jerry said, unsure whether his brother had figured it out and was turning the tables on him, pulling his leg. But no, Eric seemed as serious as ever. “That must have been the drugs talking. It doesn’t matter now, but I think the name was actually Vandelay. Dr. Art Vandelay.”

Chapter 27

Eric offered to come along. So did every single one of Brad Vogel's law partners, though they weren't actually law partners, *per se*, they simply shared office space, not profits and losses. But Jerry turned them all down. This was something he wanted to do alone as an homage to his friend.

And perhaps not quite as significant, he wasn't sure he would win his motion to join Vogel's case, in which case the entire action would be summarily dismissed. He hated to lose. Jerry readily admitted to himself that it probably said something about his character, but he would rather be alone in defeat. And if he won, the time would not be right for celebration, what with his friend's body not yet buried, his funeral yet to come.

It brought Jerry some solace that he had at least forced the Brackman-Hollis boys to make the drive down from Lexington. With the news of Vogel's death, they had all probably high-fived each other and begun filling up the void left in their calendars by the hearing that otherwise would have been cancelled. He wanted to rub their faces in it one more time. And who knew, maybe this Republican judge would take pity on an old colleague.

With a heavy heart, Jerry parked his Cherokee on the street. Two hours free parking, that would be enough. Wearing his darkest suit, his whitest shirt and an overcoat charcoal gray, he passed up the concrete stairs, past the flagpole. To his left stood the stately old Italian Renaissance courthouse, no longer in use except by the Bankruptcy Court. Jerry had stepped foot in it only once, and that was for a self-guided tour one weekday when he was home back during law school, back when he was still impressed by such things. That was before 911, when you could walk right in off the street. He paused to look at it, briefcase swinging ahead slightly with the stoppage of his momentum. There at the back was the beauty of the building, a semicircular rear wing that housed the elliptical second story courtroom. What an elegant setting that would have been for his friend to argue his poetic constitutional challenge...

Shaking his head with resignation, Jerry turned to face the modernist structure that stood before him, the New Federal Courthouse, blocky and ugly. He'd never been in this one at all. He'd never had any federal business to conduct in London and it wasn't the sort of building anybody ever thought about touring. Up a few more steps, through the squared off columns, through the metal detectors, up the elevator to the fourth floor, Jerry was appreciative to the heavens that he didn't have to talk to anyone along the way, not even a nod of acknowledgement. In his hometown, he was a long way from the more familiar halls of power in Washington, DC, ironically enough.

He stepped inside the courtroom and to the left, away from the door. Far away and high up, the judge was already conducting other business. Jerry listened for a moment...sounded like they were setting a trial date in a diversity case—a state court claim where one of the parties was from outside the Commonwealth, with a lot of money at stake. An insurance case, of course.

In his mind, Jerry had pictured this scene differently, though he knew better. He envisioned this hearing as the judge's only concern that day. He imagined the judge blocking off an hour—maybe two—for oral arguments in this landmark case, Vogel's moment in the sun. The reality was that the judge might listen to the attorneys for a few minutes, but he'd already made up his mind based on the briefs that had been filed.

And if Vogel had been here, he would have won.

Up there to the right sat Johnny Football. What was his real name? Jay something. One of the Brackman-Hollis crew. They sent the scrub to do the mopping up. He was up there with the smattering of lawyers who had other business before the court. Jerry had a feeling all of them would say their piece and go before Vogel's case would be called, and there would be no one but the judge, a couple of sheriffs and a couple of clerks to play to in this cavernous hall. Maybe also a janitor, waiting for everyone to leave so he could vacuum the carpet.

And the judge, Steve Van Doren. It was nice to see that he still sported the Republican bi-level brush cut, though his hair seemed more gray than blond now. The Republican horn-rimmed glasses were a new feature. He had been the Chief of Staff for a junior congressman from Kentucky. He and Jerry had been peers at one point, though they didn't know each other well. Jerry had met him once or twice in passing. Then Van Doren's congressman became governor of the state, then a Republican administration took over the White House. The political heavens aligned and the governor put in a good word with the President and now Van Doren was set—federal judges serve for life.

If Obama were replaced by a Republican in the next election, Jerry might have been in for such treatment himself after so many years of faithful service to the Republican Speaker of the House. That might even have been enough to make Nicole happy. But that possibility seemed but a faint glimmer on the horizon now. He would have to win this hearing and then win out in the appeals process, all the way up to the Supreme Court, to have any shot at that sort of career path. But with Vogel gone, the spirit had gone out of the thing. Could he convince the judge that the mantel had now passed to Jerry's shoulders? Could Jerry convince himself of that? Had that happened, in fact? Was Vogel's philosophy now his philosophy too?

He slinked into the back row, holding his briefcase with both hands for security, willing himself into invisibility until his case would be called. After a couple of minutes, Jerry put the briefcase down and wriggled out of his overcoat.

There was a good chance he would only get in one good lick before the judge cut him off and made his ruling, whatever it was, for or against. Two sentences, maybe three, and he wanted to make them count. He tried to think what Vogel might say, what might be his most important point. But there were no media here. The heart attack had knocked him off his game. Jerry had not alerted them that the hearing was back on. And maybe that was for the best.

It was a major step forward for Jerry when he realized that Vogel wouldn't have planned that moment, or any other moment for that matter. He would have spoken out of the moment, as the moment dictated. Which was just as well because Jerry's case was finally called and he had run out of moments.

He walked to the front and sat down at the table to the left. Johnny Football was already in his seat on the right. He was flanked by another suited man, by the looks of him an assistant U.S. attorney, probably from the local office. Someone from the DC office had been handling the case for the Justice Department. Jerry made sure he had gotten a copy of his motion, but it had been too late to get him down here, apparently. That wouldn't be a problem. The stand-in prosecutor would let Brackman-Hollis do their work for them, seeing as they were getting paid by the hour.

"Mr. Riggs," the judge said. "It's good to see you again after so many years."

At first, Jerry was flattered that Judge Van Doren had even remembered who he was, though of course with the filing of his motion to join the night before, the judge would have had ample time to refresh his memory. Jerry bobbed his head appreciatively and then glanced toward Johnny Football. He had had the good sense to wear a white shirt and normal tie to federal court, Jerry noticed...and his face was now Registering the first ounce of concern Jerry had ever witnessed on it. Why was he concerned? Jerry looked back at the bench.

"Thank you, Judge," he said tersely, as he tried to come up with his lines. He was about to say something about science being the state religion now and how it was the federal judiciary that had unwittingly installed its high priests, like the Mullahs in Iran, into positions of power that allowed them to dictate every facet of societal development; along with its unwitting propaganda machine, the media, Hollywood and Madison Avenue indoctrinating each successive generation with the efficiency of Hitler's gas chambers into a religion of death, one based on a philosophy that held that the material world is concrete and neutral, a proposition that can never be proven and is therefore a faith, which must be excluded from government under the First Amendment to our Constitution. And Vogel, if he were alive today, would have gone on to talk about—and demonstrate—how that proposition not only can't be proven but also can actually be disproven.

But after the judge's casual greeting, this was no longer U.S. District Judge Stephen Van Doren sitting up there. He was, for the moment, merely Steve Van Doren, an old acquaintance. Jerry's hope of grandstanding on Vogel's behalf was quickly deflated. High-sounding oration just seemed out of place.

And then it dawned on him: most federal judges he had ever known or seen didn't waste a single breath from the bench, certainly not with small talk like this. These guys were appointed for life, they answered to no one. They were second only to U.S. Ambassadors in their imperiousness, Jerry had observed.

Ergo...this wasn't small talk...What was it then?

No, this wasn't small talk at all. This was a signal, and Johnny Football knew it—Jerry had to admit it, the kid was good. The judge had just told both parties what his ruling would be: he was duty-bound to rule against Jerry's motion to join the case, but he had also offered him a way out. Jerry could move to have the judge recuse himself based on their past association. This motion would be granted, or at least taken under advisement, allowing him time to regroup, get his ducks in a row, recuperate from his heart attack, etc., etc., etc.

Young Jay spoke out of turn, but what else could he do? Jerry, it seemed, would have to move for the recusal—the judge wasn't going to do it himself—so he needed to get Jerry's mind away from that proposition. "You're honor," he said, "I think we can dispense with Mr. Riggs' motion with three words: He has insurance," Jay held up three fingers one at a time as he said the words, "and therefore lacks standing to challenge an individual mandate that doesn't apply to him."

"That's more that three words," Jerry wedged in there, and why not? It might be the last wisecrack he had the chance to pop off in a court of law for a while.

"And how do you know that?" the judge asked. "Mr. Riggs filed his motion yesterday. It seems to me, that sort of information should be confidential. Did you send Mr. Riggs some discovery last night, a set of interrogatories perhaps, asking him if he had insurance?"

"No, your Honor. But your Honor brings up a good point. Mr. Riggs motion was not timely filed."

"You're here," the Judge said, meaning the filing of the petition the previous afternoon had been sufficient notice to get him down to London from Lexington. "Under the circumstances, that being the death of the petitioner, I'm inclined to allow the motion." The judge looked toward Jerry. "Mr. Riggs?"

Jerry sat with his head down. He wanted to respond but his body wouldn't let him. The irony was not lost upon him that it was a physical ailment and the medical treatment he had received that now kept him from avenging Vogel's death. In that instant, he reviewed the facts. He had been put out of a job that provided the best medical benefits tax payer dollars could provide, but those benefits had yet to run out, and when they did, over Nicole's dead body—perhaps literally—would Jerry ever be allowed to let them lapse. Her lawyer had sent him a status quo agreement stating such, using legalese to say the same thing, that sat in the pile of mail beside his hospital bed. Since he had health insurance, and probably always would have health insurance, the Obamacare Individual Mandate that Vogel was challenging would never apply to him. This was a duck that would never get in line.

"Mr. Riggs?" the judge repeated.

The emotional intensity of this confrontation was too much for Jerry, too much for his heart. He was done. He would not ask the judge to recuse himself. The country was on its own. Jerry had to save himself first. In other words, his body had finally—finally—regained primacy over his head. *What the f*** are you doing to me?* it was saying and had been saying for quite some time. And Jerry finally listened.

"Approach," the Judge said. Jerry looked up, then stood up and walked forward. So did his opponent. To him, Judge Van Doren pointed and said, "Sit."

When Jerry had reached the bench, the Judge unplugged the microphone to the recording system and turned on the white noise device that ensured their conversation would not be overheard. He said, "My condolences about your friend, Jerry. I know that must have been quite a shock."

"They did that," Jerry said with some emotion in his voice, not venturing a glance back at the Brackman-Hollis representative behind him. He couldn't look up at the judge either.

"A recusal buys you some time," the judge said. "Time to get your head together. Time to work out some of these details." The main detail would be the shedding of his health insurance if he dared to.

"No," Jerry said. He looked up at the judge to let him see the pain and the physical degradation that remained in him, the sallow complexion, the drooping eyes. It was over.

"Okay," Judge Van Doren said. "Heck of a case, though. Mr. Vogel must have been an interesting guy."

When the hearing was over and the judge had left, only Jerry and Jay and the bailiff remained. Jay closed his briefcase and stopped casually beside Jerry, who was putting on his overcoat.

"There's your Johnny Football," Jay said and he didn't wait for a response before walking down the center aisle and out of the courtroom.

Jerry didn't break stride in getting his coat on. He supposed he had that coming.

Chapter 28

"Jerry."

Jerry had just left the courtroom and started on his way toward the elevator. He turned to see who had called his name. Stewart Granderson—Brackman-Hollis puppet master extraordinaire, fish lips and all—made no move to get up from the bench where he sat.

Walking back toward him, Jerry said, "Well, well, well, if it isn't Baby Stewie."

Tossing his head a little in friendly acknowledgement, Granderson said, "You mention *Family Guy* one time and you're name's Stewart . . ." he held up his hands, giving in.

Jerry stood now in front of the seated Granderson, close enough that Granderson had to look up at a sharp angle to make eye contact. With no remaining capacity for pleasantries, Jerry shrugged as if to say, *So what do you want?*

After a moment's consideration, Granderson got right to the point. "Their pills don't work anymore. Not like they used to. Especially the antibiotics."

Jerry detected a slight smile, benevolent and menacing at the same time. He was telegraphing that he knew what he was about to say would have some humor value.

"According to super ultra-top secret insider industry research, they've found that advertising helps. But it's just a band-aid. Brad would have learned all about this if he'd made partner."

Jerry removed his phone from the interior breast pocket of his suit, pressed a couple of buttons with his thumb and said into it, "Note to self: actually read a Thomas Pynchon novel."

Fish Lips smiled a little at this. Yes, he got it: he was describing a weird Pynchonian world where the unseen forces work behind the scenes to create the illusion we call the world based on warring philosophies.

Jerry may not have been moving fast these days, but he

could still think fast. This was a stroke of genius, he thought, for without turning off the voice-recording app, he returned it to his pocket. Jerry had intended to leave it all on the court, as it were, to let go of this case once and for all with its dismissal. But if he left the courtroom with one negative intention remaining, it was to stick it to Brackman-Hollis if he could, and here was Baby Stewie offering him the opportunity. If he wanted to speak to Jerry, chances were it wasn't a good thing.

Granderson was sitting on his hands for warmth. He tossed his head back and his fish lips might have turned upward just a little, perhaps in admiration that Jerry still had the wherewithal to access black humor at a time like this, and perhaps also at the accuracy of Jerry's assessment of the present moment.

"May I?" Jerry said, indicating his desire to take a seat to Granderson's left, so his voice would have direct-line access to the microphone on Jerry's phone, inside his left breast pocket. "So you're saying that all this healthcare advertisement we see today is because the stuff isn't working anymore," Jerry repeated for the record, "and Brad would have learned that if he'd made partner at Brackman-Hollis?"

"Sell the sizzle, not the steak," Granderson said.

Jerry thought for a moment, lounging back, with his overcoat open. "The steak would be the healthcare services to be provided. The sizzle would be...the disease?"

"Fear of the disease," Granderson corrected.

"Which leads ultimately to the disease and higher profits for your clients." Jerry thought for another moment, putting it all together. Advertisement...fear. "Faith," he said. "It takes faith. The healthcare system requires faith to operate."

"And people are losing that faith," Granderson said. "Little by little. It's an obsolete technology. Like the buggy whip industry when the automobile was first introduced, they see their livelihood slipping away. They're erecting barriers to entry, they're stamping out dissent, they're locking in the legal requirement that everyone pay for this obsolete technology whether they need it or not."

"Obamacare," Jerry said.

"Obamacare," Granderson repeated. "Once it's in place, they will never be able to remove it, no matter if every single American understands the world Brad Vogel's way."

There were many such precedents, Jerry considered. Subsidies for U.S. sugar manufactures, for example. The government spends millions to protect an industry that doesn't need protecting and the result has always been higher prices for consumers.

"This is what you meant at the deposition when you said that Vogel had it backwards," Jerry said. "In other words, your super ultra top secret insider research has already proven Vogel's point of view to be correct."

Jerry remembered Vogel's explanation of the Large Hadron Collider that ran along hundreds of miles beneath the ground under the France-Switzerland border, and how the scientists there were trying to prove that matter exists but had, in fact, already proven that the world is an illusion.

"Research," Granderson said. "The only recourse for the unconscious world."

"You sound just like Vogel," Jerry said.

"All this business about staph infections," Granderson said, referring to Vogel's deposition, the skin problems he had experienced.

"MRSA?" Jerry asked, wanting to know the inside scoop. "Was it MRSA?"

"It may not have even been staph," Granderson confided. "About a year before that happened, Brad contracted a bad case of poison ivy. He was very allergic to it. At that time, he took a small amount of antihistamine and that was enough to fully suppress his endocrine system. At that point, his body became almost completely powerless to fight off the most run-of-the-mill bacteria. If they'd been able to get him back on the antibiotics, they probably would have had him as a patient for life for one thing or another."

Granderson's turn of phrase echoed the billboard Vogel had pointed out to Jerry on that first day of their re-acquaintance: Your Doctors for Life.

"Brad never cared much about the details," Jerry said. "Good thing he used tea tree oil instead."

"It wasn't tea tree oil that made the difference," Granderson said.

"Then what was it?"

"Love," Granderson said.

"Love, huh."

"Skin is interesting," Granderson said. "I wish I could show you all the charts and graphs they've cooked up on this. It's really pretty amazing. For your skin to stay healthy, you have to radiate consciousness out through it constantly. And that's what love does for you. All the problems began about the time he and Candice started having problems—"

"And they went away when he met Amy," Jerry said, looking out into space as he lined up the timing of it all. He looked at Granderson. "Is that what your super-terrific insider research confirms?" Granderson shrugged his acknowledgement. "You do sound like Vogel," Jerry said. "Sounds like you might be the next standard bearer."

Granderson shook his head a little. "Too much to lose."

Jerry sat back, put his arm along the back of the bench behind Granderson and leaned in. "What about your soul, Stewie. Are you concerned about that? Are you concerned at all about losing your soul?"

Granderson tossed his head back a tick, just as he had with Jerry's other attempts at humor. "If the world is an illusion," he looked piercingly at Jerry, "what difference does it make?"

Jerry didn't know how to answer that. Remembering his voice recorder, he said, "So they had Vogel eliminated? Is that it?"

Granderson didn't reply directly. "There are factions within the government," he said. "Some are with us, some support the other view."

"Vogel's view."

"These factions have access to various facilities and capabilities, military, law enforcement, intelligence, witness protection. I think you've seen this principle in action already,"

What's he talking about? Does he mean the New Jersey police detail the COS had tapped to keep an eye on Vogel? How could he have known about that? This revelation, if that's what it was, had the ancillary effect of causing Jerry to question the COS's role in all of this and whether he was perhaps part of this cabal Granderson was describing—but to ask for further details might prove problematic. Maybe Granderson was simply fishing for information himself.

"He may have been taken out by either side," Granderson continued. He made an unplugging sound with his mouth, while at the same time gesturing like one of those children's games outside department stores, where the mechanical arm reaches down to pluck a plush toy out of the masses and drops it into a slot as a prize. "Maybe his case came along too early, before the stage was properly set. We simply don't know."

Jerry frowned, trying to take all this in. He was about to ask another question when Granderson smiled sympathetically and patted him on the knee. "Come on. My ride is waiting."

There were people in the halls, so further questions—save one—would have to wait until they got outside. "Hey, what about all this talk about nutrition and health?" Jerry asked as they got on the elevator. "Vogel was no health nut, I can tell you that."

"Anything to keep people's minds off the true source of the problem," Granderson said, tapping his temple. "Right here."

"I was hoping you would say that," Jerry said. "I hate rabbit food."

Outside, a silver Mercedes, large, high-end, waited on the street. Jerry looked in through the smoky glass. It was Jay—Johnny Football—behind the wheel.

"You let him do the driving," Jerry said.

"No, that's his car," Granderson said.

"His car," Jerry said, thinking maybe he, himself, should be the one to switch sides, not Granderson. "What is he, two years out of law school?"

"Something like that." Granderson made no move toward the car. It was as if he were awaiting one inevitable final question.

So Jerry asked it. "Why are you telling me all this?"

"Because it's fun," Granderson said. "Isn't it? Talking about this sort of thing?"

"It's fun?"

"Yeah," Granderson confirmed. "Not many people outside the firm are in a position to even grasp any of this."

"This is fun," Jerry said, incredulous. Two people were dead and this guy thought this was fun.

"And besides, it's not going to make any difference." Then, as if transitioning the conversation to a not completely unrelated topic, he said, "Pattie Dugan seems to be doing well in New York City."

"Pattie Dugan?"

"You're former intern," Granderson said, striking a reflective pose. "You know, that may have worked out for the best. You have two beautiful daughters. Remember that. Maybe you and Nicole can work on patching things up for the sake of the kids. Divorce can be so hard on them, as I'm sure you're aware. Drop all this and focus on that, that's my advice to you, Jerry." He opened the door to the Mercedes and was about to get inside. "And give my best to your lovely mother."

The Mercedes pulled away, leaving Jerry standing in the cold. He said, "I guess to lose a soul you have to have one first."

Chapter 29

"That's how they got Tupac, you know."

Brad Vogel's funeral was held in Louisville, arranged by his parents. Amy's had been in London the day before. Jerry didn't feel up to that one. He didn't know her. He'd only laid eyes on her twice in his life. With one more day of rest after the hearing, he and his mother and brother made the two-hour trip through Lexington.

Orlando Broxton and his wife, Heather, came to pay their respects. Orlando buttonholed Jerry as soon as he saw him at the visitation and with a notch of his head led him to an isolated corner.

"Tupac, huh," Jerry said. He wasn't so white that he didn't know who Tupac was: just another young rapper gunned down in his prime as far a Jerry was concerned. Apparently, Orlando saw things differently, as did many African-Americans.

"It wasn't the bullets on the Las Vegas strip that got him," Orlando said, whispering. "It was the doctors. He was in the hospital six days before he died."

Jerry looked into Orlando's eyes. This had struck a nerve, as it had with all who knew Brad Vogel. "I didn't know that, but—"

"You did the right thing getting out of there," Orlando said. "Don't believe for a minute that that dude killed Brad. They're coming for you, too. You better believe that. They won't stop, either."

After his weird encounter with Baby Stewie Granderson, Jerry had returned to his mother's house, where he sat at the kitchen table replaying the recording of the conversation over and over again. It was mostly muffled and garbled. Like their reflections in mirrors, Jerry considered, maybe it's difficult to record vampires by digital audio, too. The only phrases that were completely intelligible were "obsolete technology" and "sell the sizzle, not the steak."

And even if he got some expert to enhance the audio, what had Granderson actually said that was incriminatory anyway? Nothing really. He had been threatening, mentioning casually that he knew where Jerry's daughters and his mother lived, without ever raising his voice. And all the rest he could simply pass off as conjecture and hyperbole. Not to mention the fact that there was plenty to incriminate Jerry, himself. Granderson had the dirt on him concerning Pattie. Jerry had to admit, his prowess as a private investigator could certainly be called into question over the conduct of this entire mission, such as it was. No, that recording would never see the light of day and in fact had already been deleted.

"You may be right," Jerry said. "But the case is over...for now. I think that's what they were after."

"Maybe so," Orlando said. "But if I were you . . ."

With a little plate of crustless sandwiches, Heather sidled up beside the two men, offering them up. Orlando took one. Jerry waved off.

"You're going to start the case up again, aren't you?" Heather asked, having heard what Jerry had said. "When you get to feeling better? After all that Brad worked for, it would be a shame to let the dream die with him."

How could Jerry explain that the case wasn't Vogel's dream? That it had been Jerry who had talked him into keeping it going, without also implicating himself in his death? Maybe if Jerry had allowed Vogel to follow his instincts he would still be alive today. But then again, as Vogel had said, there are no mistakes when it comes to Consciousness. He had fulfilled his mission on this earth and as Vogel himself had half predicted, he had died a violent death. And indeed, disease had played no role in his life.

Jerry took some solace in the fact, as Eric had informed him, that Vogel's death was instantaneous. He'd been hit once in the head and once in the heart. His consort, as Eric had called her, Amy, had lived through the night.

"That case can be brought at anytime by anyone," Jerry said. "It will always be an option for anybody who truly gets what Brad was talking about. I'm certainly not there yet. I've got to get healthy on every level. I've got to prove all of it to myself by getting healthy."

Heather nodded.

Orlando didn't cotton to this side of the story. "I've got to go to the little boys room." He excused himself, leaving Heather and Jerry alone.

"The real legacy is the foundation," Jerry said. "His writing."

"You mean the blog?" Heather asked.

"That's right," Jerry said. "There's a lot there. It needs to be put into book format. I think you're the one to do that."

A little choked up by the suggestion, Heather said, "I would be honored." She placed her hand over her heart. Jerry noticed that the pale skin of her neck became pink and blotchy. She was holding in the emotion.

"There are some intellectual property issues involved with that," he said. "It doesn't look like Brad had a will, so those rights would go to his parents. When the time is right, I'm going to talk to them about it."

"Yes," Heather said. "Yes. This feels so right."

* * *

"We're Christians," Vogel's father said. "What Brad was into wasn't Christianity. And it seems he's paid a price for it."

"We've been...estranged for a while now," his mother added. Something told Jerry that she had said that only for her husband's sake. Maybe it was her tone, or maybe Vogel had mentioned speaking with his mother at some point. Her eyes were watery. Mr. Vogel's were dry. Jerry had to watch himself. He didn't have the luxury of getting upset, not with his heart in the shape it was. But he could feel his hackles rising.

"I'm not sure I would look at it that way, Mr. Vogel," Jerry said. "Your son was a great friend and a great man."

Brad Vogel had looked more like his dad than his mother. Mr. Vogel was a wisp of a man, comfortable in a suit. His mother had been a beauty in her youth but with age had put on some weight. They sat in a small private room off the main hall at the church, fitted with matching maroon couch and wingback chairs.

"Thank you for saying so," Mrs. Vogel said. Mr. Vogel nodded in grudging agreement.

"Now isn't the time to discuss these things in detail," Jerry said. "But it doesn't appear that Brad left a will. So everything he has will go to you. I spent the majority of his last days with him. I don't think he had much. One thing he did have was a website. A blog. He wrote feverishly in his last days, almost as if he needed to get everything down in writing."

"That can't be worth much, either," Mr. Vogel said.

"Jim," Mrs. Vogel said.

"There was also a nonprofit organization set up," Jerry said. "There was a lot of interest there. A lot of it had to do with the politics surrounding his court case. But that wasn't all of it. I'd like for you to consider donating Brad's writing to the foundation. I think it's the best way to see that your son's life has a lasting legacy."

"That writing will never see the light of day, if I have anything to say about it," Mr. Vogel responded.

"As I said," Jerry concluded. "Now isn't the time to—"

"Rest assured," Mrs. Vogel interrupted. "Brad's writing will be donated to the foundation." She stared her husband down. Mr. Vogel looked as if he were ready to keep up the fight, but then collapsed back into his chair. "Just you keep in touch with me and I'll make sure you have what you need."

It struck Jerry that he must have been looking at the embodiment of Vogel's peculiar views on womanhood, manhood and marriage. This must have been where all that had come from, and Jerry could kind of see it. She was clearly in charge, but not in an overbearing way. In a peaceful, open, feminine way. And Mr. Vogel seemed to appreciate it. It allowed him to concentrate on his anger and his grief.

It struck Jerry also that there was something of his own mother's way with his father that he was seeing here, too. This was just an impression picked up more from the spirit of the two people before him, perhaps, than what had taken place between them. Jerry thought he might spend a little time getting to know them in the future. Brad would probably like that, he thought. But would they? It might serve only to keep a very deep wound open.

"Your son loved you very much," Jerry said. He was looking at Mrs. Vogel when he said it.

* * *

Mrs. Vogel invited Jerry to ride with her and her husband to the cemetery in the limousine provided by the funeral home, along with Eric and their mother, too. Along the fifteen-minute route at the head of the small motorcade, the two mothers made heartfelt conversation so the men didn't have to. Jerry was proud of his mom. She knew just the right things to say under these circumstances, having lost a husband prematurely herself, never going too deep or too personal.

After a short graveside ceremony, Mrs. Vogel said, "You knew him best at the end. You'll probably want to say your goodbyes."

Jerry looked around to see if she was messing with him. But no, of course she wasn't. She and Mr. Vogel were receding back toward the line of cars. Eric and his mother had hung back from the beginning.

Jerry stood there by the open rectangular hole in the ground. The casket had been lowered but not yet covered. A heap of dirt sat ready beside the hole for that purpose. The headstone was already in place, simple elegant gray granite, date of birth, date of death.

"Can you believe this?" Jerry whispered, no one else in earshot. "This is your doing. I know it is. My brother is probably over there right now quoting something from *Star Trek 2: the Wrath of Kahn.* He's a *Star Trek* kind of guy. You would get a kick out of this. There's even a foundation, right? Just like Susan Ross. It will meet around my schedule. Nights, weekends, whenever I have time."

The wind was cold. Jerry turned up the collar of his overcoat, then thrust his hands back into his pockets. He was surprised that he did have something to tell Vogel. The casket had been closed throughout visitation, due to the head wound, Jerry imagined.

"I had a dream while I was under. I couldn't tell you when exactly. It came back to me last night. Probably because that's what we were talking about last time I saw you. I dreamed that your case had made it all the way to the Supreme Court and I was the one arguing it. I did exactly what you were talking about just before you left for Knoxville. First, I made the argument that putting 'In God We Trust' on our money and all the talk about God in our founding documents, like 'they are endowed by their Creator with certain inalienable Rights,' meant that we as a people and as a government elevate consciousness over reason. That entails an understanding that rationality can no longer wander around untethered, but rather we seek divine guidance to inform our decision-making. Be we don't seek that guidance in a magic book or a particular religion. We seek it in ourselves. And then I showed the justices just how to do that by walking them through the inner body experiment.

"They were resistant at first, but I convinced them that it was part and parcel of the philosophical contrast between a rationality-based approach and a consciousness-based approach, and they bought that. I began with their feet and went up to their heads and out to their fingertips, just the way you did it. My eyes were closed too and when I opened them at the end, five of the justices had made it all the way through—and it wasn't the five you might imagine, either—and four had left. That meant that we had won the case, that five of them were still there. I know, I know, if you do an experiment in a dream, are the results still valid, right? But anyway, I thought you might want to know that we won."

Jerry looked around. All were in their respective vehicles, waiting for the head car to get moving again.

"See you later," he said, and he walked toward the road.

* * *

They had shuttled Jerry's Cherokee to Orlando's house in Lexington. He wanted to stay there for a few days. He needed to get out of London. He needed a change of scenery. He could feel the grief coming on and he didn't want to do it down there.

"Are you sure you're all right?" Orlando asked as Jerry got out of his mother's Buick. Eric was behind the wheel, dressed in his outdated brown double-breasted suit and too-wide tie. "I don't want a cardiac patient on my hands."

Jerry assured him that he would be fine at least for the night. He kissed his mother and thanked Eric for driving.

That evening, Jerry talked some more with Heather. Orlando listened in for a while, talked some more about Tupac and then went somewhere else in the house to drink bourbon until he fell asleep. They were all three upset and dealt with their pain in their own way.

Jerry retired early and that's when his emotion came. When he sat down on the bed that he and Vogel had shared for a night, he began to cry. He cried for Vogel. He cried for his dad, whom he found that he missed more than Vogel. He cried for his girls, whom he missed most of all.

He wasn't sure but after an hour or so, he might have gotten it all out and he felt himself ready to begin healing it up.

Chapter 30

"Damn shame about your friend," the COS said. "I'm truly sorry."

And he was sorry, Jerry could see that. When he had finally returned to Arlington, Jerry called up the COS. It had taken some time for the COS to return his phone call, a period of a week or so, a week during which Jerry took the opportunity to let go of his past, his former job, clearing the decks for whatever his future might hold. A future about which he had absolutely no idea...and he was okay with that.

When he finally did return Jerry's call, the COS invited him for a walk along the Mall, the Cherry blossoms in bloom in the breezy spring weather, "and all that rot." Jerry didn't bother to dress up.

"We used him, Jim," Jerry said as they strolled. "They told us exactly what they were going to do and we let it happen in the hope of political gain."

"Jealous ex-husband," the COS said. "Fellow named Crace did it, as I understand."

"You're following the story, I see," Jerry said. "So that's the party line, is it? You're sticking to that version? No inquiry, no investigation, no publicity of any kind, is that it?"

The COS stopped him with a hand on the forearm and turned. "Politics is war, my friend. It wouldn't do any good. They would just make us look like idiots—"

"Maybe we are idiots," Jerry said.

"Sometimes you have to live to fight another day. Pick your battles, as they say. This one is too far out there right now. Too unconventional. It's never going to have the kind of resonance we need, certainly not in the near term."

"I don't care about that anymore," Jerry said, turning his back on the COS.

"We've decided to go a different way with it," the COS said.

"Big problems are coming with the system. We've made certain of that."

"How?" Jerry said. He knew the COS wouldn't answer the question.

"And as the 2014 elections get closer, we think we may have the votes to defund the whole thing."

"Defund it, huh?"

"That's the new tactic. We'll see how it goes. At any rate, your job's still open."

Jerry turned. "You expect me to come back after all this? Everything forgiven? Just like that?"

"You're a soldier. That's what soldiers do. We need you in the trenches. How's your ticker?"

It occurred to Jerry that the COS may not have known about his heart attack. "It's fine," he said. "The time off the job seems to have done the trick."

"Hanrahan's been running the show in your absence. He's been doing a fine job. You can be more hands-off."

"Hanrahan..."

Why the hard sell? Jerry wondered. *Keep your friends close and your enemies closer.* He'd heard the COS quote Sun-tze, the ancient Chinese general, many times before. A hardback copy of *The Art of War* sat prominently displayed on the bookshelf behind his desk. Jerry could do real damage to the cause—and the COS—if he chose to go that way.

But he wasn't an enemy. He was no longer the true believer he once had been, but he wasn't an enemy. Truth was, he didn't know what he was anymore, but the COS didn't need to know any of that. Having a government job where he wouldn't have to do much work for a while sounded like something he could use.

"I want double what I was making before," Jerry said.

The COS chuckled. "I can bump you up a step. That's about it. It's a government job, my boy."

* * *

Jerry reported for duty the following day, a Wednesday.

"Who's this?" he asked his secretary as they both watched the person of interest, a shorthaired variety, entering what had been Pattie's office.

"That's your new intern," Rita said.

"But...he's a guy," Jerry said.

"When Pattie left, Tim had to fill her position."

"Hanrahan? That pederast," he said. "Figures." Then Jerry thought about it for a moment: probably for the best. "Give me ten minutes and send him into my office."

Naomi said, "Tim Hanrahan or..."

"No, no," Jerry said. "The new guy."

Jerry settled into his old chair. There was something different about it. Had someone else been sitting in it all this time? Hanrahan, perhaps? It felt different somehow. As he squirmed around in the green leather, trying to re-conform it to the contours of his posterior, it came to him—his ass wasn't quite as fat as it used to be!

After his chat with the COS the day before, Jerry had continued his long stroll around the Mall. He'd been doing a lot of that the last few days. In Lexington, he'd walked up to Le Deauville restaurant to reminisce about the night he and Vogel had eaten there with Orlando and Heather. He'd ordered a bourbon as rent for his seat at the bar, but drank almost nothing of it, opting instead for the water he'd been served along side. Then he walked around downtown before heading back to Orlando's place.

A couple of days later, he'd gone up to Cincinnati to see the girls and afterwards he'd walked Mount Adams as if it might be the last he ever saw of the city. After he let go of the pain surrounding his heart, he found himself given to contemplation.

And gone too was the compulsive eating he'd used to cover over that pain for so many years. When he got back to Arlington, he walked around there too, one morning finding himself at his local Krispy Kreme. He'd stared out from under his hoodie at the hot and fresh donuts through two layers of glass but felt no motivation at all to enter the establishment. He had not consciously sought to trim down, but he'd take it.

He picked up the phone and called the IT guy. "Larry?...Jerry Riggs. Can you get my account back up and running?...Thanks."

His new intern darkened his door. "You wanted to see me, sir?"

"Very polite," Jerry said. "That's nice. Come in. You can call me Jerry."

After a bit of small talk—during which Jerry learned that his new intern Alan had graduated third in his class and was President of the Law School Republicans at Moritz College of Law at *The* Ohio State University, and that like Jerry, he was a diehard Reds fan—they got down to business.

"Alan, you seem like a nice kid," Jerry said. "I'm happy to have you here. Now let me tell you what your most important job is going to be."

"All right, Mr. Riggs. I mean...Jerry."

"From nine o'clock until ten o'clock every morning, I want you to guard that door and that phone. Guard them with your life, you hear me? I am not to be disturbed by anyone for any reason unless it's the Speaker himself. Got it?"

"What about the President?" Alan said, taking notes.

"The President will never call me, but if he does, I guess you can put him through."

"What about a Supreme Court Justice?" Alan pursued. "Or the Senate Majority Leader."

"Umm, yes," Jerry said.

"What if it's one of the members of the Ohio Congressional delegation?" Alan was very proud of this suggestion.

"No," Jerry said, thinking about it just a moment. "You know what? Let's take the Speaker off that list too. And the President, and the Supremes. You start making exceptions and you're never going to get anywhere."

"Right," Alan said, jotting it down.

"They're never going to call me anyway."

"Oh," Alan said, disappointed.

"Sorry." Jerry looked at his watch. "Here's your first test."

"Right. Thank you, sir." Alan got up. "I mean Jerry." He closed the door behind him.

Jerry had made a resolution. This was going to be his daily habit and he now understood that it would be the most important task he would complete all day. He had begun the practice at Orlando's house, where he could only tolerate a few minutes at a time, and continued when he returned to Arlington, where he managed to build up gradually to an hour each day. Now the question remained as to how he would get the job done in an office setting.

Maybe he should read a little something from Vogel's blog to get him in the mood. He tried logging into his computer again. Excellent. That Larry was nothing if not efficient.

Let's see, what was the last thing Vogel had written before his demise? Would that be too much to handle? Depending on what it said, it would not. He had avoided the blog up to this point, but now he was okay with it. Let's take a look. The final post was dated the morning of Vogel's death:

> It's interesting how often series of three come up. Among the most important of these are the three modes of life: thinking, doing and being. We spend most of our time obsessively thinking. That voice in the head never shuts up! As Lao-tzu puts it in the *Tao te Ching*, "Stop thinking and solve your problems."
>
> And then we try to keep ourselves busy with doing to drown out the voice. Whether it's a crossword puzzle, watching TV or working too much, we have to constantly be doing something. We feel like losers if we don't have something to do. Lao-tzu again: "When nothing is done, nothing is left undone."
>
> Shut off the voice in your head (it can be done, as we shall see momentarily), sit down and do nothing. Teach yourself how to just be. Focus on being, the third and most important mode of life. That's where all the answers lie.
>
> ∞
>
> Then there are the three tools of being.
>
> First, come to an awareness of the present moment. Realize the difference between the past, the present and the future. Only one of these is

real; the other two are merely ideas. The past is made up of present moments that have gone. The future is present moments that haven't happened yet. The present is the only one of these three that's real.

Whenever you become anxious, you're thinking too much about the future. Remind yourself that only the present is real and come back to it, sensing what's actually happening around you—right now. Breathing is always happening now, that's an easy entrée into the present moment. See how this present moment awareness makes you feel. It will always make you feel better.

When you're depressed, you're likely thinking about something that happened in the past that you wish hadn't happened in the way that it did. It doesn't exist anymore, let it go. Bring yourself back to the present moment and you'll feel better. Or you may be wishing your life today were as good as it was back in the day. You have to let that go, too.

Second, recognize the voice in your head. That voice is talking to someone. Who is it talking to? Identify yourself with the listener as opposed to the talker. Listen to the voice, allow it to be there—don't judge it. You will begin to realize that the voice tends to be very negative, judgmental, with a lot of "shoulds" in there: "you should do this, you should feel that." It is possible, through awareness, to shut down that voice completely. It happens gradually, little by little, and it's very easy to do once you realize that you *can* shut it down and still exist—that is to say, that the voice isn't you. It's the ego (the talker), not you (the listener).

Begin this way: never finish a sentence in your mind. Next, sit and wait for the next thought to come out, like a cat watching a mouse hole. This will produce a wordless gap in the stream of words in your head. Proceed little by little from there until that habit of internally talking to yourself has left

> you completely. Without that voice in your head, life is a lot more peaceful, and that feels pretty good too.
>
> Third, and this is the one we've talked about most, become aware during every present moment of the feeling in your body. Have one foot in your body, so to speak, throughout your day. Your body's natural state is peace, and joy automatically arises out of that peace, because in a state of peace you're able to feel the positive nature of the Universe—that feeling is joy. And joy feels pretty good.
>
> ∞
>
> The final three are the double negatives that will always work to confound your mind, bringing you back to the present moment: "Don't want, don't fear, don't resist." Any time—absolutely anytime—you're feeling bad—about anything—say to yourself, "Don't want, don't fear, don't resist," lingering just a moment on each one, feeling what each feels like and letting it go. It will make you feel better, because wanting is a bad feeling, fearing is a bad feeling and resisting is also a bad feeling.
>
> These three cover the gamut of possible reasons as to why you're feeling bad in that moment. Some will say that all three are different ways of resisting, or all three are different ways of fearing, but I've found that all three together work the best to bring me back to a state of peace.
>
> These double negatives equal a very peaceful positive.

So this was the last thing Vogel decided to say before he died. Interesting how that turned out. He couldn't have known that would be the last when he wrote it, but Brad Vogel would have said that consciousness knew. And so it was a profound epitaph all the same. That's how it felt, anyway, and Jerry now knew that was what mattered.

He turned off his computer monitor, closed his eyes and

sat back a little. After a moment, he decided this wasn't working. He got up and turned off the overhead. Not enough ambient light was coming in through the window—he'd fall asleep. He turned on the desk light. Its luminescent green shade felt soothing, just right.

He sat back again. No. This was his work chair.

He got up and sat on one end of the couch. His back was to the window. He closed his eyes...no.

He moved to the chair. He was facing the window. He could see the tops of some trees and in the distance the point on the Washington Monument. Yes, he was finally Goldie Locks: this felt just right.

He closed his eyes and began with his toes. After a moment, Jerry worked his way to the rest of his feet...ankles were next...calves and shins...knees...thighs—a lot of mass here, a lot of reality...hips; a lot of emotion stored in them, he could feel it welling up, sex always an issue, that would come out by and by...

...Abdomen—very dense, lots of room for pain to hide...Midsection; tense, anxious, but feeling it soothed, relaxed, took down the guard...

...Heart: there was still a soreness in it. And something lurked here, Jerry could sense its evil density. Perhaps this was what Vogel had called at various times pain-body, karma and original sin. This was the part of him that needed the most work. He wanted to linger here but if he did, he might never move off of it by the time his hour was complete. He would neglect the rest of his body. Jerry somehow knew he needed equal parts pleasure and pain for perfect physical and spiritual health—wisdom was creeping in. He would come back to his heart at the end...

...Shoulders; tense, relaxing now, a deep breath came involuntarily. Jerry felt like he was melting. It felt good...upper arms...forearms...hands—lots of feeling in the hands . . .

...Back up the arms to the neck: tense, relaxing now...the voice box opening though it made no sound...chin...teeth—yes, he could feel his teeth! They felt energized—would he ever need a dentist again?...

...Face: tense, relaxing, muscles he didn't know he had. Nasal cavities opening, clearing...Eyes: difficult, their density felt different somehow, but he kept with it and eventually felt the tingle in and around the eyeball. Jerry wouldn't be surprised if he never needed the reading glasses all his contemporaries were going to presently, and if he looked in the mirror later there would be no shock if he appeared ten years younger...maybe not just yet, but give it a few weeks for rejuvenation to do its work....

...Forehead, and finally brain: there were no nerve endings in there, or so he had been told, but he could feel its weight and soon it began to tingle like the rest of him. Was this the cure for Alzheimer's? Perhaps it was . . .

Jerry bypassed his heart once again to race his awareness from the crown of his head down to his feet and out to his fingertips, connecting it all together as one contiguous energy field. He felt that for a while, all together.... Wow! This was something. This was really something...

Only then did he give his undivided attention to his heart, and he held it there, warming, tingling, healing, until the negativity awakened and he was able to consciously feel the pain that his unconscious thoughts continued to generate. No specific thoughts were brought into Jerry's awareness this session, but the pain was diminished, and he knew it was only a matter of time before that nut (or nuts) would begin to crack.

* * *

Jerry opened his eyes. He noticed the tip of the Washington Monument first, which was still gray of course, but somehow more alive. The new leaves in the treetops were more vibrantly green, too. It would be nice if he could open the windows to hear the birds and the blowing of the wind. He looked around the office. The furniture had the same life to it as well, as if to welcome him into reality.

He was fine where he was for the moment, but the way he felt just then, he wouldn't be surprised if he were to spend the rest of his days meditating on a beach in Maui. If he could parlay this feeling into every minute of his day, that just might turn out to be his reality, the illusion that